PICTURES AT AN EXHIBITION

PICTURES AT AN EXHIBITION

D. M. Thomas

BLOOMSBURY

First published in Great Britain 1993
Copyright © 1993 by D. M. Thomas

The moral right of the author has been asserted

Bloomsbury Publishing Ltd, 2 Soho Square, London W1V 5DE

A CIP catalogue record for this book is available from the
British Library

ISBN 0 7475 13880

10 9 8 7 6 5 4 3 2 1

Printed in Great Britain by Clays Ltd, St Ives Plc
Typeset in Edinburgh by Hewer Text Composition Services Ltd

ACKNOWLEDGEMENT

The short third section (*Six Studies for* Compassion) is taken
verbatim from German documents quoted in *Those Were
the Days: The Holocaust through the Eyes of the Perpetrators and
Bystanders* by Ernst Klee, Willi Dressen and Volker Riess,
English translation by Deborah Burnstone (*Schöne Zeiten:
Judenmord aus der Sicht der Täter und Gaffer*), first published in
the Federal Republic of Germany by S. Fischer Verlag GmbH,
Frankfurt am Main, 1988. First English translation Hamish
Hamilton, 1991, copyright © S. Fischer Verlag GmbH, 1988,
translation copyright © Deborah Burnstone, 1991.

Reproduced by permission of Hamish Hamilton Ltd.

CONTENTS

'I had nothing to do with this technical procedure.'
August Häfner

'There should be living people who breathe and feel, suffer and love . . . Everything desires to live.'
Edvard Munch

DEATH AND THE MAIDEN

I

It was clear that Dr Lorenz was suffering acutely. His severe headaches and general weakness and tiredness were affecting his surgery. He had gone to a Berlin specialist, suspecting a tumour of the brain, but nothing had been found.

One April evening of strong wind and flurries of snow, I was summoned to visit him at home. His wife greeted me at the door and, after asking me to take off my coat and boots, led me to the doctor's study. He was sprawled in an armchair in his shirt-sleeves, listening to a record on the gramophone; I recognised the First Act of *Tristan und Isolde*, the Furtwängler recording. The voices were no more than a murmur – I assumed because the young Lorenz children were asleep.

To judge by his harrowed expression, his head sunk on his chest, the divine music was giving him little pleasure. He glanced up, nodded cursorily. 'Sit down, Galewski.'

I sat on a highbacked chair across from him. The study was simply furnished: a neat desk, a couple of chairs, some well-stocked bookshelves; the gramophone on a walnut cupboard; a family photograph on one wall: an old couple I assumed to be his parents.

I waited until the record finished; the silent grooves hissed for what seemed an eternity, then he hauled himself wearily to his feet and switched the gramophone off.

'It really is a fantastically beautiful opera!' I said.

'A few weeks ago I'd have agreed. But now, nothing seems beautiful to me.' Sitting again, he winced, pressing a hand to his forehead. 'I think it's in here,' he said, tapping with two fingers.

'What is?'

3

'The illness. I think you think so too.'

I shrugged. 'Well, the nightmares . . .'

'Yes.'

We sat in silence. He was a tall, handsome man, in his mid-thirties, several years my elder. (Though, of course, I looked much the older man.) His features were severe, almost sculptured. Normally he was broad of build, with the shoulders and neck of a discus-thrower, but over the past few months he had lost weight and his jacket hung loose upon him. Grey had begun to touch his dark-brown hair at the edges.

'I should like you to try your Freudian . . .' he waved an arm uncertainly – 'hocus-pocus on me. It can't do any harm.'

We had spoken of it before, from time to time. Rather, he had brought it up on occasions – at first dismissively, even crudely so, but lately with less antagonism. I pointed out now that I really hadn't been trained. I had studied under a Hungarian analyst in Budapest for only twelve months, after qualifying in medicine; then my father died and I had to return to my small Czech town to support my family. The collapse of my father's business left me with no alternative but to become a doctor in general practice, especially as there was soon a wife to support as well as a mounting political engagement. I wasn't competent in psychotherapy, I told Dr Lorenz.

He waved away my modesty. I was bright; he'd never regretted taking me on; I was the best of the lot; he regarded me as a true colleague. In any case he was desperate. The headaches as well as the dreams were becoming so intolerable he would soon be in a mood to shoot himself.

He would have to be completely frank and open with me, I said. I thought he might object to that.

Why so? What harm could it do? It wasn't as if I was going to tell anyone, or write up his case for some *Jahrbuch*. He managed, despite the pain he was enduring, a slight smile.

He had very rarely smiled in my presence, even in his healthy days. I always felt myself responding emotionally when he smiled, and I did so now. I owed everything to his kindness. I was very sorry for him, and for his wife. She too had been most kind, on the few occasions we had met.

What do we do, he asked. Did he have to lie on some damned

4

sofa? I said that was the normal method, but it probably didn't matter. Since there was no sofa, we could manage well enough facing each other like this.

The wind wailed, blowing the snow against the curtained window.

To begin with, I suggested, the situation he was in, the work, was stressful. He cut me short, saying emphatically that he felt no stress, apart from his illness. He enjoyed his work; he was competent – more than competent, many would say – at his job; and he had the satisfaction of a duty well performed. He greatly enjoyed the opportunity for research that his post gave him. His family life, his wife and children, brought him great pleasure. He was a fortunate, contented man.

I nodded. I agreed I had seen no sign of stress, up to the moment when an almost continuous headache had begun to plague him. Yes, he was, essentially, a contented man, and with a placid disposition, not easily ruffled. I had seen him, on my occasional previous visits, playing with little Irmgard and Seefried in childlike forgetfulness of all around him.

'Nevertheless, it *could* be considered stressful.'

'Oh, of course it's hard, it's difficult,' he conceded. 'But that only makes it more satisfying, the knowledge that I can cope and do a decent job. We're in no danger, we're decently fed; I'm very lucky to be able to have my family with me. So – where is the stress?'

'You're right.'

'One might wish for nicer surroundings' – he glanced with distaste towards the window. 'But – one has to put up with it.'

'True. So now we've got that out of the way, let's start with the dreams. Did you dream last night?'

He scowled. 'Of course! Every night unless I'm on duty. Between one and two. They always begin harmlessly enough, even pleasantly sometimes; and they always turn into horror.'

Occasionally he remembered the dream well – too well. More often the horror receded before he was fully awake.

He related his dream of the previous night.

He had been trapped on the mountains, after a fall. Dragging his left leg, he had made his way down the moraine to the valley. He'd managed to reach a farmhouse, just before nightfall; a farm near a glade of birches. There was no one about, no one who answered his cries. He'd broken a window and got inside. Silence. An air of desertion. But food in the larder; he'd gorged himself on bread and sausage. At last he'd dragged himself up the stairs to bed.

He saw the face of his mother, lying quiet, asleep, on the fresh pillow. He was surprised to see his mother in a farm under the mountain. He tried to rouse her but could not. He pulled the sheet down over her naked breasts, and further. And saw that the whole of the nether part of her body was being gnawed away, by rats.

The doctor was sweating as he revealed the ghastly end of his dream. He sighed, recrossed his legs, took out a silver cigarette case and lit up a cigarette. 'This was one of the better ones,' he said.

I waited until the smoke had formed a curl and vanished into the air. My waiting was partly from a terror at my ignorance. I had the idea that a genuine psychoanalyst would have solved his mystery with one devastating riposte.

'So what would your Professor Freud have made of that?' He slid his lips down in a grimace.

I nodded up at the portrait on the wall, the slightly faded couple. 'Are those your parents?'

'No.'

He didn't elaborate.

'The Danube,' he said after a while, appearing to be gazing through the wall, stroking the word tenderly. 'The blue Danube.'

'Are you worried about your mother, perhaps?'

'Oh, a little, I suppose. But *very* little. She's almost seventy, she's had her life. I don't want her to die, but she has to, some time. I don't think it will be yet, she's in good health.'

'When you were growing up – what were your feelings towards her?'

He replied unhesitatingly, 'I liked her very much.'

'You liked her?'

'Yes. You sound surprised. Isn't it natural to like your mother?'

I shrugged an *of course*. 'And do you still like her?'

A shade testily, 'I don't see what good this is doing. Yes, I suppose so. I really don't give her much thought. Our paths have separated. That's only natural.' Then, with a sharp look, 'Did you like *your* mother?'

An unease, a slight anguish, swept over me. I tried to nod, but my head stayed buried. Still, he interpreted me correctly.

'Well, that's good,' he said. 'That's good . . .' Sensing my distress he added, 'It's very sad. I do feel for you.'

'Thank you.'

'And your wife. I bet she was pretty.'

In a strangled voice I whispered yes.

He nodded sympathetically. Then he gave a kindly smile, saying, 'But little – Elli – uh? Now wasn't that a miracle!'

'Yes!'

I steered him back to the subject of his mother; invited him to talk about her. There was little to tell. A humdrum, ordinary woman. A midwife. A good provider. Good broad hips for childbearing. Five children altogether. A good Catholic woman. Silent over her embroidery. That was an image he recalled. His mother bent over her embroidery; usually a religious picture.

And his father? Had he liked him?

Not liked so much as respected, Dr Lorenz said. He'd come back wounded from the war, limping, one foot having been partially amputated. Yes, it was possible his limp in the dream, the leg-dragging, was related to his father. He could remember that laggard foot, as his father came home tired. He was a bank clerk; they were always short of money. But the children had shoes, even if they were passed on. Of an evening his father liked to spend the time playing draughts with a couple of his colleagues: in the summer they'd sit outside.

Of course the atmosphere had been fairly gloomy, he added. His father had been depressed, like almost everyone else. It was a gloomy, terrible time, following the war. But he couldn't say it had affected him badly; he and his two brothers had made their own entertainment, as children will. It was a mistake to think parents mattered that much.

He was talking about schooling and scouting when there was a gentle knock on the door and, after he'd said come in, his wife entered. She was carrying a tray, with cups and plates, and I caught the delightful aroma of coffee. 'I wondered if you'd like some refreshment,' she said with a pleasant smile, her kindly eyes lighting on me. 'I hope I'm not interrupting, Dr Galewski? Only this room gets quite chilly and I thought you could do with something to warm you up.'

I was conscious of blushing. Because of her tact and kindness, because of a woman's presence. 'Thank you! You're not interrupting,' I said. 'At least from my point of view. As long as Dr Lorenz . . .' I glanced towards my 'patient'. He shook his head; gestured to her to put the tray down on his desk. She cleared away papers to make space. Steam rose in two streams from the hot coffee. She handed me the cup and saucer, and a plate containing a thick slice of golden-yellow cake.

'It's marzipan,' she said. 'I made it today, the children like it.'

I took the plate, mumbling my thanks again. Her soft white hand would have looked almost as delicious, as desirable, as the cake, in more normal circumstances. She was a very attractive woman, her jolly, roundish face suffused with life; her hair, tight in a braided coronet, golden as a wheatfield; her full bosom stretching the material of her white blouse. But most attractive of all was the kindliness in her blue eyes. I sank my teeth into the moist and heavenly marzipan, saliva filling my mouth. She handed her husband his coffee and said, in a tone that included me at first but then shut me out, she hoped we hadn't been disturbed by Seefried; he'd woken up with a bad chest. She sounded a little anxious. It was understandable; there was always a worry about the spread of disease, especially chest infections. She wondered if he should have a look at Seefried, but Dr Lorenz said it didn't sound serious; he would have a look at him in the morning.

She turned again to me. 'Is it good?' She was anxious about this too, her womanly skills in question.

'It's wonderful!'

She beamed her pleasure. I was already spiking the crumbs with my forefinger. 'Perhaps,' she said, 'my husband won't want his piece!' He shook his head impatiently, waved the cake in my direction. She took his plate from the tray and eased the slice of marzipan on to my empty plate.

'Thank you, Frau Lorenz! You're very kind! It's absolutely delicious!'

'It's from my mother's recipe; she made beautiful cakes.' Then, her eyes and voice softening further, touched with sympathy, 'I expect yours did too.'

'Yes.'

'Well . . .' She grew lost for anything else to say. And to spare her I changed the subject, saying how fortunate we doctors were, and how fortunate the sick were, to be in the care of Dr Lorenz.

'Yes. He's a caring man.' She gave him an affectionate smile. It turned again into anxiety. 'Help him, Dr Galewski! I hate to see him like this!'

'I'll do my best.' I explained how I was really not properly trained in this technique. I was to an extent fumbling in the dark.

When she had gone, Dr Lorenz said, 'Where were we? I've forgotten. I apologise for the interruption, though she means well.'

'Don't apologise! It was a very kind thought. You're lucky to have such a wife.'

He knew that. He hadn't been able to be a good husband to her lately – if I knew what he meant. 'It's usually the woman who's supposed to have the headache. But she's very understanding, and doesn't complain. There's nothing wrong with the sexual side of our marriage. Isn't that what Freudianism is all about? Sex? Problems with sex? Marital problems?'

'Not necessarily. But it *is* sometimes necessary to explore that side of things.'

'Well, there's nothing to explore. I have a healthy sexual appetite, normally. But please, you must feel free to ask any questions. We must do this properly.'

I asked him if he had had relations with women other than his wife.

After a pause to light a cigarette he replied, 'I've never been unfaithful to her; not in any real sense. I did sleep for a time with a young woman who had not been lucky enough to find a husband, and who desperately wanted to bear a child; but my wife knew about that, and approved. When the young woman got pregnant our relationship stopped.'

I nodded. 'And before your marriage? Girls?'

Just adolescent flirtations; unlike his brothers and sisters he'd been fairly studious. 'Well, perhaps there was one who meant something. I suppose the first sexual experience lingers in one's memory. I worked on a farm for several weeks each year, helping with the harvest, and during my second year there, I met this girl I became quite fond of. Lotte. That was her name. Yes, she was very pleasing. We would make love in the field, under the stars. That was good. That was very good.' He stared far away.

'Is that the farm in your dream?'

'Oh, that hadn't occurred to me. No, I don't think that was the farm; it didn't look like it, didn't feel like it.'

I nodded. I invited him to tell me more about Lotte. It was noticeable that while his words evinced pleasurable feeling, a growing tension and rigidity in him seemed to contradict that. 'I'd say you felt quite a lot for her, and she for you,' I suggested. 'You feel a certain amount of pain, regret, guilt – I don't know what – for having broken with her. Forgive me; that may be nonsense.'

He stared at me. His rapid, tense breathing quietened. He murmured, 'You're probably right. Now I think of it. That's – surprising. How could you tell?'

I explained that the unconscious frequently worked by opposites; the more soft, tender, melting and yielding she had appeared from his account the more I saw her as unyielding, frozen solid, like a pillar of salt. He had chosen to name her, Lotte, whereas the name of the young woman he had helped to conceive had obviously been unimportant. 'You left Lotte behind; she couldn't keep up with you.'

'True. No woman can keep up. They keep looking behind, wondering if a child has fallen, wondering if they left the house safe.' He gave a shudder. 'I hate that biblical story. Gradually losing all sensation; conscious but unable to move a muscle.' Sweat broke out on his forehead and his arms jerked. 'That was one of my worst nightmares.' Or when you woke up, he said, and for what seemed an eternity you couldn't move. A sort of reverse of Lot's wife. 'However,' he continued, after brushing spilt ash into the ashtray, 'really the farm holds only pleasant memories. I don't think it has anything to do with how I'm feeling.'

Nothing had happened there to make him dream of finding his mother gnawed by rats?

'No. Absolutely not. The girl's not the most important memory. The farmer and his wife were very homely and kind; good Bavarian souls. There was singing round a campfire at night, after our work. A very satisfying feeling of being tired out from having done a good job.' He was silent for a time, and I grew aware that the wind and the snowfall had eased. The return to wintry bleakness had been mercifully brief. 'You see' – a flash of jealousy in his gaze – 'I wasn't lucky like you; no expensive trips abroad; no holidays at all. My mother had to take in washing so we could make ends meet. Yes, it was all very nice for you – very nice indeed!'

I acknowledged it with a bow of my head. 'You're right. I knew it even then, that there was no justice.'

'You're a decent fellow; I'm sorry.' He clutched his brow. 'This damned pain!'

'We'll finish for the night. Tell me just one more thing – when you pulled down the sheet and saw the rats gnawing, where exactly were they gnawing? At her thighs?'

'There were no thighs; they were almost up to her waist.'

'That's interesting. So you couldn't see her genitals.'

His eyes flared. 'Of course not! What do you imagine? That I had a pornographic dream? There was nothing pornographic about it. I don't have pornographic dreams.'

It had grown cold in the study, and before showing me out Dr Lorenz invited me into the sitting room, to warm myself for a few minutes in front of a blazing wood fire. Frau Lorenz was knitting – an army sweater. We chatted pleasantly; I admired a framed photo of the couple, with Dr Wirths, in evening dress at a Mess night; the Dresden china ornaments; the oil painting of a stag hunt in a forest. Then her husband showed me to the door and helped me on with my coat. The night outside was frost-black, glimmering with fresh snow as our eyes adjusted. We hovered for a moment. Then, 'See you in the morning,' he said. 'Thank you. I don't know where this is heading. I can see no sense in it.'

'Well, we will try. It takes time.'

'We have plenty of that,' he said. 'This place is absolutely full of it.'

What he meant, I knew, was that this place, this world – for people have rightly said it was a world of its own – was changeless. Changes took place elsewhere, but here time hung like a fog, a miasma. Only the seasons, the slow change from ice to mud to burning heat and back to ice, gave notice that this wasn't altogether *outside* of time, a supernal realm. As I walked back towards my quarters, crunching the spring snow that wouldn't harden, I already had a sense that Dr Lorenz's statement, though still true, was not as true as it had once been. There was a glimmer of the beginning of the end, like the two or three stars that gleamed overhead. Yet despite that slight premonition it would have shocked me – delighted me? Yes, certainly – if I'd known that another spring would see everything changed, all the people gone, nothing but a husk remaining.

I half undressed and fell into my bunk. As silently as possible, so as not to disturb my colleagues. Yet I felt that Litai was awake, facing me; I sensed his one sighted eye, burning red, staring at me. Gilchik and Lasalles were fast asleep, snoring lightly; but I knew they continued to feel hostility towards me even in their sleep. They were all jealous of my close contact with Lorenz. From the ward, next door, came a few moans. It was too normal a sound to disturb me, and I slept.

Next day, I had no opportunity to speak privately with Dr Lorenz; there was just the usual brief, polite exchange as we went about our duties in the ward.

Evening came; the day had been fairly mild, a harbinger of spring; when I set out for the Lorenz house, last night's snowfall was only an occasional crust resting on a sea of mud. Frau Lorenz, wiping her hands on her apron, again welcomed me. The doctor, she said, wasn't at home; he would be delayed. Dr Rohde had flu, so her husband had had to step in and take his place. My nostrils were twitching, drawn by an aroma from her kitchen. She smiled, sensing my hunger. 'Go into the sitting room,' she said; 'I'll bring you a tray of food.'

The log fire blazed; I was beginning to feel comfortable in this pleasant, homely room. There was something new: a sculpture in birch-wood, clearly intended to be a head of Dr Lorenz. I picked it up, caressed it. It wasn't a bad likeness. The door opened and Frau Lorenz backed in, holding a tray. Fish and potatoes. Delicious! Wonderful! And a foaming tankard of beer. Saliva filled my mouth; I tried not to look greedy.

I sat down and she placed the tray before me. Holding back for a moment, I asked after her son, and she said he was much better. The fish was fresh carp, she said, from the nearby carp farm. She hoped I'd like it. She sat opposite and gazed at me as I began shovelling in the fish and potato. I could see her relax, contented that I was enjoying her food. Pointing my fork at the stern wooden head, I said I liked it; who had done it? It was Frau Tillich, she replied. She'd been promising it for ages; indeed it should have been a Christmas present. But with a two-year-old child to look after, one had one's hands full.

The rough, tangy beer flowed like liquid honey down my throat.

It was good for the wives to have a hobby in a place like this, she said; and she thought Frau Tillich had talent. I agreed. The plate was clean. I thanked her again and set the tray aside. She glanced up at a cuckoo clock, a little edgy. Dr Lorenz ought to be back very soon.

I enquired, 'Did he have a nightmare last night?'

'He didn't wake me up, as he usually does, at any rate. I can't say. He'd left before I was awake.'

She hoped, so very much, I could help him. It was awful when he had his nightmares. He moaned and fought the air with his fists, as if trying to push something off him. And those headaches. Could I explain what I was trying to do with this treatment? 'Of course I've heard of Freud, but – you know . . .' She gave an apologetic shrug.

'Well, it's basically a search for something in the past, something the mind has suppressed because it's too painful. The repression causes the unconscious mind to create what Freud termed neurotic symptoms. That is, they're not really physical. Your husband's headaches, for instance, might be created by some childhood memory that he can't bear to confront.'

She knitted her brows. 'I *think* I understand.'

A fair-haired, good-looking lad of about six wandered in in his pyjamas, rubbing his eyes. He veered back in surprise as he saw me. 'You've met Dr Galewski before, Seefried,' his mother said. 'Say good evening to him!'

'Good evening.'

'Hello, Seefried!'

He was thirsty, he wanted a drink. She told him to pour himself a glass of milk in the kitchen, then go straight to bed. Reluctantly he turned and went out.

'A fine boy!' I said.

She blushed proudly. '*We* think so. Of course he misbehaves sometimes.'

'Don't they all?'

I took the opportunity to make some enquiries about her husband's background. His parents were very nice, very quiet, she said. She thought he'd had a happy enough childhood. Of course it had been a horrible time for everyone; the war, and after. He always spoke warmly of a Bavarian farm where he'd helped at harvest-time. She thought it was organised by a church youth group; nowadays, of course, it was a regular part of everyone's upbringing, and a good thing too. Her husband always said the farmer and his wife had treated him like second parents. He had a photo of them on the wall in his study: perhaps I'd noticed? I nodded.

She spoke of her own upbringing, on the edge of the Black Forest; her father a postman. Her parents were quite proud she had married a doctor and they'd done so well. They had come for a holiday last August, and seemed to enjoy it, though there wasn't much to do or see. 'Well, they enjoyed being with their grandchildren.'

'That's natural.'

She gave a sigh; firm breasts in her brown frock rising and falling. 'Are you happy here, Dr Galewski?'

The question took me aback. I considered. It wasn't as easy to answer as one might have imagined. 'I don't think happiness is quite the right word, Frau Lorenz. I'm used to it. I feel I'm useful.'

'I'm sure that's true. Bertold – my husband – speaks well of you; he trusts you, as you can see. Me, I'm not at all happy here. I – Ah, here he is!' The sound of a key in a lock, a door opening; she rose hurriedly, smoothing her dress down over her hips, patting her hair into place, though it was already perfectly neat. Dr Lorenz entered. I stood up.

'My dear . . . Sorry to have kept you waiting, Galewski.'

'It's quite all right.'

'I could have done without it. Dr Rohde has flu. A huge hangover, more likely.'

Frau Lorenz blushed and glanced down.

'He hates it here,' he added. 'So he drinks much too much. You may have noticed.'

'Who else was on duty?' asked his wife.

'König. Fischer. Lucas. The weather's calmed down at any rate, thank God. The air's quite soft.' He glanced at the tray I'd put down. 'Food! Good. I'm hungry, my dear.' He started to remove his gloves, his greatcoat.

'It won't be a moment.' She hurried out.

'Perhaps you'd like to wait in the study?' he suggested. 'Play some music if you want. I won't be long.'

'Thank you. You're very kind.'

I found some records of Mozart church music, and put on *Ave Verum Corpus*. The serene, golden strains brought back my father, who'd adored Mozart. I felt a sad-sweet nostalgia.

I looked along the bookshelves. Mostly they were medical textbooks, but there was also Schiller, Goethe's *Faust*, Shakespeare, *David Copperfield*, and a couple of contemporary novels by Gottfried Benn and Rudolf Herzog. Resting on its back half off the shelf, as if Dr Lorenz was in the process of reading it, was a book that took me by surprise. *Der Krieg und der Friede* by Lev Tolstoy, volume I. A handsome calfbound edition of 1908. It had a library stamp on the flyleaf, and a bookmark about half-way through.

The record hissed to its end; I turned it over.

When the music had finished I took down *Problems of the Cardiovascular System* and browsed through it. It was the area of Dr Lorenz's specialism. I became so engrossed I didn't hear him enter. He bore two tankards of foaming beer in his hands, and was smiling broadly, his thin, pale lips pulled back from glittering teeth. I replaced the book and sat down; took my tankard from him and drank.

'It's worked, Galewski!' he said.

'What has worked?'

'Your magic cure! It must have been what you said about that girl. Unlikely as it seems. I didn't have a nightmare last night; in fact I didn't dream at all. And today I've felt much better. A dull headache, no more!'

'Well, that's good.'

'It's such a relief! I could work with a swing again. So' – he plonked himself down in his chair and drew on the beer: 'Ah, that tastes damn good! – there's no need for us to continue. I don't know *how* it's worked but no matter! I shall certainly recommend you to Dr Rohde. Can you cure dipsomania too?'

'Wait!' I said. 'Nothing has happened yet. It takes weeks, maybe months. I really think we should persevere.'

Very well: we could talk for a while this evening. But if he had no nightmares tonight we would consider the problem at an end. Removing his belt, unbuttoning the tunic that had grown overlarge on him, he relaxed, stretched out his legs.

I brought him back to his farmhouse dream. I wanted to explore his relationship with the farmer and his wife in Bavaria: glancing up at the portrait. Frau Lorenz, I said, had revealed their identity. He frowned, as if irritated by her indiscretion; but the slight moodiness quickly cleared. There was little he could add. They had been happy working holidays. The farmer and his wife had been good to him; a fine couple. Herr Strauss had fought bravely in the trenches and after Versailles had joined a Freikorps. In other words, he was a patriot. In his plain, unlettered way he'd inspired him.

'But I don't see that farm as looking anything like the one I entered in my dream. You remember I crawled down from a mountain. There was no mountain near the farm in Bavaria.'

'The mountain, yes. You were injured and crawled down a moraine towards the farm. Did you climb mountains?'

Yes, indeed. He'd spent happy days in the Alps. It was one

of the curses of the war that he could no longer climb. But the day would come.

He didn't wish to say any more about Lotte; he'd covered her last night. All right, I said, but what about the other young woman, later, the one who had conceived a child by him? How had he felt about her?

He had felt sorry for her. She was a splendid type, strong and loyal and athletic. Indeed she'd swum in the Olympics. 'Tremendous child-bearing hips.' He gestured expansively. 'But rather plain, and so, no husband.' Too many young men had been killed in the trenches. He'd thought of his sisters, spinsterish, embittered. He'd really had little choice, it had practically been an order to help this deserving woman have a child. But she'd insisted on meeting Frau Lorenz to get her approval; and Frau Lorenz had been touched by that. The lovemaking had been purely functional. 'And now could we leave talking of her, please?'

'I'm sorry. Of course. I just had to – '

'I know. You have to ask questions. I understand.' He smiled. 'You can't believe you've done your work so well!'

'Well, frankly, no, I can't!'

I felt, in fact, extremely uneasy. I felt a certain satisfaction that – in really my first hour of my first analysis – I'd had a stroke of intuition, or luck, associating Lotte with Lot; but I had little idea what to do with it. I was fumbling at random. Yet here he was, convinced he had been cured, after a couple of hours' conversation.

He really *must* ask Rohde if he'd be interested in this treatment. Delicately, he would approach it delicately; but Rohde wasn't closed-minded. Not like Klein, or Entress, or Fischer.

Or Dr Stolb – now there was a real inflexible swine. Though he had maybe softened just a little since having a baby in his house.

A quietness fell for a moment; then I said, 'Why did they call her Alma?'

He glanced up at me, startled. 'Oh! – I've no idea. Well, I would think – it was probably Stolb's choice. He loves music!' He moved his arms as if playing a violin.

17

'You mean . . .?'

'After a certain orchestra leader we both know. I would say so! He probably loves *her*!'

'*Really*? You're not suggesting they've . . .'

'No, I'm not suggesting that. He's incapable of it. I've heard he's impotent.'

'Ah! That would explain a lot.'

'Yes, I don't think it was Frau Stolb's fault they hadn't had a child. Otherwise he'd have divorced her years ago.'

He had started yawning; he'd had a long day with the extra duty; he would have to dismiss me. His brother-in-law was coming for a visit, arriving tomorrow morning. He grimaced. He didn't care for him overmuch; a dull bureaucrat. But it would be nice for his wife to have his company for a few days. It almost certainly wouldn't be necessary for me to come again. He was extremely grateful. If there was anything he could do for me . . .

Dr Lorenz was not on duty the next day. I laboured to help the poor victims of tuberculosis, dysentery, fevers. For the most part I was assisting the senior physician, Dr Wirths. It was a pleasure to work with so kind and conscientious a man. Since his arrival to take charge, the hospital block had been transformed. There was now decent equipment, and the sick lay on clean sheets. The day passed swiftly and productively. During the afternoon an orderly handed me a note. It was from Dr Lorenz, asking me to turn up as before at eight. I was not surprised.

This time Dr Lorenz himself opened the door to me. I could see at once that his good spirits had evaporated, and he was in pain. 'Come in,' he said, and I followed him into the hall. There was the unfamiliar domestic sound of a cistern gurgling, and a man – I guessed he must be Frau Lorenz's brother – was padding down the stairs. A short, wiry man in glasses, in shirt-sleeves and a waistcoat. He stopped short and blinked as he saw me. 'Willi,' said the doctor, 'this is Häftling Arzt Galewski. A valued colleague. Herr Gottlieb, my brother-in-law.'

After an awkward greeting Herr Gottlieb, searching for something to say, remarked that Dr Lorenz had been showing him around this afternoon.

'And what did you think?' I asked politely.

'It's – interesting.'

'He's come to help me with my paperwork. Excuse us, Willi.'

'Of course. Don't let me disturb you.'

He bobbed his head and opened the door into the living room. I caught the murmur of Frau Lorenz asking him if he'd looked in on the children, were they asleep?

'Go through, please,' the doctor said to me.

The study held an extra piece of furniture: a slightly faded but rather elegant *chaise-longue*.

'You were right. I wasn't cured. I've had the most fiendish head all day, and a dreadful nightmare last night. Apparently I was moaning very loudly; I woke up Irmgard.'

'I'm sorry.'

'So I got this; picked it out from our store; it belonged to one of the more substantial houses in the town. What do I do? Stretch out?'

I nodded, and he sat down and tugged off his boots. Then, rather awkwardly, he turned aside and sank back, resting his head on a cushion.

'And I'm supposed to sit behind you.' I moved a chair accordingly and sat. 'Now you talk, when you're ready. About anything.'

He lay stiffly, tense. I told him to relax, unbutton his tunic. He did so.

It was a still night. No sound. I waited, determined not to prompt him. Then, out of the silence, the distant chug of a train. It grew louder, though still fairly faint. The sound stopped; a hiss of steam.

He sighed. 'I'm as relaxed as I can be. It's difficult when your head is thumping.'

Another pause, then I said, 'Go on. What's in your mind?'

'I was just thinking, it's good to be off duty; to be lying here, even though I feel a little ridiculous. I was thinking, Klein and König are on; everything will go smoothly, they're very efficient. Sometimes, if it's Rohde on, say, I worry that he'll be drunk and mess things up.'

A lengthy silence.

'Of course, Willi's arrival hasn't helped. He gives me a headache even when I'm well.' Otherwise he could have had a quiet read. He was reading *War and Peace*: had I ever read it?

Yes, I said; many years ago. What did he think of it?

Well, he found all the personal relationships, the individualism, cloying; but there was no doubt he was a good writer. 'The war scenes are brilliantly done. That's why I'm reading it. I was surprised to come upon it in the library. I thought it might offer a clue about Russian military tactics.'

'And? Is it being helpful?'

'Yes, indeed. The French just cut and ran, and that was fatal. Small guerrilla bands harried them unmercifully. We're quite right to hold our ground and fight to the death. A lot of people are saying von Paulus should have retreated to conserve his forces; but it would have turned into a rout. It has to be a relentless battle of wills. Sooner or later the Red Army will reach the end of its strength.'

He scratched his chest over his shirt; sighed again. 'But let's hope it happens soon.'

He asked if Tolstoy had had any Aryan blood. I said I didn't know. Probably.

Probably, yes, he murmured. He could write. Princess Mary was quite a touching character. She reminded him of his sister Hannah. 'Hannah was in my nightmare. Actually it didn't start as a nightmare but a very pleasant dream. I was standing outside an old monastery, looking out over some wonderful lush pastureland. Fields, woods, little cheerful dwellings. I felt good, happy, looking down at such beauty. It was about as different from the landscape here as it's possible to be. Then a monk came out and asked me what I wanted. I said my sister was a nun in there and I'd like to see her. He said that would be fine, come in, we're having dinner.

'And I came across a table groaning with food; lots of cheerful monks and nuns. Among them, Hannah, as she was about ten years ago, aged about twenty, very attractive; and also Gudrun – Frau Lorenz. I sat with them, they were pleased to see me. I ate and drank, the food and drink were delicious – '

'What did you eat? What did you drink?' I asked rather childishly.

'– Oh, I don't know. Good red wine. Duck. Yes, I think it was duck. Or was it carp? That carp last night was very tasty. It's not important.'

'No. Go on.'

'This is embarrassing. I'd come to sleep with my sister, to get her with child. I was sorry she didn't have a husband; and the Reich needed more children. My wife didn't raise any objections. Clearly I was thinking of our conversation last night. It's very unpleasant that I imagined I was going to impregnate my sister.'

I told him such things happened in dreams. It didn't mean he harboured incestuous desires.

'Well, then, after that, the dream wandered a bit.' He was mounted on a horse, and looking at the turrets and spires of Moscow, ready for the command to advance. 'That was just one thing; it became confused; lots of images; I forget them. But it came back to me entering my sister's bedroom in the monastery, seeing her shape under the sheet. I got in beside her. Monks near by were ringing a peal of bells. It didn't bother me; I wanted to do my duty by Hannah. And that's where it became nightmarish. Because as I started – you know – making love with her, I found she was just a collection of bones. A loose-jointed skeleton. The bones were rattling around in my arms. But I had to keep going, because it was still Hannah, you know? Had to keep on making love.' It was horrific; he could still see her skull grinning at him from the pillow; the hollow eyes. He had kept moving his hands around to try to find her body, her warm flesh; but encountered nothing but bones.

'That must have been dreadful for you!'

'It was! Apparently I was screaming the house down.'

'So, have you any thoughts about what it might have meant?'

Turning over on to his side, he rested his cheek in his hand.

'I can only think I might be a little worried about my sister. She's a typist in a Hamburg factory. But in actual fact I don't feel very strongly about her, she means very little in my life.'

He went to answer a call of nature, and when he came back he did not lie down but sat, crossing his legs, lighting a cigarette.

He stretched his free arm across the back of the *chaise-longue*. His headache was a lot better, he said; it was obviously good to relax. He thought his brother-in-law was mainly responsible for his bad state today. They hadn't seen him for a couple of years, mercifully, not since . . . He broke off from his sentence, looking thoughtful; the hand holding his cigarette rubbed his stubbled chin.

'It's suddenly occurred to me. I think I know where my dream took place. It's surprising I didn't see it before. Well, the scenery was different, and the building wasn't the same shape, but – yes, it has to be.'

From 1939 to '42 he had been serving at Hadamar, a mental asylum near Linburg. That was where they'd last had a visit from Willi, when he was grieving over the death of his wife. Hadamar had been a good posting. It was on top of a hill, with a charming panoramic view; the children were at an extremely likeable stage; and of course the war was going wonderfully well.

'Did your sister – did Hannah – visit you there?'

'No. I last saw her in Hamburg in – 'thirty-seven, I think. But the point is, Hadamar used to be a Franciscan monastery. Till about eighteen hundred.' His face became dreamy, wreathed in smoke. 'I'd like to have lived in that era. Well, in some ways. Goethe.' He glanced at the bookshelf. 'High civilisation. Mozart – I heard you play the *Ave Verum*. Beautiful. Did you know that, when Buchenwald was constructed, the planners left Goethe's favourite oak tree intact? They built the camp around it?'

'No, I didn't know that.'

He nodded, dreamily. It showed the Germanic respect for culture. But, coming back to Hadamar, it had been almost possible to imagine those brown-robed Franciscans flitting around the great chambers and corridors. 'So that's, I suppose, where I got my monk. We should have a drink. I dread going to bed. One drink won't do any harm, though I must be careful.'

He went out and returned with a bottle of vodka and two glasses. Poured us generous helpings and sat down again. 'My brother-in-law's gone to bed. He keeps very regular hours. I think he found today a strain, he became quite grey, and put off visiting the hospital till tomorrow. I took him through a selection, from beginning to end. I wanted him to see it's not all wine and roses for us, even though we're not fighting at the front. He was very impressed by how smoothly it all went. I told him it wasn't always like that; it only happened because of a lot of thought and planning.'

'That's true.'

'He was very taken with members of the Sonderkommando, how they did their utmost to keep the people calm while they were undressing. He followed one of them around, and heard him talking to some woman with three kids. He said the woman kept mentioning names, presumably of relatives who'd arrived earlier, and although he couldn't understand what he was telling her he knew he was reassuring her that they were okay. And so her nerves were calmed. He was very impressed by that; he kept saying to me, "But this man was a Jew himself!" He gave a wry smile.

'A half-hour later, he watched the same prisoner shearing the hair off the dead woman and her children, and stuffing bread into his mouth, quite coolly. He said to me, "Have they become hard, have they no emotions left?" I said, "I expect there's an element of that, but they're also doing their people a kindness."'

It was difficult, he reflected, this question of whether or not someone had the right to know they were going to die. Willi had let his wife die, riddled with stomach cancer, without ever telling her she was terminally ill. He and Frau Lorenz had kept urging him to tell her the truth, so that she could make any arrangements she might wish to make; but he was too cowardly. Yet even for a doctor it was hard to tell someone the awful truth.

'I remember,' he said, pouring me another drink, 'about eighteen months ago. It must have been just before you joined us in the block; I needed to section lungs while they were still alive and working, and I chose a German Jew who was going to die anyway. He was prepared for anaesthesia – I think Lasalles was the prisoner-doctor with me – and became frightened. He stared up at me and said, "You're going to kill me, aren't you?" I said, "Don't be silly, I'm just going to give you an anaesthetic,

23

you won't feel anything." "No, you're going to kill me! I'm going to die!"' He sighed. 'Well, I didn't know what to say. But then I put myself in his position and I also thought of Willi's wife. So I said to him, very gently, "Yes, you are. But we are all going to die some time, and what you'll be doing is contributing to knowledge. You will help others to live. And I promise you you will feel no pain."

'And after that, he became resigned, he didn't make another murmur. He just closed his eyes and waited for unconsciousness. Since that day, if they ask, I always tell them. If they don't suspect anything, or simply are very frightened and don't want to know the worst, I don't tell them.'

But of course, he went on, in a selection, where there were hundreds or thousands of fearful people, it was absolutely right to keep them in ignorance till the very last minute. There were particularly the children's feelings to consider.

We drank in silence, reflective. Frau Lorenz knocked and came in, bearing coffee and cake. 'Oh, you're already drinking!' she exclaimed.

'That's all right, my dear. Coffee would be nice.'

'I couldn't hear you talking.'

'We *have* been talking. Our brains are just taking a break!'

'I'm sure they need it!' she said brightly, setting the tray down. She bent intimately towards her husband. 'Willi says thank you but he'll see the hospital another time. He'll go shopping with me in the morning, and then he thinks he'll take a walk.'

Dr Lorenz brightened. 'That's fine by me!'

She turned towards me. 'My husband gets impatient with civilians, Dr Galewski!'

I nodded, smiled, my mouth stuffed full.

'Well . . .' Dr Lorenz shrugged contemptuously. 'I can't stand golden pheasants.'

'Willi isn't a golden pheasant.'

'Perhaps not.'

'Golden pheasants?' I asked, when Frau Lorenz had withdrawn.

'People who have easy postings, or sit at home making money out of other people's misfortune and suffering. I despise them. I include my brother-in-law in that category. He's an idle pen-pusher.'

And like every functionary, Lorenz said, Willi was closed-minded; his anti-Semitism was total and undiscriminating. He couldn't see that there could be exceptional people. He *might* have offered me a handshake when introduced to me as an esteemed colleague; but typically he had not. His face, coming down the stairs, catching sight of the striped uniform and the yellow and red triangles, had been a picture. A Jew and a communist, in an SS doctor's house, with women and children present! One could see he'd found it most objectionable.

A transport drawing in, distantly. 'From Theresienstadt,' he commented. 'Hungarians. There'll be a lot more.'

Anyway, enough of the unpleasant Willi; where did we go from here? The monastery of his dream-nightmare might be Hadamar, but he didn't see that it took us any further forward towards a cure.

I said it all helped. An analysis was like a huge jigsaw. We'd put two or three pieces together; they made no sense, couldn't be seen as part of the whole picture yet, but given time . . . 'Tell me more about your period at Hadamar.'

It was his first posting where he could bring his family. They had a couple of rooms to themselves; which, for them, was a paradise, after several years of separation. The staff were helpful, for the most part; had made them welcome.

The patients were insane or subnormal, but few of them were violent. He even got to like some of them. But their lives were useless, and it had been a relief when they were ordered to introduce, secretly, a euthanasia programme. But the secrecy brought problems with it; there were stupid mistakes, such as informing relatives a man had died of appendicitis when he'd not had an appendix for years. Also the local people got jumpy about the smoke pouring out of the chimney, and the smell, and the grey SS vans constantly winding up the road to the institution. The programme had had to be abandoned, though they went on gassing children. 'They were children who were really just vegetables; it was a kindness to them.'

There were odd occasions that troubled his conscience. A few patients who really were unworthy of life – 'life unworthy of life' – but, having an affection for them, he had lied on the reports, saying they were capable of humble work. On the other hand, he couldn't think of any patient, capable of the slightest degree of rewarding existence, whom he had condemned to die. With those few exceptions, where soft-heartedness had overcome, he'd done his duty meticulously.

Linburg was a pleasant town; it had some good restaurants and cinemas. Frau Lorenz had put on quite a lot of weight, from all the good food, the dining with colleagues, etc. 'She was a good two stone heavier in those days. Then, suddenly, she was picking at her food, dieting, but I didn't notice the flesh was falling off her.' He smiled. 'Till one evening, when we were going out to a club, she appeared before me in a very slinky off-the-shoulder gown, ready to be admired. And I noticed how bony her shoulders were, all of a sudden! She burst into tears when I complained – I've always liked full-fleshed women. Zara Leander: did you ever see any of her films? *Ewige Weib*, for instance? Wonderful bosom overflowing her dress. But my wife didn't know my taste for fulsome curves! Well, afterwards she started to eat properly again and regained weight.'

'She must have been bony in bed for a while,' I suggested.

He gave me a startled glance. 'Well, yes, she was – I suppose! You mean, the skeleton . . .'

I shrugged. 'It's possible.'

He glanced down at his body. 'Now it's me who's bony.'

I considered my own skeletal arms. 'You still have a way to go.'

'That's so. But you're not badly off for food, are you? I've seen you and your colleagues encourage the patients to eat their soup – but not pressing them too hard!' He gave a friendly grin.

I admitted we did that, yes. It was human nature.

'Anyway, my wife will put some flesh on you, if this goes on for a long time. How long do you think it will take?'

It was impossible to estimate, I said. Maybe a couple of months. Maybe a lot longer. I reminded him how inexperienced I was.

'Hadamar . . .' he murmured, staring into his glass, swilling the vodka around. 'Hadamar was a nice place.' From the calm of

26

Hadamar on the hill to the *anus mundi*. But you had to go where you were sent, without question. In some ways this was more satisfying, just because it was tougher to survive it. He certainly didn't feel he was a 'golden pheasant'; he was in the front line as surely as any soldier facing the Mongol hordes or guarding the cliffs of Normandy; and he had the same feeling of calm, of fulfilment.

'And, on the whole, I think I've remained a decent fellow. I think most of us have. The Reichsführer made a point of saying that, when he addressed the commandants last year. That we'd remained decent fellows, our spirit and soul hadn't been damaged. He used a Homeric metaphor, saying we steered a terribly narrow course between Scylla and Charybdis – on the one hand, losing all respect for human life, on the other, becoming too soft and dizzy and having breakdowns.'

Seeming to grow conscious of my presence, after a reverie, he glanced at his watch. 'It's time.'

I strolled back, towards the lights of the guard-towers. The sentries at the gate didn't bother to check my pass; they knew me by now. Smoke was belching into the arc-lit sky, and there was the overwhelming sickly-sweetish smell; but I was so used to it I scarcely noticed any more. I thought of Lorenz's comment about the soup. It was true, we all did it. But we *did* urge them to eat; it wasn't our fault if some of them were too weak to do so. The whole camp, anyway, was a jungle. You knew that the Kapos cut up the bread into eleven pieces instead of ten, and afterwards sold the eleventh portion. If you had banknotes stuck up your anus, in the *anus mundi*, you were more likely to survive a few weeks longer. As Marx said, it was always *who whom*. I recalled my friend, the green-triangle Kapo who was a chef, also a wife-murderer. He kept a Catholic priest alive with gifts of bread and sausage, so he could absolve him every time he killed someone in the camp. But then, the Jews were no better than the criminals. I could understand, only too easily, how a decent, civilised couple like Dr and Frau Lorenz could find most of my race unspeakable. Oh, there were the occasional Jewish saints, the rabbis who would step into the shoes of a condemned man, the mothers who wouldn't desert their children; but that was sheer animal instinct, and the saintly rabbis were thinking of their souls. They were haggling with God. It was like a bazaar to them: a bit of useless worn-out material, their bodies, for the shekels of eternal life.

They wouldn't have agreed, my fellow prisoner-doctors, asleep in their bunks.

(Litai, a Jew from Gdansk, was moaning slightly; he too suffered from bad dreams.) They thought most Jews did the best they could, in an intolerable situation. They schemed to save a few patients, and it doubtless gave them a sense of moral self-satisfaction. But they ate a little better than everyone else, and that meant someone had to eat worse. They were reasonably safe from selection, which meant the odds were just that degree worse for everyone not so privileged. I guessed that Litai's conscience was far more troubled than Dr Lorenz's.

I undressed, lay down, and found myself in a Parisian restaurant kitchen. I know it's Paris because I'm with Marie, blonde, chic, as I knew her for one summer. My uncle Jacques is also there, in his smart grey business suit. We're looking at the pheasants hanging on hooks, dripping blood. I can't wait to eat. Suddenly my father appears, in his long black coat, skullcap, black Shylock locks; his face terrible as Michelangelo's Moses. 'Shlomo, he's young,' pleads my uncle. 'This girl's a *goyim*, a *shiksa*,' Father growls. 'She's not kosher!' 'You're wrong, Father, it's kosher.' I slip the chef a hundred-franc note. There's a cow having her throat cut; her front legs slide to the ground as the blood gushes; her eyes turn up to us, sad, resigned. My uncle takes me by the lapel and says, sadly, 'Why didn't you tell us, Chaim? Why did you let your dear aunt and me go in, thinking we were taking a shower? And why did you extract my gold teeth? Why did you shear off your aunt's hair? Couldn't you at least have left that to somebody else? Shown a little family respect? Didn't we treat you well . . .?'

Marie, my first, lost, *shiksa* love, was white by now, all her blood spread over the floor. My father said, 'Okay, now you can eat her.'

I woke, moaning, to find Lasalles, the renal specialist from Rouen, leaning over my bunk, his sunken dark eyes staring at me. It was half-light. 'You were in great pain,' he hissed; 'and I've enjoyed it greatly.'

I told him about Goethe's oak, and he became more human; even brought me a mug of 'coffee'. We talked in murmurs because the others were still asleep. Wirths had told him Auschwitz-Birkenau would become the greatest agricultural research station in the east, after the war. How well it will be fertilised, Lasalles said.

He went out to take a look at the patients. Litai stirred, then pulled himself up into a sitting position, rubbing his surviving eye. I offered him the coffee, also a half-smoked cigarette I'd extracted from Lorenz's ashtray. He took it ungraciously, as though wishing he had the strength of mind to refuse it.

'You were screaming,' he murmured hoarsely. 'A nightmare?'

I nodded.

'What was it?'

He was interested in dreams. Though inclined to Kabbalistic mysticism, he sometimes made intelligent observations. I said I'd found my mother being devoured by rats.

The gaunt bald head dragged on the cigarette thoughtfully. 'I'm surprised,' he said; 'there may be hope for you. It's a profoundly religious dream. The mountain shows that. The Son, wounded by the Father's casting-out of his Bride, Holy Wisdom, the Shekhinah, the Great Mother, comes down into nature to find her; but she is being devoured by his Father's progeny. It was your guilt that was screaming; and quite rightly, quite rightly. We Jews are as much responsible as Christians for wiping out the Goddess, destroying the sacred marriage. Our souls, deprived of the feminine, are wounded.'

He paused to stub the cigarette carefully, leaving enough for a couple of draws later. 'This' – his eye flashed right and left – 'is the result. In more personal terms – well, you must decide that for yourself. How it fits in with your toadying to that swine Lorenz, for instance. *Why* do you go there?'

'I'm helping his son to learn French. Anyway, that was an interesting interpretation. Thank you.'

I hoped my thanks hadn't sounded too sarcastic. It had

been foolish to expect help from so unworldly a man. He'd obviously interpreted Lorenz's dream as though it were his own. He mourned still for his female twin, a victim of Dr Mengele; and felt guilty at having survived.

2

I was assisting Dr Lorenz in his ward-rounds. He was talking sympathetically to a factory-worker who had had his arm broken and mangled in machinery; the arm, thanks to Dr Lorenz's skill in a complex osteosynthesis, was almost as good as new, though the patient remained very weak, feverish and undernourished; Dr Lorenz pressed the man's good shoulder, standing up to move on; but suddenly his right leg gave way under him and he had to clutch hold of me to stop himself from falling.

He was rubbing the back of his thigh, still limping slightly, when I followed him into the study that evening. 'I've had an X-ray and so on but there's no problem. It's as if I've got cramp there all the time.' He lay down on the couch.

'You need a good night's sleep. It'll be okay in the morning.'

'A good night's sleep!'

'Another nightmare last night?'

He shook his head. I noticed – his hair close to my eyes – some specks of dandruff. He had the appearance of neglecting himself a little. 'Lots of turbulent unpleasant dreams, but not precisely a nightmare. I don't recall any of them. I just know they were bad. But if dreams are merely bad it's paradise. Last night, I enjoyed my bad dreams because they weren't nightmares. I was like a survivor of Stalingrad finding himself in a Berlin air-raid shelter.'

Perhaps the advance of the Russians was responsible for his stress, I suggested. It seemed to come up a lot.

No. He shook his head firmly. He had no doubt the line would hold soon. No doubt at all. He was still convinced the

31

war would be won. There were secret weapons almost ready to be used. Devastating weapons.

'Then tell me more about your earlier life,' I said. 'Where were you before Hadamar?'

'In a Viennese gaol. I'd been sent into Austria to stir things up, and I was betrayed. It wasn't too bad. I shared a cell with a communist. That's where I learned to respect your lot. At least he had a strong ideology, and was ready to die for it if necessary. We had long, very argumentative, discussions; but they always ended in cursing the Social Democrats and Dolfuss's lot.'

'Was he Jewish?'

Along my upside-down line of sight, past his scurfy hair and slightly hooked nose, I saw his lip curl up. 'No! That surprised me; I thought all communists were Jews. No, he was very Austrian in respect of his anti-Semitism. It gave us some common ground.'

'*I* had a nightmare last night,' I said. 'I met my father.'

He expressed an interest, and I recounted some of my nightmare. 'So you got out of it by bribing the chef!' He chuckled. 'That's typically Jewish!'

'I'd reverted to my fate. Everything was money in our house. Yet he'd been born poor. I don't know how he made all his money in the beginning, but we had the best of everything, plenty of servants, long holidays; my mother dripped with furs. You can only get rich through others becoming poorer.'

He swung his legs off the *chaise-longue* and sat up straight, agitated, angry. His face almost as black as his uniform. He pointed up at the faded sepia portrait of the Bavarian farmer and his wife. 'I'll *tell* you why I have that there, Galewski! They loved their land, it was their dream, they were practically a part of it. Blood and soil. But they fell on hard times in the Depression; got into hock to a Munich usurer. A Jew – of course! I went back to see them in nineteen thirty, proud to show off my SS uniform. They were no longer there. They'd had to start all over again, in poverty. *That's* why I have that photo – to remind me, if I ever doubt it, that we could do no other than this!'

'I know how you feel,' I said. 'I despise them almost as much as you do.'

I suggested he might lie down again. He did so. I waited

for him to settle himself comfortably, folding his hands over his stomach, then asked him if he'd been here when the first *Vernichtungsbau*, or bath-house, had been constructed; the one where I'd worked in a Sonderkommando. He said yes; that was in 1941; he'd been still at Hadamar but had been seconded here for a few weeks since he'd had good experience of gassing facilities.

Tell me about it, I requested. What was the building before it was a *Vernichtungsbau*?

A very run-down, poor Polish farmhouse. Surrounded by hedges, meadows, birches. *Brzezinka*, Birkenau. Birches. He remembered a delicate sky, grey-blue; a kind of crumbly-walled silence and isolation, yet so near to the camp. For a moment he was almost back at the farm in Bavaria – in terms of mud and shit and the hazy sky, not in terms of the poverty and genetic inferiority of its former owners. They had left in rather a hurry, it appeared; leaving a mess the prisoners had had to clear up. He himself had found an old photo album in a cellar; their lives, carefully posed in shabby Sunday best, had touched him briefly. And a broken doll and other toys.

There were five rooms. Sealed and proofed, he'd reckoned it could hold almost a thousand, tightly packed one per square foot, and this had proved to be the case. It was conveniently near the railway, and the bodies could be burned in long, deep pits in the adjacent meadows.

'I think we're going to have to go back to outdoor burning. Too many are coming in from Hungary. Why do you want to know about it? I'd have thought you would have had enough experience of that building . . . Sometimes, when it was my responsibility to stand inside the doors, for reassurance, I would stare at that mass of naked men, women and children, and wonder what those people in the photo album would have thought of it all, if they could come back.'

'They'd probably have said, "Thank God the old farm's still doing something useful."'

He barked a chuckle. 'Yes, the Poles are certainly not crazy about the Jews. Nobody likes them. You know – I had to smile – our maid, who's a Jehovah's Witness from the Danzig area, told my brother-in-law, as bold as brass this morning, that she thought it was right for the Jews to die, because of what they did to Christ! My dear brother-in-law was very taken aback! So you see, they're hated by everybody. The Jews ought to ask themselves why it is everyone hates them.'

'I was wondering, because of the birch trees,' I said, 'whether this was the farmhouse you dreamt about, a few nights ago. Where your mother was gnawed by rats.'

'The Jews as rats . . .? It's possible. It had something of that feel about it. That's clever of you. I'd never have thought of that. You Jews *are* clever. That's what makes you so deadly. I sometimes think the Jews and the Germans are the only clever races.'

'I don't necessarily mean the rats stood for Jews. We ought to think longer about it.'

He had tensed; his shoulders under his jacket tautened. 'They were under the bedclothes, they'd already devoured her genitals. Yes! They'd have loved to do that. I watched them pawing my mother as she shopped. That smell they have! Puh! And they say dogs smell! You know, Galewski, I once shot a beautiful wolfhound because it had gone wild and was attacking a prisoner. It was early on. Then I looked at the beautiful dead body, and at the miserable cowering smelly Jew I'd saved. And I resolved never to be so stupidly sentimental again.'

Since Darwin, he continued, it was ludicrous to consider our species sacrosanct. The wolfhound he'd shot had been more intelligent by far, as well as more graceful, energetic and purposeful, than the idiot children he'd had at Hadamar. Yet the liberals, the democrats, placed a pale around the human species, saying thou shalt not kill. It was pure self-seeking. We could torture and destroy animals to our hearts' content, yet we mustn't touch the most degraded and destructive human animal, except in war.

On 1 May, dear to my heart, panic struck the hospital block. Gilchik, squat, round-faced, spectacled, rushed in and told us there was going to be a selection. Rohde, the worse for drink, had dropped a heavy hint. And it was true the ward was bursting at its seams; but that was common. We rushed around, getting everyone out of bed and out of the block who was capable of moving. They protested, they cursed us, they wept; and some adamantly refused to budge. Or were really incapable of surviving outside.

There was an even riper smell of shit than usual, for the prisoners felt our tension.

The SS troops arrived, surrounding the block. Two empty lorries drove up. Then Dr Lorenz strode in. Even my friends knew it could have been a lot worse; we'd expected Entress. His face lean and ascetic as a priest's, his mind sadistic.

Lorenz called us aside. We had to make a list of the hopeless cases. He would wait. He sat, nursing his leg.

Lasalles, Litai, Gilchik and I made separate lists, then compared them. Theirs were all in low single figures, I had twenty down. They argued, they cursed me in whispers. I told them if they gave Lorenz their lists he would laugh at them. And he'd do his own check and we'd lose not twenty but forty at least.

They wouldn't listen; insisted on a democratic vote. Gilchik gave Lorenz their joint list – five hopeless cases – and he laughed.

He went from bed to bed, shuffling the medical cards. At the end, he gave me a pile of about forty cards and asked me to get them ready for a selection. I had to implore them, order them, to get up and remove their shifts. Many could not stir, but just gazed up at me, uncomprehending. Others staggered out, skeletal figures, moving disjointedly. Mussulmans. So termed because they resembled Indian fakirs. The skin stretched tight over their bones. Their heads looked unnaturally large, their eyes sunk deep, luminous. Sores all over them. I got them all into a line.

Dr Lorenz, a white coat over his uniform, stood on a wooden box; then gestured with his stick. The naked men had to run past him. It was as always an absurd, grotesque sight. Running skeletons, pumping their arms, trying to stick out their chests as if they were Olympic sprinters. Many of them had swollen swinging testicles which bounced as they tried to run.

One of the figures who staggered past the doctor like a marathon runner on the verge of collapse, his legs criss-crossing as he walked, was the factory prisoner whose arm he had saved by complicated osteosynthesis. Lorenz pointed him towards the larger, shivering, chest-heaving group who had been selected for special treatment. I admired, in a way, the SS hardness.

Twenty-eight Mussulmans were led to the waiting trucks. I knew Lorenz had been kind. Most of the other twelve or fifteen were really hopeless cases. If I had presented my list of twenty he would probably have nodded all right, or at worst chosen another two or three as a matter of form.

I pointed this out to my colleagues when the trucks and the troops and Dr Lorenz had gone; but they didn't want to recognise the truth, which was that their stupidity had cost several men their lives.

'It was good of you,' I said to him later that day, in his study, 'not to select more.'

He considered before replying. 'No, it was just.'

He seemed unusually saturnine. 'How is the headache?'

'Bad. All day.'

'I'm sorry.'

'And last night there was a nightmare again. I thought I was over them.'

'Tell me about it.'

His old university tutor of anatomy sent him to fetch a kind of doll with lifelike organs. He opened the cupboard and the doll fell on him; only it was actually the corpse of Heini, an old schoolfriend from Passau, his eyes bulging. Lorenz couldn't push him off him, and his piercing chill stole all through him.

'*Why do I always dream of death?*' he burst out. His brow was bathed in sweat. '*Why do I always dream of death?*'

'I don't know. We must find out.'

'It's not that I'm obsessed with it. I don't give it a thought. It's the inevitable end of life, that's all. All that matters is the race, the *Volk*.'

'Tell me about the university tutor. And Heini.'

There was nothing much to tell. The tutor was, unusually, a supporter of the Weimar régime; rightly got the sack ten years ago. But a harmless, decent tutor for all that.

Heini, his schoolchum, had loved philately. Dr Lorenz had envied his large collection. He thought he might even have stolen a few of his stamps, one time. Heini had cried, and

36

he'd always had a guilty conscience about it. Especially since word came that Heini's father had been killed at Verdun. Like three hundred thousand others, for nothing, for a few square kilometres of soil. Dr Lorenz had given Heini some of his toy soldiers to make up for the lost stamps and his father.

He spoke about his feelings of ecstasy and pride at every report of German advance in that war; and the devastating blow it had been to a sensitive adolescent, the news of humiliating defeat. His dream, which I wanted to explore, became lost in politics; we achieved nothing, like the armies bogged down in the mud of France. I craved food, did not concentrate, drawing a mild rebuke. At last nourishment came, in the form of a layer cake filled with cream, and hot strong coffee. My patient, sitting up, said jokingly he was surprised there was any cake left, given his brother-in-law's appetite. Frau Lorenz, smiling, said he was out hiking all day so it was no wonder he ate heartily. She was glad, he was missing a wife.

The cake was deliciously soft and moist, but left me craving more. It pained me that Dr Lorenz ate his piece. Frau Lorenz was good at baking cakes, he said; he recalled a cake shop in Passau in his youth, at the corner of a pleasant cobbled street. It had marvellous cakes in the window, and after school he would press his face to the glass. But of course they couldn't afford to buy there, once the inflation started booming. I could guess, he said, who owned that cake shop.

I needed to go to relieve myself. He excused me. I climbed the stairs and went to the bathroom. When I came out I was drawn by the half-open door opposite. I knew it was a child's bedroom. I peeped in. Night had not quite fallen; my eyes adjusting, I saw a sweet blonde girlish head on the pillow. Irmgard's thumb was in her mouth and she clutched a doll. I gazed at her for a few moments, wondering if she was enjoying an innocent dream.

Linoleum cracked outside the door. I glanced out and saw Frau Lorenz. 'What do you think you're doing?' she hissed. 'Come out!'

Tiptoeing out, I whispered to her, 'I thought I heard a noise; I was checking to see if she was all right.'

'You could have frightened her to death,' she scolded, a little less angrily.

'I'm sorry.'

My arms hanging at my sides, my shoulders hunched, I grew conscious of my striped prison garb, my shaven skull.

'All right,' she said, relaxing. 'But don't do it again.'

When I entered the study again and sat behind him, Dr Lorenz said to me, '*Ewige Weib*.'

'Pardon?'

'Sorry – my nightmare about the rats gnawing at my mother. It's suddenly struck me we saw a film, a few weeks ago, called *Ewige Weib*, which compared women in history with rats.'

'*Women* with rats?'

'Jews. Did I say women? I was mixing up the films. *Ewige Jude*, of course. I had in my mind an image of Christina Söderbaum, who was ravished by a Jew in *Jud Süss*. Have you ever seen one of her films? She's adorable; winsome and snub-nosed, truly *ewige weibliche*. But anyway, yes, I'm sure the rats gnawing at my mother are Jews.'

'So, we have you coming down from a mountain, dragging your leg,' I said pensively. 'And we know that leg reminds you of your crippled father. And then the farmhouse has suggestions of the old converted peasant farm here at Auschwitz. And you find your mother in bed, half-eaten by Jews. It's beginning to make sense.'

'Is it? Then why is my head still throbbing?'

'It takes time.'

He pointed out that his father hadn't been exactly crippled; indeed he'd come out of the war quite lightly. Compared with the severely brain-damaged ex-soldiers at Hadamar, for instance. 'It distressed me, Galewski, having to sign their lives away; even though it was a blessing for them. But the worst was that our soldiers in the east got wind of what was happening, and were understandably uneasy about the same thing happening to them, if they got badly wounded.' That was why the euthanasia programme had been a mistake, or at least premature. He'd been relieved when they'd called a halt to the adult killings.

I waited in vain for him to pursue this line of thought. After a period of silence I said, 'I'd like to go more deeply into your mother.'

He became slightly irritated. He'd told me everything. She was a simple good woman, devoted to *Kinder*, *Küche*, *Kirche*; the best kind of Aryan wife and mother.

'Is she very religious?'

'Quite religious, yes.'

'Forgive me, this is a rather personal question: are you still a Catholic?'

He shook his head.

'Do you believe in God?'

He hesitated. 'I'm a Godbeliever, like most in the SS. I'm not sure what that means. But there must be Someone, I think, taking care of the world; saving the Aryan race, for instance, from the flood which overwhelmed Atlantis, their original *Heimat*. I also admire certain great religious figures, in particular Luther. He identified the Jewish problem early on. Set their synagogues on fire, he said, strip the poisonous worms of their belongings and drive them out of Germany for all time. That's very good.'

He interrupted my next question by saying it was time to finish: pulling himself upright and tugging at his uniform.

The next evening I moved us at once to his mother, asking him to give me a mental picture of her, from his childhood. He evaded my request, speaking instead about the hard days those had been for everyone: yet no harder than for the youthful Hitler, struggling for existence against the Jews of Vienna. Lorenz's pre-war cell-mate, the Austrian communist, had told him an interesting anecdote he'd picked up from an uncle. His uncle was sure he'd seen Hitler at a railway station, gathering up luggage for travellers. It was known that he had done this, in his poverty. 'He described to his nephew a scruffy figure, with long, unkempt, greasy black hair, and wearing a long, ragged black coat he'd probably bought at a Jewish pawn shop. He carried the holiday suitcases of my cell–mate's uncle, who tipped him. Tipping the Führer! It's a strange thought. Life is very strange.'

'Yes, it's intriguing . . . But coming back to your mother – do you have a photo of her?'

'Not to hand. If you want an idea of her, open the top drawer in the bureau there' . . . he pointed. 'You'll find some postcards. Give them to me.'

I did as he said. Without rising from the couch he riffled through them, then handed me one. A reproduction of a painting, it showed three women, two old and one young, in peasant dresses and hats, at worship in a church. Sitting devoutly, two bent over their Bibles, one straightbacked; large gnarled hands joined in prayer. All their hands were overlarge and used to hard work. The young woman, white-aproned, was big-boned and ungainly, a virgin and fated to continue to be.

'That's my mother.'

'Which?'

'The one in the apron on the left. I bought it in a picture gallery in Hamburg, some years ago. Hannah dragged me along, I'm not really terribly fond of paintings. But I liked that one. Hannah could see it too – that it was our mother. Usually she'd be sitting with one of my aunts, and sometimes a neighbour, in the church. This is during the war, I'm talking about, when the men were mostly away.'

It gave me an impression of a strong, simple, devout woman, I said.

He was about to say something else, but closed his mouth. 'Go on,' I urged. It was nothing important, but he remembered now he'd seen three prisoners sitting, three women, who'd reminded him very strongly of that picture. It was last Christmas. Did I recall the families who'd been arrested in the town on Christmas Eve, by any chance?

'Yes.' Even in Auschwitz it had been a scene hard to forget. I'd been summoned around noon that day to Block Eleven, a block whose windows were sealed up. Victims of camp selections were shut up there for days, waiting for the gas, often without any food or water. That festive day the camp orchestra, its girls in bright dresses, was playing in the open air near by. Strauss waltzes, carols. I remember 'Stille Nacht'. It was a drizzly, chilly morning. When I entered the block, there were many SS soldiers and doctors, and six badly beaten-up civilians in rough everyday clothes. Dr Lorenz was present.

Three of the prisoners, I learned, a married couple and their son, were German. The man, who was one-armed, had worked for the Polish railways and had been settled in Oswiecim, with his family, years before it became Auschwitz. The town had long been a major junction.

Just after the camp had been set up, a Polish family by the name of Korczak came to share the German family's home. They were supposedly relatives – a couple of a similar (middle) age, and their teenage daughter. None of the Polish family looked very Jewish, but this is in fact what they were.

They had kept a discreet profile, seldom leaving the house. But someone in their street had betrayed them. A lorry-load of SS soldiers had turned up outside their house on Christmas Eve morning. The Polish male was ordered to drop his trousers, and was found to be circumcised. A search produced a Torah and other Jewish articles.

These, then, were the frightened people in Block Eleven who sprang into my memory when Dr Lorenz invoked that Christmas past.

'When I arrived to examine them,' Dr Lorenz said, 'I saw the two women and the Jewish daughter sitting on a bench by the wall, hunched over. The German woman was reading a Bible. Although they were all younger than the women in that postcard, I had the feeling I'd seen such a tableau before. Then I recalled the Hamburg painting. The resemblance gave me an odd, prickly sensation.'

I invited him to tell me everything he could recall.

'Why, do you think it's relevant? It just crossed my mind – a coincidence.'

I said one never knew what might be relevant.

'All right . . . I examined and questioned the German couple. They were badly cut and bruised; there was no excuse for that as they obviously hadn't resisted. I made a note of it, and the NCO in charge was confined to barracks for a week. Well, they told me these Jews were friends of theirs from Cracow; decent people. I told them every German knew of at least one "decent" Jew, but in fact they were all our dire enemies and had to be wiped out. The woman, who I must say was very brave, said to me it was terrible what we were doing in here. I remember she said, "When I see the smoke and the fire, I think

perhaps Christ is being killed again." She shed tears only when
begging me to spare her son.'

It was obvious none could be spared; but he hadn't wanted
the German family, whom he'd rather liked, to be hanged
in ignominy. He also – it was perhaps a weakness – didn't
particularly want to be involved in killing, especially killing
Germans, on this festive occasion. He knew Stolb and Tillich
had no such compunction, and no family lunch planned, so he
left the executions to them. He expected them to use phenol.
'But as I'm sure you recall, they didn't.'

He waited for a response, seemingly; when I made none
he said, 'I'm still not entirely clear what happened. I've heard
different versions; I'm sure there was a cover-up.' Outstretched
on the *chaise-longue*, he looked back at me over his shoulder. 'I'd
like to hear what really happened from your lips . . . Don't
worry, this is between us. The affair is closed, it won't be taken
any further; I'm just curious.'

'Well,' I said, 'Dr Stolb and Dr Tillich were just a little – '

'Drunk? Yes, I'd already gathered that.'

They had wanted some fun. And Irma Grese had turned up,
brandishing her whip; blonde, plump, ravishingly beautiful,
wearing a cream-coloured suit and slingback shoes that were
probably a gift from Canada. A creature from another world.
I surmised she had a date with Dr Mengele, but meanwhile had
some time to kill.

'Dr Tillich,' I said, 'told the prisoners they all deserved death,
but as a seasonal gesture the commandant had decided to spare
half of them.'

'That was a lie.'

'He said they could have the choice. Each should write down
the names of the three people they thought should be spared. I
had to give out pencils and paper.'

A 'Kovno-style choice', Tillich had called it. He had been in
the Lithuanian city when the SS told the ghetto's Judenrat they
could choose four hundred who would be given 'life-permits'.
Once they'd chosen the four hundred, each person had to select
three relatives to survive with him.

'He and Dr Stolb,' I continued, 'read out the prisoners' lists
aloud, after I'd collected them, and calculated who was to be

spared. On a points system. But then Tillich went out and came back a few minutes later, saying that now only *one* was to be spared, they'd have to vote again.'

'That's pure sadism,' Lorenz hissed, with an angry shake of his head. I recalled the sobs and the abuse, as friendships and loyalties between the families dissolved in an instant. The male Jew had written down the names of the German family, but his wife and daughter had chosen their own family.

'And I gather the Jewish girl was spared,' Lorenz said. 'I was told she wasn't actually Jewish; she claimed the two men had kept her locked away in order to abuse her sexually. Stolb didn't believe her, so ordered her to sleep with the Jew – the man claiming to be her father. Stolb did this thinking it would soon establish her as a liar, but she proved him wrong. This is what he told me: is that how it was?'

I hesitated. Should I tell him *I* was responsible for saving her life? She wasn't pretty but something had touched me about her: perhaps her fierce lust to live. 'I must live!' she'd whispered to me, her eyes wide and glazed from terror. Tillich, Stolb and Grese were bent over the pieces of paper, grinning broadly. While they were distracted I whispered to the girl, 'Here's a way that might work . . . It's *Nacht und Nebel* with those brutes . . . You have to disown your family . . .' Over her protests I said, 'Leave it to me, I'll say it for you . . .'

I decided not to tell Lorenz this. For the girl's sake, not mine. 'That's correct,' I replied. 'I think she was telling the truth.'

The Jewish couple had started moaning as I conveyed, first in German then Yiddish, their daughter's 'accusation'. Grese's whip lashed out at them. The Jew was ordered to undress, to lie on his daughter. She, Judith, was weeping. The mother had fallen to the floor and was tearing her hair. The man couldn't get an erection. I crouched and whispered, 'Take his penis in your mouth; do whatever you have to, everything depends on this moment.'

And she succeeded. I think her father himself realised, eventually, this was a possible way of saving her life. After he had entered her – with some difficulty – he kissed her very tenderly on her brow. This was the farewell caress; the rest, you could see, was a nothingness, a physiological reflex. Tillich called out, 'Give us a Messiah, Yids!' Tears coursed down both their faces – It was perfectly obvious to everyone that this was father and daughter, and that the girl had been a virgin. Irma Grese's eyes were firmly fixed on her, and beads of sweat stood on her brow. She would want this girl. I knew then that her life would be saved.

'What's happened to her?'

'She's working in Block Ten.'

He nodded wearily. 'And then she was ordered to shoot her abductors?'

'Yes.' My head swam, remembering. Not all had been shot; and only one – the boy – mercifully, in the back of the head. Sexually stimulated, the three SS had stretched their imaginations.

'Thank you. The truth at last. Or as much as you dare release to me. It was barbaric. They're brutes. A woman too! Grese is a swine. But I feel it was partly my fault; I should have stayed and done my duty, rather than hurry home to my family lunch; it would have been a dignified and painless execution in that case, you know that.'

'I know.'

I suddenly remembered my 'kosher' dream. The death of the German woman, her throat slit, had crept unawares into that dream.

The Christmas massacre had been unusually extravagant and baroque, almost Bayreuth. Even Stolb and Tillich, at the conclusion, had looked furtive, as if aware they had exceeded their physicians' role. Meanwhile, of course, some eight hundred Polish Jews were choking on gas; but that was normal; it could not be compared, in sadism, with Stolb's revolver pressed to Judith's neck, commanding her to fellate her German 'abuser', as he hung from a wire noose.

Irma had given the girl, as she got dressed, a bar of chocolate.

I brought Lorenz back to present reality. The three female prisoners had reminded him of the Hamburg painting. And his headaches had begun at around this time. 'Can you remember exactly when?' I asked. 'Was it before those arrests or after?'

'I don't remember.'

And now it was time to finish, he said, swinging his legs and sitting up. I was startled that our session had been so brief; and disturbed not to have had the chance of some food and drink. I thought the abrupt finish might indicate that we were touching upon something critical. Lorenz's explanation, as we hovered outside the front door looking up at the murky twilight, was firmly pragmatic. He had an important meeting he must attend – to discuss the problem of fuel for the pits they were going to have to use as an extra to the crematoria. Fat from the burning bodies would provide some, but would not be enough. It was a serious problem.

We heard a train pull up, then the hiss of steam and a dog's bark. 'From Italy,' he observed. 'Well, they'll have to wait. It's all getting too much.' He passed his hand wearily over his eyes; his face looked sunken and ashen. Even my estranged colleagues were saying, with satisfaction, that Lorenz had aged ten years in the past six months. He clutched at his skull with both hands.

'Bad?' I asked.

'Yes. Bad. I don't know if I can go on; I'm near the edge. With the problems that are going to get far worse, one needs to be fit. Are we any nearer a solution, Galewski?'

'I believe so,' I lied.

I still had absolutely no idea what was making him feel ill.

Warm weather had come. He asked me one day to visit his house in the afternoon, since he was to dine with the commandant in the evening. I felt, for the first time in two years, a glimmer of physical well-being as I approached the pleasant avenue of bourgeois houses. I knew it was because of the extra food; I was now just over a hundred pounds in weight, and looked – and no doubt felt – much better than my colleagues. It didn't endear me to them. Also, though smoke belched behind me, flames leapt from the chimneys, and the warmer weather made the smell of burning flesh almost unbearable, I took pleasure in the flowers adorning the front gardens. Everywhere else in Auschwitz's vast expanse was mud.

I lingered by the small front gardens, breathing in the scent, savouring the gay colours. I wished I could identify the different flowers, that I'd been more curious about nature. Too many towns and cities in my life. Next door to Dr Lorenz's house I saw a yellow ball bounce out of the half-open front door and trickle down the step on to the concrete path. It stopped by the gate. Out of the door came a toddler, a little girl in a short blue short-sleeved dress and a napkin. Her legs and feet were bare. A chubby, rosy-cheeked child. My heart missed a beat: could this be Elli? But at once I knew it couldn't be; this child had dark-brown hair. Blinking in the sunshine, she took an uncertain step, saw the ball, carefully climbed down the doorstep and tottered down the path towards the gate. I stopped, smiling at her. She stooped and picked up the ball in both hands, holding it towards me, large brown eyes taking me in.

'*Ball,*' she said, holding it up.

'*Ja!*' Leaning over the gate I ruffled her hair. '*Schön!*'

A woman appeared in the doorway, a bath towel draped around her naked body. *Schöne* also, long chestnut hair, newly washed, handsome features, glistening-damp, opulent shoulders and bosom. She scowled at me. Smoke at that moment covered the sun and the flowers dimmed. 'Renate, come here this moment!' she scolded. Then, to me, 'You! Kike! Go away! Be off!'

I moved on past, and opened the gate leading to the Lorenz door. I rang the bell. An elderly woman prisoner opened the door and offered me a suspicious, unfriendly look. 'Go into the study,' she said, pointing a skinny hand. I knocked, and Dr Lorenz called, 'Come in.' He was writing at his desk. 'A moment,' he ordered. 'Please sit.' He blotted his page, stood up, rubbed his thigh, then limped to the *chaise-longue.*

'Thank you for coming at this time. We're saying goodbye to the current commandant and welcoming back the old one. Commandant Höss is returning for a couple of months to help organise the Hungarian action. He's a superb organiser and a fine man; totally conscientious. The problems we've had here were not of his making. It will be good to see him again.'

He stretched out, and lay in silence for some time. I was grateful for the respite; my emotions were overcharged by what had just happened: the child, and then finding myself responding sexually for the first time in this place. It was wonderful what a

46

little food could do. I'd believed myself permanently impotent, and it hadn't seemed to matter.

'I had a terrible morning,' he said with a heavy sigh. 'The headache when I woke up was indescribable. I even thought of shooting myself. I took a sedative, and fortunately it's eased somewhat. But I didn't know what to do with myself on the ramp; I almost envied those who would soon be at peace.'

'I'm sorry.'

'Well, this doesn't seem to be working, Galewski. I'm sleeping a little better, and my weight seems to have stabilised at a hundred and fifty pounds; but the headaches are worse and I'm limping badly, as you can see. I think we should call a halt to this.'

I became alarmed. I desperately needed these sessions.

'Often a patient gets worse before he gets better in this therapy, Dr Lorenz,' I assured him. 'We've only been going a short while, and the improved sleep is really a very good sign, a very positive sign that you'll get well.'

'Truly? Well, then, we will continue. I do find that lying here talking to you seems to calm me. You're a good listener. I'd be sorry to give it up.'

Much relieved, I asked him if he could think of any particular reason for his having felt worse this morning.

Well, he had had some unpleasant news from home. His sister Eva, hitherto the soul of honesty, had been arrested for theft. She worked at a grocery shop, and had been caught smuggling food out in her clothing. His parents were terribly upset; none of his family had ever been caught in a criminal act before.

'Of course there is hardship; but that's no excuse. We Germans have to set an impeccable standard of honesty. The state has enough problems on its hands without some middle-aged spinster from Passau giving them extra paperwork to do. I feel very angry with her. Our parents are not young; this will put a strain on them.'

Also, he'd been upset in a different way, not personal, by something Willi had admitted to Frau Lorenz on the last night of his stay. Willi had felt guilty, and wanted to share his burden. During his wife's illness, when she lay in hospital fading away

47

from cancer, he had found solace with one of her nurses. 'When my wife told me about it, I felt despairing about humanity, Galewski. Where was his loyalty? He has none. Sitting by his poor wife's bed, holding her hand – and then going back home with the nurse and fucking her. You must excuse my coarse language, but that's what he was doing.'

So these two instances of gross disloyalty – his sister's towards her employer and the state, and Willi's to his wife – made him feel that there were no moral values left any more. 'What are we fighting and dying for?' he asked. 'We're taking on the immorality of our enemies.'

You even occasionally found disloyalty among the SS – cases of theft of state property, acceptance of bribes, and so on; though in general the SS was staunch, they kept the blood-oath.

'I've never let my parents down. I can say that at least. We are not close, but I've never been disloyal to them.'

Nor to Frau Lorenz. Though there were some problems. Even before the headaches their intimate life had grown less satisfactory. It was probably his fault, much of it: excessive preoccupation with work. Perhaps they should work towards another child. Frau Lorenz, too, had been a little broody when Frau Tillich had had her baby.

I said, 'Do Dr and Frau Tillich live next door?'

'Yes. Why?'

'I saw Frau Tillich as I came. And her child. Renate?'

'Renate, yes. Frau Tillich is a good woman; she looks after her well. I can't say the same for Dr Tillich. It pains me to criticise a colleague, but – well, I don't have to tell you what he's capable of, particularly when he's drunk too much.'

Didn't he behave decently at home? I asked.

Not always. He oughtn't to tell me this. They sometimes heard the sound of blows, Frau Tillich sobbing. And once he had shot a prisoner who was putting up some kitchen shelves. The prisoner had tried to steal some food, apparently. That had to be punishable by death, but surely not in your own house, with a small child present.

We returned to the subject of his marriage. I supported the idea of another pregnancy; Frau Lorenz struck me as a very motherly woman. Dr Lorenz gradually cheered up; even chuckled now and again.

His wife served us tea and cakes in the living room. As she bent over, her plump breasts overspilling the bodice of her sun-dress, I felt that stirring again. It warmed me almost as much as the tea.

'I'll walk back with you,' the doctor said. 'I've some papers to pick up from the hospital.'

We stepped out to an afternoon glowing with warm sunshine from a blue sky. The smoke had stopped belching for a while and the air was clear and fresh. We both, as one, paused to fill our lungs with it. A bird was singing; bees hummed among the flowers. He gazed up at the sky, crinkling his eyes. 'Yes, how can anyone say there's no God?' he murmured. 'It's an astonishing universe.' Then to my surprise he chanted some verses from Genesis: '"And Jacob awaked out of his sleep, and he said, Surely the Lord is in this place; and I knew it not. And he was afraid, and said, How dreadful is this place! This is none other but the house of God, and this is the gate of heaven."'

We walked towards the camp entrance. An Arbeitskommando was just being led towards it, and we stopped to let them go past: prisoners, guards, dogs. '*Arbeit macht frei,*' Dr Lorenz murmured. Most of the prisoners walked with a spastic gait, and their bald, over-big heads on skinny necks gazed upwards, almost without exception. I'd seen it many times; it wasn't only the fine day; in any weather the Mussulmans, not long for this world, looked upwards. I remarked upon this phenomenon to Lorenz.

'I hadn't noticed it. But you're right. I wonder why it is. Is it some neurological response, or psychological? It would be interesting to find out.'

As we reached the block he said, 'Thank you, Galewski. I thought this morning we were going downhill; but you really do make me feel better. I'll see you in the morning. Goodbye.'

I said, 'There's something you could do for me, sir.'

'Yes? I'll try.'

'I'd like to see Elli. Just once. Just for a few moments.'

He stood frowning. 'Elli . . .? Ah!' He smiled. 'The miracle-child!'

'Yes. Is there any way you could arrange it for me?'

'Absolutely impossible. Frau Stolb never lets the child out of her sight. The only thing I can suggest is, do a favour for Dr Stolb. He's very jealous of Mengele's twins, and my heart-bypass experiments. Why don't you approach him with some psychological experiment? – He's interested in that aspect. Perhaps the Mussulmans' upward gaze? But make him think it's his idea . . . Then, you never know, he might let you see her.'

'Thank you,' I said. He nodded, and turned towards his office.

3

I should tell you about Elli – though that is no longer her name, if she still exists, somewhere in the world. I was arrested in Slovakia in February 1942, as a communist agitator – a Jewish communist agitator – and taken to Theresienstadt for questioning. There, I expected every day to be shot or hanged, but was only constantly beaten up. At the end of March, I was sent off on a transport of many thousands of Jews to an unknown destination. In fact, Auschwitz. On the way there was the usual overcrowding and starvation, resulting in hundreds of deaths.

When we arrived at last and the bolts were pulled back, the dead and the half-alive tumbled out on to the ramp. The Dantesque scene has been described many times, and there is no point in adding to that list. The black-uniformed SS, the scarcely held-back dogs barking; 'Throw everything out, line up at once! *Raus! Raus! Schnell!*'; and weirdest of all, in a way, those spectral, skeletal, bald-headed figures in striped prison garb, weaving in and out of this, sorting us into fives; bobbing, deferential almost. 'Leave your luggage; it'll be brought to you.' It was dusk, and there was no colour, only various tints of grey between the black of the SS uniforms and the dirty-white of the snow lying on the ground. We were all dazed, starving and racked by thirst, deafened by the sudden noise.

I heard an officer shout, 'Doctors *austreten!*' But I had been warned that they killed all Jewish doctors at Auschwitz, so I didn't move out of my group. We shuffled forward slowly, and approached a point where a tall, stout, superbly elegant officer – Tillich, I later discovered – was standing on something, and pointing with his thumb left or right. The old and the very young, or women with children, always seemed to go left, towards a line of trucks. As I came under the haughty gaze I could hear him whistling softly, a well-known Franz Lehár tune. The thumb was going right – right – right constantly now, because I'd travelled with about two hundred young Slovak men. We had to walk. Some envied the people on lorries, but most were glad to stretch their legs.

In the reception block, I learned what was happening to those, the vast majority, who had turned left. The first reaction to that news is total disbelief and then immediately numbness. I was luckier than most in that I had travelled alone. I undressed, and was shaved and deloused; they had not yet introduced systematic tattooing. I was then sent to a stinking barracks where I shared a narrow bunk with three others. One of them died during the night, and I woke to feel a frozen body next to me.

We two hundred young Slovaks had the honour to be chosen as the first Auschwitz Sonderkommando. Our task was to dispose of the gassed bodies. We also, as the summer wore on, had to dig up the burial pits at Birkenau, the village of *Brzezinka*, the place of birch trees. We had to drag the corpses, who had breathed their last poisonous fumes in an old converted peasant farmhouse, to the new crematoria. Auschwitz was still quite virginal. The work was terrible, but we could steal food from the clothes of the victims. Not many of us committed suicide.

But how long would they let us live? It was obvious we were seeing too much. And how long would our minds or our souls live?

If a young man committed suicide by throwing himself into the flames, it was usually because he had just dragged his own child, brother, wife, father, mother, out of the gas-chamber.

One warm May afternoon that happened to me. The word had been given to draw back the bolts. Corpses tumbled out of the doors and the Sonderkommando began the process of dragging the naked bodies out. Among a small group of old, grey-bearded men I found my mother; after her, my wife, and she held our baby Elli to her breast; and I saw that our baby was still alive, eyes closed, sucking at the nipple. Her little plump hand, creased at the wrist, was moving.

Could I be hallucinating? No, she lived! I tore her from

the breast and hugged her; I looked around, panting, like an animal at bay. A few comrades stopped what they were doing and stared at me. 'She's alive!' I cried. 'My baby!' They thought I'd gone crazy. I had, of course, but soon they saw that I was speaking the truth. A guard roared at me, threatening to shoot me, but I shouted at him, 'This one is alive!' The guard would have shot the baby, but fortunately Dr Stolb was striding towards us. I told him she was alive, and she was my baby; she'd been sucking at my wife's breast. He gaped, looked grey. It had never happened before, and he was responsible. 'It's a miracle,' he said, moving his gloved hand to his collar as if to make the sign of the cross. 'Give me it.'

I handed Elli to him; holding her at arm's length he strode away, towards the red-brick crematorium, and vanished.

The rest of the day passed in a delirious haze; I was convinced Elli too was dead. That night in the block I made up my mind a dozen times to go out and walk into the electrified fence.

Towards noon the next morning our Kapo, a mass-rapist from Cologne, pulled me roughly away from a female corpse and growled that I was to go to the hospital at once. Dr Stolb wanted to see me. Dizzy, shitting my pants (a frequent occurrence), I set off. Stolb was known as especially brutal and sadistic; perhaps he wanted to show me Elli's little body horribly mutilated; and would then no doubt shoot me or inject me.

When I had found the block I was welcomed with a hug from a kindly middle-aged prisoner. 'I'm prisoner-doctor Loewenberg,' he said.

'You're a doctor here? I didn't think they had Jewish doctors.'

'A few; I was lucky. Look, Stolb will be here any minute. Come with me.'

He led me down the ward – if it could be called that – past piles of Mussulmans, silently staring or moaning. The smell of my own diarrhoea blended into the total overpowering stink of gangrene, sweat, shit. I followed him into a cubicle. 'There!' he said. 'The miracle of Hell!' I saw a cot – and in it my Elli, on her back, pink-cheeked, her lovely blue eyes open. With a sob I bent over her, stroked her cheek and talked to her. 'We've not much time,' Loewenberg said. 'Stolb brought her in here yesterday to examine her. Essentially to cut her up, find out how she survived. But by sheer chance his wife called in, and she fell in love with her at once because your baby smiled at her. Well, who *wouldn't* fall in love with her?' He bent beside me, touching the fine blonde down on her head. 'What's her name?'

'Elli,' I sobbed.

'Elli. The fact is, she's desperately broody – Frau Stolb. They can't have children, and now their best friends, the Tillichs, have a fine little baby girl. So she's crazy with jealousy. Well, I overheard her talking to her husband, begging him to let her adopt Elli. They can't believe she's a Jewish baby, with the eyes and the hair – he's coming.' I followed his gaze out of the window; Stolb, a white coat over his uniform, was striding towards the block. Loewenberg seized my arm and dragged me out of the cubicle. He faced me, eyes staring deep into mine. 'I lost my two. If you want your baby to live, even in the hands of an SS brute, you must tell him she's not Jewish.'

My brain was reeling. He let go of me; turned away in the direction of the door. It opened and Stolb entered. Eyes of a dead carp, bulbous nose. 'Dr Stolb, this is the prisoner,' Loewenberg said.

Stolb gave a curt nod, surveying me. His stare confirming my unmistakably Semitic appearance, gloom settled on him. 'Do you speak any German?' I nodded. 'Good. Come.' And he led me into an office.

He sat behind his desk, folding his hands in front of him. Suddenly there was a pleading look in his carp-eyes. 'That baby is really yours?'

'Yes.'

'But she can't possibly be Jewish.' The pleading look became almost desperation.

'No,' I said.

The tension drained from his face and his shoulders. He smiled. 'I knew it!'

His mother, I explained, had been only a quarter Jew. And she'd had an affair with a Finnish businessman.

'Finnish! Ah, that explains the colouring!' Well, it had truly been a miracle. I wasn't to worry about the baby, she was alive and well, and a German female prisoner was breastfeeding her.

His wife felt sorry for the poor little baby, and they were prepared to adopt her. In the circumstances, he didn't suppose I'd have any particular feelings, but doubtless I would be glad that my wife's child would have an excellent home.

I expressed my gratitude. He rose to dismiss me. I said, 'By the way, do you know that Häftling Arzt Loewenberg has glaucoma?'

He frowned. 'How do you know that?'

'Because I'm a doctor and I looked him in the eyes.'

And that was how I became a *Häftling Arzt*. A few days later the Slovak Sonderkommando was gassed *en masse*.

There was another selection in the hospital, a small one. Dr Lorenz had been too charitable. Stolb took it. He asked for my list of hopeless cases and I gave him it honestly. Twelve men. He accepted it because he knew it was honest. If I'd said six he'd have had them running past him naked and would have taken fifteen or twenty. The twelve men were given benzine injections. After he'd finished I asked if I could see him for a moment in his office.

'Well, what can I do for you, Galewski? We're out of aspirin, if it's that.'

'I wanted to say, Dr Stolb, I'd be honoured if you'd let me assist you in your psychological experiment. I have some experience in psychology.'

He blinked rapidly three or four times. 'What experiment?'

'Forgive me, I've been listening to gossip. I heard you are very interested in trying to cure homosexuals. And I'm afraid I jumped to conclusions.' I said I had recalled his brilliant insight at Christmas, in knowing that a young Jewish virgin had the heart of a Messalina, and skill to match. Putting two and two together, I assumed he planned to use her with homosexuals. I thought it was a wonderful idea and I'd be very interested to take part. However, it seemed I'd got it wrong and I was sorry for wasting his time.

He was doodling on blotting paper. At length he said, 'You're not a follower of Herr Freud, by any chance?'

'No. I don't rate his psychology at all highly. I'm a keen supporter of Dr Jung.'

'Ah, yes! I've heard of him.'

'And I also admire the work of the Reichsmarschall's cousin, Dr Göring.'

Stolb doodled a little more. I wasn't entirely wrong, he said; he did have some sort of experiment like that in mind. It might be possible to involve me. He would let me know.

The days were drawing out. Now it was still warm and sunlit when I arrived at Dr Lorenz's house in mid-evening. On one such visit I found the doctor absent once more, summoned to the ramp because Mengele was indisposed. Frau Lorenz told me to wait in the study and entertain myself with some music. She brought me bread and sausage and coffee.

Savouring the food slowly, I listened to that tender, melancholy Schubert quartet, *Der Tod und das Mädchen*. Meanwhile I glanced through all his records. He seemed to admire Handel greatly. There was an unknown work called *Wilhelm von Nassau*. Curious, I put on one of the many records, and heard a familiar chorus from *Judas Maccabaeus*. I could see how difficult it was to eradicate all Jewry from German life. Next I put on a soprano aria from *Messiah*: 'I know that my redeemer liveth', since it brought back to me a Christmas in Paris, with Marie, my *shiksa* girlfriend. I'd heard her playing in a performance of the oratorio with the Sorbonne student orchestra. She was a violinist. I sat in the front row of the half-empty hall, and drew in the silent music of her hair, the candelabra's lights creating tremolos in its long, soft waves, down over her shoulder as she swayed to the rhythm of the bow. I had loved her. I had lost my virginity to her in a dark, quiet corner of Notre-Dame; in order, she'd said jokingly, that she could go immediately to confess her sin.

Lost in those memories, I was unaware that Dr Lorenz had entered. Not till the scratchy 78 had finished, and I'd raised my eyes from my palms, did I see him standing there. He too looked rapt; his eyes were open but they stared into space. He jerked himself into awareness and said, 'I'm sorry I'm so late.'

'It's given me the chance to hear some more beautiful music; and to conjure up beautiful memories.'

'It touched a chord in my memory too. I'm not sure what. It's something on the edge of my memory's vision, so to speak.'

He hobbled painfully to the couch; and stretched out, sighing. '"Though worms destroy this body," he murmured, "yet in my flesh shall I see God . . ." Absurd, but very touching . . . Did Stolb get back to you?'

'Yes, as a matter of fact.'

'Are you going to be assisting him with some research?'

I hesitated, finding it slightly awkward. 'Yes.'

'The Mussulmans?'

No, I said. You might term it a psycho-sexual experiment. He'd insisted on that area.

'Naturally!' said Dr Lorenz drily. What was the experiment?

It was a comparison, I said, of different racial responses to fear, in a sexual context. The French termed orgasm the little death; Dr Stolb wanted to bring little death and big death together. Thirty or so young, healthy Jews, suitably well-fed for a couple of days, and the same number of purple triangles, conscientious objectors, would be forced to sleep with the Jewish girl under laboratory conditions. They would be told that if they could continue for ten minutes without ejaculation they would live; if they failed they would be instantly shot. Needless to say, the girl would be required to do her utmost to make them come as soon as possible.

What was the point of it? Lorenz asked. It sounded highly suspect.

'The point is that the Jew is believed to be much more of a slave to his animal instincts than the Aryan. Dr Stolb believes a higher proportion of the Germans will be able to distance themselves from their instincts and so survive. In which case the thesis will have been scientifically proved.' The Germans wouldn't in fact be shot, I added. They would be told they would be, but it would not happen.

He frowned. 'Is it a sincere experiment? Is it valid scientifically?'

'Yes, I think so,' I lied.

'I dislike the voyeurism of it.'

'So do I.'

I also disliked the inevitable outcome in most cases. I doubted if any normally heterosexual young man could copulate for ten minutes with Judith Korczak without reaching the point of no return, even in the face of terror. I consoled myself that I had tried my hardest to get Stolb to accept the harmless homosexual experiment, but he had insisted on this devilishly sadistic alternative. In any case, I told myself, the Jews would otherwise have been gassed straight away; I was giving them a few days of good food and rest, followed by the chance to sleep with a girl of immense erotic power. If I had to die, I knew which death I would choose.

'However,' Dr Lorenz reflected, 'I suppose it would be useful scientific evidence of something we merely know in our bones.'

'I think so.'

'And will he let you see your daughter?'

'Yes. For a moment.'

'Well, that's good; I'm pleased for you.' And I could tell that he meant it. 'I suppose we should get on; though I'm tired. We'll keep it short.'

He had had another Jew-dream. Very unpleasant. It had started well. He was on leave, visiting a holiday resort. The signposts said Padernice. It was a nice town, scrupulously clean; excellent facilities; and by no means overcrowded. No Jews, he had observed; and it made a wonderful change after Auschwitz.

However, while he was taking a shower in a hotel room, suddenly a door closed on him and he couldn't get out. He could hardly move in the cubicle. 'And suddenly lice – actually little black beetles but I thought they were lice – poured out of a crack in the tiles and swarmed all over me. They covered me from head to foot. I screamed. My wife woke me up.'

Well, it was quite clear, he mused, the Jews were the black lice. Padernice was a significant name; it was the name of a nonexistent town given to Jews in the ghettos who enquired where their relatives had been sent to work. There were no Jews in Padernice, it was a wonderfully clean city: yet they *were* there, lurking, disguised as insects.

We explored the dream further for a short while, without finding anything unexpected. Then I brought up again a youthful homosexual contact, which he had confessed to me previously. A youth in a Bavarian Freikorps. It appeared to have been just normal youthful experimentation.

Suddenly he was struggling to breathe, choking, fighting with his whole body to push something away from him. I was frozen to my seat, frightened for us both. I'd just managed to rise from my chair and taken a step towards the door when the choking fit subsided as swiftly as it had come. He panted, 'It's all right, it's all right; sit.' I returned to my chair.

He calmed down. It was the third time that kind of thing had happened, he said. A sort of asthma attack.

'You must get some rest, Dr Lorenz. Let's finish.'

He pulled himself erect and rubbed his eyes. Then he said, looking at me, 'My mother is dying. I had a telegram this morning. A stroke. She's not expected to live more than a few days.'

'I'm sorry.'

'I blame Eva's thieving. The scandal was too much for my mother. She's a very conventional woman. They both are – both my parents. They hated it when I joined the SS, and really we've not communicated much since. I'm taking compassionate leave to say goodbye to her. And then I have some business in Berlin. You won't see me for a couple of weeks.' Rising awkwardly he added, almost shyly, 'I shall miss our evenings. I shall miss you.'

I missed him too – in a way. Missed his wife's food, certainly. Yet it was also a slight relief not to have to confront my own floundering incompetence. After my initial stroke of intuition – which seemed more than ever now like simple good luck – I had absolutely no sense of direction or purpose: except to survive and eat. At times, when he was feeling slightly better, Dr Lorenz seemed to enjoy the explorative process more than I; even surprised me now and then with an intelligent perception.

Only one thing was more important than to eat, and that was to see Elli. That prospect made the horror of Stolb's laboratory experiment bearable.

One brilliant early June morning, after our session, Stolb detained both Judith and me, saying he had an extra duty for us outside the camp. I felt an uneasy prickling in my nape. The Allies had just landed in Normandy, and he might want to get rid of witnesses. I even felt, reviewing the session, that there had been a climactic air about it: for besides Stolb and a cameraman there had been Irma Grese in attendance, watching keenly, and Dr Niemans, the camp pharmacologist. (The mere rumour of having been involved in a sadistic sexual experiment may have been responsible for Niemans's unusually heavy sentence of six years' imprisonment pronounced by a Cologne court in 1957: even though the suffering of the Jews and German pacifists – who were not, after all, spared – was as nothing compared with the daily horror of the camp, or the more 'legitimate' experiments.)

I was fearful at Stolb's order; but there was nothing I could do. 'Pick up an emergency medical box,' he said to me. He said to Judith, 'Today you are the prisoner-doctor's nursing assistant.'

Two armed soldiers escorted us out to a grey van and we climbed in. The van started off, through the camp, and out of the gates. Then it pulled up again and I glimpsed the colourful flower gardens of the staff-houses. A few minutes later, three female prisoners got in; one of them the severe-faced, violet-triangled servant of the Lorenz household. A soldier handed in after them a large box, like a picnic hamper. We drove off again. I felt a little easier; it seemed unlikely they'd be shooting these women too.

After a couple of bumpy kilometres, we could glimpse trees – countryside. We stopped. 'Out you get!' said the soldier, opening the doors; but not as they did at the ramp. Grass, flowers, birches, a pool! We stood dazed, blinking. The soldiers threw themselves down and removed their helmets, fished out their cigarettes. They weren't interested in us. 'What are we here for?' I asked them.

'Wait. Enjoy yourselves. Have a swim.'

Judith was an innocent girl again, blushing as she pulled off her heavy men's boots and ragged, ill-fitting dress. Even the sour Jehovah's Witness stripped to her underwear after a slight hesitation, and we all dashed into the pool. Ecstasy – the cool water, the sun, the dappled birch leaves!

Afterwards we stretched out in the sun, chewing grass, plucking buttercups idly.

Judith and I chatted. Our hopes and dreams. She would have liked to become a dress designer, perhaps. Irma Grese had such beautiful dresses, where did she get them from? They were from all the best couturiers of Europe, I said.

'And her perfumes! They're always different, always so mysterious!'

Her perfume, yes: flooding the lab; flooding Block Eleven at Christmas, as with frankincense and myrrh; blotting out even the smell of burning flesh.

'Always? How often have you seen her?'

A shrug. 'A few times.'

'You're lucky to have survived.'

'It's because I'm plain. I'm told she only kills the beautiful prisoners.'

Sometimes, though, she didn't answer me; stared sullenly into the distance. There was an ambiguity about her, as there was about the doctors, indeed all of Auschwitz. How could it have been otherwise?

'Irma did things to you in the brothel?'

She shrugged, plucking and giving me a harebell – I was ignorant of its name till she told me. 'I suppose so . . . She had me dress in a nun's robes. I don't know why. She said she'd beaten the nun to death. Do you think she did?'

'Yes. Are you in love with Irma?'

'Isn't everyone in the camp in love with her?'

She drifted off into a reverie, not answering if I spoke. But then she touched my hand and said, 'You saved my life. I think. I'm not sure if there's a life to save, any more.'

I laid my hand over hers, and caressed the bony knuckles. 'Yes,' she whispered, 'you've saved me and destroyed me.' She looked into my eyes with naked hate. 'Often in that obscene room I wish it was you lying on me.' She dropped her gaze. 'You may take that as you wish.' Just then the sound of car engines broke the stillness; everyone pulled themselves up into a sitting position. Through the trees came two staff cars, one after the other, driven by soldiers. There were women and children in the cars. Three women, four children. The cars pulled up behind the van; the drivers jumped out and opened the doors for the passengers. We – the girl and I, the servants, the lounging soldiers – jumped to our feet.

Three women: Frau Lorenz, Frau Stolb, Frau Tillich. And their children. *My* child in Frau Stolb's arms. My heart leapt. How changed she was! Golden curls, and so pretty! Tears stung my eyes.

The three servants scurried around, taking rugs, towels, folding chairs, from the cars. The three blonde women fussed their children then took off their robes; underneath they were wearing bathing suits. They glanced in our direction but gave no acknowledgement of our presence. Even Frau Lorenz pretended not to know me. I did not care; I had eyes only for Elli. It hurt me when Frau Stolb called out to her, 'Alma! be careful of the pool!'

The servants opened the picnic hamper, spread out a table-cloth on the grass, and took out a feast. Lemonade was poured into cups, and some was given to the four soldiers; we prisoners licked our parched lips. Then the three German women swam, with Irmgard and Seefried, while the servants took care of the tots, Renate and Alma – Elli. Feeding them baby foods.

'That's my daughter there!' I whispered, swallowing a lump in my throat. And instantly could have bitten my tongue. 'You mustn't tell a soul.'

I told her the story. She had heard a rumour of a miracle-baby who had survived the gas-chamber. She was moved; tears glistened. 'I would draw her for you if we had any paper,' she said.

'You can draw?'

'I was good at it at school. I like drawing.'

I fumbled with the catch of the medical box. Evidently our excuse for being here was in case of an emergency. Stolb had been kind, for once. There was a stubbly pencil and a prescription pad along with the bandages and lints. Resting the paper on the box, she sketched the child, pretending to be looking at the tree behind her. She tore the page off the pad and gave it me. Even at a distance, she had caught a likeness. 'Thank you!' I said. 'That's wonderful!'

I buried it later near the hospital block.

The other child, Renate, bronzed now, naked except for her napkin, tottered towards us, and stopped a few yards away. 'Hello!' I said; and she pointed at me. '*Jude*,' she piped, but it meant nothing to her, of course. She put her thumb into her milk-smeared mouth.

Her mother rose out of the pool and called, 'Renate! Come away!' Renate turned and headed back towards her prisoner-nanny, a woman with the black triangle of asocial behaviour.

I ached for Elli to come up to us, but she did not.

After their swim, the SS wives and older children settled on the rugs and were served their picnic. Some food was sent to the soldiers. At the very last, when the debris was being cleared into bags, Frau Tillich stood up, and threw two pieces of bread in our direction: just as if we were dogs. It didn't matter; we fell upon the bread, and it was good bread.

They lazed; the older children climbed trees and went exploring; the toddlers were bathed in the pool. Then it was over; they got back into the cars, which reversed, then drove away. I watched Elli fade into the trees.

'I'm cured, Galewski!' Dr Lorenz said, greeting me on the evening of his return. He had not lain down but spread himself at ease on the *chaise-longue*.

'Cured?'

'No headaches, no nightmares, for a week – and you can see how I can walk! I cured myself, I didn't need your Herr Freud after all!'

He looked well, I had to admit. Blooming with health and vitality. Heavier too. I'd noticed it in the hospital, when he'd briefly put in an appearance during the afternoon, suitcase in hand, fresh off the comfortable train . . .

'Well, I'm delighted to hear it. How is your mother?'

'Still clinging on, but there's no hope.' Thoughtfully he pulled out his cigarette case. 'But we were reconciled. She can't talk but she was able to squeeze my hand. That was good. And my father and I talked, and – ' he nodded several times – 'I think we made it up.' He pointed to the wall behind me. The photo of the farmer and his wife had gone; there was a different, younger couple, dressed as for a wedding.

'Your parents.'

He nodded, bent over his silver cigarette lighter. He drew in on the cigarette, puffed out the smoke, rubbed his chin. 'It was painful riding through Germany. Those bastards! What they've done to our cities! No doubt the news from the West has cheered you?'

I couldn't deny it, I said.

It would be very different when they came to the Rhine. They would see what the German spirit was really like, when up against it. In the end the English and the Americans would see reason and join them in attacking bolshevism. It was only a matter of time.

'So what cured you?' I asked.

'Well, actually it did have something to do with our sessions, indirectly. You remember you were listening to that Handel aria, "I know that my Redeemer liveth"? It affected me, it stirred up something.'

Returning home after many years, to a sad household, had clicked on the memory like a light. He was about nine years old, playing with an older boy he didn't know very well. They were exploring the church, its graveyard, its crypt. In the crypt they came across a deep tomb, on which you could just read the name Rosen. He must have been a stinking old Jew, his companion said. What was he doing here in a church? Under his name was the phrase 'I know that my Redeemer liveth'. ('I checked this out: it's still there.') Let's turf his bones out, the older boy had said. There was a crowbar lying near by, left around by some builders who were repairing the walls. The boy had crammed the crowbar under the tomb lid and managed to ease it off.

'We were both shit-scared, only neither dared admit it. He dared me to get in and hand him the bones. So I climbed in; it was very dark and quite deep. As I was feeling around for bones, he slammed the lid on me. I could hear him laugh, and his shoes scuffling the stone steps leading up. I was alone there in total darkness, with no air. I panicked, and started heaving at the lid with all my weight, hitting it with my fists, my head. There were insects on my face and hands. I was choking for oxygen. Eventually I must have blacked out. The boy came back and dragged me out just in time.'

'It must have been a horrible experience.'

'So horrible that I forgot all about it. Fancy doing that to someone! I wasn't even sure if it was a dream or a memory; but my father and my sisters confirmed it had happened. Once we all started talking about it, I felt a tremendous release, and my headache went.'

'I wonder why you developed the symptoms so suddenly, at Christmas.'

'Oh,' he said, flicking ash, 'Frau Lorenz gave me the *Messiah* records then.'

I felt slightly foolish. 'I did tell you I wasn't at all experienced,' I said.

He chuckled, and said that all the same I had helped him. I'd set him off thinking about his childhood, and I'd played that record.

Frau Lorenz came in with cheese, potato, beer. She was wreathed in smiles and friendliness. When she'd gone, he asked me about the racial experiment. I said I was glad he'd brought it up as I had a big favour to ask of him. Dr Stolb was terminating the experiment prematurely. He would give no reason. Lorenz interrupted to say he'd heard a whisper that it was all kaput. One theory was that Stolb was frightened by the war situation; another was that someone, possibly Irma Grese, had sent Frau Stolb an anonymous letter.

'Saying what?'

'Oh, you can imagine – that her husband's getting too much fun watching a Jewish slut screwing.'

'So which do you think it is?'

He shrugged. 'Frau Stolb is a fierce woman, a hard woman; probably harder even than Stolb, who's a coward at heart. And she's jealous. But who can say? It seems a pity if it was going well. Was it?'

I said I thought, apart from his bypass experiments, it was probably one of the most important experiments in Auschwitz. It had great possibilities for development in all sorts of directions.

'Well, I'm afraid I carry no weight with Stolb. I couldn't – '

'I don't want you to try to get him to change his mind, Dr Lorenz. It's just that the girl's to be told she'll be shot the next time someone lasts the ten minutes or remains impotent. He wants to get rid of her.'

'And you don't want that?'

'No. I feel responsible for getting her into this. She's co-operated fully.'

He frowned, looked dubious.

'And besides, I like her. A lot.'

He smiled almost roguishly. 'Ah, I see! Well, that's different . . .! I could pull strings to get her back to the brothel.'

'She doesn't want that. Also, it's still too close to Dr Stolb.'

'She might be found a place in the hospital. Working under me personally, so that Stolb wouldn't dare touch her. And close to you, hmm?' He winked.

That would be unwise, I said. My colleagues had an inkling of what had been going on. I wasn't their favourite person in the world, to say the least. The girl's presence would inflame the situation. I suggested she could go to Canada.

'Canada! I see. Yes, that's as good a Kommando as any. All right, I'll see what I can do.'

He got to his feet, and I thought he was going to dismiss me. I felt a sense of panic; I realised I would not only miss his wife's food and drink acutely, I would also miss these evenings of intimacy, however restricted, with that awesome black Death's Head uniform – compared with which even death was a maiden in white. But the dismissal was not to be quite yet; he merely wanted the vodka bottle. He poured us generous measures, then sat down again and hooked one black-booted leg over the other. He was in a mood to chat.

He would get Mengele's support to foil Stolb's plans. Mengele was a good fellow; a thoughtful officer. Though his obsession with twins and dwarfs was a bit excessive, and personally he found his collection of eyes creepy. It was unkind of him to have Häftling Arzt Litai's blue eye where the former Polish gynaecologist could see it. His sister's eyes too? That took obsession much too far. He was basically a good fellow, nevertheless; everyone liked him; and of course all the ladies were in love with him, the women prisoners too. Mengele would support him against Stolb and save my sexy little friend.

He lifted his head, listening tensely. Relaxed after about

66

a minute. 'I thought I heard a plane,' he said. 'The fires are an open invitation to the Allies, it's amazing they haven't bombed us more. I guess they think we're doing their dirty work for them.'

I asked, wouldn't it be possible to extinguish the pit-fires during the brief summer night? They had to be visible for thirty kilometres around. He shook his head; the pressure was too great; even now, transports were having to wait half a day or more before being unloaded.

But my question seemed to make him more thoughtful, even a little oppressed; and he murmured, 'Out of the east cometh the whirlwind, and cold out of the west.' He smiled grimly.

Where was that from? I asked. The Book of Job; he believed he had slightly misquoted it.

But even if the war ended in less than total victory, as was possible, and even if some details of the Jewish action came out, this place would be forgotten in fifty years. Perhaps less. People would not wish to think about it; they would be involved with their mundane affairs – kids, jobs, love, holidays. He saw the Crimea as the future playground of Europe, with a great autobahn running all the way to London. America would be washed up, destroyed by its Jews, Negroes and liberals. Russia would be a poor client state east of the Urals. Japan would control the Orient.

'Everything will become tamer and more conventional. Even the Reich's policies. These years have been a necessary *Blitzkrieg*, Galewski. And yet, something heroic will be lost in consequence. Even this place, with all its grimness and suffering, has a kind of tragic grandeur about it, don't you think? A very Germanic grandeur and purity. Those of you who survive won't find anything to match it.'

He was silent, sombre, for a moment, then gave a wry smile. 'Yes, my friend, you and I might bump into each other on a Black Sea beach in fifty years' time, should we be lucky enough to live that long! Bald and pot-bellied, no doubt!' He gave a shrug as I ventured to say I thought it unlikely. 'As a matter of fact,' he continued, 'I've sworn an oath to go there in nineteen ninety-two! Fate sparing me, naturally. Two years ago I gave a helping hand to the Bata Shoe Company; they wanted a supply of water and I rounded up a few thousand inmates to drain some ponds. They were so delighted they threw a wonderful party for us; and we got talking about the future – life – you know how one does when drunk – and I said, "Let's repeat this on the Black Sea in fifty years' time! I'll only be eighty-five!" It was just a joke, but someone said, "You're on!" And before we knew what we were doing, some of us were drawing blood and swearing!'

He chuckled throatily; poured us another drink; hunched over his glass.

A faint sound of a whistle, barking dogs. He lifted his head again. 'They're unloading,' he said with satisfaction. 'Those people are lucky, if they only knew it.'

'Why is that?'

'Because if they'd arrived at Belzec, Sobibor, Chelmno or Treblinka, not one would survive.' Here, a few score would survive a few weeks or even months. He gulped; gestured to me to knock my vodka back; poured again.

There was a faint knock at the door, and his wife entered, holding out an envelope. 'A telegram came for you,' she said. She looked anxious.

'Thank you.' She withdrew and closed the door quietly. Moving to his desk he picked up a paperknife and slit the envelope open. He removed the telegram and scanned it. His face paled.

'Excuse me,' he muttered, and left the room.

For a while I could hear nothing except the faint noise of barking from the ramp. And then I heard a cry, a whimper, from Frau Lorenz. Her husband came into the study; he wore the vacant stare of a Mussulman. 'My son Heini has been killed,' he said, 'by an American bomb.' He rested his head against a bookshelf.

'I'm so sorry! I didn't know – '

'You didn't know what?' he harshly interrupted.

'– that you had another son.'

'What business is it of yours? Do you think I'd tell all my business to a Jew? . . . Even a decent one,' he added more quietly. 'You did know there was another child. He was just six years old. Probably some kike dropped the bomb that killed him, some filthy American kike!'

Forgive me, he added, he wasn't blaming me personally. He moved away from the bookshelves and went to the window, staring out at the blood-red sky. He wiped a tear from his eye. He said in a tremulous voice, 'Would God I had died for thee, O Absalom, my son, my son!'

I said, 'I'll go; you must comfort Frau Lorenz.'

'Oh, it's not *her* son. She's crying for me; and for the mother too. She knows what she must be feeling. Coming round in hospital; being told her only son is dead.' His voice broke for a moment. 'But yes, please, go. I shall work. There's a huge backlog of paperwork.'

Outside, the evening sky was fading, that part of it which was not filled with a smoky red glow. I walked towards the flames. I was in the Sonderkommando again, and it was those minutes when the people packed into the gas-chamber waited, not knowing what was going to happen. There was always a wait, so that body-heat could raise the temperature, which made the gas more efficient. I had an instinct which told me the wait was now, for those Hungarians. And you knew your turn would come soon, but you were grateful that this time it wasn't; you munched the bread and sausage you found in their clothing.

As I walked, a distant, forgotten memory awoke. I was shearing the hair of some Dutch children, aged from about seven to sixteen, probably brothers and sisters (I'd already dealt with what might have been their grandparents); and when the guards weren't looking I was poking around to see if they had anything hidden in their private parts. The bodies were in a pretty filthy state, smeared with shit and even menstrual blood in one case. They were also very thin, though not by Auschwitz standards; the teenage girl had no bosom and her hip-bones jutted out. Dr Lorenz had walked over and stood above me, hands behind his back grasping his stick. He had gazed down at them with what might have been disgust or pity or both, and said, 'Son of man, can these bones live?'

Rage blinded me to all discretion and I replied in his language, 'O Lord God, thou knowest.'

His face turned red as the crematorium walls; he lifted his stick to hit me; then controlled himself, smiled faintly, and walked away.

JEALOUSY

I

I know what you're thinking: you're thinking, who's this fat middle-aged woman I shall have to stare down at four times a week for the next few months, why did I ever agree to it? . . . I *am* fat, I'm huge, look at this handful of fat; don't try to patronise me. I hate fleshy people. If I were you I'd keep my eyes closed. Maybe that's what you're doing.

So how do we start? With a dream? Isn't that the usual thing?

Well, I don't dream.

When I saw you worked in an office block, I almost turned back. But I assumed you'd at least make it fairly comfortable. When your wife, or whoever it was, gave me an address in Holborn, I pictured something a little smarter.

Your curtains are appalling. The repro of the *Maja nude* isn't bad, but it's terribly insulting to female patients. I'm an artist myself; or rather I'm in art admin. Unless you're a man you stand no chance in the artistic rat-race; I found that out very early on.

You don't say much, do you? You're very young. I wanted a woman. I have very little faith in analysis as it is, but if I have to do it I'd rather it was with a woman. But Oscar, Oscar Jacobson, said he couldn't recommend any at present; the good ones all had full case-loads. So he gave me your number; said you were still in training but quite promising. Are you?

Do you know Oscar? . . . Why can't you tell me? It's ridiculous . . . Okay: well, the answer is I *used* to know him quite well; but I haven't seen him for, oh, it must be fifteen years or more. My father was his batman, or driver, or something, during the war, and they kept in touch after through Christmas cards. I come from Yorkshire, and my parents don't travel far, so Dad's never met Oscar since. But when I wanted to transfer

73

from my art college in Leeds to London, Dad asked Oscar if he could help. Or rather, if his wife could: Myra. She was a tutor at the Slade. She got me an interview. As a student I used to visit their house quite often; they were very kind to me.

Is this what I'm paying for? Silence?

I enjoyed visiting the Jacobsons, it made a break from the student hostel. There was always plenty of booze, and Oscar would play jazz records. Mixed up with classical which I didn't understand. But he wasn't solemn about it; I remember there was one piece of music he played a lot, a vocal piece, about a young man who wants to run off with a gypsy. It's for tenor voice, very screechy and high, especially at the end. The singer on the record couldn't really reach it. And Oscar would jump up from his chair, throw his head back and try to sing it too. Scream it, rather. He had an appalling voice! But he knew it, and was laughing at the same time! He could be lots of fun. It's tragic to think he has motor neurone. But then, he must be eighty at least, so I suppose one has to expect something. Myra's much younger. She's at Brighton College of Art, teaching part-time, but on the verge of retirement Oscar said.

After I finished at the Slade I went off to the States. Fell in love with a Vietnam vet. who'd had his legs blown off; got involved in liberation movements; had a great time. I stayed there about four years. When I came back I met Oscar and Myra a few times but it wasn't the same. People change. Well, and Oscar's politics irritated me more than before. Pretty right-wing. Not Thatcherite, not quite like that fascist, but – sort of mushy wet conservative. I couldn't take that crap any more. Also I got involved with the man who became my husband. Steven. He's a QC. We have a son, Phil, who's fourteen. Quite bright. We live in Holland Park.

But I did hear Oscar give a talk on the radio, six or seven years ago, on the psychology of mass unemployment, and he sounded much more radical. Steven heard it and was quite impressed.

. . . What do you want to know about him? Steven's one of the few men I know who isn't a male chauvinist pig. He helps as much as he can.

. . . Why do you want to know? What has my age got to do with anything? I'm fifty. Women have had it when they're fifty.

Steven's a year older but still attractive to women. He wants to go into politics. He's looking for a Labour seat. Obviously his charm is an asset. I've thought of standing for the council myself, in the past; but I had a responsible job and a son to look after. If your child gets sick, it's the woman who bears the responsibility.

Do *you* have children? No, I suppose you're too young.

. . . Yes, they're both still alive. Very working-class. Dad's retired now, of course. Mum's not retired; women never retire. We went up to see them a couple of weeks ago, during Phil's Easter break. Just for a weekend. That's enough.

My head's thumping. I was in the Poll Tax demo in Trafalgar Square, and got bashed by a truncheon. We might just as well be living under Hitler. What do *you* think of the Poll Tax? I think it's dreadful that decent politicians like Martin Luther King or Robert Kennedy get assassinated, yet vermin like Thatcher get away with it. The IRA missed her by about three seconds, in Brighton.

What do you think?

Fuck. Why can't you answer one simple fucking question?

. . . Well, that was a nice speech. I can see that. Up to a point. But surely there should be some kind of dialogue, for God's sake.

. . . I get a need to eat a lot. When I say a lot I mean a lot. I need to stuff myself until I'm sick. It's as if there's a great big hole in me and I can't fill it. And I wake up in the middle of the night, feeling quite suicidal, and can't get back to sleep again. I'm depressed. I don't want it to affect my marriage, which is strong; or to hurt Phil.

That's it. – So what do we do?

. . . Oh, about a year. I've tried meditation, even tran-quillisers. They don't help. Our GP said what about some psychoanalysis; but I resisted. Then, a couple of weeks ago, I was turning up some old photos and so on, and found one of Oscar and Myra. I thought if anyone knew of an analyst who could help me, he would. I didn't imagine he'd take me on him-self, as he's so old. For all I knew he might have been dead. No, I suppose I'd have read obituaries and so on. Anyway, I wrote.

I'd like to see them again. I don't know how mobile he is. I could ask them to dinner, perhaps.

. . . Oh, it can happen any time. In the middle of the night or at work. I'll go to the canteen and eat three or four jam doughnuts. I'm a vegetarian; we all are. I loathe meat; loathe the smell of it cooking. That's one reason I don't visit my parents more often; there's usually a disgusting smell of a roast dinner cooking.

But if I'm desperate, I'll eat anything. I once – no, I can't tell you this . . . OK, I was out walking in the country and I found I didn't have any food with me. This was at Christmas. We were with Steven's mother in Hertford. She's very posh, a great snob, in spite of being a Labour Life Peer. I needed to get away. But I was desperate for food. So I found a beetle on the ground and ate it! I didn't tell anyone. I threw up. You're the first person I've told. I just needed to get something in my stomach; anything.

. . . That's depressed me even more. I also saw an African painting this morning, which depressed me. It showed children, babies really, lurking in ditches each side of a country road in Africa; and they were all staring down the road. It was very sinister. I found the story behind it in a catalogue. The story goes that children who've been killed at birth or aborted hide by the roadside outside Deathsville, waiting for their mothers to come . . .

Only a man could have made up that legend.

. . . I don't dream . . . I'd have thought it was plain enough. I don't dream. Well, I do have a sort of recurrent nightmare. I guess I've had it two or three times in the last couple of years. I'm in a room where there's a sort of porthole, and it's shut. Then it's opened, and I press my nose against the glass, expecting some lovely view, and I see these horrifying faces. They're distorted, and like squashed against the glass, their eyes bulging, staring at me. Really evil, wicked faces. Their noses all flattened sideways, and their lips. I know what that reminds me of – the Hillsborough football disaster, a couple of years ago. Those horrifying pictures, do you remember? Crushed up against the barriers, unable to breathe. Because the pigs, the police, are more worried about crowd control than people, working people, dying, and won't open the gates.

Yorkshire again. Ripper country. It's an evil place; men totally dominate. But maybe I should have stayed there; lived next door to Mum and Dad; got a job in a bank and married a bus conductor. Eating whelks at Scarborough. I've only had the nightmare since Hillsborough. It affected me a lot.

But at least it's still a community up there; people have caring, socialist values still. I went up to help during the miners' strike, and it was wonderful to feel that closeness again – especially with the wives; they really blossomed during the strike. For me it was like going back thirty-five years, to when I was Lily Rowbottom. Those little bleak two-up and two-down terraced cottages . . . Though actually we had three bedrooms and my parents own it, which is unusual. Or used to be. I think Dad bought it with a legacy from his grandmother.

But it's just two different worlds. It was a huge culture-shock when I came to London as an art student. So much wealth! Taken for granted! I'll never forget when Mrs Jacobson first took me home with her. It's in Golders Green. They're Jews, of course; though completely secular. Oscar's family came from Czechoslovakia originally, but he's very English. Myra's Polish, and still had quite a strong accent. Where was I? – I was saying about their house. You don't see it first because of the trees along the drive but then there's this vast red-brick Victorian house – at the time it looked like Buckingham Palace to me! And then the interior: masses of books and paintings, Persian carpets and even a clavichord! I remember Wanda Landowska playing it, at a party. But to them, and others I met there, it was all quite normal, even modest.

And I suppose, now, I'm used to that sort of house too. Though ours is much messier, more of a junk-heap. Ah, well.

I didn't mean to go on about the Jacobsons. It was just being in touch with them again; it's brought back memories.

I don't know what you want me to talk about. My schooldays were pretty ordinary. I used to go up to Uncle Jack's farm quite a lot, helping out. It's on the edge of the moor. *Wuthering Heights* territory. I used to sketch the – it's time? We don't seem to have started even. Well, I guess I'd better come on Thursday again; I'll give you a chance. But I warn you, I won't stand for any crap.

★

Do you know, you've got a cuckoo in your drive, Oscar? Listen a moment . . . No, you can't hear it from here. It suddenly rang out, right above my head in one of the elms, as I was walking up! Marvellous! You could almost be in the country, turning off the road into your drive. So balmy, after my poky little office and the fumes of the tube. And May is such a wonderful month! Even your cleaning lady had a smile on her face when she opened the door!

The garden looks fabulous, thanks to Myra.

I like the new wallpaper in the hall – I hadn't really taken it in before. The sunlight really makes it glow. And that little bureau . . . It's fresh, yes, very delicate and graceful . . . Oh, *French*. It's lovely. Sotheby's? I keep meaning to go there – just to have a look, of course, we couldn't possibly afford to buy anything. But I always seem to be too busy.

Well, let's see . . . I had a dream about Martin Luther, last night. We were strolling in Cornwall, and I thought, I'll never be able to match his wit, his intellectual gifts, his charm. We were heading for a sort of castle-door; you know, kind of arrow-shaped at the top; but I turned left, which was the wrong direction, and he went in alone. But then, I was inside, and standing by his bed, and he said, Why not join me and have a talk? So I got into bed beside him.

Oh, and there was a car-journey. We were going to a village on the moors called St Buryan. Luther was in the passenger seat beside me, and there were a couple of other people in the back. I told them I'd honeymooned in Cornwall; it was a beautiful county but getting spoiled; and they kept saying what a great guy Luther was.

Well, let's consider it. I started to work with Lilian Rhodes last evening, and she happened to mention Martin Luther King. It was in connection with assassination. How good people, like King and Robert Kennedy, got killed, whereas the IRA plot against Margaret Thatcher failed.

The dream is about my father, of course. Eloquent after-dinner speaker at Rotary Club dos, etc. One of the people in the car said Luther's tongue could cut like a scalpel, he opened your mind up. You know how Dad felt about me becoming a shrink, Oscar. I didn't go through the castle gate into neurology, but turned left, as it were, into a career he considers second-rate and vulgar. He wouldn't say that to me, but I know he feels it.

. . . That's right! Castle Street, Winchester. The castle door. I didn't think of that. I hated that house, it was so dark. His house in the country is much better, don't you think? He's rather let the garden go to seed, since you and Myra were last there.

Dad rang us at the weekend saying he'd booked a cottage in Cornwall for the last two weeks in August. He hoped we'd be able to join him. Sharon feels a bit pissed-off because we went there last year, as you know, and we didn't have a great time. Our car broke down twice, the washing-machine flooded – but there were no floods in the bedroom . . . Even though Belinda was with her grandparents in Northampton, and it should have been a kind of second honeymoon. Well, of course, you remember; you said second honeymoons tended to be like second-hand cars! But we've had to say yes to Dad, because otherwise we simply wouldn't be able to afford a holiday. Things are tough, what with the bloody Poll Tax and Belinda's school fees. When I think we've got another thirteen years of education to pay for – and at the infant stage it's relatively cheap! We can't possibly afford to have another baby.

We're arguing a lot these days. We're in a bad way. That's St Buryan – the marriage is buried.

. . . Well, no, really it's not that bad; but the danger is there. It's funereal, at least . . . I'm sorry, I didn't catch . . . It's not your voice; it certainly hasn't deteriorated, Oscar: I'm getting tinnitus quite badly. I think it's all the stresses . . . Oh, about money, mostly. Like, does she *have* to have her hair done every week? Does she *have* to keep buying trashy paperback novels when we have a perfectly good library? And – well, the old problem. She thought, after med. school, I'd have more time. Which was stupid, because if I hadn't chosen to go in this direction I'd be in some hospital working all the hours God sends. I'm beginning to think it's simply impossible to live a full professional life and be married. She'd rather I was a brickie like her Dad, so I'd come home in the evening, strip to my vest, and watch TV with her. Freud didn't know how lucky he was, having a wife who knew her place, was happy in it, and made everything run smoothly for him.

She's got too much time on her hands. I see no reason, now Belinda's started school, why she shouldn't go back to work. She's a top-class secretary; Dad would give her a marvellous reference. We're really up against it financially, I'm not joking. I'm very grateful to you for getting me Mrs Rhodes, it's a great help. I know you could have recommended Rachel Brandt to her; she wanted a woman; thanks for the helping hand. But I still only have three patients. She says a five-year-old needs her mother to be at home after school. *I* think the real reason is that she's got used to a pleasant life, pottering about from eight-thirty till three.

You'd think she'd have plenty of energy for a decent sex life. But it's not working out that way. Very prone to headaches these days. Or rather nights. Last night I said to her, okay, just touch me a little, and tell me about Klaus. But she just snarled. Did I tell you she goes to an encounter group in Hampstead on Saturday afternoons? It's supposed to help people who are related to analysts and patients – mostly patients. I can't see it's helping her one bit. In fact she seems *less* in sympathy than she was before. And since I'm playing cricket it means paying to take Belinda to a play-group.

I'm sorry. My problems are very small, compared with yours. When I think of you, I . . .

I know; I promised not to feel sorry for you. I feel tremendously lucky that my training analysis is in your hands. You can say more in five words than most other analysts in five hundred . . .

No, I don't think there was any erotic feeling in my getting into bed with Luther. Comfort, maybe. I have wondered if, after my mother left us, I sometimes got into Dad's bed, for comfort.

I wish I could lie down with my mother, just once. I wish I could remember more than flashes of her. I'd like to know if she's alive or dead. Why did she leave like that? Are you absolutely sure she gave you no inkling? Myra was very close to her; didn't she suspect *something* was up?

Ah, well . . . I can believe Father was hell to live with, and very probably knocking off some nurse; but why didn't she take me with her? A child of seven! Ah!

JEALOUSY

Fuck her! Fuck her!

Ah, Myra! Hello! . . . I could have moved him; I was being very selfish and thoughtless. Can you manage? . . . It *is* a lovely day, you're right. I was telling Oscar you have a cuckoo in your drive. Yes, one can really feel the sap rising.

. . . So where were we? Oh, my mother! Well, that's a bore. You must find it so.

Dad's retiring next week. I'm going down for the presentation on Tuesday, so I'll have to miss that session . . . You're right – that could have been in my mind with St Buryan. Although I think he's quite looking forward to it and has plenty to occupy himself with. Including a book on neurological research. But he's going to be buried in the country quite a lot, on his own. Buried, yes! Yes, it's a big life-event. He keeps asking after you.

Talking of authorship, I sense there's a strong homosexual component in Bill Hamilton. I'm really enjoying our sessions. He's a very likeable rogue, and he talks so fluently, even when he's drunk – which is most days. A very unhappy man. A successful writer, till the alcohol got to him. And he talks, on the couch, as if he's dictating a novel. This morning he was recounting a wartime sexual experience. He was an aircraftsman in the RAF. Late one evening, he said, he was standing outside a dance-hall waiting for the station-bus to come and pick them all up. Nearby, in the dark, a WAAF officer was kissing her boyfriend goodnight, very passionately. The bus came, and they got on. Hamilton found himself sitting with the WAAF officer standing pressed up against him, as the bus was crowded. It seemed rather rude of him, I thought, to sit while she was standing, but still . . . She had her feet apart to steady herself.

It was pitch-black in the bus, he said. As they set off he let his hand stray between her knees. The bus veered, and his hand sort of accidentally brushed against her stocking. He moved it away, but the next time it touched her he kept his hand there, to see what she'd do. She did nothing. He removed his hand from contact, after a while, but raised it higher under her skirt, and when the next jolt came and his hand brushed against her thigh she still didn't move away or say anything. So he let it rest there; and then, gradually, grew bolder, till he was stroking her bare thighs, and twitching her suspenders. And eventually he had his fingers in under her pants, and inside her. She gave a slight hiss at this point, and moved against his fingers. Presumably her boyfriend had got her in the mood. She was sopping wet, Hamilton said, and he ran his hand all over her – to her anus, to her belly up under her girdle, smearing the wetness around.

When they reached the airfield he removed his hand and she got out, without acknowledging anything. He went back to his hut and of course sniffed his fingers and masturbated.

What troubled me was that it excited me too, Oscar. He told it so graphically I could feel myself in his position. And I sensed he knew I was excited; and perhaps intended me to be. Maybe he even invented it. I hope not. Once he used the phrase 'flirted with her suspenders'. I asked him why he'd used that verb. He couldn't say. But he was pretty clearly flirting with me.

But that's disturbing. That I got excited. I still feel we ought to be Olympian, objective.

You're dead right; we *are* only human.

I don't know what my impression is of Mrs Rhodes. Or *Mizz* Rhodes. Lilian. She talked a lot about you and Myra. She obviously likes you both very much. She has no idea I see you. She told me Myra helped her get a place at the Slade, and she knew you both well. Is that true? It took me a little by surprise. Of course there was no reason why you should tell me you knew her before. She must have been decent-looking when she was young. I don't like those quaint spinsterish specs. They're deliberately intended not to flatter her. They're saying to everyone, Keep off. And I thought dungarees had gone out.

I think she'd like some contact with you. She feels bad about having lost touch. Why don't you let her visit you? You're too much alone, you and Myra.

I think the dream I told you about also concerned you. This house is your castle. And I'm very worried lest we have to bury you – lest we lose you. I'm very conscious how inadequate I am compared with you. I lie down with you, in a sense. *For* you, at least.

When Bill talks about the war, I feel impoverished. It seems almost cosy, and those English war films reinforce that impression. Noël Coward, Celia Johnson, plums in their mouths; John

Mills, the rougher type, heart of gold. WAAFs and WRENs emerging from their basement ops-rooms, all sensible shoes and sexy uniforms, blinking in the sunlight, saying to the handsome stubbled officer at their side, Good heavens! it's daylight! And accepting his invitation to breakfast. All I have is the Falklands really. We've missed out. Of course I shouldn't be talking like this; when Myra went through hell. As Lilian moaned non-stop about England I felt like saying to her, Ask Myra how it compares with Auschwitz! and *your* war wasn't exactly a picnic, was it? No, my God! And so many of your family, on the continent, wiped out. Forgive my stupidity.

Here's old Castro! Good boy, we've almost finished! . . . I wonder sometimes if we're getting anywhere. Apart from your razor-sharp remarks I don't feel I'm discovering anything new about myself. Perhaps I simply don't have many problems, and there's nothing to discover. I love my wife and daughter, and if we row a lot – doesn't everyone? It's no worse than most marriages.

I sometimes feel these sessions must be terribly boring for you. I'm sure you must look forward to Rachel Brandt coming; she's led a rich life – well, in the sense of having been in the civil service, dealing with people's problems. It's probably a very good idea to become an analyst at a mature age. I feel she probably has a lot more to offer than I.

Well, I'll see you on Friday. Thank you.

My dear Lilian,

Thank you for your further, very kind letter and invitation. I know it is immature of me to feel embarrassed about meeting old friends in my present condition; but even an aged analyst must be allowed his immaturities. It would be good to see you, but – no, I am sorry, I could not bear it. Besides, it's difficult to eat, and I find it painful to talk for more than a few minutes. The two hours I spend with my patients, almost every day, drain me; and they are used to my voice and also capable of 'filling out' my brief remarks. With Myra, of course, I can communicate almost by telepathy.

Having said that, I must add that I have been moved quite deeply by your re-entry into our lives, and I would very much value being able to write to you. May I? Time weighs heavily on me. I could enjoy writing to you, pouring out some of my thoughts which otherwise are stifled by dumbness. You need not reply at any length – I know how busy you are, and even busier, now, having to find time to take analysis. A postcard would do; one of your postcards of interesting pictures. You always chose so well, there was always something intriguing to explore in them. I've still got a couple of the postcards you sent us from NY – the Met.

I am glad your first session with Christopher James went reasonably well. You should not be put off by his reticence in responding to your questions. The analyst has to be a kind of blank screen for the patient, so that you can project upon it the image your psyche requires. If you got to know him personally, your knowledge, however slight, would interfere with that requirement. So I'm not in the least surprised he would not admit to knowing me. We *have* met, as I said; I know his father quite well, we were for a time colleagues on a working party trying to bring neurologists and psychoanalysts closer – a vain effort – and we became friends. From reports I've had of Christopher, I felt he might be good for you, despite his youth and inexperience – and in the absence of a suitable female therapist. I hope I was right.

He would be more interested in finding out *why* you wished

to know if he was acquainted with me. Perhaps he thought you might be less willing to confide in him if you knew he was acquainted with an old friend from your past. I am guessing. It would be unwise, I suggest, to tell him we are corresponding. Analysts are not immune to jealousy, and he might fear that an older, much more experienced analyst was trying to interfere. It goes without saying that I shall never seek to do so.

You asked how I spend my days. Well, they vary little. Myra gets me up at about eight, and it takes her until almost ten to wash, shave and dress me and give me some breakfast. Then I am ready for my first patient. This exhausts me, so that I am ready for a snooze. Sometimes lately, if the day is fine, such as we have been having, Myra will wheel me into the garden and I doze off there. As you know she is a keen gardener; I've never been drawn to it but I take a dreamy pleasure, these days, in watching her going around, spraying, weeding, doing arcane things to borders. I can become quite rapt, staring at a daisy beside my foot! Imagining its unimaginable, humble life. Wishing, in a way, I could be that daisy, to whom inactivity is natural.

My second patient comes at twelve. Both these people would be quite demanding, even for a younger, healthy analyst. One of them is in grave danger of a full-blown psychosis; the other harbours transsexual urges – but neither is as yet aware of their problems. At one, Myra gives me a light lunch, and together we watch a soap on BBC1 – *Neighbours*; you must have heard of it. It's totally absurd; families without bedrooms; but it exercises a weird fascination. We've become hooked on it. I imagine the banal ordinariness of these suburban Australian lives compensates me, to some degree, for the abnormality and tedium of my own life.

I snooze, or rest on my bed, for a couple of hours, while Myra does a little painting or gardening. After that, I read or write letters. At eight we have dinner. My appetite is very small these days, and it takes all of Myra's good cooking to tempt me. Afterwards, maybe a little television; and so to bed, at around ten.

An exciting existence!

Today one of my patients was unable to come; so I am

writing to you instead. This is the second departure from routine: at around seven I was awakened by church bells. My first thought was that they were celebrating Dunkirk, fifty years ago. Yes, fifty years ago today I was lying half-dead in a Kentish fishing-boat, being carried back to England. Lying in that little boat, I *thought* I knew what depression was. But if that young officer could have visualised himself fifty years later . . .

Well, it doesn't bear thinking. That dreadful war overturned so many plans. But for it I should not be with Myra; but for it I would probably have specialised in the heart, my early interest, rather than the mind. So many thoughts and regrets whirled in my mind as the Dunkirk bells rang out.

Later, my female patient, who is a Jewish Catholic (odd combination), informed me it's Ascension Day; so that must be why the bells pealed. Ascension Day! Extraordinary irony.

I try to think as little as possible of my useless and dying body, Lilian. Sexual desire, I believed, had quite vanished. But a few days ago one of my patients conjured up an erotic story. A memory of wartime and the services. Perhaps for that reason – I knew the little ships were gathering for a sentimental return – the story evoked enormous pain in me. I was in mental agony, listening. I imagine it was deliberately sadistic on his part, since he has transferred hostile feelings towards his father on to me.

Those were brave days. I was proud, though a Jew and only marginally accepted, to fight for England. But now! You are right in what you wrote about Thatcher's Britain. Enormous greed and selfishness. Breakdown of all communal values. I know you did not expect me to agree; you used to tease me about my 'right-wing' views. But things are not always as they seem. Myra and I did not disagree with you politically as much as you thought. No, not by a long chalk.

Well, I must move on to a somewhat more painful task: writing to a godson of mine. He's HIV positive, the result of injecting drugs. It's so terribly sad, as he's a highly talented young man. He does not dare to tell his parents, poor lad. Actually, I blame them: they stifled him with privileges and expectations. He needed to tell someone, and I'm glad he could trust me. But what can I possibly say to him to give him consolation? That with luck he'll be run down by a bus before he develops full-blown AIDS?

I shall consult Myra; she's very good at finding the right words. She's preparing lunch – there's a pleasant smell of vegetable soup emanating from the kitchen. I have enjoyed writing to you and hope I may do so again. Time and separation have curiously little effect on true friendships. It is as if we were squatting on the floor again, passing around the joint. Drinking that rather nice claret we used to get in bulk from Collinsons. You remember? That's gone, long since. It became a boutique for a time in the Beatles era, when you'd deserted us for America; then a deli; more recently an estate agent's when house prices exploded. And now they've had to close too and it's empty. Ah well!

Shalom!
Oscar

2

The tube was packed. I think a train had broken down. I could hardly breathe and some man groped me. I almost didn't get off at Holborn, as I was trapped. I was tempted to say fuck it and go straight on to Holland Park. It was crazy, the way people were struggling to get on and off, showing no concern for others. Naked Thatcherism!

Anyway, I'm here.

I hate your office. Loathe it, loathe it. Why can't you work at home? Are you afraid you'll reveal something of yourself? You want to watch out some woman doesn't knife your Goya.

Tell me something: supposing you find out what's wrong with me, will you tell me?

. . . Because I got a letter from Oscar, and he said something which really put me off analysis. Not that I've ever been *on* it. He said one of his patients was heading for a psychosis, and the other had an urge to change sex, and neither of them knew about it. I thought, shit! what are they paying him for, then? Why doesn't he fucking tell them? It would be like a doctor diagnosing breast cancer and deciding to keep his patient guessing . . .

So what you're saying is, it's better for the woman with breast cancer to find it out for herself? I think it's crazy. There's this person who according to Oscar is heading for a psychosis – which means going mad, right? – and Oscar doesn't want to tell him; he must find it out for himself!

Or her. It's more likely to be a woman. Our lives are enough to drive us crazy.

So I'm not at all sure I can trust you. You're going to have to earn it. If you're trustworthy you're only about the second or third man I've ever met who is. I trust my husband. Well,

I *think* I can trust him. I've never had any need to worry about other women. But on Sunday, we were slopping around in the garden; I put my hand in my pocket for a tissue and found instead a piece of paper. I pulled it out and there was a name and phone number on it in Steven's handwriting. Jenny, the name was. I realised I was wearing his jeans. We often wear each other's at the weekend; he's not very tall and he can get into my jeans and I his. I didn't think anything of it, I just gave him the slip of paper and said, This must be yours. I assumed Jenny was a client or something; but he blushed. He looked like Phil does when we catch him out in something naughty. – Oh, yes! I must tell you about that! That was Saturday, our little episode with Phil. Anyway, Steven looked sort of caught out. I didn't ask him about it, I wouldn't ever dream of doing that. It was probably something quite innocent.

Saturday. Yes. I went to the shops early to stock up for the weekend, and we had people coming to dinner that night. I left Steven making the beds and running the Hoover over. Phil had gone for a piano lesson. When I got back, Steven met me, holding something behind his back. Then he brandished it at me. It was one of those porno magazines you see on the top shelves in newsagents. He said he'd found it under Phil's bed.

I got very upset. I know boys look at these things in school and pass them around; but it upset me that Phil wasn't grown-up enough to resist the pressure. Steven persuaded me we should play it cool; and I'm glad we did. Because, poor boy, he was terribly embarrassed when we showed it to him. We made him sit down at the kitchen table and we took him through the pages one by one. Steven was very good; he said, at every page, almost as if he was taking someone through their evidence: Now, what is there here that you like looking at? We're not condemning you, we'd just like to know what appeals to you about this. Of course Phil was tongue-tied and very red-faced.

Then, together, we tried to show him how degrading this was to women; how the models were totally unlike real women; they were being exploited for money. I said I knew he masturbated and that was perfectly okay; but we'd much prefer him to use his imagination. And he did begin to see. Steven offered him the magazine back, but Phil said he thought it should go in the waste-bin. I don't think we'll find any more under his bed. But it's appalling to think children get exposed to porn like that. A few of us are trying to do something about it, but it's like spitting into a hurricane.

Steven's very good with him. Better than I am, really. He was determined he should go to the local comprehensive, which is a really good one, rather than suffer a public school as he had to do. And he loves it there.

He works terribly hard. Steven. He's asleep these days before his head hits the pillow. Saturday afternoons he goes to a Free Legal Advice Clinic, helping poor people. He's more and more involved with the Labour Party. He's in an important working party, ACCELERATE: the Advisory Council towards a Common European Law based on Rational Values. – I don't know who thought up that mouthful. And of course he's terribly conscientious at his job. He's taking on more and more cases involving abuse of women, as his record's so good in that area.

You can see he's tired and stressed, though; and I don't suppose my depression helps. I've tried telling him to ease up, but he won't.

This is getting us nowhere. I don't even think you're listening. I get the feeling your mind is somewhere else.

Lovely weather we've been having. Do you think we're going to have a drought? Why do I want to know whether you think we're going to have a drought? – Go on, say it!

Yawn, yawn.

This council Steven's on is currently discussing domestic rape. Probably about ten million women are raped by their husbands or partners in the EC yearly. It's unbelievable, don't you think? Steven's put forward a radical idea which he thinks could cut it down by two-thirds. Every female over sixteen would have a personal code, perhaps based on their National Insurance number. Before making love she would call a central organisation and speak her number. It would be an indication that she consented to sex. If someone was using force or intimidation, she would give a wrong number; and this would carry heavily at any subsequent trial. Most couples would have access to a phone, and it would actually take less time than putting on a condom. And it's just as much safe sex. If she didn't ring through, and later made an accusation, that would be a strong presumption of guilt, unless they were on a mountain in Sardinia or something.

A man would think twice before raping his wife or girlfriend if this was in operation. And in some cases it would allow the police to forestall the rape. I think it's a wonderful idea, but he says there's opposition from some of the right-wing members, on grounds of interference with personal freedom. I simply can't see that argument. What freedom is there for the poor woman who's raped regularly by a drunken husband? It would also be a safeguard against men being wrongfully accused – although I think that's mostly a myth; women don't lie about a serious thing like rape. But, okay, if a woman phoned her consent through and then accused her partner of rape, it would be some defence for him; although there'd always be the possibility that she'd changed her mind.

It's loathsome the way the dice are loaded against us. We had a couple of ethnic social workers round for dinner on Saturday. Nice people. We got talking about that debate in Parliament a few weeks ago, about abortion and foetal experimentation. We were saying how incredible it was that anyone could object to a small bundle of cells being experimented on, when the result could be an end to congenital defects. We should be far more worried about what happens to children when they're born. Our friends told some horrific stories of incest among the families they care for; and, as it happens, Steven's just finished a case at the Bailey involving child abuse and incest. A bloke with his seven-year-old stepdaughter. Steven had to defend him. He was relieved when the jury found him guilty.

Traffic noise. I'd never realised quite how relentless it was until I started coming here. I guess it'll be going on long after we're dead.

I've not been over-eating, though I almost weakened last night. Steven was late home and had bought pizzas. I had an urge to stuff a whole one into my mouth; and the camembert, and apples, oranges, peaches. I suddenly felt that emptiness and insatiable craving to fill up the whole. But I resisted it. That was a tiny victory, I guess.

Something's bugging you. I feel it. I'm very intuitive.

Oh, well . . . If you say so.

Did I ask you if I could borrow that Goya for the October exhibition I'm organising? . . . Thanks . . . No, no, repros are fine. I've just been promised a good print of Munch's *Madonna* – do you know it? That's just a rhetorical question, I don't expect you to answer it. A woman with jet-black hair, piercing eyes, a screaming mouth. And a tiny homunculus in the corner of the picture, near her hips. It's perfect for the exhibition because it exactly conveys the male vision of a predatory female. If you have sex with her you will be destroyed. Her black hair will wind about you and strangle you. He absolutely loathed women.

. . . No, I don't think so. If you're looking for dark events in my childhood you won't find any. It was a perfectly ordinary, Yorkshire working-class childhood. Of course the moors can be very dismal. The Brontë shades haunt it. I'd sometimes glimpse Catherine galloping over the moors, with Heathcliff after her. And Plath is buried in Heptonstall. Among thousands of black overturned gravestones. In death she's Sylvia Plath Hughes. Don't you think that's monstrous?

Trapped like my mother. Monday: she'll be taking the washing off the line about now. Straining her old tired bones. Dad'll be sitting in the kitchen window, reading the *Express*, waiting for his supper.

I was born in Sheffield, but I've no memory of it. It's nowt but grime. I was a war baby. Mum worked in munitions; my grandparents were there and helped look after me. She and Dad moved to Heptonstall when he was demobbed. I was four years old. I can vaguely remember sitting on a box surrounded by furniture. That's really my first memory. And then I remember Ted being born, how jealous of him I was; but I've very few memories of my childhood. I'm always suspicious of people who claim to remember a lot.

I did have one of those curious, vivid memories of smell yesterday. I'd taken Steven's leather jacket out of the wardrobe to see if it needed dry-cleaning. Well, no, I'd better be honest, he'd worn it out the previous evening and I smelt it to see if there was any scent on it. Isn't that awful? And I checked for hairs

. . . Anyway, as I smelt the leather I had this powerful feeling I'd smelt it before, some time in my childhood. I seemed to be sitting on a floor, and there was this pungent smell of leather. It was a warm and comforting smell. I can't get beyond that.

I wish I *could* get back. To the working-classes. I was chatting to Brenda, my home help, over a coffee yesterday, and I said, Of course Dad was only a lorry-driver. It was about higher education for girls, how tough it was in our day, and I was trying to say, My father wasn't educated and didn't value education. Brenda kept on chatting, but her face was flushed. Then I realised her husband is a long-distance driver for Bird's Eye Frozen Foods. I could have kicked myself. And a few weeks ago I was talking about rates of pay for part-time art teachers, and said it's chicken-feed, it's only fifteen pounds an hour. She agreed with me, that it wasn't much. But later I thought, God, we only pay her a fiver an hour. It's above the going rate; but why do I do it? Why do I get myself into these embarrassing predicaments?

I'm sure your mind's a million miles away. Okay, it's incredibly boring, but I *am* paying for this, you know!

. . . Pardon me? God, you haven't become a mute! . . . No, that was all he said. Just that he had these two patients, and one was the wrong gender and the other was borderline psychotic; he didn't give any details about them. Why? Do you know his patients?

I forget I mustn't ask questions. That's your privilege.

It's time? Thank Christ!

I've been thinking quite a lot about that dream, Dr Jacobson. The one I had a couple of weeks ago. You know, where my sister and I were sitting with Ruth when she was dying, and Sarah admitted to me that Ruth was my child not hers.

And I don't know if you remember it or not, but I wondered why she thought it would be a big surprise to me, since I'd known it for seven years.

Well, it seems to me I was thinking of my namesake in the Bible. Rachel. She was in service for seven years before she bore Jacob a child . . . Yes, I'm sure you were perfectly aware of it. I was stupid not to think of it before. It's forced me to admit I was jealous of Sarah. Not because of her husband . . . God knows, he was nothing to write home about! I don't think Sarah loved him, and I'm sure he didn't love her. Though they'd probably have stayed together if Ruth hadn't died. But I was jealous about Ruth. And that makes me feel enormously guilty.

She was such a brave little girl. I'm sorry.

It's okay. I'm all right now. Your garden's looking beautiful, Dr Jacobson! Your wife works very hard on it. Did she tell you we bumped into each other the other day? Your godson, Tristram Dahl, was playing at our church. He played beautifully, they all did. One would never have thought they were still students. I've been meaning to ask you how he is? . . . Oh, that's good! It's such a terrible tragedy, this AIDS. But he hasn't developed it yet, has he? Let's hope . . . Well, I pray for him.

I also saw Chris James yesterday, on a tube train. He was probably on his way here. He didn't see me. I thought he looked very strained and red-eyed, almost as if he'd been crying. Is he okay? . . . I don't think I've seen him since that lovely party you had here, a couple of years ago. No, that's not true . . . he was at the Manchester conference, but we were in different groups. I was probably mistaken in thinking he looked stressed, his eyes might have been red because the wind was blowing dust everywhere; my own were quite sore. I might even have a stye coming. I'm feeling quite harassed at the moment, actually.

Though I'm getting on quite well with my patients. I think. Jason seems much more confident, and I'm beginning to make some headway with Sue.

Are you comfortable? Would you like me to move you?

JEALOUSY

I realise I'm . . . I'm prevaricating. Forgive me. I simply don't feel like talking about my relationship with my father today. I don't know if it's a defence, I don't think so, it's rather that my mind is filled with that project I mentioned to you. I really want to talk about that, not my feeble little psyche. Do you really think there's a chance they would consider creating a museum in Byelaya Tserkov? It would be wonderful if that were to happen! It's as if those little cousins of mine keep whispering to me, begging me to try and do *something* so they won't be completely forgotten.

I could so easily have been one of them. Sometimes I feel I have no right to my life, Dr Jacobson. Do you understand that? Sarah thinks I'm being sentimental, and living in the past; but I don't see it that way. I've brought for you that German book I mentioned, with the extracts from military documents and so on. I can't tell you how much I've wept over them.

It's . . . it's unbelievable that human beings could . . .

I'm sorry.

But I know *you* understand, and I bless you for it.

Do you mind if I read you something from it? This is from the Catholic Divisional Chaplain: *I submit the following report to 295th Infantry Division: Today in the afternoon towards 14.30 hours Military Chaplains Tewes and Wilczek, Military Hospital Division 4/607, came to the Protestant divisional chaplain and myself and reported the following: They told us that German soldiers had drawn their attention to the fact that Jewish children aged between a few months and five . . .*

I'll leave it with you.

. . . Yes, if you don't mind. Thank you. I'll be better on Friday, I promise. Can I just sit here for a while?

Please keep the book. I went to Hatchards and bought a second copy.

Would you mind terribly if I got myself a drink of water? . . .

Thank you. You must think me awfully stupid. I've wasted your time today.

You give so much of yourself. I've wanted to say for a long time if there's anything I can do in return . . . please ask.

Pardon? . . . Yes, of course! Which is it . . . the bottom drawer? Are these the keys? . . .

Oh, yes! That's very fine! It's . . . it's you! Am I right? . . . It's wonderful; why don't you display it? . . . Well, okay, it's not a great work of art, I guess; I really wouldn't be able to say, I'm no judge of these things; but it's striking. You were a very handsome man, Dr Jacobson! Very severe, very military . . . Are you all right?

Mrs Jacobson! Mrs Jacobson! . . . Dr Jacobson's not well. He's shown me this. I think it's upset him . . . No, I won't, I certainly won't speak of it. But I'm very honoured he wanted to show it me. I'll see myself out. Ring me if he's not up to it on Friday, won't you?

My dear Lilian,

Thank you so much for your card . . . Botticelli's *Spring* was a thoughtful choice. And your message. Yes, they were good years, the sixties. But I can't help feeling, in retrospect, those liberation movements that sprang into life then, such as feminism, gay rights, black power, are rather like weird exotic blooms, in place of the great forest of communism I thought would last for ever and spread over the world.

That will surprise you! I always gave you the impression I was a sort of vaguely rightish liberal, I know. But that was far from the case. I feel in a confessional mood.

I was a bit of a rebel at school. In the holidays I returned to Birmingham you see, where my father's factory was, and I could see the appalling poverty. My marxism then was all pretty adolescent stuff; but during my years in Vienna after the war I began to think more seriously about the world. I met a number of splendid, idealistic communists; I saw what was happening in America . . . Dulles, the military-industrial complex, etc . . . I didn't become converted, but I was close. I also learned about the naked capitalism of the ghettos. In Warsaw, if you were rich, you could eat every day a three-course meal for fifteen zlotys, and gaze out at wretches stumbling skeletally past, who could only afford two zlotys for thin soup; and they in turn stepped indifferently over the bodies of people who could not afford even that. In the death-camps it was even more naked, as Myra could tell you.

Then, back in London, married to Myra, a certain well-known art historian at the Courtauld, where Myra was studying, thought I'd be a good chap to take on the analytical work with intelligence officers, etc., who were suffering from breakdown. Their previous chap was about to retire. I was beginning to make a name as an analyst; I was 'clean', I had fought 'gallantly' in the war, with my MC.

Don't get me wrong; I never betrayed my country. But, while genuinely helping these men and women psychologically, it was not difficult to broaden my patients' political outlooks, over a year or two years' analysis, three or four times a week.

I was sufficiently harmless for Blunt to be able to reveal I was a communist, when he was found out. I was questioned, and they soon realised I'd done nothing more than make a dozen or so Cold Warriors a degree or so more flexible. However, part of the deal was to continue to disguise my political views, so as not to make them look even more of a laughing-stock after Philby, Burgess, Blunt, etc. But I absolutely trust your discretion, Lilian. I was proud of the work I'd done for communism. The analysis of other patients, with their trivial personal problems, seemed very small beer in comparison.

Oh, I had some troubling times. Prague. The revelations about the Gulag Archipelago. But I survived them. I saw them as setbacks, possible mistakes, along the difficult road to Utopia. But now . . . It's all ashes, Lilian my dear. Communism is dead. I find the events in Russia and Eastern Europe infinitely depressing. The onset of my disease coincided with Gorbachev's accession to power. I sometimes wonder if that is significant. Certainly I could bear my personal dissolution if I could feel that the faith I have served was flourishing. But the forest has burnt down, in just twelve months. Just a few blackened trunks left – China, Cuba, etc. Christianity took two thousand years to die, and it's still not totally dead. My faith has managed less than a century. Indeed, less than the span of my own lifetime. It's ghastly. The sight of those first 'refugees' from East Germany, pouring over the Czech border into the West, before the Wall was breached – I could hardly bear to watch it. They were so happy! And I had dreamed that one day the opposite would happen.

A market economy in the Soviet Union!

I am sitting in the garden, a rug over my knees. The clouds look rainy, but rain declines to fall. The grass is brown in patches. Myra bends over, weeding, a few paces away, her back to me. Her sturdy bare legs are planted wide. Sensible lace-up shoes. An old blue skirt swinging; her white blouse draping round it, loose. Her short black hair tinged with grey. Muscular brown arms; a swinging motion. She looks like a peasant; a worker on a kibbutz or *kolkhoz*.

East Germany, Czechoslovakia, Hungary, Poland, Bulgaria,

Romania . . . They toppled, so swiftly, and with such evident rejoicing. What can we say? Were we wrong?

The principle was right. But it evidently could only have worked if there had been a world revolution when Lenin came to power. In a world divided between capitalism and communism, the former was bound to win. Because, with its ferocious competitiveness, the most successful were bound to reach a prosperity that a less competitive system could not rival. And people are greedy. Imagine that life had also begun, those billions of years ago, on the moon. But somehow the primitive life forms had chosen to evolve not by competition but co-operation. By now, I imagine life might have evolved as far as the chimpanzee. The moon full of chimps. Gentle creatures, eating bananas and other fruit. No viruses, microbes, amoebas, toads, rats, etc. No sharks in the lunar seas. Dolphins, perhaps; dolphins feeding on algae. An infinitely gentler, softer, more equal planet than ours.

But mankind, the successful capitalists of our planet, would land there and colonise it. And the chimps and dolphins would think, This is right and proper: see how far they have gone beyond us!

And we would bring them the viruses and rats, like the pornography that's flooding into Hungary.

Mention of rats brings back something unpleasant, a nightmare. Up until the past few weeks I've been blessed with good sleep, but lately I've been having a few nightmares. And last night's was the worst. I woke Myra with my attempts to scream. To cut it short, I dreamed I found my mother, when young, being devoured by rats. They'd eaten everything up to her womb. The weird thing is, I dreamt this once before, almost half a century ago. How amazing the psyche is. Then, I didn't understand it; now at last I'm beginning to. Understanding doesn't lessen its horror. Quite the reverse.

I am very depressed, Lilian. Both my patients were in a bad way today. Perhaps my mood affected them. I showed one of them a wood sculpture I haven't shown anyone since I brought it out for you to see, some thirty years ago. A head of yours truly. I don't suppose you remember it. Carved in the delirium and destruction of 1944. I was thinking of

you as I showed her it. Perhaps one day you will understand why.

The rats led me adrift: forgive me. I was saying, the great
dream has faded and we are left with the trivial; people with
marriage problems, problems of sexual identity, hangovers
from their abhorrent parents. Trivia. My other patient was
obsessed today with an affair his wife had three years ago! But
he actually *begs* her to relive it for him, since his life today is so
dull! Imagine it! Trivia . . .

Or perhaps not trivia. I don't know. I don't know anything
any more. I come back to my own life, my own 'trivial'
problems. I have another small confession, my dear. In those
distant days, before you vanished from us, I loved you.

I can picture your surprise as you read these words. I don't
think you ever suspected. I was very good at concealing my true
emotions and beliefs. Certainly you could not have suspected
it from that evening when Myra was running your drunken
boyfriend home and we were alone in the house. We'd had a fair
amount to drink too, and when I made a pass at you you didn't
reject me. I recall that night so clearly, yet possibly you will not
even remember it. After all, nothing happened. I remember I
went to the bathroom and when I entered the bedroom you
were pulling your dress off; for a few moments it was trapped
in your magnificent thick chestnut hair. My heart missed a beat
– many beats – seeing the beauty I had longed for and dreamed
of for more than a year.

Shyly you revealed that mount of Venus that concealed, yet
offered, a treasure that for me was richer than all the Torah.
Then, just at the moment you sat on the bed to finish undressing
and remove your earrings, I said something brutal, like, 'This is
wrong; get yourself dressed.' And left you to go into the living
room, light a cigarette, and immerse myself in *Rosenkavalier*.

Our relationship was never quite the same after, I think, and
I don't blame you. Now, close to death, I feel I must explain. I
should say in some self-defence that we didn't know then about
your other entanglement, with your uncle back home, trapping
you as your head was trapped as you undressed; I hope and
believe I would have spoken more gently had I known of it.

I think I'd loved you from the first evening Myra brought

you home. You were so fresh, such a delightful country girl, with that charming Yorkshire burr! You'd dressed up, had a flouncy blue frock on, and were embarrassed because we were casually dressed as always. You brought a joy to 'Padernice'.

Of course, I knew you had boyfriends of your own age; and I don't think it occurred to me that you might feel something for me until that night when I let you down so humiliatingly. One reason why I told you to get dressed was my secret life; an affair would have been a terrible complication. Myra would not have minded; we made no secret that our marriage was fairly open. I kept, for safety, to short, light-hearted relationships in the main; with you I would not have been content with that.

But the main reason for my change of mind was something more personal. We had just received a letter from an old friend of ours who had known my Czech cousin, Chaim. Chaim didn't survive the holocaust. During his time in a camp he lost his baby girl in an agonising and quite extraordinary way.

When I saw you getting ready to sleep with me it suddenly struck me that you were roughly the same age as his daughter would have been. Well, I just couldn't go on; I was too overcome with emotion. It would have been like sleeping with my own daughter, in some way I can't explain but you will perhaps understand.

Why did we lose touch so totally, my dear? I thought perhaps you blamed me, later, for the termination I helped you with; or perhaps you were simply terribly upset and didn't want to see anybody. Then we learned you'd gone off to the States. Upon your return, three years later, you were friendly but things were never quite the same. From our side too, I'm sure. No one's fault: we simply couldn't pick up the traces.

It may be you will want to talk about some of this to Chris. Supposing it stirs up any memories, good or bad, in you. Feel free to do so, but you must disguise it so that he does not suspect you are referring to me. For the reason I explained to you in my last letter and – well, it would not be wise.

I've become terribly thin. My bones stick out, making it uncomfortable even to sit. But I mustn't give way to self-pity.

I'm exhausted. Myra will wheel me inside now, and lay

me on our bed. That bed in which, thirty years ago, after you had left red-eyed from tears, I too cried for what might have been.

Oscar

3

The atmosphere's pretty poisonous at work. The young women there are so scared of Mick Masterson they won't even admit I was right to lay a complaint against him.

But we can't just lie back and take it, like the Titian *Venus* in the Uffizi. Do you know it? She's got a little posy in one hand and her pussy in the other. Just lying back waiting to be screwed. She's some man's pet, just as the dog curled up at her feet is hers. I've managed to find a good eighteenth-century copy of it for my October exhibition. Copies are better – they don't have the distraction of being 'masterpieces', whatever that means; you can see the naked chauvinism.

In my lunch-break I joined some friends of mine at Smith's in the High Street. We marched up to the magazine rack and swept all the porno mags on to the floor. *Penthouse, Mayfair*, all that shit. We sat on the floor and said we weren't moving till they promised not to stock them. We got a lot of support from the customers, though one woman pissed us off by assuming we were Pro-Life. A Jesus-freak in a grey plastic mac. I won't repeat what Hannah said to her. If you think I'm militant you should hear Hannah.

But I felt so tired after. And ravenous. We went for a coffee and I stuffed four cream buns into my mouth before I could stop myself. Then I went to the loo and brought them up again.

What does your wife think about porn? I take it you're married? You're – how old? – about twenty-eight? Perhaps thirty. You look older than when I first came. Actually you don't look well. Are you sickening for something?

Just curiosity again. Just simple bloody *concern*! Trying to see you as a human being. I guess 'seeing' isn't the right word, since you insist on sitting behind me, gazing down at me stretched out here, like the Titian *Venus*, like the *Maja nude*. Shit, why did I ever agree to do this?

I'm sorry I didn't bring a posy to hold in my right hand; but I can let my left hand rest on my crutch. Is that okay? Would you like that? You could put your hand on my shoulder and tell me what a good girl I am, like Masterson does in the typing-pool. Actually you're a bit alike, except he's older; he's freckled too; his hair's a bit more auburny. A real Mick.

Do your friends call you Christopher or Chris?

Chris! Ah! You said that almost as if you're human! God, this surely is a red-letter day!

Chris. Christ. Suffer the little children to come unto me, and forbid them not, so I can have a feel of their little pussies.

Red-letter days. Jamie, my friend in LA, calls them that. Yes, I'm on my period. They're very irregular now.

We get thrown away like a used tampax. Feminine disposal.

It caught me on the hop, this morning. I had to rush out and buy some. We shouldn't have to pay for them, of course, they should be on the National Health. *I* can afford them, but poor women can't.

Steven's come to a very brave decision. He's decided he won't in future defend a man who's accused of violence against women . . . Because he thinks it shows a lack of solidarity with the majority of his clients, who are abused women. He's sure to get a lot of flak for it, but he doesn't care. He plans to announce it next week. I think the *Guardian* will want to do an interview with him.

I'm still wondering who Jenny is. It's not been mentioned since. If he was having an affair it would seem so stupid to have a piece of paper with her name and phone number in his jeans pocket, when he knows I often put his on. And it would be unlike Steven. He's one man I didn't think would cheat. I don't feel I can ask him straight out. If I was going to I should have done it at the time. After a fortnight I can't suddenly say, Oh, by the way, who's Jenny? And in any case he would presumably have some story ready.

I received a declaration of love, a few days ago. I haven't been sure whether I should tell you. It's nothing important. When

JEALOUSY

I was a student I used to see quite a lot of a married couple, Richard and Angela. They were friends of the Jacobsons. I was poor, living on a grant, and I used to earn a little pocket-money babysitting for them – they had two young kids. I had no particular feelings for Richard. I was going out with a guy called Jeremy, who was President of our Student Union. I really fell for him. At that stage I was still practically a virgin. Jeremy was my first lover. Before him there'd only been the usual clumsy fumbles back home in the local flea-pit, or behind the chapel wall.

Then he left college and I only saw him now and again. Then not at all, for weeks. When I'd almost given up on him, he left me a note in my pigeon-hole saying could I come with him to Richard and Angela's; they'd invited us to dinner. The joy I felt! He picked me up on his motor-bike, and I was wearing a new suit and thought I looked really nice. He apologised for not having rung, said he'd been busy organising a Trotskyite cell. It seemed convincing. He groped me under the table at dinner and I thought everything was on again. But then, as he got drunk, he started paying attention to our hostess. Angela. Who was really quite plain. Oscar – Richard got pissed too, stretched out on the sofa. Then Angela manoeuvred the situation so she could run Jeremy home, since he was far too pissed to use his motorbike; and when I stood up to go she said, No, you stay, the night's young. And there was nothing I could do about it; she was my tutor after all . . . Well, yes, it was Oscar and Myra. Stupid of me. Don't ever let on to them I've told you.

That was when I discovered what it means to be jealous. I hoped she would crash her car on the way back and have a serious accident. I went to the bathroom for a cry – I could cry in those days: stupid little cow. Anyway, I let Oscar make a pass at me. I didn't want him. He smelt of garlic. But I wanted revenge on Jeremy. But then, when I was undressing, he suddenly turned nasty, telling me to put my pants back on.

It was a very distressing experience for a twenty-year-old girl. But now Oscar has explained. It seems he was in love with me. But he'd been researching the holocaust that week and he thought of all the children who should have been

105

alive, and – desirable, like he found me. He felt too upset to go ahead.

I was quite moved by his letter. There were other things, personal things, that explain a lot and make me see him in a different, better light. Totally surprising things. I couldn't tell you. He said I could tell you the rest, if I wanted, but to disguise his identity. Well, I blew it.

Of course he's a great MCP; it was clear from his letter that he regarded me as a sex object. But one has to make allowance for his age; and it's moving to think he loved me all that time, and never revealed it. Had he told me at the time I don't know what I'd have done. I might have responded; I don't know.

I found myself, last night, playing over a scratchy old jazz record that I first heard at their house. King Oliver.

. . . No. No, of course there were no children. I only said that to put you off the scent.

He *must* have cared for me. I remember – I think it was the second or third time I went there – he took me into his study and took out of a drawer a carved head someone had done of him. Myra was in the kitchen making us some supper. He seemed not to want her to know he was showing me it. It was rather crudely done, even as a student I could see that, but it was recognisably him. Younger. He made me run my hands over it. He was fairly pissed. I thought it was odd he wanted to show it to me. His eyes were moist, and he said something like, if I only knew the history of it. I'd forgotten it until he mentioned it in his letter. Apparently he'd never shown it to anyone else until a few days ago, when he showed it to one of his patients.

. . . Yes, I suppose so; what *might* have been if he'd met me when he was younger. I don't know. He was already quite grey and with a straggly beard; I really didn't think of him in that way.

. . . No, I certainly *didn't* see him as a father-figure! God! If you could see my father! I'll race thee back to t'house! . . . He'd say that when we'd been out collecting frogs. He collected them to send to laboratories; got a shilling a hundred for them; something like that. I'll race thee back to t'house! Poor old Dad.

. . . I don't know if Myra slept with Jeremy that night; he

never contacted me again. I went off men for a long time.
Till Jake, in New York, five years later . . . Oh, I did have
a sort of – 'holiday' boyfriend in Yorkshire. I let him give
me a couple of knee-tremblers after Jeremy ditched me, out
of sheer sexual frustration. But nothing, really. Also I was ill
for several months; had to have leave of absence from college.
I spent most of it with Auntie Mabel and Uncle Jack, on their
moorland farm.

Phil isn't well, he's been off school for two weeks. We're a
bit concerned about him. He had a sore throat, which seemed
to pass off normally; only it came back and he feels awful, poor
kid. Can hardly drag himself up the stairs. And he has exams
coming up. It's a rotten time for him to fall sick. Our GP's taken
a blood test.

So I had a disturbed night, getting up for him. And then I
had a bad dream. I'm afraid I dreamed of you. You were stalking
me on the Yorkshire moors, coming for me with a knife to kill
me. I was trying to hide behind rocks, not knowing where you
were. Once you leapt on my back but I managed to throw you
off and run. In the end I heard you crawling towards me and
I leapt out from behind a rock and hit you over the head with
a stone, very hard. You screamed. Your head was all mashed,
like tripe. I'm sorry.

Mother used to serve us tripe every Thursday. And now
you're serving it.

That's probably very unfair. I'm sure you're doing your
best. Now and again you say something I think is quite
sensible.

. . . Pardon me! Oh gosh, I'm sorry! How embarrassing!
My stomach gets very heavy these days; dragging down. And
a period makes it worse.

How stupid of us women to get embarrassed because of
an involuntary fart. Men fart all the time. Steven and Phil
are always farting. But we're supposed to be genteel. I can
remember a concert in the Sunday school. I must have been
about ten. A man had just finished a solo, with a lot of flourishes,
and the pianist, Ivy, was just poised to play the concluding
chords. And in the pregnant silence while we waited for her,
I farted, very loudly. We'd had sausages and beans for tea. I

could see people trying to appear as if they hadn't heard, but their faces were lowered and some of them were shaking with laughter. I just curled up, wanted to die.

It was like a comment on the solo, which was probably pretty ghastly.

After the concert, when we got home, Mam said, I wor that ashamed of you, our Lil! But Dad and my brother laughed. It wor the best thing in t'whole concert! Dad said.

We had a gramophone and three or four records of brass band music. No books except the Bible. God, it was awful!

Oh, yes, and Mrs Mills! A fat pianist! *Mrs Mills*! They thought she was wonderful. Liberace was wonderful too, they wouldn't miss him on TV for the world. Ay! he can't half rattle them ivories! Dad would say. Ey, Steven? And Steven would have to say, You're right, Arthur! He hates visiting Mum and Dad. I can understand it; it's just not his scene.

Mrs Mills! All those chins and bosoms wobbling! I'd forgotten her. They thought she was fantastic. Quick, Mrs Mills is on, Annie!

Now, my Uncle Jack, he was different, he had a bit of taste and a bit of feeling. Only he wasn't musically educated, of course. But you could see he really *felt* the music, if there was an extract from some popular classic on *Family Favourites*. Like the *Dream of Olwen* or the Warsaw Concerto. He'd close his eyes and listen intently, and afterwards he'd say Ay, lass! with a kind of sigh, as if to say, that's another, more beautiful world. And he loved nature too. On our way back from milking he'd stop, so we could look over the moor, up at the stars. He helped *me* to appreciate nature too, standing there with him in the silence. Ay, lass! He could be crude, effing and blinding. Belching and farting. Boy, could *he* fart! But deep down he was a sensitive man. Auntie Mabel, well, you couldn't call her sensitive, but she was kindly. They should have had children but I don't think she could. I think they probably felt very sad about that, though they never said. They liked having me visit, and I felt they loved me. I felt good up at the farm; perhaps because it was so high up, and isolated, I had a sense of the seasons passing and the earth turning; a bit magical, almost.

I don't know. I don't know. Life is strange.

JEALOUSY

You look back over it and you wonder, Was that me? How could I have done such a thing?

And you think, Maybe we don't have control over anything; maybe it's all just fate. That it all has to be. I don't know.

It's time? Okay. I'm almost sorry; I was just beginning to relax.

Dreadful . . . I'm still feeling dreadful, Oscar . . .

I think I'm far less normal than I like to imagine. What I've learnt from you in the past eighteen months is that I look at people through glass. And that's pretty horrible. I guess it started in those awful summer hols in my teens. Coming home to a grim succession of housekeeper–mistresses. I dreamt the other night about Kim – I've told you about her, I believe. Fat and lifeless: except at night when I could hear her moaning in Dad's bed. We hardly exchanged six words all that summer. Dreadful isolation. But none of the others were much better. Castle Street. The dark house and the detested housekeeper.

I took Sharon out to dinner last night. A sudden impulse. A little French restaurant that's opened around the corner from us. Very expensive. Thought I ought to make up to her for the past week; all my tempers and crying spells. We couldn't really afford it; with the baby-sitter and her taxi fares it's set us back nearly a hundred quid. But we had a nice candle-lit meal, and by the end of it we were holding hands. We got rid of the sitter pretty quick and headed for bed. Everything was fine to start with; then I made the mistake of saying, So what else did you get up to with Klaus? And straight away she stiffened, turned dead cold and angry, and pushed me out of her. I said, What have I done? You said you would talk about the past, it isn't as if I was asking you to fantasise about the future . . . But she just kept her back turned to me; wouldn't answer.

Why can't she accept it's something I need? She ought to be grateful; most men would rage at their wives if they found out they'd been unfaithful; even leave them. And it hurt me too, when I first found out. All those times in Vienna when she couldn't make love because she had headaches . . . And really it was because she was in love with a fucking gym-teacher. It was excruciatingly painful – but also tremendously exciting. Sharon's not the most glamorous of women; I'd never imagined she could get involved with someone like that.

We've had some amazing nights when she's been willing to talk about it, share it with me, tell me where they had it, what they did, and so on. Why's she suddenly turned cold on me about it?

After all, she has a lot to make up for. I was humiliated in front of a couple of our friends in Vienna. Jenny Townshend in particular – you know, she works at the Freud Museum; she was in Vienna for a few months while we were there and we saw a lot of her. She and her Austrian lover, Karl. They covered for Sharon. She was supposed to be with them when really she was in bed with Klaus. When I think how often the subject of infidelity and affairs came up in our conversations, in connection with psychoanalysis, when the four of us were having a drink together – and they kept perfectly straight faces though they must have been laughing at me secretly! That's the most painful thing about being betrayed: the secret laughter. Klaus too, of course – he sometimes joined us for drinks. Everyone knowing but me. I'm sure Jenny knew absolutely everything that went on, because Sharon got very close to her, she was the only English girl she knew in Vienna. I imagine they still talk about Klaus and Karl, and giggle about those days. And yet *I'm* not allowed to ask her about it.

Anyway, after turning her back on me like that she soon fell asleep. I was thoroughly roused, of course, and felt I had to relieve myself if I was to get any sleep at all – even though I've hardly slept for a week, as you know. I tried to do it gently, recalling something she'd told me, about her and Klaus screwing in our bath; but it woke her, and she snapped at me. So I had to stop. After that I tossed and turned for a couple of hours, and eventually dropped off.

It could hardly be called sleep. Just an opportunity for violent sexual dreams.

It was the war, and I was in disguise, trying to escape from the Nazis. At one of the checks there was some confusion about change I owed them – I don't know what for. Not knowing German well I gave them the wrong change. This aroused their suspicions, but I managed to pass myself off as a Swiss. They let me go.

Then they were coming after me. I came to what looked like a big grey flower with stone petals. Between the stone petals some people were crouched, trying to hide by blending into the stone. So I too crouched on all fours. The Germans came. One of the soldiers started to 'frisk' me, as it were, to find out if we were humans or stones. I had disguised myself as a woman, and he frisked me by running his hands up under my skirt – up to the hips. It felt not unpleasant; but he stopped and gave way to a female Nazi, and I was a little disappointed by that.

Then I was in a group of several French whores, making love to one of them. My mother was there. I don't know why I'm sure it was my mother, observing me. She said, Be careful, put some cream on her down there so you won't get a disease. I said, I can't do that, she's already creaming. There was a kind of thick white cream all over this whore's cunt. She was a mass of flesh. I was pumping away in her. It was delightful but at the same time rather frightening; it was all a bit – excessive, immoderate.

Well, I think a lot of it is obvious. I've felt as if demons were pursuing me this week; and Klaus was very Nazi with his fitness-fanatical blue eyes and his splendid muscles. I walked out of a newsagent's without picking up my change yesterday. That scene is typical of my confusion and sense of persecution at present.

Then, this big grey flower . . . Jung would have called it a mandala-symbol. Stone and flesh. I hid among the stones, pretended to be stone. I *feel* like a stone, much of the time. Sharon makes me feel like a stone, calling me inhuman. But I didn't feel stony when the Nazis started frisking me under the skirt. I think this must have been a memory of Bill Hamilton's story of the WAAF officer – remember? But I seemed to enjoy it more when the male soldier was doing it. That's worrying. That seems to show homosexuality very clearly.

. . . Of course! You're right! I wasn't male at that point so it was perfectly natural to prefer the male hands running up my thighs! It's not homosexuality as such, rather an urge to be female! Yes!

Ah! . . . Right! – Change! Money was the wrong change – I wanted a *sex* change!

It's not something I've ever suspected in me. But unconsciously . . . It could be so. Perhaps – perhaps I feel that had I been born a girl my mother would not have left me, she'd have stayed on or taken me with her. Yes!

You don't know what a relief this is! Jesus!

. . . Well, I can tell you now. Lilian Rhodes revealed something you'd said in a letter that scared me to death. You said –

or so she claimed – that you had two patients, one of whom
had transsexual urges and the other was heading for a major
psychosis; and neither of them was aware of their problem. She
shouldn't have revealed something you'd written in confidence,
but there it was . . . I couldn't tell you before. Knowing Rachel
Brandt's rather mannish walk, I assumed *I* was heading for a
psychosis. Instantly I began to feel I actually was!

That's why I've been such a pain, Oscar! Why I've been crying all over the place; convinced I was heading for a breakdown.
Or worse. Madness.

Jesus! . . . Jesus! . . .

What a wonderful day it is!

Believe me, I can live with transsexual urges, very easily! It
just gave me an interesting dream! And – yes – now I think of
it, when Bill told me of his experience I guess I identified with
the officer, her feet planted wide, swaying in the dark, feeling
the caress of an anonymous hand.

The rest of my dream was just reassuring me that I'm not
homosexual, don't you think? And giving me a great deal of
pleasure. Though there was danger in it, and the stickiness of
the whore was frightening. The messiness of sex. Well, it's all
a great mess.

I worry a little that Klaus may have given something to
Sharon.

You can't imagine the relief! It's as if my mind has been
cramped into some intolerable position and has now been
moved, released!

I'm also feeling happier with Lilian. Beneath her neurosis
there's a pleasant woman. She'd been abusing me and all men
as usual when, suddenly, she broke wind. And was terribly
embarrassed. Suddenly, in her confusion and embarrassment,
she seemed very human and almost lovable.

She's an hysteric, of course; as surely as Freud's Dora.
Classic.

Maybe I'm liking her better because I can see her extreme
views as part of her mental problem now. It seems to me that
hysterics no longer develop physical symptoms, as in Freud; no,
they take up man-hating feminism. Do you think? . . . Well,
anyway, Lilian's beginning to open up about her past. She had

a letter from an elderly man called Richard – a friend of yours, I think. He's dying, as no doubt you know, and he wanted her to know he'd loved her when she was young. She's been very moved by his belated admission. Had he declared his love at the time, she says, she might have responded. Well. Probably you knew about it. I'm sure not much escaped you.

My tinnitus is bloody awful today. Dad rang this morning, and I thought he said he'd brought Sharon joy for her birthday. He'd actually said he'd bought her *Joy* – an expensive perfume.

Now that I've had this relief from my anxieties, I can concentrate on my patients better. Jane is extremely dependent. It distresses her enormously that we'll be breaking off for several weeks.

For that matter it distresses Sharon too. We can't really afford not to have their money coming in. Therapeutically it's necessary, I know. I shall miss my sessions with you.

I must try to lay off Klaus. Show her I can make love in silence. But she doesn't go out of her way to support me. Take the cricket on Saturdays. All the other wives are at the match making the tea and sandwiches – but not Sharon. She prefers to rub noses at her bloody encounter group. Which, if you ask me, is really just a chance to get together with Jenny afterwards and talk about Klaus!

My cricket's been lousy this summer. Top score, fourteen. I can't concentrate. I'll just be shaping up to a bowler when a phrase of Adler or Reich comes into my head – and I'm a goner. Fortunately we're all third-raters or I'd be out of the team. Of course Dad could have been a first-class cricketer if he'd wanted. Century for Glamorgan Seconds when he was sixteen. Bloody typical.

And *you* were a fine cricketer, weren't you? Didn't you hit a century against Harrow? . . . I thought so. I imagine the war put paid to that side of things for you.

Okay . . . Gosh, I feel a bit dizzy. Thank you for this session, Oscar; it's made all the difference to my peace of mind.

Would I what? . . . It's my ears. Would you type it? Here, let me wheel you to your desk. Shall I put the paper in? That's it!

. . . That would be wonderful! Let me just check, but I think . . . We've got our two weeks in Cornwall with Dad, late August . . . Everyone we know is off to Tuscany or the Bahamas, but we can't afford to look a gift horse in the mouth. At least we'll have the Daimler instead of our old banger. Yes, we're back on September first. The eighth, let's see . . . We're playing Dulwich Corinthians, our last match, but I'll have missed the two previous matches: so, yes, we'd love to come. As a matter of fact, Lilian has been talking about Munch. She hates him. I really don't know his work; it'll be interesting.

I've a confession I want to make: do you mind me staying a couple more minutes? – Castro! Good dog! good dog! I feel jealous that you confide in Lilian and not me. Of course I know you can't, while I'm in the training analysis; it's irrational. And then, well, she told me about a carved head that you showed to her and also Rachel. I felt hurt that you showed it to Rachel. So I start to think, he's dying, he can only move one hand, life must be unbearable for him – why not slip the poor old bugger a few pills and put him out of his misery? That's awful, isn't it? Terribly childish.

I'm sorry, Oscar. But now I feel so much better – you can't imagine!

Do you need to be pushed anywhere? . . . Okay. I'll see you tomorrow.

Golders Green
July 3

Dear Lilian,

Thank you so much for your card. I've not had a chance to write to you before because, as I'm sure you'll realise, it's a full-time job looking after Oscar. This term I've taken retirement, two years earlier than I need have done. I suppose we could have got someone in to look after him, but travelling down to Brighton I'd be away most of the day, and he's not very good with strangers. His condition embarrasses him greatly. I try to tell him he's being stupid, but he's always been a proud man, as you know.

Anyway, it did him a great deal of good to be in touch with you again. I hope you are feeling a little better; Chris James is going to be a fine psychotherapist, Oscar says, and I'm sure he'll help you. You are also helping him, of course.

Oscar is not so well today; he is having a lie-down; it's raining – very dreary for July, but then we had a splendid spring, didn't we? At least the rain gives me an excuse not to be working in the garden. I suppose, to be honest, I use it as a temporary escape. The strain of being constantly with someone you love who knows he is slowly dying is horrific.

He's terribly envious of those who are active. There's a girl in an Australian soap we watch, who is in a wheelchair. I can see his eyes boring into the screen, thinking, You don't know how well off you are, being able to move your arms, talk, eat! It's very sad.

At least twice a week we plan his funeral. The latest is strongly Mahlerian: the last movement of his Eighth Symphony. *Das Ewig-Weibliche zieht uns hinan* . . . Also Kathleen Ferrier – do you remember that scratchy old record? – singing the end of *Das Lied von der Erde*. Heartbreaking. Tomorrow he is as likely to choose some Johann Strauss and jazz.

At least your card brought back a happy memory. Our honeymoon in Florence. May 1950. We both stood transfixed before this painting in the Uffizi. When we read the painter's name, Artemisia Gentileschi, we couldn't believe it. A woman! It really is a wonderful, ferocious picture, isn't it? I hadn't seen it since our last visit to Florence in 1975. It struck me afresh

116

with its genius – and its savagery – even on a postcard. That wonderful fixity of the two women's gaze on the point of interest – Holofernes' neck! I'm sure Gentileschi was influenced by the rape she'd suffered; she was avenging herself on Tassi.

And then one looks at the victim. Eyes and mouth wide in panic; the blood already spurting; he knows it's inevitable. His legs are wide apart, and his scarlet cloak is like a woman's skirt. A man, for once, is in the helpless female position.

It probably seems strange to you that we associate our honeymoon with this painting; but there it is.

In connection with another disturbing artist, Munch, we want to invite you to Brighton. I enclose an invitation. Can you make it? Do come, and bring your husband and son as well. I did some research for the Munch film a couple of years ago – someone in Oslo noticed I'd written a couple of decent essays on him. This showing at the Art College will be the first in England. It should be good, and the Norwegian embassy has been tremendously helpful in arranging an exhibition. Mostly prints and minor works, but it should be worth seeing. I don't know if Oscar told you we have a flat down there; bought it before the prices explosion. We haven't been able to enjoy it as much as we hoped, because of Oscar's illness; but we still occasionally manage to get down, by taxi; and very fortunately it's a ground-floor flat, and just a two-minute walk from the sea. I thought we'd take advantage of the film-presentation by inviting a few friends down and having a party. Well, to be honest, I've been desperate to persuade Oscar to meet people. He won't have friends come to 'Padernice', but he knows we could hardly invite people all the way to Brighton for an art-film unless we threw in some sort of party. So do say you'll come. We both know it may be his farewell.

Now that I've retired from teaching, it would be nice to think I might paint. I don't know. It takes courage to pick up the brush again – seriously, that is. How about you? You were so promising. I don't think I ever quite had enough talent. But your postcard has given me an idea, or at least brought one to the surface. Why shouldn't I try to portray Auschwitz? It's easily the deepest experience of my life, yet I've never dared to touch it. Much too horrifyingly painful. But the *Judith* brought back a memory . . . Well, I might as well admit it came to me first when we saw the picture at the Uffizi. I was truly amazed that a woman had painted it, but not at all amazed that women could hack a man to death with such ferocity.

I've seen it myself, you see. I saw two skeletal women sawing away, with their last remaining strength, at the neck of a Belsen guard who'd got himself trapped in barbed-wire. A tommy had given them his bayonet. They'd been with me on the death-march from Auschwitz in the winter of 1944.

I confess when I saw that painting in the Uffizi my knees buckled. I remembered the guard's screams. I think at the end he thrust at the blade, because he knew, like the Assyrian general, there was no hope, and he wanted to end his agony quickly. The two women died of starvation a few days later. They probably met their victim again on the bank of the Styx.

'I have supped full of horrors.' Who wrote that? Most people ask me about Auschwitz and Belsen sooner or later; you were one of the sensitive ones, my dear, who had the grace not to ask. It was too bad we seemed to lose touch. Of course it was understandable, after all you'd been through, you wanted to get right away. It's difficult to measure pain; I'm sure you felt as much pain over the abortion as I in Auschwitz and Belsen. And perhaps you may have felt that we *oughtn't* to have offered our help, but let you go ahead with it and have it adopted by your aunt and uncle. Yet it seemed to be what you wanted.

How do we survive?

Looking back on my life, it's a miracle I ever recovered from my experiences. Oscar was my miracle. Why he fell in love with me I shall never know – I looked ghastly. But 'the heart has its reasons that reason knows not of'. I could never repay him. What I am doing for him now is nothing.

I took a break then to go in and see if he was all right. He's still asleep. He looked so thin and drawn. And once he was so strong and handsome. Well, you know; he was still handsome when you visited us. But you should have seen him in his thirties! I was so proud of my distinguished English major!

And so terrified of meeting his family. But then of course – did we ever tell you this? – we drew up in a taxi in the street where he had lived, and he couldn't believe his eyes. His house

– gone! Blown up in one of the last raids on Birmingham. Only his mother alive, and she, in the hospital, blinded and half-demented, barely able to recognise her son.

At least we were able to make her comfortable for her last few years; and she did recover somewhat mentally. Fortunately there was some money, which enabled us to train for careers, and buy nursing help for her. But money means very little; we would have given every penny just to have one of our relatives alive.

Or for the chance to have children. I even wished – no, it's too painful, for both of us. Well, that we could have adopted your little baby ourselves. But probably I'd have made an awful mother. After you left for America and another close woman-friend of mine left for Canada, I had a breakdown. Oscar dragged me through that too, with his understanding.

What a terrible century we've lived through. It sickened us to hear that the Lords have thrown out the bill to have war criminals eligible to be tried in English courts. It's to be hoped the Commons reverses it next year.

Enough of this gloom, I must put on some soup for Oscar; he can't swallow solids any more. For myself, I've discovered M & S do quite delicious snack meals. There's no point cooking for one. Today I'm going to have their chicken tikka; it's *very* tasty – have you ever tried it?

Affectionately,
Myra

4

Jenny, this is Steven. It's Saturday, six p.m. I thought I ought to warn you, Lilian might ring you. She found out I haven't been going to the Free Clinic. Some poisonous typist at her office told her she'd seen me with a woman. It was revenge because Lilian had complained about her boss who's a chronic toucher. Anyway, I got it in the neck when I arrived home, and she immediately charged me with seeing someone called Jenny . . . She knew your name because she found a slip of paper with your number on it. I explained that you run an encounter group for partners of people in therapy; of course she didn't believe me and she took it into her head to check with Chris James. Sharon took the call, and confirmed it! So she was terribly remorseful, and terribly grateful I'd wanted to learn about therapy and help her. But in case she has second thoughts and decides to ring you, I thought you ought to be prepared. She's extremely edgy and unpredictable since her sessions have ended for the summer. Thanks, darling. Cheers.

Fowey,
Cornwall
Aug. 25

Darling,

My first letter to you. I'm sitting in the tiny kitchen with a bottle of wine at my elbow. I volunteered to wait in for a plumber, since our loo is blocked. We're very lucky to find one who'll come out at a weekend.

As we've driven around, my heart has lurched every time we approached a phone-booth. Some of them are still red around here. Red for passion. I've wanted to say, stop the car, I need to ring my lover! Oh, I know you couldn't have said much, but it would have been some contact. Is your secretary truly discreet? *I* was, as Alan's secretary, and by God I needed to be! He's always been an awful womaniser. I was very surprised, at first, when I met his son, and found him very reserved and shy with girls.

I'm using Alan's Amstrad, which he brought with him to work on his book. Before starting this I looked at what he was writing, and it depressed me rather. It's about animal research, and I know it's necessary (tho' not for cosmetics), but I sometimes had to type horrible stuff for him and yet it had such a cool scientific style you almost forgot you were writing about creatures suffering.

Oh dear, this is serious! And I didn't mean to be, but reading that upset me a bit. And yet Chris's Dad is a sensitive, compassionate man in normal life.

Now I'm quite enjoying the feel of typing again. Is your sec. really thinking of leaving in December? And do you think I could do the job? I've no experience of legal work, though I suppose medical secretary isn't so very different? It would be wonderful.

I wish you were here! I'd let you undress me, I'd lie down, open my legs, and let you eat raspberries out of my pussy. With Cornish cream, if you liked! Has it all been too sudden? We don't really know each other, do we?

I'm stroking my cheek, which is still a little tender. Chris thinks some bloke at Jenny's group flipped his lid and gave me a whack! I think of it as a flower of passion. I know you

121

wouldn't do it unless I said it was all right. I can feel the love and gentleness behind it. Passion *is* a bit raw and violent, isn't it? I dreamt one night we were together and you were biting my tits and I loved it!

I want to be lying on a Cornish beach with you, completely naked, with the surf crashing over us! Very Daphne du Maurier, I know – she lived near here – but it's my major fantasy. Well, that and making love to a virile, brawny seventeen-year-old life-guard! (I don't mean it. I shouldn't tease you about your age.)

How everything cheers up because of a little sunshine! Till now it's been cloudy and drizzly. On our one hot, muggy day, Wednesday, we had a bit of a panic. Chris drove us to a ruined castle not far from here – well, it's called a castle tho' there's not a stone to be seen, sod-all in fact. I was in a foul mood, because we'd been last year, and I was missing you too. Alan suddenly collapsed in a faint. He soon recovered, and thinks it was just the heat, but it gave us a scare.

God, I won't see you properly for another two weeks. Can't bear it. Jenny might let us meet at her house when the cricket season's over. She's very romantic, and she's always felt I should have a fling. When we were in Vienna together, she tried to get me off with a thicko gym teacher. He wasn't my type at all; I'm afraid I go for the brainy sort. She had me matched with Simon at the group – do you remember a tall, gangling young man wearing filthy corduroy trousers? But as soon as you walked in that day I knew you were someone special. Well, at any rate, the moment we were paired off in that exercise and we had to hug each other.

I don't know how I feel about your wife. It was certainly an awful moment when she rang. She sounded so upset I thought you'd had an accident on your way home and somehow she knew you'd been with me. I don't know how I'll feel when I face her in Brighton. Presumably she doesn't know Chris and I have been invited too? It will be painful – and yet there's a weird desire to see 'the other woman'. And I'm really looking forward to meeting your son. Poor lad. I'm sure he'll grow out of it. It sounds to me as if he needs lots of hugs and kisses. (Like me.) Perhaps when your wife starts her new job she'll feel happier and able to give him more attention. I don't think Chris knows about the new job, by the way. From what you've said there's a *lot* she hasn't told him.

She's phoned him a couple of times since the panicky Saturday, and told him she'd spoken to me and why. He was very taken aback, asked me why I hadn't mentioned you were in Jenny's group. I said we didn't use surnames, so I hadn't known. I described you as short and balding. Sorry, darling! I didn't tell him you had marvellous eyes, or that your voice would turn Mary Whitehouse into a sex maniac. I bet the women jurors are sitting on damp skirts when you address them. They'd have lots of damp knickers for you, why don't you ask them! Perhaps you ought to tell your wife you've suddenly realised who the short-arsed brunette in Jenny's group is. I'd feel less uncomfortable, I think, if she knows we've met.

– I had to break off to let the plumber in. He was cheerful and fat and had athsma (is that how you spell it? it doesn't look right). I made him tea and pretended to understand his thick Cornish accent.

When he'd gone, and I was using the newly-flushable loo, I decided to give you a treat. Though God knows why you should get a buzz, as you call it, from it. However, I don't mind. They're coming in a jiffy – which I had thanks to my friend Ann who sent me down a tape of Queen I'd asked for. This is the first and last, darling, like the pub at Land's End, so make the most of it! I don't want to know what you do with them! Only hope to God your secretary *does* respect packages marked Private . . .

I *will* wear sussies for you some time, only it's awkward on Saturday afternoons; Chris might notice and wonder why I was tarting myself up to go to Jenny's group. Especially as he knows we do a lot of rolling around there. He's even suspicious when I put on a skirt. Like I told you, he's extremely jealous and we have to be careful. But we've been quite safe at the flat, I promise you; Tina would *always* ring if he left the cricket for any reason. She's discreet and doesn't ask questions; and I've given *her* an alibi a couple of times. She's a character! She got home one night and found Bob, her husband, in a foul temper, as he'd been bowled out for a duck. She said to me she thought of telling him she'd been out for a fuck!!

P.S. (Evening) There was a great panic then. I went to make a coffee before printing this and posting it, when suddenly I heard the Daimler! Hours before they should have arrived back. I just had to pray Alan didn't want to use the Amstrad. Belinda had been crying a lot, complaining of feeling hot; and they couldn't deal with it. Two doctors! I think she has a slight tummy-upset – Alan cooked her oily chips last night while Chris and I were out for a meal. She's fine now, I've put her to bed and the men have gone to the pub. Why is it men can't stand to hear children crying? My Dad's just as bad.

Can't wait to see you – even tho' we shan't be able to do anything. I send you a long, slow, wet kiss.

Lots of love,
Sharon
xxx

My dear Lilian,

Thanks for your card from Aldeburgh; it brought back a happy memory of taking tea with Ben and Peter.

We have been spending a few days at the flat. Myra has been preparing for the film and exhibition, and contacting caterers for the party. But also, she wants me to tell you, she's been sketching and painting. The College let her retain a studio for her private use, but this is the first time she's taken advantage of it. She's delving into her experience of the death-camps. I can see her descending into the depths. For myself, I prefer the way of Lot rather than his wife – even though it's I who look like the pillar of salt. We change, we live in the moment. There seems little point in regretting the past or bewailing it.

Still, I shouldn't discourage her. I think she's always felt slightly disappointed in her art. She's even said she wished she'd kept to her original ambition to become a dress designer. Didn't she design and run up a dress for you once? There was a time when Myra could look quite stunning. But over the years her mind has concentrated more and more on essentials.

Anyway, I have been alone much of the time, and have tried to ease the boredom by writing up a case study on one of my two remaining patients – the one whom I described as an unconscious transsexual. Actually I've modified my views on that; she just has an inordinate identification with the penis, thanks to a father who exposed himself to her frequently. At the same time she shrinks from sex (she is a divorcee). Her other obsession is with the Ukrainian branch of her family, which was wiped out in the holocaust. I sometimes have to restrain irritation, since she was too young ever to have met or have any contact with them. – Not only too young; her parents wanted nothing to do with Ukrainian riff-raff. I would find the obsession more understandable if she'd been in my situation with regard to my Czech relatives, whom I knew and loved. Yet even so I know one has to put a line under the past.

'Look not behind thee, neither stay thou in all the plain; escape to the mountain, lest thou be consumed . . .'

However, it is those obsessions that are not easily comprehensible which are the most interesting psychologically. It's as if she is *jealous* of their suffering, and even their deaths. Because she spent her wartime childhood safe in the Highlands of Scotland she feels emotionally deprived!

There may even be a link between her penis-envy and her envy of the more emotionally potent (in her vision) experience of the European Jews. Or maybe not. In any case, this is what I'm using to pass the bleak hours here. It's hardly the traditional idea of Brighton! My poor 'working' finger is weary.

I had a bad beginning to the day. Read in *The Times* a short obituary of Margarita Holstein, one of the founders of the paraplegic games. I knew her slightly. She swam for Germany in the 1936 Olympics, then gave birth to a handicapped (but delightful) child. He was killed in the bombing on Berlin, and Margarita was badly injured too, losing both legs. But these tragedies didn't quell her spirit. In memory of her son she endowed a fund to teach handicapped children to swim – a fund to which I gladly contributed.

I'm longing to see you, Lily, in ten days or so. (You're still Lily Rowbottom in my imagination.) Though that too will be painful, in a way. From the acceptances there should be some nice people that I think you'll feel in tune with – spiritually minded and creative people, concerned for environmental issues and so on. Tories and hard-nosed businessmen should be conspicuous by their absence, thank God.

But in the words of the old song, I'll only have eyes for you.

Love,
Oscar

Brighton,
Sept. 3

Dear Rachel,

Many thanks for your letter, but I'm sorry you're unwell and probably won't be able to come next Saturday. I merely wonder whether you have brought on the flu deliberately (though of course unconsciously) for other, psychological reasons. I.e. your fear of crowds and strangers. If that is the case, I think you should try to come if at all possible.

I say that, in spite of the fact that the guest-list, with a few exceptions, fills me with ghastly foreboding. There are far too many WANKRS (Well-heeled Artists for Neil Kinnock's Revisions of Socialism), and MUESLIS (Morally Unimpeachable, Ecologically Sensitive London Intellectuals). But they're the tribes that our vocations have attracted and that we've had to pretend to belong to.

I wanted to let you know, in case you don't come, that I've written to my acquaintance at the Soviet Embassy, putting forward very strongly indeed your suggestion for the museum in Byelaya Tserkov. *Is* there a white church there, as its name implies? I enclosed photocopies of those deeply affecting extracts from *Schöne Zeiten*. My mind flashed to those documents when my wife, who has been busy helping with the exhibition, etc., showed me six studies for Munch's painting called *Compassion*. In their own way, I suppose, five of the six protagonists in Byelaya Tserkov were being 'compassionate'.

I'm reading Sereny's book about Stangl, the Treblinka commandant. He killed a million people, yet she makes it clear he was *fundamentally* quite a nice man. Go into your local at a busy hour, and somewhere there – given the wrong circumstances, ambitious, frightened, obedient – is Stangl. Instead, not having been put to the test, he is perhaps planning a charity run.

I still hope we'll see you here. Be brave. Summer flu can vanish with a breath of sea air.

With best wishes,
O.J.

SIX STUDIES FOR COMPASSION

I

Catholic Divisional Chaplain   Division command post
to 295th Infantry Division   20 August 1941

I submit the following report to 295th Infantry Division:

Today in the afternoon towards 14.30 hours Military Chaplains Tewes and Wilczek, Military Hospital Division 4/607, came to the Protestant divisional chaplain and myself and reported the following:

They told us that German soldiers had drawn their attention to the fact that Jewish children aged between a few months and five or six years, whose parents are said to be executed, are locked up in a house in intolerable conditions under guard by Ukrainian militiamen. These children can be heard whimpering continuously. They said that they went there themselves and had confirmed this fact but had not seen any members of the Wehrmacht or any other authority responsible for keeping order here or carrying out guard duty. They reported that there were only a few German soldiers there as spectators, and that these men had expressed their indignation at this state of affairs. They asked us to report to our headquarters.

Their description of these incidents made it reasonable to suspect that this was an arbitrary action on the part of the Ukrainian militia. In order to be able to report the matter accurately, I myself, accompanied by the two military chaplains and the Protestant Divisional Chaplain, Wehrmachtoberpfarrer Kornmann, paid a visit to the house, where we discovered the following:

In the courtyard in front of the house the crying and whimpering of children could be heard very loudly. Outside there were a Ukrainian militiaman keeping guard with a rifle, a number of German soldiers and several young Ukrainian girls. We immediately entered the house unobstructed and in two rooms found some ninety (I counted them)

*children aged from a few months to five, six or seven years old.
There was no kind of supervision by the Wehrmacht or other German
authorities.*

*A large number of German soldiers, including a sanitation officer,
were inspecting the conditions in which the children were being kept
when we arrived. Just then a military policeman, who was under the
command of the Ortskommandantur or the Feldkommandantur, also
arrived. He stated that he had come only in order to investigate a case
of looting which was said to have been carried out by guards from the
Ukrainian militia.*

*The two rooms where the children had been accommodated – there
was a third empty room adjoining these two – were in a filthy state.
The children lay or sat on the floor which was covered in their faeces.
There were flies on the legs and abdomens of most of the children,
some of whom were only half dressed. Some of the bigger children
(two, three, four years old) were scratching the mortar from the wall
and eating it. Two men, who looked like Jews, were trying to clean the
rooms. The stench was terrible. The small children, especially those that
were only a few months old, were crying and whimpering continuously.
The visiting soldiers were shaken, as we were, by these unbelievable
conditions and expressed their outrage over them. In another room,
accessible through a window in one of the children's rooms, there were
a number of women and older children, apparently Jews. I did not enter
this room. Locked in a further room there were some other women,
among them one woman with a small child on her arm. According to
the guard on duty – a Ukrainian boy aged about sixteen or seventeen,
who was armed with a stick – it had not been established whether these
women were Jews or not.*

*When we got back into the courtyard an argument was in progress
between the above-mentioned military policeman and the Ukrainian
sentry who was guarding the house. This guard was being accused of
the looting and also of destroying several passes which had been issued
by the German military authorities to other Ukrainians (who were in
fact women). The pieces still lay scattered on the ground. The military
policeman disarmed the Ukrainian guard, had him led away and then
went away himself. Some German soldiers who were in the courtyard
told me that they had their quarters in a house right next door and that
since the afternoon of the previous day they had heard the children crying
uninterrupted. Some time during the evening of the previous day three*

lorry-loads of children had already been taken away. An official from the SD had been present. The lorry-driver told them these were the children of Jews and Jewesses who had already been shot and the children were now going to be taken to be executed. The execution was to be carried out by Ukrainian militia. The children still in the house were also to be shot. The soldiers expressed extreme indignation over the conditions in which the children were being kept; in addition, one of them said that he himself had children at home. As there were no Germans there in a supervisory role I asked the soldiers to make sure that nobody else, particularly members of the local population, entered the house, in order to avoid the conditions there being talked about further.

Meanwhile a senior medical officer from the Wehrmacht whom I did not know had visited the children's rooms and declared to me that water should be brought in urgently. In such conditions the risk of an epidemic could not be excluded.

I consider it necessary to report this matter to my HQ for two reasons: first, there is no German watch or supervision at this house and second, German soldiers are able to enter it any time. This has indeed already happened and has provoked a reaction of indignation and criticism.

Dr Reuss
Military Chaplain

2

Wehrmachtoberpfarrer Kornmann   O.U.
Protestant Divisional Chaplain   *21 August 1941*
to 295th Infantry Division

I submit the following report to 295th Infantry Division:

Yesterday (20 August) towards 1500 hours two military chaplains from a military hospital unit in this area came to see me and the Division's Catholic Military Chaplain and reported to us that near by, some 500m away, about 80 to 90 children from babies to school-age were being held in an upper storey of a house. The children could be heard from a long way off shouting and crying and as they had already been there 24 hours, the soldiers quartered in the neighbouring houses were being sorely disturbed at night. The two military chaplains had been made aware of the presence of the children by the soldiers themselves. Together with the two chaplains and my Catholic colleague, I went to the house in question and saw the children lying and sitting in two rooms. They were partly lying in their own filth, there was not a single drop of drinking water and the children were suffering greatly due to heat. A man from the Ukrainian militia was standing guard downstairs. We learned from him that these were Jew children whose parents had been executed. There was one group of German soldiers standing at the watchpost and another standing at the corner of the house. Some of them were talking agitatedly about what they had heard and seen.

As I considered it highly undesirable that such things should take place in full view of the public eye I hereby submit this report. The two military chaplains were from Military Hospital Unit 4/607 and were named Wilczek (Protestant) and Tewes (Catholic).

Kornmann
Wehrmachtoberpfarrer

F.d.R.
signed: signature
Lieutenant and O.1 (l. Ordonnanzoffizier)

3

295th Infantry Division   Division Command Post
1. Generalstabsoffizier   *21 August 1941*

Report on events in Byelaya Tserkov on 20 August 1941

*On 20 August at about 16.00 hours the two divisional chaplains
reported to me that some ninety Jewish children had been locked up
in a house in the town for twenty-four hours without any food or water.
They reported that they had gone to investigate the conditions there
after they had received reports from chaplains from the military hospital.
These conditions, they told me, were intolerable and an attempt to
induce the Ortskommandant to intervene had not met with success.
The divisional chaplains recommended that the conditions should be
remedied urgently as numerous soldiers were visiting the house and the
sanitary conditions were liable to have dangerous repercussions. This
was confirmed by a senior medical officer from the military hospital.*

*Upon receiving this report I went at 16.30 hours together with
the ordnance officer, Lieutenant Spoerhase, Divisional Chaplain
Dr Reuss, and an interpreter, Sonderführer Tischuk to the house,
which was situated down a side road set back some fifty metres from
the road. From the road one could see the house and hear children
whimpering. There were about twenty NCOs and men standing in the
courtyard. There was no guard post in front of the house. A few armed
Ukrainians were standing about in the yard. There were children lying
on the window-sills, but the windows were not open. On the landing
on the first floor stood a Ukrainian guard who immediately opened the
door of the rooms in which the children were accommodated. In the three
interconnecting rooms there was a further Ukrainian guard armed with
a rifle. There were about ninety children and several women crammed*

SIX STUDIES FOR COMPASSION

into the rooms. A woman was cleaning up the farthermost room, which contained almost only babies. The other rooms were unbelievably filthy. There were rags, nappies and filth all over the place. The half-naked children were covered in flies. Almost all the children were crying or whimpering. The stink was unbearable. A German-speaking woman was claiming she was completely innocent, had never anything to do with politics and was not Jewish.

Meanwhile an Oberscharführer from the SD had entered the house. I asked him what was going to happen to these children. He informed me that the children's relatives had been shot and the children were also to be eliminated. Without making any comment I went to the Ortskommandantur and demanded an explanation from the commandant. He told me that the matter was out of his competence and that he had no influence over measures being taken by the SD, although he was aware of them. He suggested discussing the matter with the Feldkommandant, Lieutenant-Colonel Riedl. I then went to see him accompanied by the Ortskommandant and the O.I. The Feldkommandant reported that the head of the Sonderkommando had been to see him, had notified him about the execution and was carrying it out with his knowledge. He stated that he had no power to change the Obersturmführer's instructions. I asked the Feldkommandant whether he thought that the Obersturmführer had also received orders from the highest authority to eliminate children as well; I had heard nothing of this. The Feldkommandant replied he was convinced of the correctness and necessity of this order.

I then requested that the area around the house be sealed off so that the troops would have no possibility whatsoever of seeing what was happening inside. I pointed out that the soldiers who were quartered in the vicinity of the house had heard the children whimpering throughout the night, which had already given rise to considerable criticism on their part. I further asked that the transport to the executions should be conducted inconspicuously. I also offered some of the men from the division for guard duty if the Feldkommandantur did not have sufficient manpower. I further stated that I would immediately instruct Army Group to come to a decision as to whether the execution of the remaining children should proceed or not. (According to the Feldkommandant, a number of children had already been eliminated the previous day by the Ukrainian militia on SD orders.) The Feldkommandant gave his agreement to this arrangement . . .

137

Conclusion:
1. The troops have been trained by their officers to have a decent soldierly attitude and to avoid violence and roughness towards a defenceless population. They are fully aware of the need for the toughest intervention against guerrillas. In the case in question, however, measures against women and children were undertaken which in no way differ from atrocities carried out by the enemy about which the troops are continuously being informed. It is unavoidable that these events will be reported back home where they will be compared to the Lemberg (Lvov) atrocities. The troops are waiting for their officers to intervene. This is particularly true for older married men. An officer is therefore forced to intervene out of consideration for his troops where such things take place in public. In the interest of maintaining military discipline all similar measures should be carried out away from the troops.
2. The execution could have been carried out without any sensation if the Feldkommandant and the Ortskommandantur had taken the necessary steps to keep the troops away. This unfortunate state of affairs was caused by the failure of both commanders to take the necessary action. During all the negotiations the impression was given that all the executions could be traced back to an initiative of the Feldkommandant. Following the execution of all the Jews in the town it became necessary to eliminate the Jewish children, particularly the infants. Both infants and children should have been eliminated immediately in order to have avoided this inhuman agony. The Feldkommandant and the Obersturmführer declared that it was not possible to provide alternative accommodation for the children and the Feldkommandant declared several times that this brood had to be stamped out.

(signed) Groscurth

4

Protestant and Catholic   *O.U.*
Military Chaplains   *22 August 1941*
to Military Hospital 4/607

We hereby submit the following report to 29th Infantry Division as instructed:

On 20 August 1941 at 13.00 hours we heard from German soldiers that quite a large number of children had been locked up in intolerable conditions in a house near our quarters. A Ukrainian was said to be guarding these children. As we suspected this to be some arbitrary action on the part of the Ukrainians we went over there straight away. We found about ninety children packed together into two small rooms in a filthy state. Their whimpering could be heard in the vicinity of the house. Some of the children, mainly infants, were completely exhausted and almost lifeless. There were no German guard or supervision present, only a Ukrainian guard armed with a rifle. German soldiers had free access to the house and were expressing outrage over these frightful conditions. As these events were taking place under the aegis of the German Wehrmacht and would therefore damage its reputation, we immediately went and reported to the Ortskommandantur. The Ortskommandant went with us to the house, inspected the conditions and then took us to report to the Feldkommandantur. At the Feldkommandantur none of the competent gentlemen was available for us to talk to and we were advised to call later. As the matter seemed to us to be one of utmost urgency and we assumed that the divisional commander of 295th Infantry Division stationed in the area was the most senior-ranking officer, we went to see the two divisional chaplains of 295th Infantry Division and informed them of what was happening so that they could report to their HQ.

Tewes, Military Chaplain
Wilczek, Military Chaplain

F.d.R.
(signed) Spoerhase
Lieutenant and O.1

5

From the Commander-in-Chief   Army Headquarters
of Sixth Army   26 August 1941

Ic/A.O.
No. 2245/41   3 copies
9. Kdos   copy 2
Statement on the report of 295th Division
on the events in Bialacerkiew [Byelaya Tserkov]

The report disguises the fact that the division itself has ordered the
execution to be interrupted and had requested the consent of the army
to do so.

Immediately after the division's telephone inquiry, after consulting
Standartenführer Blobel I postponed the carrying out of the execution
because it was not organised properly. I gave instructions that on the
morning of 21 August, Standartenführer Blobel and a representative of
Army Headquarters should go to Bialacerkiew to inspect the conditions.
I have ascertained in principle that once begun, the action was conducted
in an appropriate manner.

The conclusion of the report in question contains the following
sentence, 'In the case in question, measures against women and
children were undertaken which in no way differs from atrocities
carried out by the enemy about which the troops are continually being
informed.'

I have to describe this assessment as incorrect, inappropriate and
impertinent in the extreme. Moreover this comment was written in an
open communication which passes through many hands.

It would have been far better if the report had not been written at all.

(signed) von Reichenau

Distribution:
Army Group South = *2nd Copy*
295th ID = *2nd copy*
Files = *3rd copy*

f.d.R.d.A

(signed) Groscurth
Lieutenant i.G. (im Generalstab)

6

. . . Then Blobel ordered me to have the children executed. I asked him, 'By whom should the shooting be carried out?' He answered, 'By the Waffen-SS.' I raised an objection and said, 'They are all young men. How are we going to answer to them if we make them shoot small children?' To this he said, 'Then use your men.' I then said, 'How can they do that? They have small children as well.' This tug-of-war lasted about ten minutes . . . I suggested that the Ukrainian militia of the Feldkommandant should shoot the children. There were no objections from either side to this suggestion . . .

I went out to the woods alone. The Wehrmacht had already dug a grave. The children were brought along in a tractor. I had nothing to do with this technical procedure. The Ukrainians were standing round trembling. The children were taken down from the tractor. They were lined up along the top of the grave and shot so that they fell into it. The Ukrainians did not aim at any particular part of the body. They fell into the grave. The wailing was indescribable. I shall never forget that scene throughout my life. I find it very hard to bear. I particularly remember a small fair-haired girl who took me by the hand. She too was shot later . . . The grave was near some woods. It was not near the rifle-range. The execution must have taken place in the afternoon at about 3.30 or 4.00. It took place the day after the discussions at the Feldkommandanten . . . Many children were hit four or five times before they died.

(signed) SS-Obersturmführer August Häfner

THE LONELY ONE

She had to pause and take a grip on herself before she entered the gallery. It was comfortably full of small groups of people, chatting and sipping drinks, and of others – students mostly – flitting from picture to picture around the walls. She had always had a problem with claustrophobia, and hated being in rooms without windows. For that reason she had rarely visited art galleries, theatres or cinemas. She was very uncultured, except she read a lot. She felt frightened of betraying her ignorance before these sophisticated people, almost all of them strangers. Munch was no more than a name to her; glancing around, she thought his pictures looked weird.

She took one step inside the door, and stopped again. She smoothed her dress down over her stomach, conscious of the bulge she couldn't get rid of. She'd tried aerobics, but lacked the determination to pursue it properly. The plain black dress she'd bought at M & S had seemed slimming, as she looked in the mirror; but now she thought she'd bought a size too small and her ungainly figure was all the more apparent. She hitched at her tights through her dress, even though they hadn't sagged.

Looking round for someone to talk to, she saw no one she knew, apart from Dr Jacobson, of course, so obvious in his wheelchair; and Mrs Jacobson. They had three or four strangers clustered around them and she lacked the courage to go up to them. She took a few steps towards the table where a steward was serving wine. Her steps dragged, it was like wading through that grey sea outside; she still wasn't completely over the flu that had dogged her for most of the summer. Normally she strode confidently and energetically, not at all a lady-like walk. The habit came from those walking holidays with Father. Poor Father.

'White, please,' she said to the young man poised over the bottles. He looked nervous too; a student at the art college probably, earning an extra couple of pounds. 'Thank you very much.' She flashed him a smile but he was already turning towards a well-filled T-shirt saying *No Gulf War*.

— The young and the beautiful. She was neither.

Sipping the wine, she gazed around again, her heart fluttering with anxiety. At that moment she saw another familiar face; it belonged to Chris James, a fellow would-be analyst. A tall, earnest, sandy-haired young man; rather handsome, and with a shy, freckled, boyish charm. He'd go far. He was turning his head, looking straight at her while chatting, and she was sure he recognised her. She gave a hesitant smile across the room, but his vague expression didn't alter; he turned back to his companions. Rachel tried to remove her smile but it remained on her face like a kind of *risus* for several moments.

She stepped up to one of the pictures. *The Lonely One*, she read on the card adjoining it. 1896/7, hand-coloured mezzotint. The delicate, mournful picture edged into Rachel's loneliness. She had never had as slim a waist, bound with a black belt, as that young woman gazing at the grey sea, her back turned; never that long straight shimmering hair, the colour of bright sunlight. The shore she stood on grey, with a few vague rocks tinged with the gold of her hair; the sea a lighter grey, almost the shade of her long dress. Greyness everywhere, except for those flashes of gold. Gold even touched the hem of the dress.

You couldn't see her face. It struck Rachel that the great feeling of loneliness came from that absent face.

She was aware of herself gazing at the picture; her ungainly ageing body and short mousy hair. She was standing behind herself, observing. She'd had that feeling quite a lot lately.

Turning away, she noticed that the crowd around Dr Jacobson had thinned out. Apart from his wife, there was only a tall, elderly, strikingly suntanned man leaning on a cane. Mrs Jacobson spotted her, gave a hint of a smile and a waggle of her hand. Rachel moved towards them.

She'd never seen her analyst in a dark suit and tie before. Over the last months, in their analytical sessions, he'd usually been in pyjamas and dressing gown and she'd got used to him like that. Now the way his suit hung on him, and the white starched collar gaped around his scraggy neck, shocked her. She covered her reaction well as he recognised her, his head lolling, his lips parting in a smile and his tongue protruding slightly in the effort to say hello.

'Racheniceyoucome.'

'I was determined to make it.'

'Are you feeling better?' Myra Jacobson asked. Her hand

148

rose to the back of Rachel's neck. 'Your label's sticking out, my dear.'

'Oh – thanks. Yes, I'm a lot better.' The deeply sun-tanned man was smiling at her pleasantly and she smiled back. Slimly built, in a light blue suit; dark hair touched with silver; deep-brown eyes, bushy grey eyebrows, a cleft chin. An attractive man; distinguished; like one of those ageing but ageless Hollywood actors you watched on the Wogan Show and thought, My God I could still go for him! His hands were clasped together over the top of his cane.

'Let me introduce you,' Myra said. 'This is Dr Becker, a very old friend. He's come all the way from Damascus to be with us today. Anton, this is Rachel Brandt. She's in analysis with Oscar. – A training analysis. One of the two people he still sees.'

There was strength in his hand-shake. Probably well into his seventies, Rachel judged, he was still fit and vital, still in the world of the healthy. The contrast with Dr Jacobson, not so much older, saddened her.

'Delighted to meet you!' he murmured in a strongly accented voice.

'Hello!' She wasn't sure where Damascus was, exactly. 'You live in Damascus?'

'Yes. I've lived there for – oh, four hundred years.' Myra intervened to correct him: forty. He could speak in German, she told him: Mrs Brandt knew the language. Rachel said not well, and would he speak slowly? He continued in his native tongue, 'I haven't seen Oscar and Myra in all that time. Longer!' He encompassed them both in a sad smile. 'But I had to come for this occasion.'

'How did you meet each other?' Rachel asked, her eyes straying beyond him.

The young woman on the grey shore took a small step forward.

'I was an officer in the Wehrmacht. After the war, there were vast medical problems among the refugees. I met Major Jacobson at one of the camps; we worked together. And, of course, that's where we both met Myra.'

'Enem – friends,' Oscar mumbled.

'Please?'

'We weren't enemies but friends,' Myra explained. She took Dr Becker's hands in hers, gazing into his eyes with warm affection.

'Enemies became friends,' Rachel said almost at the same moment.

'Ah, yes! Exactly! We became friends.' The old doctor's lean, lined, tanned face grew emotional; he nodded several times. 'Friends.'

The yellow-haired young woman drew up her long skirt in handfuls and crouched. A yellow stream burst from her.

A footfall on the rocks attracted her attention. She turned her head, still crouched over, and saw a young man in a black suit just behind her. She gave a slight nod and turned away again, staring at the grey sea.

A trickle of yellow ran across the picture from the woman to the sea.

A trickle of speech came from Oscar's lips. 'We've changed a little!' Myra interpreted; and Dr Becker grinned broadly, exposing perfect teeth save for one gold filling at the front.

'Yes, a little! We all have. But in the spirit – you are that same handsome man! And Myra – I would have known you anywhere.'

Myra blushed, gazed down at her navy-blue trousers and sensible shoes.

'Are you here in England for long?' Rachel asked.

'No, alas. I must fly back tomorrow.' He grimaced. 'Though I am old, I try to keep busy. I've had a wonderful three days with Oscar and Myra and it's not possible to stay longer, I'm afraid. Have you ever visited Syria, Dr Brandt? – Is it Dr?'

'I'm afraid not. To both questions. I'm plain Mrs.'

'Certainly not plain! Your husband couldn't be with you?'

She flushed at the no doubt insincere compliment. 'We're divorced.'

'It's so common these days.' His brown eyes crinkled at the corners, gazing at a *Madonna* lithoprint, or through it. Then he redirected his gaze back to Rachel. 'You have children?'

'No, unfortunately.'

'Ah, they can be a comfort. I have a son in Damascus, and

two grandchildren. They're Syrian, of course. As was my wife. She died of cancer last year, though she was only fifty-three. I think I've lived too long. Perhaps it would have been better if I had died in the war, like so many millions of others.' His eyes veered to Myra, holding her gaze; his closed lips gave another mournful twitch.

He asked where Rachel lived, why she had decided to take up analysis in – he hesitated, seeking the right, the tactful, word – in mid-life. She explained how a desk job in the civil service had seemed empty and dull, after her divorce. The urge to help people. Yet she was increasingly unsure if she could cope with it.

She was standing apart from herself again, listening to herself speak. Dr Jacobson had not looked at her as she had confessed her uncertainty about her fitness to be an analyst. She looked at the *Madonna*, while the conversation drifted to other, mundane matters.

The swirling black hair of the *Madonna*, extending to her hips where the picture cut off. The coils circled her naked breasts, were echoed in the black circles around her closed eyes. The lips closed, full, dreamy; a dark shadow under the firm, tilted chin; the body arched at the slender waist.

At her side, tiny in the corner, clutching strands of hair pathetically, a curled-up hollow-eyed foetus.

'She's wonderful, isn't she?' said Dr Becker, intercepting her gaze.

'Yes.'

'You can pay half a million pounds for a good lithoprint of the *Madonna*,' Myra said. 'The Japanese are collecting Expressionists, and they don't have many Munchs.'

'Iscraze.'

'It's crazy. Oscar's right.'

She's trying to tell me something, Rachel thought, staring at the black-haired woman. What is it?

The wheaten-haired woman on the shore had stood up, letting her skirt tumble down into place. The young man came up to join her, and without touching hands they walked together nearer to the grey sea.

It was very nice having a flat in Brighton, but they couldn't use it much any more; it was rather a waste. And the Poll Tax. Did Dr Becker know about the Poll Tax? They had to pay twice over, which didn't seem fair. They would sell it when . . . Myra's eyes met her husband's, and her voice tailed away.

She held a glass half full of red wine to Oscar's lips, which trembled as they sipped.

Dr Becker excused himself to go and look at the pictures. He gave Rachel a short bow.

She had started to say how proud they must be to have drawn their friend all the way from the Middle East, but she stopped in mid-sentence. Dr Jacobson's tired and bleary eyes were gazing past her; they had widened, become almost animated. Looking round, she saw a woman in a brown suede jacket over white slacks. She was beaming. Hand in pocket, a nonchalant, almost masculine air. Unmade-up but attractive; short brown hair on the turn to grey; John Lennon specs. Fiftyish, at a guess, but unfazed by ageing. Ignoring Rachel, she bent over and grasped Oscar's lifeless hands. 'Oscar!' she exclaimed warmly.

'Li-Li!'

The woman released his hands and straightened, turning with the same warm smile to Myra, who hesitated. 'It's Lilian,' the woman prompted.

'Lilian! My *dear*! How stupid of me!' She embraced her. 'I *ought* to have recognised you. So good to see you again!'

'Yes, it's been much too long. Steven'll be here in a minute, he's parking the car.' Lilian glanced from Myra to Oscar and back, smiling still, drinking them in.

'This is Rachel Brandt,' Myra said, as if just noticing the awkward presence of an outsider. 'Lilian Rhodes, another very old friend of ours.'

'Hello,' Lilian said, shaking hands; turning instantly away. 'So how *are* you? Thanks so much for your letter, Oscar. God, we've had an awful journey – the traffic was absolutely mad!'

'Yes,' said Myra, 'so everyone says.'

'And where's the green countryside there used to be? We'll soon be one solid mass of housing. It's so depressing.'

'You haven't brought your son with you?'

'He wasn't up to it, Myra. A friend's looking after him.'

'Poor child! Though it's really not very exciting for a teenage boy.'

'Nowaba,' Oscar said.

Rachel could see the warmth in his gaze, directed at Mrs Rhodes. He'd never looked at her in that way. She moved a little apart, and gazed at a picture.

Morning (A Servant Girl), 1884. The dark-haired girl sits on her rumpled bed, legs crossed, her right arm reaching over her knee and lifting her heavy skirt slightly, her feet bare. She stares to her right, to the morning glow at the window. She is about to pull on her stockings; there's a long day's toil ahead, and no pleasures except to glimpse the light through windows. She is resigned, contemplative, neither sad nor merry; grateful to see the morning light.

'Nowaba,' Oscar repeated as Lilian frowned.

'No way back,' Myra interpreted.

'I still don't understand.'

'He means the traffic, the housing estates.'

'Oh, I see! I guess you're right.'

But it was getting too much to stand. She and her husband were thinking of buying a cottage in Suffolk. They'd seen this tiny cottage for sale in Aldeburgh. Somewhere to get away to.

'The original painting is in Bergen,' Myra said, noticing Rachel's gaze. 'It's less interesting than his later style; still very naturalistic.'

'I like it.'

She wanted to be that pensive, tranquil servant-girl, dead these fifty years and more.

'Yes, it's nice.'

'I loathe that picture,' Lilian said, gazing at the *Madonna*. 'God, how he hated women!'

A man ghosted up beside her, wine-glass in hand. Short, balding, perspiring. A white suit, pink-and-white striped shirt, with a red bow-tie. Lilian introduced him. Shaking his sweaty hand, Rachel thought she'd seen him before somewhere. Myra solved the puzzle by mentioning a *Guardian* interview. That was it; he wasn't going to defend any man accused of violence against women. She'd thought it was admirable in a way, and yet . . . And yet she didn't take to him. She didn't like the sleek smooth fleshy double-chin nor the bow-tie; didn't like the pompous voice; she could imagine it haranguing a jury.

The precious moments of silence and contemplation ticked away; the light kept fading and brightening imperceptibly through the hazy clouds.

They were discussing the cottage in Suffolk.

'Is it centrally heated?'

'It has night-storage heaters. Terribly damp in places. I don't know, I don't know. It would be nice.' Steven swung towards his wife. 'Should we buy it?'

'Well, it's reasonably priced; now's the time to buy, we'll never get a better bargain.'

The morning light filtered through an almost transparent water-jug on the window-sill. Dreamily she rubbed her ankle; the left hand clasping the right forearm as she rubbed. Resignation. Simplicity. Picking up the thick stocking she started rolling it on to her foot.

Rachel stood at the edge of the group, speechless, ignored; toying with her almost-empty glass. 'If everyone bought a second home,' she said, 'then that concrete jungle you've been complaining about would have to stretch over the whole country.' But she didn't say it.

She glanced around the room. The chattering knots of people, self-consciously holding the stems of glasses as though they were flowers. How she loathed the English middle-classes, her own class. She loathed the *Telegraph*-reading brigade of Tories, the Wimbledon strawberry-eaters, splenetic Majors and their twinsetted wives. At least she *thought* she loathed them, until she was with her own kind, the socially conscious do-gooders, the engineers of equality. Which somehow never involved *them* in any pain. Dr Jacobson had warned her what to expect; it consoled her that his blank face hid similar thoughts. Yet his wife seemed comfortably a part of them.

'You'd have to pay two lots of Poll Tax, as we do,' she warned.

'Oh God, the Poll Tax! The Thatcher tax! That woman makes me feel ill! Even more than Munch's *Madonna*!'

Saying 'Excuse me,' though no one noticed, Rachel wandered off to refill her glass.

She stood before a picture she knew. The only one she had recognised. *The Scream.* 1892. Original in the National Gallery, Oslo. Is she a woman or a man? This hairless figure, hands pressed against the head like an inverted pear, eyes like holes, mouth stretched open like an egg. A bridge. Two men in long black coats walking sinisterly up behind her. Yes, surely a woman. And the sky a swirl of reds and blues. Reds mostly.

> *One evening I was walking along a path – on one side lay the city and below me the fjord. I was tired and ill – I stopped and looked out across the fjord – the sun was setting – the clouds were dyed red like blood.*
>
> *I felt a scream pass through nature; it seemed to me that I could hear the scream. I painted this picture – painted the clouds as real blood. – The colours were screaming.*

'It's very powerful, isn't it, Mrs Brandt?'

She looked aside, startled. The cane. The Wogan show evergreen film star. Becker. Boris Becker in about fifty years time, perhaps.

'Yes. It's always frightened me. I've only seen it in books before.'

'I too. It seems like a – my God, I'm forgetting my own language! *Prédiction* . . .'

'*Vorhersage –* '

'Exactly! Your German's very good; how did you learn it?'

'My husband was German.'

'– I see. Like a prediction of the twentieth century. It's a very realistic portrayal. We saw many like that in the refugee camps, your therapist and I. Stick-people, no longer human.' He sighed. 'And those men in long coats – well, I've seen them many, many times. Gestapo. I was lucky, I served with Rommel's Afrika Corps. There was still chivalry; I've seen our soldiers queue up to give blood for a seriously wounded English prisoner. Of course, war is always horrific; but we had no idea what was being done at home. It's no excuse, I know.'

However hard she pressed her hands to her ears, the scream rang out louder; and the steps echoed louder on the wooden bridge.

Oscar and Myra were being greeted by a man with a gold chain around his neck. A local official? the German asked. Rachel nodded. 'The Mayor.' 'It's so dreadfully sad to see Oscar like this,' he said. 'Myra wrote to me saying he might not live very much longer. I'm glad I came. How do you find him in your – your meetings with him?'

'He's wonderful,' she said simply.

'Yes, he's a wonderful man. When you think what he lost in the war, because of my country, and yet I never once sensed anything but friendship from him.' He added after a moment's pause, 'I too suffered. I lost my first wife and – well, too much. But it was my country that caused the war; I can't really complain.' His gaunt, wrinkled face seemed to flinch, still, from some terrible memory.

But his suffering was the same, Rachel said gently; and then tried to correct herself; suffering was – incomparable, she wished to say, but Dr Becker had to help her with the German word, *unvergleichlich*. Her niece had died five years ago of leukaemia, and she'd thought no one could possibly grieve more than she had. Yet in truth her sister, Sarah, grieved much more.

'But I also know,' she continued, 'that not even my sister's pain can compare with what our continental relatives went through, in the war.' She felt a nervous tic start up in her cheek as the old German soldier enquired politely where they had lived, and what had happened to them. 'They were Ukrainian,' she said. 'My grandfather was the only one who left, in nineteen hundred. He settled in Glasgow and started a tobacco business. He wanted to assimilate totally; changed our name from Slavchenko to Slater; converted to Catholicism; and hardly kept in touch with his family in the Ukraine. When we were growing up in wartime, my sister and I hardly knew anything about them. But one day, after the war, there they were – a couple of half-starved uncles – standing on our doorstep. They were the only ones who'd survived, out of twenty or thirty.'

'So you and Oscar have a lot in common,' said Dr Becker

gravely. 'Immigrant families, and the European branch all but wiped out.'

'That's right! He's found it too painful to visit Czechoslovakia; but I went to the Ukraine a couple of years ago, and Dr Jacobson very kindly used his influence to get me a visa to visit the family home, which was in Byelaya Tserkov, a village about seventy miles from Kiev. It was a very moving, painful experience.'

The nerve in her cheek started twitching again. She felt compelled to tell the story, every time she mentioned that village, that family house; and she did so now. The house was no longer a house; it had been converted into a *kolkhoz* store. And no one would go near it after dark. It was reputedly haunted. The peasants heard the whimpering of children. 'There were cousins of mine among them,' she said in a choking voice. 'The Wehrmacht troops stationed there even made complaints about the terrible conditions. I stood in that house; I . . . I'm sorry, you must forgive me.'

Touching her arm, he said in a deep, compassionate voice, 'I understand! Believe me, I do.'

She confessed that Dr Jacobson thought she'd become too obsessed. And it was true it affected her feelings extraordinarily. Every time she entered some civilised gathering like the present one she couldn't help comparing it with that house of dying children. It made everything seem shallow and unimportant.

'*The Scream*,' said a voice behind them, interrupting her. She turned, startled, and saw Chris James. 'It gave me a sleepless night the first time I saw it. How are you, Rachel?'

Blanking off her inner vision she said, 'Oh, fine, thanks. Well, I've had the flu, but I'm just about over it.' She introduced him to Dr Becker and they shook hands. Chris asked if he'd ever been to Brighton before and he said no, nor ever to England. Brighton seemed a pleasant, lively town.

'It's where the English traditionally come for dirty weekends.'

Chris had been to Cornwall on holiday. The weather had been mixed.

His wife came up to join him. Rachel recalled her vaguely from a party at Dr Jacobson's before his illness. A short, dark-haired, pretty woman in a red dress; Chris slid his arm round her shoulder. They spoke of Oscar; the sadness of it; he could still take some pleasure in life, but soon . . . Dr Becker, nodding, said that in a truly liberal society – Holland was perhaps the only one – Oscar would be able to ask a doctor for an assisted death. He was quite sure he and Myra had their plans, but it was tragic that Myra would have to risk prosecution, even imprisonment. You're right, Chris said, euthanasia would have to come. Rachel, for whom the idea of legalised death was for some reason a frightening concept – and had been so long before she'd stood in that Ukrainian store-house – couldn't find words to express her emotion, and the right moment passed: the men, as so often, driving in another direction, considering that the last word had been said.

Chris's wife was staring short-sightedly at *The Scream*. 'I know I should like it, but . . .'

It made them all gaze in silence; uncomfortable. Three students flitted by in front of them; then Lilian and Steven came up.

'Hello,' she said to Chris. 'This is a pleasant surprise!'

'Hello! Good to see you, Lilian!'

'My husband: Steven.'

A handshake. 'Chris James.'

'I've heard a lot about you, Chris.'

'This is Sharon, my wife – Lilian.'

The two women stretched, across Rachel, touched fingers. Sharon said, 'We've talked on the phone.'

'Yes, we have. And you two know each other.' She glanced from her husband to Sharon. They nodded at each other pleasantly.

'In rather different circumstances!' Sharon said with a smile.

'That's true! You've watched me pounding a pillow a few times!'

'I've done my share of that too.'

Rachel said, 'Have you met Dr Becker?'

'Anton,' he said; 'please.' He shook their hands. He seemed, to Rachel, to greet Lilian Rhodes with particular warmth; he spoke her name, said Oscar had mentioned her. His expression both warm and sad. He's looking at his wife, she thought: Lilian's about her age when she died.

As though confirming her thought, he said in a husky, emotional voice that they must please excuse him, he would look at the pictures. She saw the glint of a tear before he abruptly turned away. He gazed, unseeing, at the nearest picture. She, too, looked at it, making sure she didn't intrude into his grief.

Embracing Couple, 1890. Pen and ink. A tender, naturalistic love scene. The youth's head buried on the girl's breast; her eyes are closed, her head resting on a raised pillow; their arms are round each other. A water-jug on a bedside table. The old Afrika Corps soldier gazed at it absorbed. He's recalling his *first* wife, Rachel thought, across the decades. And she remembered *her* husband, that time when it was good, the hotel in the Cotswolds.

'What time do you think it is?' the girl asked drowsily.

Her lover half opened his eyes and lifted his head from her breast, looking at the window. 'It can't be more than four. The sun is still bright. We've plenty of time.'

'Mama will wonder where I've got to. I should get dressed.'

'Not yet.'

He buried his mouth to her breasts again, seeking her tender nipple. She gave a sigh, and her arm tightened around him.

She opened her thighs readily to him and he entered her.

It was beautiful. Again.

When they had moved apart, he got out of bed and went to stand near the window. He looked out at the grey fjord, down at the grey rocks. He saw a young woman in a grey dress standing there, yellow hair streaming down her back and tinting even the rocks and the hem of her dress with its colour. She seemed indescribably sorrowful and alone.

Dr Becker moved away; Rachel turned back to the small group. Lilian Rhodes was saying earnestly to Chris's wife, 'You should try for it. Secretarial skills don't just vanish. And Steven's a very kindly employer – aren't you, darling?' She swung to look at him.

'I don't beat my secretary if she makes a mistake! At least not more than twice a week!'

Sharon grimaced. 'I don't know.'

'Go for it,' Chris urged her.

'Here's my card,' Steven said, slipping it from his breast-pocket into her hand. 'Think about it.'

'Yes, all right. Thank you.' She dropped the card into her handbag. Changing the subject, she asked the couple how their son was.

'Still not at all well, alas,' Steven replied. 'We don't know what's the matter with him. He missed almost the whole of last term. He has his GCSE's coming up, it's extremely worrying.'

'Yes, it must be.'

'He could try harder,' Lilian said. 'His mind's on other things. He's not in our good books at the moment. I went home in the middle of the day to see him – when was it? Tuesday. Our cleaning lady wasn't due until three, and my neighbour, I knew, was out, so I was a bit worried about him, on his own. Well, he didn't hear me come in and when I opened the door of his bedroom he was in bed with a pair of knickers over his face. It was quite frightening.'

'How old is he?'

'He'll be fifteen in a week's time.'

'Well, it's natural for teenagers to experiment,' Sharon said. 'I shouldn't worry about it too much. It must be awful for him, lying at home sick, missing his schoolfriends, missing you.'

'He was smelling you, my love!' Steven said with a rosy smile.

'He wasn't! They weren't *my* knickers; they were black; I don't wear black knickers, you should know that. I told you they weren't mine.'

Steven didn't remember her saying that; he must have been distracted. Whose were they then?

'One of your clients'. Well, I assume so! Unless you've a secret admirer! I assumed they belonged to the miner's wife.'

He looked puzzled.

'I haven't told you this; I didn't want you to get terribly angry with him. I got it out of him last night. They were in a packet addressed to you. It was while you were working at home a couple of weeks ago; your secretary brought some mail around, remember? Phil says he opened it by mistake, he was expecting some computer game. I don't think he's lying about that. He just saw a jiffy-bag lying on the hall table and – '

She paused; Sharon had coughed at the wrong moment, sending out a spray of red wine, splashing her husband's shirt. 'Christ, Sharon!' he muttered.

'I'm sorry.'

'Soda water,' Rachel said timidly; 'that's good for red wine stains. Or salt.'

'It's OK,' he muttered, dabbing at the small spots with a handkerchief.

'– so I assumed it was evidence being returned from that trial. The knickers found at his lodgings.'

'Yes,' said Steven; 'yes.' His cheeks had reddened. 'That must have been it.'

'– Steven was prosecuting a rapist, but the man was cleared because the defence brought up her past during the miners' strike, when she'd been forced to advertise her used knickers in a magazine for perverts. In order to feed her kids. This monster claimed he'd sent for them then. – That's right, it was in the *Guardian* interview.' She turned towards her husband. 'Though I was puzzled why they weren't sent back to her solicitor.'

Steven opened his mouth; closed it; waved his free hand. 'They're always getting into muddles.'

'Are you okay?' Chris asked him solicitously. 'You look pale.'

'I'm fine. Fine. It's warm in here.'

'I've washed the knickers, you'll be able to send them back. Not that I guess she'd want them again. They were in a frightful state. They were – well, you can imagine!' Lilian screwed up her mouth. 'They hadn't been washed since the rape. And Phil's been – you know! *Adding* to it! There probably *was* a note with them, which would have indicated they came from a rape trial; I didn't ask him about that, but I assume there was.' She put a hand over her eyes. 'It's truly disgusting. Maybe that's what turned him on!'

'It's quite understandable,' Rachel said, but her timid words were lost as Chris said at the same moment, 'Boys do these things; adolescence is an awful time, and especially in that sort of situation, as Sharon said.' He glanced around, but his wife had glided a few steps away and was gazing at a picture.

'See you later,' he said to the couple, and moved after her.

Her cheeks were flushed too; she had moved past *The Scream* and was staring at *The Sick Child*.

Rachel stood with Lilian and Steven, and didn't know what to say. They didn't know what to say. Steven was staring down into his almost-empty glass. She should move off, but felt rooted to the spot.

'Another drink?' he asked, coming out of his trance. 'Same again?'

'No, just a mineral water. Thanks.'

Lilian covered her glass. 'I'm fine.'

The two women fixed their eyes on Munch's embracing couple.

'Children can be a problem,' Rachel said.

'You're right.'

They were silent again.

Steven thrust a glass into Rachel's hand, said 'Jolly good' and sipped his wine. All three of them sipped. Then Steven said to Lilian, 'Well, shall we move around?'

'Yes.'

'We'll see you,' he said to Rachel. 'You're staying for the party?'

'Yes.'

'Good.'

They sidled off. He looked flushed, ill at ease, she thought. Stiffly, her legs dragging, she moved in the opposite direction.

She came to a girl propped up in a bed.

The girl brought back vividly, achingly, Rachel's niece, her sister's child, dying of leukaemia, her skull as hairless as a small baby's.

The girl's tender, resigned face, turned sideways, is almost as white as the almost-vertical pillow. The woman beside her, at whom she is gazing, clutches the girl's hand; her head is bowed in despair, bringing into view the bun at the nape of her neck. The child's eyes, in gazing at this woman, are also directed at the light, coming in through a window. She wears a green bed-jacket, the coverlet is green, the curtains, drawn-back, green. The painting is scumbled and crumbly like a Renaissance mural.

'Death,' said a voice behind Rachel. 'It haunted Munch all his life.'

She turned to see a tall, gaunt man in black, almost like Death himself. 'I'm Sven Sorensen,' he said with a shy smile; 'I'm from the Norwegian Embassy in London.'

'Rachel Brandt.' They shook hands.

'Laura Munch, his mother, died of TB when he was five. When he was fourteen, the sister Sophie, closest to him of all the children, died of TB too. She was fifteen. He could never forget those deaths. This is clearly Sophie, and the grieving woman is their aunt, who had come to look after them.'

'That's very sad. It's a beautiful picture.'

'It's the only Munch in a public gallery in London. And where do you think it's hung? In the basement of the Tate! You English prefer pictures of horses!'

'I can't deny that.'

'You can have my Cindy doll, Auntie,' Ruth says, barely able to whisper, yet smiling like an angel. 'You like her, don't you?' Great Ormond Street Hospital.

This Munch was telling her something; he had been sent to her; she wasn't sure yet what he was telling her.

Then suddenly she heard his voice. 'You must get out of this mess, this crazy fucking mess. The people here don't like you, feel uncomfortable with you around. You're a loner, and that's awkward for them, you don't fit in.'

'I know that.'

'Well, it's not for me to tell the English what to like,' said the Embassy official. 'We are a small, thinly populated country, far to the bleak and sunless north. It's natural you shouldn't be very interested in us or our art.'

'Did you arrange this exhibition? It's splendid!'

He looked pleased, sliding a hand up and down his lapel.

'The film is very good,' he said. 'You'll like the film. Of course, that had nothing to do with me. There are some wonderful scenes. The mother's death in particular. She wrote her children a letter, you know, a few months before her death. After the birth of her last child. In it, she tells of her fear that she may not see her beloved children again in Heaven, but that she will beseech the Lord to save their souls. That letter was read to them over and over, by their gloomy father. You may imagine how it must have terrified those children. Any sin they committed – the slightest – the most natural . . .'

'Yes, they must have been terrified.'

'Terrified to death!' He smiled sadly.

Glancing down the room she saw a plump white-haired man in a raincoat shaking hands with Chris James, putting his arm round Sharon.

'Still, our century has abolished Hell,' the Norwegian said.

The white-haired new arrival was threading across the room, making for Oscar. The cuffs of his pinstriped trousers flapping, he moved swiftly for a man of his bulk, a man in his 60s; he was good-looking, robust, bright-eyed. She saw the warm greeting as he embraced Myra and grasped Oscar's limp hand.

'And this one – this one is terrible, don't you think?'

Death in the Sick-room. Lithograph of 1896. Study for the painting of 1898 in Oslo's National Gallery. Death has touched not only the background figure, her face hidden, in the high-backed chair, but all the family, who are mourning already. There is no window or door to the room; they are locked in their grief. A pigtailed girl sits in the foreground, in profile, head bowed and hands clasped. Behind her, an older sister standing, hands clasped.

'That's his sister Inger,' the Embassy official said, pointing. 'She's on the verge of tears. Almost like Egyptian art, don't you think? And that's Edvard behind her, his back turned, gazing at Sophie. Oh yes, the sick girl is Sophie.'

The whiskered father looms over the girl, his hands raised beseechingly. An aunt rests her hand on the back of the chair, head bowed. Another figure, a young man, rests his forehead against a wall.

'They're totally isolated in their grief. None of them can help each other.'

Myra's voice: 'Mr Sorensen, I wanted you to meet Alan James.'

'Pleased to meet you,' the Norwegian said.

'Alan's a very good friend of ours, only we don't see nearly enough of him. He lives in Winchester.' Myra made it sound like Damascus.

'Ah! Winchester. I've never been there. What do you do, Mr James?'

'I'm a surgeon. Well, I *was* – I've recently retired. Now I guess I'm a writer and a layabout.'

'I'm sure you're not that! Oh, this is Mrs Brandt.'

'Hello.' His handshake was soft as cream, a surgeon's hand. It held hers for a half-second. His bright blue eyes were uninterested; they veered back to Sven. 'I hear you're responsible for the exhibition. It looks marvellous; they hit you as soon as you come in.'

'Thank you. It wasn't easy, getting them all together at short notice. Mrs Brandt and I were just discussing this picture. He re-created this scene over and over. He was an obsessive. All his key images were created over and over and over. He was obsessed with death.'

'We Welsh are obsessed with rugby.'

'I wouldn't have guessed you were Welsh, from your accent.'

'Your English is pretty good too.'

'Ah!' He blushed. 'You're very kind. My parents are great anglophiles. I was brought up on Thackeray and Kipling. Kipling was obsessional too.'

Myra lifted her brown arm to glance at her watch. Rachel caught sight of a tattoo. A number. It gave her a shock, seeing it for the first time. Whenever Myra opened the door to her, at the charming detached house in Golders Green, Rachel always hurried past with head lowered, seeing nothing but – in her mind's eye – Dr Jacobson and the beige couch.

Myra is thinking not of Kipling, and certainly not of Auschwitz, but of the film, which she saw this morning. It pleased her.

It opens with a child's bedroom; night; a thin moon through the drawn curtains; a wind sighing. Into the sighing of the wind blends gradually the crying of a child.

The door opens slowly and a heavy figure enters, a lighted candle fluttering before him. The bearded, nightshirted man puts the candle on a chest of drawers and bends over his son. 'What's the matter, Edvard?' he says. 'Are you weeping for your mama?'

Tears on the boy's cheeks. He shakes his head.

'Then what are you crying for?'

'I woke up, Father, and I didn't know where I was. I wondered if this was Hell.'

The man, groaning, ruffles the boy's hair. 'No, my son, this isn't Hell. Hell is infinitely worse than any suffering we've had to bear: even the day your dear mother died. Get out of bed, get down on your knees, my son.'

The boy, wondering, climbs out of bed, and father and son kneel together.

'We must pray.'

They compose their hands and close their eyes.

'O Lord, we beseech thee, grant that in thine infinite mercy we not be punished as we deserve, and that we escape the pains of Hell . . . And that the mother of these little ones . . .' The sweat is bursting from his brow, the candle flame's reflection is fractured into a score of devilish fires in his demented eyes, filling the screen.

His voice continues, fading, as the scene changes to a cloud-swept, intermittently sunny day; a fjord; a rowing-boat bearing two men in their thirties. The plashing of the oars.

There is no dialogue for some time. An island shore draws near; a solitary house.

Munch, to the man who is rowing: 'You say there's no hope for her?'

A brief headshake.

'Poor woman! I don't know what comfort *I* can bring her.'

'She just wants to see you once more.'

'Do you think women love more deeply than we do? It's sad, but she means nothing to me any more . . . Yet all that beauty, that vitality – in a short while to be non-existent, as if it never was . . .'

'Perhaps,' says his friend, 'she *won't* be non-existent.'

'You mean an afterlife? I find it difficult to believe that. I can't imagine all those people resuming conversations with friends and relatives: Hello. Good morning. Do you remember Asgardstrand? Do you remember when we shot at one another in Morocco? . . . But *something* of us goes on. Like crystals dissolving and reforming.'

The oars are raised as a shingle beach draws close; the boat grounds.

A simple bedroom with a view of the fjord. A young woman lies in the bed, still, eyes closed. Munch enters, removing his hat, placing it on a chest of drawers by a water-jug. He bends over the woman: 'Tulla! It's Edvard . . .'

Her eyes open; she smiles; tries to draw him down in a passionate embrace. Munch springs back.

'You're not dying; you're not even ill; this is a trick! You bitch!'

She scrambles up in bed, her nightdress high around her thighs, reaching for him. 'Edvard! I can't live without you! We can straighten everything out; I need you!'

He turns, grabs his hat. She pulls a pearl revolver from under the pillow. 'If you leave me I'll kill myself!' She presses the gun to her temple and he springs, trying to wrest it from her. They struggle. The gun goes off and he cries out; blood sprays from the middle fingers of his left hand . . .

A dark ill-lit street in Kristiania. Munch in the shadows; his left hand, bandaged, grasps his dark cloak at the throat. He sees an amorous couple draw near, on the opposite side of the street. The woman fondles her lover's beard as he fumbles a key into a lock; they giggle and sway drunkenly, then disappear into the house; the door closes. Munch's face, contorted with jealousy, the eyes burning.

'Did he marry?' Alan James asked, his gaze on the sick-room's frozen figures.

Myra shook her head, and Sven Sorensen said, 'No, he feared commitment too much. He usually became involved with women who were already married; it was safer that way. But also torturing. He painted scenes of jealousy time and again. There were some violent moments.'

A noisy room; wine-bottles, glasses, smoke. Three men, including Munch, sitting. An elegant, mischievous-looking woman has pulled down her bodice to reveal her breasts to the onlookers. Her husband or lover, enraged, presses a revolver to her forehead. She goes on laughing, teasing, leaning over Munch, cupping her breasts with her hands as if to say,

Taste! Her husband pulls the trigger; an explosion; she falls in a shower of blood as he turns the gun to his own forehead and fires. He slides to the floor beside her.

Munch is kneeling. The dead woman's black hair is spread over his lap. The crimson blood-splashes in her hair become the bright red lights in a Christmas tree. It's the home of Munch's childhood. His mother, wearing a black silk dress, sits pale and ill on a sofa, supported by a pillow. She coughs blood into a handkerchief. Her black-bearded husband, pacing, comes and sits beside her. The children sit or stand around, looking lost despite their Christmas toys and dolls. Laura Munch summons Edvard with a gesture, a smile; he comes, and she puts her arm round him.

'Sing for me, my darling,' she says.

He pipes up, 'Silent Night, Holy Night.'

'That was lovely! Don't be sad, my dear. Live well, so that in time we can be all together again in Heaven, as we are now, only much, much happier, and for ever.'

Her words merge into a fit of coughing. Outside, as the scene dissolves, Christmas bells peal.

A small art gallery. Munch, aged about twenty, and friends are hanging pictures, mostly they are realistic Norwegian landscapes and portraits. There is a shout: 'Edvard!' He looks aside towards the doors, startled. 'Your father's coming!'

Munch rushes to pick up a large white sheet, and he flings it over a painting of a young black-haired girl, nude, staring with a frightened, wide-eyed expression, her arms crossed timidly to hide her pubic area. A black phallic shape, seemingly composed of innumerable strands of black hair, emanates from her pelvis.

Dr Munch, his beard beginning to grey, marches in grimly; Edvard greets him silently and gestures at a snowy landscape. His father gazes, then pats his son's arm, and marches out.

The Munch house; a shuttered bedroom. Dr Munch, in his shirt-sleeves and collarless, kneels, lashing his back awkwardly with a whip, and moans.

A studio room. Munch at a canvas, painting feverishly. His father's moans can be heard. Models – a young girl and a staid middle-aged woman – are posing for *The Sick Child*. As the moans rise briefly to a scream, the models show alarm.

Munch: 'Don't be frightened. My father will get over it and be none the worse. I've had two gifts from my parents: sickliness and tuberculosis from my mother, and madness from my father. I should do very well.'

He attacks the heavily-encrusted canvas with a knife, hacking away flakes; smears on more paint and rubs it in with his hands, dementedly. 'I must bring her back to life. It's still not quite how it was . . . That's better!' He relaxes, drops his arms, smiles at the models. 'When it's perfect, she'll live again!'

The older woman, her lips trembling: 'Your sister was a lovely child.'

Oscar in his wheelchair, the pupils of his eyes lifted high to counteract his lolling head, gazed at *Puberty*, a pen-and-ink study for the oil painting of 1893. Rachel stood behind him. She recognised her own emotional self, at thirteen, in the tensely staring, fearful girl, haunted by that brooding shadow. It had almost a life of its own. The girl's arms, crossed near the wrists, were unnaturally long; the breasts were barely developed.

'Maya,' Oscar dribbled. 'Limaya whenfirstma.'

'Maya?'

'Myra,' he pronounced with difficulty.

'Ah! She's like Myra when you first met her?'

'Ya! Ya!'

'I can imagine that. Your wife is still beautiful.'

'Ya. Only thi – thi – '

'Only thinner. That girl is thinner?'

'Na. Na. Maya thi – '

'Myra was thinner.'

'Ya. And eyes; eyes lar – lar – '

The eyes of the girl in the drawing were huge, wide-opened, scared.

'Myra's eyes were larger?'

'Ya.'

'I like this one a lot. He seems to understand how the girl feels.'

'Blood.'

'She's bleeding? It's her first period?'

His head slumped even more in a nod.

'He understands females. He feels compassion for them. Yet have you seen *The Vampire*, Dr Jacobson? I'll take you to it. It's frightening. A red-haired woman, her mouth clamped on a man's neck as if she wants to bite it right through.'

'Blood.'

'Ya – yes.'

Suddenly Oscar seemed to gain strength from somewhere, and spoke more clearly and at greater length. He was reminded of her dream that she'd told him about during their last session of the summer – how she had menstruated through her clitoris, since she no longer had a vagina. Had she had any follow-up dreams?

No, Rachel said.

He'd thought it was something of a breakthrough.

Myra appeared, standing at Rachel's shoulder, an index finger caressing Oscar's cheek. She stooped to kiss his bald crown. 'Are you okay, my dear? You're not too tired?'

'Na.'

'That's good.'

He moved a finger, indicating the picture. 'Freudbehere.'

'Yes, that's terribly Freudian. He should be here, you're right.'

Rachel thought of his comparison of the adolescent girl and Myra. It was very difficult to see the likeness now. Myra with her strong square-jawed face and prominent nose, the lank greying hair; her tan, from all the hours of gardening in the brilliant summer, accentuating the network of fine wrinkles; the sturdy form, her sagging full breasts straining at her blue silk blouse. But of course Dr Jacobson had met her in a refugee camp, still weak from Auschwitz; bringing her a few choice items from the officers' Mess, helping her regain her strength out of compassion for her youth, he had fallen in love with her. It was a moving tale Rachel had first heard before ever meeting Dr Jacobson, in a TV documentary about the holocaust. Yes, Myra would have been thinner than this slender girl; her eyes appearing even larger in her bony, tragic face.

'Did I tell you, darling,' said Myra, 'he claimed he'd met Freud in a train once? Or at least he hinted it was Freud. It's hard to tell, as he'd just come out of a mental clinic in an alcoholic daze. It's in the film; you'll see it.' Reminded, she glanced at her watch. 'It's about time to go to the cinema.'

As she moved to steer Oscar towards the exit their path was barred by an old man leaning on a walking-stick, an old man in a deerstalker hat, shabby sports jacket and grey trousers. He smiled, lifting his hat to the two women, then staring down at Oscar. 'Excuse me,' he said, 'would you be Oscar Jacobson?'

'Ya.'

The smile broadened, false teeth gleaming. 'Does the name Tubby Collins mean anything to you?'

He waited; Oscar stayed frozen.

'Well, it wouldn't! We last met sixty years ago! I was in your form at Radley.' He waited again hopefully. Oscar showed no reaction. The smile faded a shade. 'I almost got expelled for betting on the gee-gees once; that's probably my chief claim to fame there. No?'

'My husband can't talk very well,' Myra explained.

'Of course, of course. I attend an evening class at this college. I retired ten years ago – I owned a betting shop, how about that! – and moved here. And I saw the announcement in the student paper and thought I had to pop in to say hello to my famous old school chum.'

'That was kind of you,' Myra said.

'I nearly fell off my chair when I heard you on the radio a few years ago. You gave us the impression of being a plodder at school – like yours truly. Only you were a whizz on the games field, as I never was. Well, you fooled us all, and good for you, old chap. Bit like Churchill I suppose. Late developer.'

Sensing Dr Jacobson's unease at this unwelcome intrusion from the dark ages, Rachel turned away, turned to *Death and the Maiden*. The naked woman is being embraced by a skeleton under bare trees. Beside them hover, one above the other, two meagre children with the overlarge heads of famine victims.

She felt Dr Becker loom up at her shoulder. They gazed in silence together, yet she sensed they were seeing two different pictures. He seemed very moved by the one he saw; he was blinking rapidly and she thought she saw a moistness about his eyes again.

'Do you like it?' she murmured at last, in German.

He didn't reply straight away. When he eventually spoke his voice trembled. 'I've written about this picture. Not about this picture exactly but what lies behind the figures. I gave it this title, but I was thinking of the Schubert. I wrote it last year after my wife, my second wife, died. It helped to fill the gap.'

She started to say, yes, her sister had done some writing – but his voice carried over. 'This meeting with Oscar and Myra is very moving, very moving.' He started to rub the area between chest and shoulder, under his jacket. He sighed, and she saw him glance along the wall to where Lilian Rhodes, standing alone, was staring at the *Madonna*. 'I must write about the *Madonna* too. Before I die. A lady strewn with lilies . . . Forgive me, I'm thinking aloud; it's a dreadful effect of old age. But my mind's not too bad when I write. At present there's no time, with the Kuwait crisis.' Pensioned-off old men like him were being called back into service in case of a national emergency. To ensure the safety of water supplies, sewage, etc.

As his tremulous voice talked of water supplies and sewage his eyes were still gazing past her, and they seemed to be fixed as much on Lilian Rhodes as on the *Madonna*. She recalled how warmly he'd greeted her – no doubt because he knew this woman meant so much to Dr Jacobson. The voice buzzed around her, and she felt the walls encroaching. She turned, her head spinning, and saw a deerstalker hat being lifted in farewell, and then Dr Jacobson being pushed by his wife towards them.

Mrs Jacobson slipped her arm into Dr Becker's, saying, 'It's time to go to the cinema.' Her statement, her smile, took in Rachel too, as an afterthought. She was sorry, Rachel said, she didn't think she could see the film. 'I hate rooms without windows and doors – Dr Jacobson knows that. This hall has been almost too much for me.'

'That's a pity – but I do understand. And it's so hot in here.'

'I'll get a taxi to the station.'

'I can't allow that! We can't have you missing the party! Why don't you go straight to the flat and wait for us? Relax, have a lie down: I'll give you the key.'

Well, if she was sure . . .

She was sure; and Oscar said she must stay. Myra searched in her handbag for the door-key, then remembered it was in her raincoat pocket and gave her instead a whole bunch of keys. She told her the address to pass on to the taxi-driver, and said they'd see her in a couple of hours. She was to help herself to drinks, make herself at home.

Rachel warmed to her; she had always considered her a rather cold woman, but now there was a homely Jewish motherliness about her. It couldn't have been easy, remaking her life, all her family lost, in a strange country. Still, after forty-odd years, her accent was slightly foreign.

'Thank you! Enjoy the film!'

After she'd collected her rather shabby coat, Rachel thought she had better go to the loo. Her vague need became desperate as she saw a queue of ladies, in the concourse outside the toilets. She joined the end of the queue. She tried to focus her thoughts on something else: what she could buy Sarah, her sister, for her birthday.

'Hello! Haven't we met?'

A resonant, cultured male voice. Her vaguely gazing eyes focused on a well-built man of about sixty. The clothes struck her first: Savile Row, impeccable, rich, brooking no argument, Tory, home counties. A strong-chinned, ageingly handsome, weatherbeaten face confirmed the diagnosis. He wore a thin-lipped smile. 'Didn't we meet once at Oscar's? At a party a couple of years ago?'

She remembered. And she'd gone weak at the knees then too, drained of energy by the effortless upper-crust power and grooming. This was that other, infinitely older English establishment; and while she was merely irritated by the younger one, the care-workers and poly lecturers, she went to pieces before this kind.

A Permanent Secretary. Top of the tree. Meissen crockery.

'Charles Dahl,' he reminded her, shaking hands.

Was she going already or had she just arrived too? He'd had a polo engagement with Prince Charles, which had delayed them. One could hardly turn that down! With a slightly ironic lift of his bushy brows, disarming any suggestion of name-dropping.

Claustrophobia. Ah, yes; he'd never suffered that, but Oscar had cured him of agoraphobia, early in his career. So he understood.

'The exhibition is excellent,' she said.

'Oh, is there an exhibition too? I'll push on in and take a quick look. So nice to have met you again.' A genial nod, then he glided towards the front of the queue. Rachel saw him hunch over, addressing a few words to a thin, furred lady, who nodded. He strode off towards the hall.

Munch whispered to her again: 'I don't want shits like him looking at my pictures.'

'How do you know he's a shit?'

Because Norway had been full of such men. Conservative, happiest in their all-male clubs discussing finance and taxes. Privileged, closed off to feeling and to women. What could he possibly see, looking at the servant-girl pulling on her stocking, or the girl reaching puberty? 'I hope Charlotte Corday knifes him . . . You look desperate.'

'I am.' She hoped Dahl hadn't noticed her clenching her thighs together. His intimidating presence had made her bowels loose too.

There had to be other toilets in a college, maybe she should make a dash for the stairs and go hunting. Fortunately the line of ladies dwindled fairly rapidly all of a sudden, and she was inside the toilet and waiting outside a cubicle. Her panic eased, and with it the need, a little.

The stream was gushing from her; it was a sweet relief, not least to be alone for a few moments, locked away from the crowd of strangers. Now she could enjoy a bowel movement at leisure. She gazed fascinated at graffiti. Surely no man had a cock as long as that?

My friend Anita likes me to piss on her.

Keep it for pissing on Thatcher.

How times had changed. Never anything like this in the girls' toilets at South Glasgow Tech.

God, how much hatred that woman attracted! She thought the intensity of it neurotic. She didn't care for some of her policies, nor that cut-glass voice; but the way she could suddenly revert to childhood and Lincolnshire with a snarled phrase like

'You're *frit!*' suggested a very different essence beneath the mask. She was a radical, a lonely woman.

Pulling her tights up, flushing the toilet, Rachel had an impulse to add to the graffiti; something really filthy. She contented herself with staring at the huge cock. The trouble with most people she knew, they wanted sex tame and orderly; hence referred to it in such terms as boobs and bonks and vibrators. They were frit . . . She wondered if those manic blue eyes had ever stared close-up at that kind of member. It seemed likely. She'd have to do everything with total enthusiasm.

But you're frit too – she told herself, gazing at her wan, age-ing face in one of the mirrors. The conjunctivitis that had been plaguing her had cleared, fortunately. Now the light-brown eyes were simply fearful and obsessional like the girl's in *Puberty*. She slipped on her coat and went out into the concourse, empty now. She pushed out through the swing doors and breathed in the sweet cold air, prickling with a hint of rain.

She was cruising in a black cab along the promenade, gazing at the grey sea. There was a beach for nudists.

A small anti-Gulf War demonstration was taking place by the pier. The taxi-driver, who had driven in silence, suddenly burst out, 'Load of poofters and yobs! We ought to ship them off to Kuwait, see how they like waiting for bloody sanctions to work while their families are being tortured and shot! God almighty, I don't know what this bloody country's coming to!'

The train runs alongside the grey North Sea. The sky is as grey as the sea. Two middle-aged men sit across from each other by the windows. One is in a wretched, bedraggled state; his suit crumpled and stained, his beard and hair matted, his eyes red, feverish, haunted in his pale, gaunt face. He is drinking Schnapps, straight from the bottle. The other man is soberly dressed and his grey beard is neatly groomed; he wears glasses and is reading.

The train stops at a small German station. A few ladies in Edwardian dresses, and a few soldiers in the uniform of the Kaiser, are glimpsed. Doors are heard opening and slamming shut. A whistle. The train moves off.

The respectable man, removing his glasses, says, 'Will there be war, do you think?'

Munch, startled, shrugs his shoulders, drinks.

'Are you going far?'

'To Norway.'

'So you won't be involved. Who will you side with?'

The door of the carriage slides open and a soldier enters. He sits near the door, staring straight ahead, his rifle between his knees.

'Germany, I should imagine. France has been good to me, with food, women, drink . . .' He waves the bottle. 'But Germany's been kinder to my art.'

'Ah, so you're an artist.'

A nod. 'And you?'

'Psychoanalyst. From Vienna.'

The door opens again and a beautiful young woman enters. She is naked except for long black gloves and a black ribbon round her slender, pale throat. Her fair hair is piled high; from her ears dangle long golden earrings. She sits opposite the soldier and stares ahead, straight through him. No one in the compartment gives her more than a cursory glance.

'I suffer from bad nerves,' Munch says. 'I've been in a clinic.' He pats his head with his left hand, two fingers of which are seen to be scarred and misshapen. 'Electric shocks, you know.'

'Symptoms?'

Munch rubs his right leg. 'Numbness. Hallucinations.'

'Nervousness is bad. Long cure. Diet. Schizophrenic existence.'

Munch drinks, then offers him the bottle. He shakes his head.

'Your art must be a therapy.'

'It's also part of the cause. Art is the heart's blood. If it's not that it's nothing.'

The psychoanalyst nods. 'But don't forget the mind. The mind is as mysterious as the heart. Now we've thrown out the delusion of a God, the mind becomes even more mysterious. Life becomes more mysterious.'

'That's so.' He has drained the bottle. The young woman, moving for the first time, makes a gesture requesting that he give it to her. Munch stretches forward, handing it across. She opens her legs, begins masturbating with the bottle-neck. It enters her.

'Women,' he says. 'The Sphinx. They want all of you.'

'But the mind and the heart are old-fashioned concepts, my friend. We've seen their time, I'm afraid. The future belongs to toys and ideologies.'

Munch isn't listening. He is staring at the naked woman.

'The man who lives with a woman kills something in himself. Yet she is a miracle. I don't want to paint anything else.'

Silence for a time; then the train jerks and slows, and draws in to another small station. The woman withdraws the bottle-neck swiftly, closes her legs, stands up and gives Munch back the bottle.

'Thank you.'

'Don't mention it.'

She slides open the door and goes out; hesitates a moment; heads right.

Rachel hesitated in the flat's small entrance-hall, then opened the door in front of her. It was a broom-cupboard. She backed out, closing the door, and opened the one to her left. It led into the drawing room. She went straight to the window, unfastened it and slid it wide open. She took deep breaths, gazing out at the pleasant, lawned square of terraced Regency houses. Beyond them, to her left, outlined against a thin beginning drizzle, the dome of the Royal Pavilion.

Her temple throbbed with the warning of a headache. Kicking off her shoes she lay down on the sofa and closed her eyes. Her mind drifted in and out of a drowse. The throbbing eased.

Opening her eyes, rising on her elbow, she surveyed the room. Her scalp prickled not unpleasantly. Loneliness, she sometimes found, became a kind of excitement in a strange house or flat; became an opportunity to delve into someone else's life. It was something connected with puberty, with that girl, her wrists crossed over her sex. And this was the Jacobson flat; though it was just a holiday flat, it would contain elements of his personality. Like every analysand, she wanted to know everything about him.

This room was sparely furnished. A three-piece suite and a couple of cane chairs; a walnut drinks cabinet; small TV, video recorder and sound system. Three small abstract paintings were signed M. Jacobson. Rachel didn't care for them. The books in the low pine bookcase – in contrast to the massive and packed teak shelving in Golders Green, which intimidated her – were disappointing; mostly paperback novels by such people as Jilly Cooper and Jackie Collins, and a few art books.

In the rather cramped and dark dining room, a tablecloth had been thrown over a buffet – clingfilmed plates of cold cuts, cheeses, salads and desserts. A small marble bust of Karl Marx, more beard than face, stared from the sideboard.

In the bedroom she relished the sinfulness of opening drawers, but found nothing of interest. Dr Jacobson wore white boxer shorts.

There was an inner door. Thinking it was probably the bathroom she turned the handle but the door proved to be locked. She took Myra's bunch of keys from her raincoat pocket and tried a few of the smaller keys, and eventually one of them worked; the door slid open. She found a room little larger than a spacious cupboard – maybe it had been a dressing room originally – but it contained office equipment.

Desk, chair, filing cabinet. On the desk were an old manual typewriter and an artist's portfolio.

She opened the portfolio. Skeletal, bald female figures, wearing what looked like striped pyjamas. She turned over a page. The same figures, suspended from a gallows. On the next page one of the figures was depicted in close-up: the rope, the broken neck.

Auschwitz, she thought, as her own nape prickled.

She shut the portfolio.

She tried the desk-drawers but they were locked. The smallest of the keys on the bunch opened them. The top drawer held nothing of interest: stationery, postcards of Brighton, a paperknife, three or four letters to the Jacobsons which she resisted the temptation to read.

The second drawer contained sadomasochistic magazines. The extremely violent and perverse pictures disturbed her; yet analysts had to consider the whole of human nature; nothing human could be alien to them. There was also, naturally, some excitement in the discovery.

Buried underneath them were a couple of large unused brown envelopes. She found, in the first, some polaroids showing a redheaded young woman naked on a bed, bound and gagged. The second contained half-a-dozen attractive, detailed charcoal drawings. The topmost showed a plump girl in coat and cloche hat, crushed by surrounding people in what seemed a bus or tram. Her hand was raised in the act of touching or perhaps taking off an earring. Her eyes were wide, as if in a trance. Rachel liked the sketch; it was a relief after the lurid and violent pictures. The other five in the set showed the same young woman, broad-hipped and big-bosomed, in various stages of undressing; the final one, nude, outstretched on a bed. The tightly braided blonde hair, and particularly the clothes, identified the period as the thirties.

She was just replacing these rather charming pictures in the envelope when she heard a door open and shut. She froze. There were voices, male and female. They were approaching the bedroom. She had no time to do anything but push the door as far as it would silently close. Trying to keep absolutely still, fearing that her hammering heart would give

179

her away, she looked out through the slit between door and jamb.

She saw Chris James's wife, and right behind her a thickset form. Chris's father. He was breathing heavily, stumbling a little; Sharon was saying, 'Here, sit down on the bed, let me get your shoes off.'

Rachel breathed a shade more easily. It might have been the Jacobsons; she'd have been disgraced, her career over before it had begun. Mr James sat, then lay down, his chest heaving; Sharon pulled off his shoes and helped him remove his tie and loosen his collar. Rachel gathered that he'd felt ill and Sharon had brought him to the flat to have a rest. She sounded anxious: should she ring for a doctor? No, no, he said, he would be all right. He was sorry to have spoiled the film for her.

'Don't worry about that; to be honest I wasn't sorry to have an excuse to leave. It was dreadfully stuffy in there, and I didn't find it exactly riveting.' Rachel saw her perch on the bed beside him and take his hand.

'You *looked* rather bored,' he murmured. 'You looked as I felt, *cariad* – that the interval couldn't come soon enough. Well, I couldn't let you suffer, could I now?' Grasping her by the shoulder, he drew her face down to his and kissed her. She pulled away.

'You pig!' she gasped. 'You're not sick at all!'

He chuckled.

'My God! You've imitated that woman in the film!'

'That's right!'

'Bastard!' Yet there was amusement in the word.

'But I don't have a revolver to threaten to shoot myself with.'

'No, but you've never needed a revolver. I've never been afraid you've had a gun sticking into me! But really, Alan, you're a senior citizen now; you're too old for such childish tricks.'

Rachel saw her shake her head in exasperation.

'Now, that's unkind! That's very depressing.'

'What about this woman you're seeing? Deirdre? What would she say?'

'Oh, Deirdre's nothing. Lie down with me.'

'No.'

He'd just wanted to be alone with her for a while; to talk to her. He hadn't realised someone had gone on ahead of them to the flat. But the Lord was good, she'd obviously gone out for some sea air. Not even bothering to lock the door. You could see she was in a state.

All right, if she wouldn't lie down, she could sit. She let him take her hand. It had been a shock for him to see Oscar, he said. He felt very sorry for him. He'd always been a caring person behind a rather cool exterior. 'I remember once, when I was coming up to Harley Street one day a week, Oscar dropped in to see me. I was showing out a mother who had a little boy who was very spastic. I wrote up some notes and when I came out I saw Oscar wiping his eyes. He was very upset. He explained that he'd known a little boy like that, and it still affected him.'

'I've always quite liked him, the few times we've met. Myra makes me nervous, though, somehow.'

'Yes, I know what you mean. But she's been through hell.'

His voice became urgent and emotional. Why had she avoided being alone with him in Cornwall? He'd found it hurtful. At first she denied it; but after a while she confessed she was involved with someone.

Disbelief, amused curiosity and jealousy mingled in his response. Steven Rhodes! That lefty! 'His wife's Chris's patient!'

'Yes, it's embarrassing.' But there was something even more embarrassing: Steven had been badgering her for ages for her knickers and . . . When she'd finished the story he cawed a chuckle.

'It's not funny, Alan.'

'No, I can see that.'

'Phil must have my letter. Steven's shitting himself.'

Was she in love with him, Alan asked, his voice trembling slightly. Rachel saw her shrug. 'I think so.'

His voice grew sadly tender, more Celtic. It hurt, hearing those words. He'd never stopped wanting her; loving her. If that was true, she said tartly, he ought never to have encouraged her with Chris while he had an affair with that massive-boobed radiologist.

'It wasn't like that. You were so young. I felt it wasn't fair on you, *cariad*.'

'That's a load of balls! . . . I must have a pee.' Rising to her feet, she took a step towards the door of the office, but he said, 'In the hall, second on the right.'

He felt as lonely as that grey woman on the shore, touched by yellow light. Alone with just the live-out housekeeper in a rambling country house. It had first struck him overpoweringly at the earthworks in Cornwall, as he and Chris paced separately around it, isolated in the silence and heat and sense of chasms of time. Castle Dor. Once King Mark's palace. Loneliness, and the humid heat, had overcome him. Chris and Sharon thought he was having a heart-attack.

He'd always been lonely. Lonely in the Valleys, essentially English in the big house on the hill, and mostly away at school and college. Lonely on his wedding-day – screwing that bridesmaid. He'd dragged Angharid, once so chapel-prim, into confused relationships, encouraged by Oscar and Myra. Andrea Dahl, so unattractive now, whom he'd glimpsed entering the college cinema – he and Angharid had rolled about with her naked in Oscar's house, on a bed piled with coats, jazz floating up from downstairs; Chris, parked for the night, sleeping in a carry-cot next to the bed. It wasn't surprising she'd made her own secret life.

The thickening rain at the window told him another autumn was here; reminded him of that early autumn of 1967 when his wife had simply vanished. She'd gone to London, taking a return ticket on the train; she and her cousin Bron from Bexhill were going to the theatre, and she would stay the night with Bron. It happened a couple of times a month. But she hadn't returned to Winchester; Bron knew nothing of a theatre trip, nor of all their previous meetings dating back to before Chris was born. She knew only that Angharid had a long-term lover in Golders Green.

To Alan now, twenty-three years on, it made no difference whether she was drinking Campari in Benidorm or mouldering beneath some moor off the M1. He thought the latter more likely, and so had the police. With her long auburn hair and miniskirt – they'd just come in – she'd have attracted attention that evening. Some bogus taxi-driver, aged now, probably kept *her* knickers – and bra and suspender belt – in a box, along with others, where his wife wouldn't find them.

As far as Oscar was concerned, well, he'd denied any affair, unconvincingly, but it really didn't matter anyway. What *had* come as a shock was when, on a skiing holiday with the Jacobsons in Yugoslavia, Chris, adventurous like most teenagers, had fallen badly; and who had helped out the inadequate local hospital with an O-negative blood transfusion but Oscar . . . Nothing was certain in this life, but it was a very strange coincidence.

Alan sensed Sharon's shadow, and opened his eyes. She'd freshened her make-up. Lie down with me, he said; but her red, tempting lips said, no, let's go in the lounge. Lie down, he repeated, pulling at her hand. Just to talk, I promise.

She kicked off her shoes and stretched out.

'You were miles away,' she said.

'I was thinking of Angharid. Seeing Oscar again today, it's hard to think of them screwing.'

She sighed. 'I've too many secrets from Chris; so have you. I wish you'd never told me. Why did you tell me?'

'I hoped it might make you feel better about Belinda. She would have been part-Jewish if . . . One wouldn't need to be anti-Semitic to have found that a bit uncomfortable.'

She shrugged. 'I wouldn't have known. I've sometimes wondered – did you want to take revenge on your wife by getting someone else's wife up the spout? And the only suitable victim you could find happened to be your daughter-in-law . . .'

'That's unfair!'

Yes, she said more gently, it was. She ought never to have let him stay the night, with Chris away. Or else not got drunk and thrown caution to the wind. She sighed again.

Belinda was a love-child, he murmured; however unfortunate the circumstances. He'd felt dead from the feet up until a certain cheerful, vibrant girl from the Midlands turned up at his office . . . He'd still felt she was there for him, even after Chris, and though they hardly ever made love. But now . . . His voice tailed away.

'It's better this way. If I can think of you as simply Chris's dad I can cope with my guilt. Please accept it.'

'I'll try. The trouble is, you have this amazing effect on me. Deirdre can't get me quite hard. Yet you, without doing anything, just by lying close – you see.'

A faint chuckle. 'Yes, there's no problem there!' But it was no good, she felt so awful seeing him and Belinda together. She was trying to get him out of her system.

'So is that why you've . . .?'

'Probably.'

'Ah, *cariad*!'

He slid his hand along her thigh, over her dress. 'Tights.'

''Fraid so . . . No. Please.'

'Just let me touch you. One last time; one for the road.'

Distant voices. 'They're here, Alan.' 'That was well-timed.' Sharon stood up, smoothing her dress; he slid his feet off the bed, zipped himself up and reached for his shoes. The voices came closer, outside the room. 'Alan! Are you all right?'

'Yes. Much better.'

'He's okay,' Sharon said. 'But he *must* get himself checked over. It's the second time it's happened in a month.'

'Dump your coats in here,' Rachel heard Myra say, glimpsing her solid shape for a moment. She shrank back, sick to the stomach, her head thumping again; Myra *must* notice the door wasn't shut tight.

There were many voices, familiar and unfamiliar; shapes flitted into view, coats piled on the bed, and the voices, close now, medleying like autumn branches in a wind.

'What a lovely flat, darling!'

'You okay, Dad? Thanks for looking after him, Sharon.' Chris's arm encircling her.

'Lilian, did you meet Tim and Lavinia Braithwaite?'

'How's your mother, Lavinia?'

'Not too bad, considering she has Alkaseltzers. That's her own name for it! We were down last Sunday; they look after them very well there.'

'That's nice . . . The coats go in here, Peter!'

'Loved the film! I was thinking, we ought to put it on at LWT. I'll have a word with Melvyn if you like.'

'Would you? That would be great!'

'Marvellous, the way they did the explosion and all the glass shattering! That was fine camera-work.'

'It reminded me of the night the IRA tried to blow up the Cabinet. We happened to be here. It woke us up, made the windows rattle like fury. You remember it, Oscar?'

'Ya. Greanight.'

'Sven, do you want to leave your briefcase and your umbrella in here?'

'Thank you. I was looking at your books. I'm surprised you don't read Thackeray and Kipling.'

'It must have pissed you off when you found out Thatcher was okay!'

'It pissed everyone off, I think, Peter.'

The hidden woman, the lonely one, kept expecting, hoping, the tide of sounds would recede; but every slight lull was followed by another ring at the doorbell and, a moment later, a distant babble of voices. The bell had just rung again as she heard Oscar, inside the bedroom, ask, 'WhereRacheBran?'

'Yes, where *is* she? . . . Andrea! How good of you and Charles to come!'

'Oh, we wouldn't have missed it! It was *extremely* good.'

'*I* thought so. How's Tristram?'

'Oh, fine – *so* sorry he couldn't come. God, look at my hair! . . . He's in Bolton. Has a recital in the Purcell Room next month: he's frightfully pleased about that.'

'Wonderful! You must be so proud of him. Is that the phone?'

Rachel heard the scuffle of Oscar's wheelchair at the door; Myra's voice receding. She glimpsed the beetling form of Dr Becker, removing his black overcoat. Then he helped Andrea, a thin, bosomless woman, take off her rainsoaked fur coat.

'Thank you! What a shame it's turned like this, when you're here for such a short time. We've had a marvellous summer! Charles and I almost wished we hadn't booked a gîte in Provence.'

'*Der Sommer war sehr gross!* Our summers in Syria are always too gross. I would been disappointed if it not rains in England.'

'Steven! My dear, you're soaked! Have you met Dr Becker?'

'Yes, we met.' He spoke slowly for Dr Becker's benefit. 'We were in the middle of a very interesting conversation. Will Syria stick to the coalition, do you think?'

'Who know? That depend how does Israel. What you think in England? We shall have war or peace?'

'Oh, it doesn't matter what we think! Thatcher wants a war, so she can win another election and fuck us up even more.'

Myra's voice again. 'It was Adrian and Jenny sending apologies. They were let down by their child-minder. Dump your coat in here, Naomi.'

A harlequin figure in multicoloured trousers, elasticated at the ankles; voluminous white lace blouse; white hair from which she flecked raindrops. 'Thanks, darling. We had trouble parking.'

'It's always a problem. Did you enjoy the film?'

'To be perfectly honest, I found it a trifle morbid; but the Norwegian scenery was lovely. I love that blouse, darling!'

Steven, drying his bald-spot with a handkerchief, 'Myra, where's your loo? I'm absolutely dying for a pee.'

'Second door on the right, lovey.'

'He seemed rather obsessed with death,' the harlequin figure reiterated.

A call. 'Is there any Perrier, Myra?'

'I ordered some. It should be there, Charles. I'm just coming.'

At last the last people had left the bedroom; the ineffable symphony of middle-class English voices faded to a low hum as a door was closed.

Trembling from head to foot from muscular strain and emotional stress, Rachel settled on to the floor; moved on to her side; curled up like a foetus.

Snow blankets the solitude around a large wooden two-storey house. Moments of stillness, a frozen Nordic landscape. Suddenly a huge explosion, sending a shock-wave almost visibly across the snowy contours; the glass of the house's windows shatters.

Munch, aged yet unstooped, painting a grey-dressed woman by a grey sea, is rained-on by glass fragments.

We see him wandering in the snow outside, hugging himself to try to keep warm; blood trickles from a cut on his cheek; on the horizon there is the glow of burning fires. He coughs.

A German SS officer, greatcoated, monocled, stout, is walking through empty rooms whose walls are filled, from floor to ceiling, with paintings by Munch. There are many sick girls, many chambers of death, many dead mothers, many redhaired vampires, many murders of Marat, many lonely wheaten-haired grey-dressed young women, many scenes of jealousy and passion. The windows, devoid of glass, gape, letting in blasts of wind. We see, waiting outside, a staff-car with a driver.

The officer descends stairs, and walks through the downstairs rooms – again all empty of furniture and filled with pictures by Munch, besides printing presses and lithographic stones. He pauses before *The Sun* of 1911; the sun's radiance filling the canvas, turning sea and cliffs into light.

He enters a bedroom. It is murky; the windows have been boarded up. Apart from the bed on which Munch lies under a blanket, there is a wicker chair, a small table with water-jug and glass. The walls are dense with nude women.

The officer comes forward, makes to sit in the wicker chair.

Munch, his voice frail yet commanding, 'Please don't sit there. My sister died in that chair.'

The officer hesitates, then perches at the foot of the bed. The old man struggles weakly to lift his head from the pillow. He glances at the wicker chair. 'I have to paint her again. Must bring her back to life, you see.'

'Your pictures are amazing!' the officer says. 'I am grateful to you for letting me look around.'

'I could hardly stop you. But you are not welcome. I am not a Quisling.'

The officer looks pained. 'What have you Norwegians got against us? This is merely a temporary occupation, we have no designs against your country. You're only harming yourselves in blowing up docks, and making life for your people generally unpleasant.'

He waits. Munch stares up at the ceiling.

'Soon there will be peace, Herr Munch. Then our nations will be friends again.'

The dying man tries to chuckle; it turns into a racking cough. Then, 'Peace! I came here thirty years ago for peace. I gave up women, alcohol, drugs, for peace. And peace has ruined my art. No passion any more. Just technique.' He sighs, removes his arms from under the blanket, gazes at his gnarled hands.

'You've still time to rectify that, if it's true,' says the officer. 'Artists can be productive into their nineties – look at Titian. You will travel again, you'll come to Germany. We'll provide you with all the women and wine you want. I don't know about drugs, but maybe those too!'

He smiles, tries to touch Munch's arm, but is rejected. Shakes his head sadly. 'I came to see how you were; for no other reason. You've admitted yourself, Germany has been good to you. Dr Goebbels even sent you a telegram on your seventieth birthday!'

'You changed your mind about me. I suddenly became degenerate. All my paintings were sold off, to pay for armaments. You've seen it here: the exhibition in our National Gallery, Art and Non-art.'

An apologetic shrug. 'There are stupid excesses. It happens with any revolutionary mass movement. We shall buy your pictures again, after the war. In fact, I would like to buy one of them for myself, right now. The one you call *The Sun*. I like it a lot. It's full of the Aryan spirit. Name your price.'

He unbuttons his greatcoat to reach in.

'I don't sell.'

'But you have thousands of pictures here!'

'They are all my children.' A tear rolls from his eye.

'My sick children.'

The child stretched out her arm along the floor; her hand reached up over the skirtingboard with difficulty, and she began scraping at the dull paint and then at the plaster till flakes came off; and she continued to scrape so that her nails became broken and her fingers were raw and bleeding.

She didn't know where she was. She didn't know where Mama was.

Her mouth filled with dust. She whimpered.

SCREAM

I

Abbey Hospital,
London

Sept. 20 1990

Dear Dr Jacobson,

I am a sick girl. I bleed. I am the world. I ask God, Why the holocaust? Why leukaemia? Why the death of children? And he only answers, Why do you want to know? Or else, It's time.

Rachel

Heptonstall,
Yorkshire

Oct. 8

Dear Chris,

Thank you so much for your letter of sympathy. It was a kind thought. My mother is in a state of shock, understandably. Ted didn't bother to fly home, just sent a wreath, which hurt her quite a lot. She says Steven's been like a son to her. He and Phil have gone home, as he has an important case coming up, and also a selection meeting with the Slough Labour Party. He's been very supportive. This has brought us even closer together, if anything. I'll be staying here for a few more days; I'll let you know when I'm back.

Phil is terribly upset. I was just hoping to get him back to school, but while he was here his ME or glandular fever or whatever it is got worse, and he feels rotten. It shows there's a strong emotional element in his illness. But it's very worrying, as he should be starting GCSE work. Steven keeps indulging him with gifts – computer games, CDs, etc. – which isn't like him. I tell him you can't buy a child happiness. He's with his grandmother in Hertford for a few days, till I get back.

Life seems utterly pointless and random. A few seconds earlier or later leaving the Home, and Dad would have been here now, alive and well, reading the paper.

The irony is that Auntie Mabel, who was in the passenger seat (Dad was bringing her home for lunch) is unhurt except for bruises. She doesn't know what happened, being senile.

I keep remembering Dad's face, the last time we saw him, at Easter. Wearing his old yellow cardigan. So sorry to see us go. Yet Steven and I were glad to get away, driving like the devil to get on to the motorway and back south. I feel very guilty about that. I hope he realised I did love him.

Just a week ago I was with you, moaning that everything was hopeless, couldn't be worse. I'd give anything to be able to go back to that – it seems like happiness now.

It was a very nice funeral, as those things go. The chapel was packed, and good singing. *The day thou gavest . . .* and *Abide with me . . .* It brought back my childhood, and of course lots of old people I hadn't seen for years were coming up, putting their arms around me. It felt good, in an awful, griefstricken way.

Mum and I didn't go to bed that night. We sat up talking and drinking Auntie Betty's rhubarb wine. I could have done with having you there next day – there's a lot I have to talk to you about. Mum revealed something to me that totally shattered me. On top of losing Dad it was too much, but I can't blame Mum because she was overwrought. Losing Dad brought back the death of her first child, Jane, who only lived a few days and is buried in Sheffield. She feels guilty because she never goes there any more. So everything came pouring out to me. I'm still in a state of double-shock. I'll tell you when I get back. I'll only say it's beginning to make a little more sense of things that have always puzzled me, like why I have artistic interests and talents when there's never been anything of that sort in the family.

I had to break off then. Mum wanted to go to the grave to see the flowers properly and read the messages. When we got back I gave Steven a ring at his chambers. He didn't get Slough, unfortunately, where he would have had a chance of winning the seat; it looks like it might have to be Bath, where he won't stand an earthly in an election, but he says it will be good experience and it's a nice place to get a second home in, for a while. He says the idea is he'll win his spurs there, and then they'll find him a good by-election seat to fight. It all seems terribly unimportant to me at the moment.

He also said Sharon's looked after his briefs amazingly well during his absences. She seems to have settled in well. I'm glad it's turned out like this. She's a vast improvement on his last secretary he says.

This had to happen just as *I* was about to start a new job. But they're being very understanding, and told me not to start until I feel ready to.

Oscar and Myra sent a wreath, which was kind of them. I suppose it won't be many months before I'm going to his funeral. It was a terrible shock seeing him looking so ill, wasn't it? – and then, to think what happened. When I got the phone-call saying Dad was in a coma and not expected to live, I thought of that moment in the flat. How peaceful it all was, with some nice music playing, and then Rachel coming in and stepping over people's legs heading for Oscar, bending over him, as if to whisper. Even though she looked weird, in that wig and with her mouth chalky, it didn't seem to sink in that there was anything wrong with her. All so calm – and then that awful scream from him, and blood trickling down over his collar!

It felt just like that when my ordinary dull depression that day was changed into something terrible. Sometimes I think life is so unpredictable and threatening, it's a wonder we survive at all.

I'm going to make Mum a cup of tea and then I think I might borrow our neighbour's bike and cycle up to the moor. Might have a look at Auntie Mabel and Uncle Jack's old farm; see what the new owners have done to it. I need to get away on my own.

Regards,
Lilian

I feel very nervous lying here again, Dr Jacobson . . . Oscar. You're being so kind, I can't believe it. If my sister hadn't forced me to ring up, I'd never have had the courage to face you. I thought you'd never want to see me again, ever. But my sister said, Rachel, he's a kind man, he'll understand why you did it if you're honest with him. Yet it was unforgivable. Do you think it's still possible I could become a psychotherapist? Tell me honestly.

. . . That's wonderful! You really don't think I'm psychotic? I don't *feel* that I am, most of the time; but then, I'm on quite powerful drugs.

They were very good to me, at the hospital. Especially the priest, he was a great comfort. And it's lovely having Sarah with me, she has a calming influence.

Is your wife at home? . . . Ah. I really wanted to apologise to her too, and to thank her for looking after me. I didn't know until I woke up at the hospital that I'd blacked out and Mrs Jacobson had put me to bed . . . No, absolutely nothing: between entering the living room and waking up in hospital. It's a complete blank. I had to be told what I'd done.

But I *did* remember unlocking the door in the bedroom and being in the office. Did I leave it very untidy? . . . Oh, I'm glad of that. I've no excuses. The Munch pictures affected me a lot, I felt very peculiar; I didn't like being with all the people, at the exhibition; I felt shut in. And then, when I got to your flat, it was such a relief I think I reverted to childhood, or at least adolescence; when, for reasons you've already explained to me, I made a fetish of going where I wasn't supposed to go; searching where I wasn't meant to search. Munch's *Puberty* really got to me, for that reason. So I'm afraid the unexpected office was too big a temptation. It even overcame my claustrophobia. Though I had a panic attack later when the door closed on me and I thought I was locked in.

Your wife's pictures really upset me, coming on top of the Munch. They're extremely powerful and frightening. At first I glanced at the ones in the portfolio, and they were frightening enough. Except I liked those sketches starting in the tram, they were very beautiful. But later, after everyone had arrived and dumped their coats and gone into the living room, I found the others, in the filing cabinet.

. . . Yes. Those.

I'm sorry; it still upsets me, even remembering them. But I don't mean to criticise them, don't think that for one moment. I can see their artistic power. But . . . Well, it wasn't only the pictures; I accidentally saw and heard things. It's embarrassing. But Sarah says I should tell you everything. It's about Chris James. Or rather, his wife and his father. They came in while I was in the office. He was pretending to be sick, but it soon became clear he had other ideas in mind . . . And not only that, I gathered they'd had an affair and that . . . God, I really can't . . . Well, Chris's wife is involved with Steven Rhodes . . . I'm absolutely sure. Sharon made it quite clear. Apparently she'd – she'd sent him her knickers and they'd gone astray. Got into the hands of Steven's son. Chris's father laughed about it, thought it was a big joke. But he was upset too, you could tell; he was jealous. They had oral sex, him and Sharon, just before everyone came back.

No, *she* . . . she performed fellatio.

There are other things too. Perhaps next time. You know I don't like talking about these things. But I did feel very sorry for Chris. And for Steven's wife too. I was so sorry to hear about her father. Was the young man in the sports car drunk? . . . Ah yes, it's terribly sad; for *his* family too. I know you're very fond of Lilian and I'm sorry if this upsets you. It's all the more unpleasant in view of Lilian's being a patient of Chris.

. . . *Is* she? His legal secretary? That's coolness for you! Sometimes I think I don't belong to this cynical world.

Well, where was I? After seeing and hearing those things, I felt more disturbed than ever, and turned my attention to the filing cabinet. And there was oral sex again, though with – well, what looked like violent death too. It was too much. It wasn't those pictures alone, it was the accumulation of shocks. I'm a rather squeamish person, Dr Jacobson; I'm not sure I'm cut out for this profession.

I found the wig, with the newspaper cuttings of your wife in the student rag carnival. I don't know what made me put the wig on. I must have been in a precarious state. To my knowledge I was just going to come in and apologise, making up some excuse, like I'd been taking a walk for some fresh air. But then, why would I have the red wig on? . . . Of course. Munch's *Vampire*.

I had no reason to blame you for any of it. Yet I attacked you viciously. Do you still have the marks? . . . Well, thank God for that.

I know. It's obvious why I chose you to attack. But shouldn't I have come through the transference by now? You're *not* my father, you're *not* my ex-husband. You're a man who's always been wonderful to me; who's saved me. I love you very much: do you mind me saying something so simple and so straightforward?

I had a dream about you and Mrs Jacobson a couple of nights after I left the hospital. I was inside her womb, curled up; and Chris James was with me. We were twins. There were these strong contractions and he was forced out; I followed. You were hugging Chris, who was naked. I was choking for breath; no one seemed to be taking any notice of me. At long last Sue Grant, my patient – well, my former patient – picked me up, shook me and hammered me on the back, and I breathed. A priest came and blessed me.

Well, I'm clearly jealous of Chris, despite all his troubles. I must think you prefer him to me.

. . . It's kind of you to say so. That makes me feel better. I *do* feel you like me, sometimes, very much. But then I have doubts. After all, he's well educated and I'm pretty ignorant. I'm not cultured anyway, I don't know about art and music.

The twins partly came from an article I read in the *Sunday Telegraph* soon after I came out. I was going to cut it out for your wife to read, but I forgot. It was about an SS doctor called Tillich. The name struck me because of the theologian, I wondered if they were related. Have you read about it in any of the other papers? I wondered if Mrs Jacobson had come across this doctor in Auschwitz. He's been discovered in Paraguay, and the Lithuanian government say they'll ask for his extradition if and when they get their independence. He helped destroy the Kovno Jews before he went to Auschwitz. The article said he was a colleague of Dr Mengele; and it mentioned Mengele's experiments with twins.

I still had your wife's pictures in my mind; so I've been thinking a lot about the holocaust. I told your old friend, Dr Becker, about my visit to Byelaya Tserkov. I had several dreams about it while I was in hospital. I also dreamt about those two Ukrainian Jews who turned up on our doorstep after the war. Father gave them a little money but made it clear he didn't want them around. The holocaust embarrassed him. After they'd gone, I asked Mother what it was all about; she said Jews had had a hard time in the war, in Eastern Europe, but *we'd* had a hard time too, with rationing and air-raids. I still find that an incredible thing to have said. Though characteristic of my mother.

– Pardon? Oh, I liked him. A very distinguished man. The very best type of German . . . Pardon me? He gave you your training analysis? Gosh! He should have told me. He was obviously thrilled to see you again, after so many years . . . And your wife, yes, of course . . . You were what? You were rivals for her? Good heavens! But you won . . . You *lost*? I don't – Oh, I see, it's a joke! You still have a bonny sense of humour, it's wonderful.

. . . Really? Is it good? . . . I like *your* collection of case studies, it's very helpful for beginners. I've started to read again, which is nice. Still the old topic, I'm afraid; the holocaust.

Hermann's aunt Berta, from Frankfurt, came to visit us last week. She's eighty but amazingly active; is always off somewhere on holiday, on her own. Terribly independent – insisted she could sleep on my studio couch. They were very strongly anti-Hitler; her husband was a conscientious objector, in fact, and died in Auschwitz in 'forty-four. A whole group of them died, and no one knows how, except that they were in the experimental block so one can imagine it was something hideous. She's very kind to me; the fact that I'm no longer married to Hermann makes no difference, I'm still one of the family to her. I said to her, Why did the Germans hate Jews so much? She pointed out, of course, that it wasn't only the Germans, in fact they'd been less anti-Semitic than most. Then she said, Well, you say you're going through bad times here, but imagine it's a hundred times worse. Besides that, your country's been devastated by a war and a lot of your territory taken away. Never mind that you were responsible for the war. There's no work, your children haven't enough food. How do you feel? You're very frightened; you've lost control completely of your life.

Remember, she said, I'm imagining this is England, today. You belong to the left, and you see that a huge amount of the capital that's grinding you down belongs to men in turbans. The shops you can't afford to buy from belong to men in turbans. Or you're on the right, you're patriotic and conservative, and you see that your beloved country was very nearly taken over by an internationalist conspiracy called communism, and its founder and many of its leaders wore turbans. They're a huge threat. You long for secure, traditional values, and you see society being ruined by men who are soft on homosexuality, divorce, abortion, pornography, etc., and many of these so-called liberals wear turbans. You look in your newspapers for comfort and direction, but almost all the journalists wear turbans. You go to a lawyer to try to redress some wrong done to you by someone in a turban, and the lawyer wears a turban. You yearn for the old life of the quiet, beautiful countryside which is being destroyed; and who are the people who don't care for the country and never live there, but on the contrary are thriving from urbanisation and industry? Men in turbans. Never mind that you forbade them to own land in the country.

It was weird, Dr Jacobson, but as she said all this, trying to explain, I began to see hatred even in *her* eyes! For us Jews!

Turbans, turbans, turbans, she said! Driving Porsches – you don't see the ones who are poor too – with their veiled wives beside them wearing fur coats; while you rot without a job and your tubercular children cry for bread.

Don't you think, she said, you English would envy them and fear them? Even though they're as frightened as you are, and with more reason. Fear is the mother of hate, she said, terror is the father of terror. And we were sick; sick enough to let a madman win power. He gambled recklessly, and amazingly England and France let him get away with everything; so we thought how great he is, he's Superman. That's the story of our century.

She went on for hours. How people felt even more threat-
ened when the Jews started to assimilate, started to become
German. I even had the curious sensation of hating my own
people, Dr Ja – Oscar! For their stupidity in not realising how
they *had* to inspire envy and hatred.

. . . Oh yes, I know that. The Jews were in a vice; and they
couldn't help being sober citizens who saved their money rather
than dissipating it on drink and loose living. They couldn't help
being smart.

Aunt Berta's a very remarkable woman, I would like you
and Mrs Jacobson to meet her. She's gone to stay with Hermann
in Manchester, but will be coming back to us for a couple of days
before returning home. If you'd like to meet her I'm sure you'd
find her interesting. I've told her your wife was at Auschwitz;
she's always desperate to meet survivors to see if they know
anything of her husband's fate.

. . . I understand. It was only a thought.

My sister was very shaken. She's written a short article called
Turbans and sent it off to the *Sunday Telegraph*. With my aunt's
permission, of course. She likes to write; it's filled a little of the
hole left by Ruth's death. She's had a couple of poems published
in small magazines. But I don't suppose she'll stand much chance
with the *Telegraph*.

I don't know, I don't know . . . Do you think the Lords were
right to reverse the Commons bill on prosecuting ex-Nazis?
Will the Commons still go ahead? And should they? . . . It's
so difficult. In the article about Dr Tillich, they showed a secret
photo from Kovno, and I thought, Oh my God, yes, get him!
But then I thought, it's so long ago, and here's this frail old man
– they had a photo of him with some Bolivian estate workers –
who's been harried from country to country, and now they want
to put him on trial – and what's the point? They're not even sure
it's the right man. In any case we're all different people now.
Why not leave him to die in peace?

You lost relatives too – people you'd actually met, stayed
with; what do *you* think? Should one forgive if not forget? . . .
Yes, I suppose it has to be a personal choice.

. . . My Byelaya Tserkov dreams, you mean? Usually I was
in the house, hiding, and unable to help my cousins and the other

whimpering, wide-eyed children. I tried to keep repairing the plaster – because as you know they were eating it. I thought, at least it's food of a kind, if I can keep plastering the walls. Once I was digging a tunnel, trying to lead them out. Oh, and I dreamt of the long mound, out in the fields near the forest, where they and their parents are buried. The mound was glittering with wheat, and it was pulsing, heaving, as if it was some huge insect trying to break out of its cocoon.

I found some bones while I was there – did I tell you that? It's very common, apparently, for bones to be ploughed up.

And, once, the house seemed to be mixed up with yours. There was your harpsichord, and – clavichord: sorry! and that statuette of – I think you said it was Hermes? – in your living room. I was with little Anya, my cousin, in that dream, and we were trying to tunnel out. I guess that was because you're Jewish too; I don't normally want to *escape* from your house; I really love 'Padernice'; I'd like to spend all my time here! Well, a lot of it! It's so light and spacious, and so cultured and comfortable.

Pardon? I didn't quite – Oh yes, I suppose it could have been that. Though I'd have thought my defences were well and truly down by now.

Aunt Berta had done a little digging for me, concerning Byelaya Tserkov. Two of the Catholic chaplains involved, Reuss and Tewes, were made bishops after the war. Reuss in Cologne and Tewes in Mainz. Reuss also became a professor of Moral Theology . . . Yes, I wondered that too: whether he ever considered the moral theology of his report. I don't know if you remember, but he gave two grounds for his complaint – that there was no German supervision, and German soldiers could enter the house at any time. Nothing about the morality of murder and genocide.

He should have sat down naked amid the shit, with a bairn in his arms, and screamed. And gone on screaming.

It's time? I feel utterly exhausted. I shall go home and go to bed, I think. I'll see myself out. I didn't know whether to wear a coat, but it's getting quite chilly out . . . Do you like it? It's only from Oxfam, I'm afraid, but it's quite nice, isn't it? Well, it's warm, that's the main thing. Thank you again, so much – Oscar. You look – quite well. Shall I see you again on

Thursday? . . . I'd love to give you a kiss, to thank you. Only I know I mustn't.

Really? . . .

Life is beautiful, though, isn't it? Despite all the horror. We mustn't always dwell in tragedy. October's a wonderful month: that burnish on everything. Look at the sunlight shining on those laurels! I've been more aware of the preciousness of life since my illness . . . Oh, how insensitive of me! It can't seem very beautiful to you. I'm sorry!

I love that photograph of you in your uniform! You have such a lovely smile in it! . . . I prefer it, for that reason, to the sculpture you showed me. And I like that photo of you on one of the dust-jackets, of you climbing in the Cairngorms. You *were* athletic, you're right! Such broad shoulders! . . . Pardon? – '*and at even thou shalt say, Would God it were morning!*' Is it Proverbs? – Deuteronomy, that's it. Yes, we should live in the day and take no thought for the morrow.

Thank you! Thank you! God bless!

Golders Green,
November 1 1990

My dear Lilian,

Thank you so much for your phone-call to Myra and now your letter. I assure you I'm fine now – relatively speaking; my neck has quite healed. Only a psychoanalyst's internal battle-wounds!

Poor Rachel has left the psychiatric hospital, and seems much recovered. Her sister has come down from Scotland to take care of her. I have never thought there was anything terribly wrong with her; I now find she was upset by witnessing a blow-job!! (But what else would you expect in Brighton!) Oh, and hearing something about a pair of knickers that had been sent by a woman to her lover. You would think an analyst in training would have more stomach, wouldn't you? But it's because the poor woman has no one who would want her knickers or for her to give him a blow-job.

But let us turn to you, my dear. You have been much in our thoughts in the past few weeks. I'm glad your mother appreciated the flowers, also our note of condolence; glad, too, that Steven has been a tower of strength, and Chris helpful. The pain will fade: though, as Freud said, something changes at the deepest level when a father dies, and you must not expect to get over it quickly.

And how terrible for you to have to face a second shock so soon after the first. It was a bad time to be told such news, though I can understand how your mother (for she is, in all essentials) would have felt totally vulnerable and distraught, and how things that were never intended to be spoken came tumbling out. To answer your question, yes, I did know about it, but it was never my place to tell you. I'm sure you appreciate that. But I'll tell you now all I know. I can add very little to what your mother has said about it.

I'd been a liaison officer behind the Russian lines with Zhukov's troops. A couple of months after VE day, trying to rejoin my regiment, I found myself at Belsen and I saw at once I was needed there far more than I was by my infantry regiment. The misery was appalling, and there were far too few doctors. Also I was a rather good linguist, and could be useful

202

in interrogating some of the SS swine who were pretending to be honest Wehrmacht soldiers or even ex-prisoners. I was allotted a driver, a young man called Arthur Rowbottom. I saw almost at once what a fine, honest man he was; I liked him enormously, and found his company much more congenial than my fellow officers. I'd grown accustomed to the greater classlessness of the Red Army.

I was only with your father for a few weeks, before he was demobbed; but in that time we became quite close, and I found I could rely on him totally. Sheer Yorkshire grit! And I think he found he could confide in me too. He told me how his wife, your mother, had lost a baby after a difficult birth, and how she probably wouldn't be able to have another. And that, unhappy and lonely, she had got involved with a GI, like so many thousands of English girls. And he also said it served him right because he himself had had a fling with a Belgian girl called Yvette in 1940. Very much a one- or two-night stand, under the imminent threat of death, with the British forces being pushed back to Dunkirk. I sympathised; I'd been in that retreat too.

He told me, just as your mother has said, that he'd tried to retrace the girl during the allied advance; and discovered she'd been killed about a year before by the Gestapo. And that there was a three-year-old daughter in an orphanage. Your father visited it, and found a half-starved and filthy little girl. It had upset him greatly. And everyone who'd known and admired Yvette told him the child was his; there'd never been any doubt of it in her mind.

So – he wanted to adopt her, take her to Yorkshire. He thought his wife would accept the child, even grow to love her; and they could put the past behind them, start afresh. He wanted to leave Sheffield, find a job somewhere else. All I did – and I don't regret it – was 'milk' some money from an SS fugitive, to help him with that new start. You'd had such a bad beginning to life you'd hardly begun to speak, he said. Just a few very basic words of Flemish. It wouldn't be hard, in some new place, to pass you off as their normal legitimate offspring, if he could get documentation. There were false birth certificates and other documents flying all round the place. I had a word with a real expert, a Captain Fortescue. He was, I believe, killed later in Korea.

That's all I can tell you, Lilian my dear. Your father kept in touch, and I learned that everything had gone better than expected, and what a delightful little girl you were. I saw the delightful little girl for myself, when Myra brought you home from the Slade! I shall never forget that moment; I was very touched.

It *has* occurred to me that some of your recent emotional problems may well relate back to your earliest years. For that reason it may be as well that the truth has come out at long last.

You are bound to feel like a displaced person. We are all displaced, everyone who was touched in any way by Nazism. The important thing is that your mother in Yorkshire has loved you and loves you very much. Also you can feel proud that your biological mother was a heroine of the resistance. And very beautiful, your father said. I'm sorry, he didn't tell me exactly where she had lived, nor showed me any photos. No one was taking pictures of girlfriends in the days before Dunkirk.

Probably I shouldn't tell you this, but the circumstances are exceptional: this ought to bring you closer to Chris. Did you know that his mother abandoned him when he was seven? Only in your case there was no abandonment, you have merely found there is another, tragic and mysterious and caring, mother-figure in your life.

But I don't, in the least, seek to minimise the additional pain and upset this has brought to you. I wish I could hold you in my arms and comfort you. Or do I mean comfort myself?

What a monstrous web that spiderish Swastika spun. I have been indulging lately in some violent fantasies. The Germans still have absolutely no idea what they did; only survivors like Myra do; you have to suffer it to know. In my fantasy scenario, the police of various nations will swoop on all the German tourists lounging on European beaches next summer – fifty years after the beginning of the holocaust. They will be told to leave their bathtowels on their deckchairs, to keep them booked, but there are some anomalies in their passports. They have to assemble at the nearest railway station. They are bewildered but they go, for Germans are nothing if not orderly and obedient. They find themselves, even more bewildered, locked up, a hundred at a time, in cattle-trucks. And they set off for an unknown destination. It's happening simultaneously in France, Britain, Italy, Yugoslavia, Spain, etc. The transports chug for a while and stop, interminably; move on and stop; the Germans become desperate, they have no food nor water nor sanitary provisions. Of course, unlike the Jews from the ghettos, they are quite fat and in good condition, so they're in not much danger of starvation.

At last, after many days, they hear the bolts being drawn back; alsatians and wolfhounds barking; 'Out! Out!' And they emerge, those who still live, blinking in the light and stunned to see an exact replica of Auschwitz or other death-camps. And SS doctors standing, lordly, while a camp orchestra plays a merry tune. At last it begins to sink in. It really did happen! It felt like this! *Arbeit macht Frei.* They are selected – all in one direction – and taken in trucks to a crematorium disguised as a bath-house; told to undress, are given towels and soap. Then they are shut in the bath-house, hundreds together with no space to move an inch; and they wait . . . And wait . . . And wait. They know at last how it feels.

Some of it. Not nearly enough. And only a few million would die instead of the forty million which would be proportionately the just number. No, certainly not an eye for an eye and a tooth for a tooth. But we'd settle for it; we're not savages.

But what about Germany itself, you'll be saying? They'd never permit this to happen . . . Well, they'll have no choice; the nuclear powers will threaten them with annihilation – *Vernichtung* – if they try to interfere.

I'm reading the reflections of a German statesman. Who do you think wrote this: 'Germany must compose the nucleus around which Europe will federate'? Willi Brandt? Schmidt? Kohl? Wrong: Adolf Hitler. Night of Feb. 22 1942; one month after the Wannsee Conference decreed the final solution, and within a few days of the inauguration of a new crematorium in a converted farmhouse at Birkenau. It's working out perfectly for him; it's Germany that's making the running for a federal

Europe, though most of its neighbours, including France, are happy to oblige because they're still terrified. Yes, Hitler would settle for this, the consequence of his terrorist *Blitzkrieg*. Of course this Fourth Reich, lasting a thousand years, will be a more liberal fascism than he imagined; but he'd settle for it. German domination, in a *judenrein* Europe, though co-operating with Jewish plutocrats abroad! An impregnable conservative-liberal-social democratic castle. No daring, no adventure: tameness, peace, apathy. I shudder at it. I'm glad my life is almost over, my dear Lilian.

I didn't mean to get carried away into politics. Forgive me. Don't imagine I'm xenophobic about the Germans; some of my best friends are Germans.

I get very aggressive, sitting in this chair unable to move. Actually, Hitler's *Table-Talk* is quite entertaining; one can see his charm, even occasionally his humour. My poor old lips have twitched into a kind of chuckle a few times. Complaining, for instance, that Ukrainian girls working in slaughterhouses were up to their ankles in blood! The killer of my race can make me smile! But then, as Kafka said, 'What have I in common with Jews? I have hardly anything in common with myself and should stand very quietly in a corner, content that I can breathe.'

Myra all day raking up leaves, tidying up for the winter. She's about to come in. There are premature Guy Fawkes bangers going off, scaring poor old Castro to death.

I hope your new job goes well. If there's an unpleasant atmosphere at work, one should really get the hell out. The people at the Race Relations Board ought to be friendlier – after all, that's their job! At least you went out with a bang – your Lambeth exhibition seems to have caused a good deal of controversy. Myra's hoping to see it next week.

I've spent longer than I meant boring you with this letter. But I realise I've missed writing to you. If you care to, write to me, or send us your delightful cards.

I am rather depressed.

Love,
Oscar

I'm wondering whether we should use real doctors or actors at our English facsimile Auschwitz? Actors, I think; Anthony

Hopkins, Jeremy Irons and Kenneth Branagh have the arrogant good looks that would make them most apt. Can't you just see Irons with a monocle?

Ach! So much lost, so much lost! Beloved, vivid faces – vanished.

2

I'm sorry I'm a bit late. I've been glued to the television.

I thought this was the day I'd be rejoicing. It's unbelievable, Chris, isn't it? Thatcher! Gone! All the people at the office were delirious, dancing on the desks. No one did a stroke of work; we got some wine and lager in and stared at the telly all day. But I couldn't feel as my colleagues did. Oh, when the newsflash first came I felt great; it was the first good news I've had in weeks. And I thought – poor old Dad would've been so thrilled. But as I watched her in the Commons I had a very strange reaction. I actually started to feel sorry for her, and even admire her. She's got guts, you have to say that.

I'll miss her. God, I never thought I'd say that! The hole in me feels bigger. I've spent ten years filled with loathing for her, longing for this moment; yet now it's happened there's a huge sense of loss. Who's that woman in the Greek myth, with the snakes in her hair? . . . That's it. Maybe we need someone like that, I don't know. Someone to hate. I always felt that Steven saw a lot of his mother in her, even though his mother's a socialist. – Well, of a sort. Steven couldn't very well shriek at his mum for giving him a sod-awful childhood, so he could use Thatcher instead. I guessed it but felt she deserved it anyway. And she *did* deserve it, so why do I suddenly feel like I'm on her side?

. . . Ah yes! Why didn't I think of it! Betrayal, rejection. The stab in the back. Yes, you're right! – when she came in, and the Tory back-benchers stood up and cheered her, I *did* think, They're all hypocrites and half of them are Steven lookalikes.

He's cockahoop, of course. He had the nerve to ring me at work and say isn't it great and couldn't we meet for a celebratory

208

drink? I told him to go fuck himself. The bastard. I still feel sick to the stomach at his treachery, his sheer fucking hypocrisy. All those months. And God knows how many others there were; I don't expect it's the first affair, do you? He swears it is, of course; or was. He says he's not seen Sharon since I walked out – do you think that's true? And that it was just an aberration – that's the word he used – an aberration; he wanted to find out if he was still attractive to women. The usual excuse.

He's terrified I'm going to make a stink and ruin his political career before it's begun. Well, I couldn't be bothered.

He's full of crap. All this guff about not defending men accused of violence against women – he hates women. When we first got together he used to like wearing leather and treating me rough. We had to – he had to work hard to control that side of his nature, and I thought he'd managed to, but now I don't think he ever did. There are hints of it in Sharon's filthy letter. It wouldn't surprise me, either, if he wasn't secretly queer. He was great buddies about ten years ago with Edward Caufield, the actor; and you probably know there are strong rumours that he's gay . . . You didn't know that? Just because he looks a tough guy on TV? He and Steven went to Paris for a weekend – they *said* to see a rugby international.

I'm better off without him. It was just such an enormous shock. I have Oscar to thank for letting me know, unwittingly – he's very upset.

How are you and Sharon getting on? – and don't ask me why I want to know . . . So *that's* her line, is it? What sort of a woman *is* she, to send her smelly knickers to someone! God! And have them end up being sniffed by a spotty sex-mad teenager – I hope your wife's proud of that. Still, I really got her going that day, with my husky voice, saying, Is Steven there? Could you tell him Mandy called? And there's a private packet on the way by first-class post please tell him to expect it in the morning . . . She was pissing herself, I could tell, wondering who I was. I knew right then it was true. And even *then* he tried to deny it when I confronted him, his face like a red pepper, his mouth gobbling and gasping. I let him protest for a good half-hour and imagine he was persuading me, and then I said quietly, Phil's admitted it, he's given me her letter; and I took it from my handbag.

And then he started crying. The miserable toad.

Yes, that was a good day. Well, no, it was a shitty awful day, but I made him suffer too, and I made your wife squirm. Not enough, though; I really hate her guts, she's a dreadful woman. If you could have read her letter. I don't know how you can go on living with her, Chris.

. . . I've told you a dozen times I don't want you to be hurt more than you have been already. It was a filthy letter, let's leave it at that. I really do feel concerned for you, you know that, don't you? Oh, the first couple of days I hated you too, and I felt like never seeing you again. But you're also a victim; and apart from the emotional aspect I dare say you'll miss her salary, won't you?

They were a bloody cool pair, weren't they? In Brighton? And what idiots we were! They must have laughed their fucking heads off.

I shouldn't have tried to kill myself, I should have killed *him*.

But I won't do that again, I promise. I promised Hannah; she said if I was going to overdose again I could do it somewhere else. She and Juppa have been very good to me. I don't know where I'm going to live. I should have the house; but I don't think I could cope with Phil on my own, the way he is. I don't even know if I *want* to. I still can't get over the thought that he blackmailed his father for ten weeks.

Hannah and Juppa say I can stay as long as I like. I'll stay for a few more weeks and then look for a flat. He can buy me something very expensive, it'll serve him right. And by then, perhaps, I'll feel better about Phil and he can move in with me. But just for the moment I'm better off on my own; Hannah and Juppa don't mind if I withdraw into myself. Though I do miss having a proper bed.

Darkness. I hate winter.

My exhibition seems to be drawing good crowds. If all this hadn't happened I'd no doubt be very upset at how some of my friends reacted – well, I thought they were friends – but now I don't give a shit. Saying it's pandering to men's craving for pornography – it's absurd!

I've lost everything. Father, mother, husband, son, home.

You think you're down as far as you can go, and then you plunge deeper. That bonfire night when we took Phil to the Trades Union barbecue, I felt very miserable. Yet I forced myself to look fairly cheerful for the family's sake. Now, looking back, I didn't know how well off I was; I didn't know that in the morning Oscar's letter was going to hit me – wham! I got nausea very badly at the fireworks display. That old problem of a fire blazing up and meat cooking. I vomited, even though I hadn't overeaten. I wonder if my mother and I were in a bad air-raid in Belgium, and I smelt human flesh being roasted? Well, I'll never know; I can't trace her.

I've dreamt I was lying on a bed, naked, with a young English soldier taking off his uniform to lie with me. There were explosions and flashes outside. As he came to me I saw it was my father – as he is in his army snaps. I said to him, I'm an open city.

And then, well I had that awful nightmare again, that I told you about. I haven't had it for over a year. I'm in a young woman's arms. Last night I actually saw her face – she was very striking, and had long light-brown hair floating around me. She made me look into a kind of port-hole, and I expected some attractive view, but instead there are these heads, their eyes bulging, pressed up against the glass on the other side. Demonic faces, yet they seem as scared to see me as I am to see them. I don't want to look but my mother makes me – I'm sure it's my real mother. Yvette. She clearly loves me dearly, yet she's forcing me to see this.

Chris, before I forget, I've a confession. When I told you I'd found Steven was having an affair, and then said it's Sharon, I enjoyed your pain. I suppose it was a way of spreading my hurt. I deliberately kept you waiting before dropping the name in . . . You think it's understandable? I wish I could believe you.

But I don't feel that way any more. I hope you and Sharon work it out, I really do. Belinda should help.

At least I've still got good friends . . . And you, yes. Are you my friend?

The people at work have been great. They're a terrific bunch of people. And the last couple of days I've been able to take more interest. There's a horrifying case of incitement to racial violence come up, a piece in the *Sunday Telegraph*. Nobody in the office reads it but we had over a dozen complaints on Monday morning. It was written by someone called Sarah Fitzpatrick; no one's heard of her. But it's a dreadful article. It set out to compare the Jews in Hitler's Germany with the Muslims and Sikhs in today's Britain; and it manages to insult both. The Jews were responsible for the holocaust! And the implication is that our Asian communities are equally obnoxious and culpable, and therefore to be pilloried and attacked. Vicki, our director, has put me in charge of it. The paper's offered to print an apology, but they won't get away just with that. Not if I can help it. There'll be mosques burning before we know where we are. This country's swarming with racists, you know. I'm going to nail that woman to the wall.

I'm not looking forward to the weekend. It's going to be very crowded in the flat; Hannah's ex-stepdaughter is coming down from Newcastle with her boyfriend. They'll have to park their sleeping-bag in the hall, so we'll be tripping over them every time we go to the loo. They're joining us for the CND demo in Trafalgar Square. Do you realise war could be only seven weeks away? I can't believe even Bush will do anything so mad; oil prices will go sky-high, the environment will be polluted for decades, thousands of young Americans and Brits will be killed. And for what? Well, we know what. For oil.

Juppa wants us to go out to Saudi Arabia and join the peace-camp. Do you think I should? . . . I think they'd give me leave of absence.

But Juppa doesn't have children, whereas Hannah and I do. It makes a difference.

Incidentally, did you see that Dr Becker's photo in the *Guardian*? Oscar's friend. It was at a meeting between a Pentagon general and a Syrian diplomat in Damascus. Becker was in the background with two or three others; the caption called them advisors. I'm sure it was him. What's he doing at a meeting like that? I wonder if Oscar saw it. I should have cut it out and sent it to him.

. . . Some sort of public health inspector, he told me. That could mean anything in Syria. But he said he'd been retired for ages.

I found him a bit strange. In Brighton I mean. He took my hand between his and gazed into my face, saying what a pleasure it was to meet me. Oh, it was – harmless enough, but – a bit creepy. Sort of very *personal*. Almost as if he fancied me; though in fact he was perfectly courteous and correct. Maybe all the weird Munch pictures affected me.

Oscar seems very depressed; and it takes the form of a tremendous xenophobia towards the Germans. I can understand it but one has to forgive.

Do you know if he was married before? Before Myra? . . . No, it's just that I was thinking back to the old days and I recalled him hinting that it wasn't his first marriage; and that he even might have had children. It was obviously painful; I wondered if there was a divorce. No. You don't know.

Actually, I got the impression, at the time, that they were lost in the war. That he simply didn't know what had happened to them. It was one of his drunken evenings, he was driving me to my digs, and he never mentioned it again. It was very muddled, I may have got it all wrong.

I'm sorry. I'm tired. I almost drifted off. I *was* asleep? Are you sure?

Is it time? I *must* have dozed off.

It's a really tedious journey to Herne Hill. I still don't know why you didn't walk right out too. For me, it's the ultimate betrayal, unforgivable. And how can one be sure they used condoms? Even if Sharon hasn't played around before, how do I know *you* haven't? Have you ever been unfaithful? . . . Have you injected drugs? . . . Well, I'll have to take your word for it, I suppose. Have a nice weekend.

Sharon's gone, Oscar. She's gone. I miss her so much.

It happened a couple of nights ago. We'd gone out for a pizza – old Miss Wainwright baby-sat for us. And afterwards, we started to make love. And to talk about her and Steven. It was painful; and yet a part of me wanted to talk about it, and so did she. You understand. We'd been avoiding the subject for a week. Well, she told me how they'd met, where they went on meeting. Once it was at my office; they made love on the couch. That gave me a very odd feeling. Recently, in his chambers after work, as well as Saturday afternoons at the flat while I was watching Chelsea. It was my fault, she said for the umpteenth time, for being so preoccupied and distant. I agreed with her, and said I'd change my ways.

She wanted silence then, and for a while it was good, it was natural and even wild. I could and should have come then. But I wanted to prolong it; I slowed it up. And started to think about her and Steven again. I said, with a twisted grin – I could *feel* it was twisted, as my lips were trembling – Was it as good as this with him?

She stiffened, turned her head away. For once in our marriage I wanted her to say no, it wasn't as good. I think. But she didn't say anything. I said something else along the same lines, I can't remember what exactly, and she said, very cold, Look, just concentrate on me. I said, But I am. And we were okay for a while, till I said – lying – I knew it would make her angry, it was a demon in me – I read your letter to him; the one you sent with your knickers; it upset me. How could you write such things? And she sighed and said, still stiff and annoyed, she was drunk when she wrote it.

I was trying to be understanding; I even said she could have stayed on as his secretary.

She was hardly moving by now, and her head was turned away and covered by her arm. I said, I'm sorry, I won't mention him again, this is beautiful, I love fucking you. She started to move again, and even kissed me, and I felt I was building up to a climax. I said, But we can talk about Klaus, can't we, sometimes?

I'd have been happier talking about Klaus. At least, that's how it seemed at the time. Klaus was safely behind us.

Well, that did it; she tore herself away from me and got out of bed; fumbled into her bathrobe. There was never anything with Klaus, she said. He never even touched me. She was very angry.

I heard her thundering around in the kitchen making tea. I lay back, my erection dwindling, feeling angry too and humiliated. All that romance I'd built up about Klaus and she'd been conning me!

I did wonder what kind of monster I was, that I needed it. I knew it was my fault. I wandered out to the kitchen and put my arm around her; but she shrugged me off and said she was going to sleep on the sofa. I didn't go after her; I didn't offer to change places. After all, it was *I* who was hurt, who'd been cuckolded. If I sought to compensate with a little perverse pleasure, in talking about it, she ought to be glad to oblige; that's how I felt.

At breakfast we barely spoke. I went off to the office and tried to cope with Bill. All the time thinking of Klaus, how I'd built him up in my imagination until he was absolutely real; and how angry I felt with Sharon that she's destroyed the illusion. I rang home, and didn't get a reply. I got worried, and decided to call it a day. I felt a creepy sensation as I climbed the stairs, passing old Mr Morgan in his carpet slippers and ragged dressing gown, going down for the milk. I think I had a vision of being like him in my old age, solitary, abandoned. I knew before I opened the door Sharon had left me. There was a letter for me on the mantelpiece. It said she couldn't stand it any longer, and was going to live with Steven. He'd been asking her to move in but she hadn't wanted to. She wasn't sure it would work, but I'd forced her to try it. Nothing could be worse than living with me.

In a daze I found Steven's number and rang. Sharon answered. I begged her to come back. She said there was no way. She would come round on Monday when I was out to pick up some more stuff. We would sort out later how I could see Belinda.

I walked from room to empty room, for about an hour. Then I got into bed. I curled up like this, and even sucked my thumb. Oh, and I had Belinda's teddy bear with me. I really felt like I was a child again, and my mother had gone away. I started remembering scenes. I remembered the smell of cut corn, my Welsh granny who'd come to look after me; she took me for a picnic to Cheesefoot Head, where they've been finding the corn circles. I asked her when Mummy was coming back and she said, very sadly, Chris dear, we don't know where Mummy is. We're not sure she *is* coming back. And I said, What, ever? And she nodded. Ever. Ever seemed like a long time even then. Cornfields still make me feel sad.

I kept a scented handkerchief of hers for years. I even took it with me to school, and would smell it in the dorm after lights out. Dad kept her clothes for a long time. I probably got into the wardrobe and smelt them, held them against me. I think I remember that. And I remember once, on a Saturday afternoon in Shrewsbury, walking behind a woman with long auburn hair like my mother's, and catching her up to see if she was her.

I guess I'm reliving some of that grief.

What the *hell* happened to her, Oscar? It still tortures me . . . *Canada*? Really? There were rumours she went to Canada? . . . But why didn't Dad ever tell me that?

. . . Pardon? Va-cunt? Vascunt? Oh, it's a vast country. Yes. I suppose it is. If she didn't want to be found.

And now Sharon might as well be in Canada. I got up in the evening to make myself a cheese sandwich. Then went to bed again but didn't sleep; my mind just drifted, trying to work out what had gone wrong.

When morning came I forced myself to dress and go out. I went to that place in Jermyn Street you mentioned, where they'll let you dress up; I thought I'd try it. I guess I was still worried I might be heading for a psychosis, and wanted to persuade myself I had transsexual leanings. I couldn't get in; I've booked for next Friday. Then I went to watch Chelsea. For a time I lost myself in the game.

The gloom only descended when I returned to the empty flat with darkness closing in. I threw myself on the bed and cried. But later I forced myself to go out and get a take-away and a video. It wasn't much good but it passed the evening. I went to bed about eleven and read awhile from Kafka's Diaries. I'm glad you loaned me them. They should have depressed me, of course; but he was such a miserable man it cheered me up slightly.

I went to sleep and dreamt about Hitler. He was a lumber-jack, swinging a huge axe in an arctic waste. He offered me the axe. I swung it but it missed the tree and dug into the ice.

I woke. It was the middle of the night. I listened intently, thinking Belinda was crying and that had woken me. Then I felt empty space beside me and I realised I was alone. I lay in the dark thinking about my dream. I recalled a phrase of Kafka's, read last thing. Something about art being the axe with which we attack the frozen sea within us. Obviously that had given me the image. But why Hitler? Why old Adolf? . . . There's a good story Cilla Black tells . . . She hosts *Blind Date* – it's a cheap game-show Sharon watches – God, Steven'll hate it . . . about a radio disc-jockey who asks general knowledge questions between records, and he asked this girl what was Hitler's Christian name. And when he came back to her after the next record she said, 'Was it Heil?'

Where was I? . . . Yes, waking up, thinking of my dream and the axeman.

I thought, it's not only artists who wield an axe against the frozen sea. Charismatic leaders do it too; indeed everyone who feels driven. Thatcher, Lenin, Hitler, Freud. Each of them thinks he's attacking a different enemy – socialism or capitalism, the Jews or the scientific establishment. But in fact it's always the same frozen sea.

I got out of bed to make myself some tea. I – I put on her clothes. Feeling slightly crazy. She's left quite a lot behind. Even – well, some make-up. And earrings. It was a way of getting her back. Of course they didn't fit, I had to leave the skirt unzipped, etc. Stuffed the bra with socks . . . It calmed me a little. It wasn't a sexual feeling at all. I just felt calmer and a little creative. With the electric fire on, and a whisky, I sat and thought about Kafka. And Hitler. And really interesting, original ideas flowed in, Oscar. It wasn't just the softer clothing, it had something to do with being open to the earth, a deeper, more organic wisdom.

I went to bed again about six and slept for a few hours. Then I had a lazy day, reading all the heavy Sundays and just drifting around in my dressing gown, almost like Kafka. I spoke to no one except my father. I'd realised it was his birthday, and so I phoned him to apologise for having forgotten it. He was very upset to hear about Sharon's going, but I assured him I felt fine. I had another bad spell as darkness fell and rain swept down, but nothing I can't endure.

I feel free. I don't have to talk to someone when I don't want to. But at the same time, I miss her, Oscar, I miss her dreadfully. I miss her scent in the bathroom; I miss the cheap vulgar sounds of Radio Two when I wake up.

I've even started to miss her cooking. I find I don't bother much for myself. When I was coming here I found myself staring hungrily at an advert in the underground for potatoes! Just simple potatoes! But they were golden and sprinkled with parsley, and I felt my mouth watering. Sharon's a bloody good cook. I really resent Steven having the benefit of her cooking. Myra's a good cook too, as I remember – that's a simply divine smell wafting through! She told me it's carp; you had it in the war in Poland and really loved it. And of course it's soft and bland, isn't it? . . . No, I've never had it. I suppose it's all in the ingredients; Myra says it's got Burgundy, garlic and onions with it . . . No, no, I couldn't possibly do that; but thanks for asking me.

She doesn't look well, though – Myra. Very strained. Are you sure she's up to the Christmas Eve do? You've been so lucky to have her, Oscar.

I feel sure Sharon won't get on with him. I think I forgot to tell you, but Lilian said he likes rough sex, and might even be gay. She said he was very close, several years ago, to Edward Caufield. Who apparently is gay . . . I agree, it seems highly unlikely, he's been married three times and plays swashbuckling rakes; but that's what she said. Someone ought to warn her. I'm almost tempted to myself, but she wouldn't believe me. I don't think I believe myself. Her parents will loathe him; they're among the C2s that kept Maggie in power. And Sharon, though she's not interested in politics, doesn't have much time for Labour or feminism. What does she see in him?

I'm sorry. I was thinking of Belinda. Poor little girl. How confused she must be.

At least she's mine. She's about the only thing that *is* mine. He's not going to take *her* away from me. I shall ask for custody. Though God knows how I'd look after her.

Is *every* woman in my life going to leave me? Although I think my mother may have been driven to it. Not only by other women. Dad's going to be working again. Has a year's contract with the government, doing research. When I asked him what it involved, he said, putting cats' heads into missiles, so their eyes can home in on the target. I think he was joking; I hope so. It's more likely to be an extension of his research on brain injury in the fifties and sixties. Did he ever tell you what he was doing, Oscar? I read about it in my teens, but tried to put it out of my mind, it was so horrific. He scalped live chimps, then struck the naked brain to check the pattern of damage it caused. Making it wobble like a jelly. He's a fucking monster. I reckon my mother felt she had to get the hell out.

This defence contract's to do with the Gulf situation. If there's a war, there'll be dangerous low-flying missions, he says. Lots of possible brain injuries. He's highly delighted; thinks it might get him a knighthood, to top up his OBE, if he can help save British lives.

Oh, and I'll tell you something else he did; in the States; in the fifties. Subjected dogs to a thousand blows of a mallet, on all their legs, to find out how they responded! And – I remember this distinctly, even though I read it sixteen, seventeen years ago – three dogs that were brought back to the lab for a second go at them, twenty-four hours later, expired on the table before a blow was struck . . .

Well, that was extremely interesting data! My delightful dad, with his smooth healing hands!

Yes . . . I feel quite sick; I shall cancel Bill I think and go to bed.

Golders Green
Dec.9 1990

Dear Sharon,

I have been wanting for some time to express to you our good wishes for the future. It is not pleasant for an old couple like us to find one's friends breaking up, and we were sad to hear of the split between you and Chris. But these things happen, and increasingly so. In the old days I think we believed more strongly in fate than in happiness; now that is reversed, and probably a good thing too. We hope you will be very happy.

I wanted to tell you, since I may not see you again, how very much we both like you. We thought Chris was very lucky to have you as his wife, even though some people believed he had married 'beneath' him. Idiots! We thought it was the other way around, if anything. I remember, on our first meeting you, you admitted you'd cried when the ships came home from the Falklands and the band played *Rule, Britannia*! and *Land of Hope and Glory*. We warmed to you instantly. All our 'friends' are totally without patriotic feeling – can't even begin to comprehend patriotism. While Myra and I have tears in our eyes listening to the Last Night of the Proms, these people have tuned in to Radio Three and are listening to Stockhausen! They're faithful enough to their equally boring spouses – or pretend to be; though leaving a trail of divorces and unhappy children; but essentially they are faith-less, having no transcendent vision, no generosity of soul. All they seem to care about is adding a few more years to their miserable lives by wearing condoms, avoiding red meat, and not smoking. Myra and I have never smoked, not for health reasons but because smoke has unpleasant connotations for her; but we're both feeling now like starting! She tells me there was more sense of spirituality at Auschwitz than there is in modern London. I can believe it.

You, my dear, are a wholly natural, unpuritanical person, totally without pretensions. I hope you'll always stay like it.

I hear from Chris that Phil has taken to you wholeheartedly, and is even back at school. That's marvellous – a credit to your warm, affectionate nature. As for Steven, I don't know him well; we only had a few minutes' conversation in Brighton;

but London is a village, as you know, and I have heard of him over the years, and never anything but good. Most notably, he reacted with superb dignity, in everyone's opinion, to the rumour some years back that he was in a relationship with Edward Caufield. I've no idea if it was true and I don't care; we are all, as Freud said, bisexual. But the gossip *could* have been damaging, yet by common agreement he behaved with self-restraint and honour, and there was never any question of his career suffering. Rather he was appointed QC not long after. It is greatly to his credit. And now a political career beckons; you will be a politician's – partner. (Or wife, I assume, in time.) Judging from my brief glimpse of him speaking at the Labour conference, and my knowledge of his abilities generally, I am sure he will have a seat within two years and a Cabinet post, in some legal office, very soon after. You will be an important woman at his side, linking hands and singing the Red Flag.

Sadly, I shall not be here to see it. Life is increasingly a burden, but it will soon be shuffled off. We have had an offer for the Brighton flat, thanks to a ridiculously low price; but at least Myra will not be destitute.

She sends her warm regards, as do I.

Oscar

3

Hello, Chris, it's me – Lilian. You really should change your answerphone message, it's awful. Why does it have to be so pompous? It would make one of your patients suicidally depressed even if they weren't already. Anyway, I just rang to say I'm sorry I couldn't keep my promise, but it's all too much.

You've done all you could. Well, if we could have slept together perhaps that would have helped; I'd have felt on slightly more equal terms with those pricks who've got my house and my son. As it is I can't stand lying on that lumpy sofa where I know they fucked.

I should've thrown myself on the bonfire on Guy Fawkes Night, like I was tempted to. At least I'd have still believed in Steven. But I'm a coward – pills are much easier. I'm pissed. Hannah and Juppa are out. I'm lonely.

Thanks for trying, anyway. Goodbye.

It's all in the melting-pot again, Oscar. I had a call from – Pardon? Oh, she's okay. She rang me this morning; was just out of hospital. Says she feels shaky on her legs, but feels much better mentally. I've invited her round for a pre-Christmas drink. She's very lucky I came home early from the cricket club dinner.

I was saying that – the dream? What dream? Oh yes! we hadn't finished discussing it. Well, I don't think there's much more to say. I can't deny the homosexual component; my skirt – I think it was one of my mother's, that I used to snuggle against in the wardrobe – was up above my hips and Steven was thrusting into me in time with the thrusts on the video. But all my attention was on him and Sharon fucking. The video was astonishingly sharp and clear – sharper than Kate and Damien's holiday video from the Bahamas; sharper than life. It was pure agony watching them.

And then when Steven came, or rather when they came on the screen, I did too. My first wet dream since adolescence. Since those nights when Father screwed the fat, moaning Kim in the next bedroom and I longed to be in his place, vanishing into her vast and sulky flesh.

Yes, you're right, this situation's like a return to adolescence. Puppy fat, sexual ambiguity. And limitless possibilities opening out; frightening but also marvellous; whereas previously it seemed as though everything in my life was essentially fixed. Marriage pins you like a butterfly.

The problem is, I'm still fixated on her. I think I'll always be.

Oh yes, there was one thing I didn't mention. Steven hissed in my ear, What would Oscar think of his little girl now, h'mm? Meaning me. But that's obvious enough. Of course, you're like a father to me . . . No, I wouldn't mind at all being a Jew.

I think I preferred you to my father as early as ten or eleven. You'd joke, you'd play funny April Fool jokes, you could have fun.

The video was probably because Steven mentioned cam-corders, the afternoon I bumped into him near Claridge's and we went for a drink. He was piled high with parcels and so we got talking about presents. He said he'd bought Phil a video camera. He'd been on at Lilian and him for months to buy him

223

one; it would be educational; there was a film-making option in his GCSE art.

I was thinking to myself, he doesn't want it for art, he's hoping to video you and Sharon screwing. He's obsessed with sex. He was home, sick, on his own, for weeks; he's very likely drilled a hole through into the bedroom.

Still . . . poor lad . . . Lilian's not exactly been a great mother to him.

Do you really think my mother could be in Canada?

. . . You don't sound convincing. Well, I'd never find her anyway . . . There's an old photo of you in our family album, with Myra and my mother, taken in your garden, and I started to imagine a resemblance. All very silly and very Freudian! When you first mentioned Canada, last month, I misheard country as cunt! I wanted you to have known her sexually.

Yes, yes, I could quite fancy being a Jew . . . Maybe a Jewish woman . . . By the way, I meant to tell you, there are obscene anti-Semitic leaflets being circulated. I picked up one on the tube the other night. It warned against a Zionist plot for a multi-racial takeover of Britain; said police have been searching a synagogue carpark for the body of a murdered Christian child; it calls the holocaust the holohoax! Lilian would be better off finding the authors of this sick trash than persecuting Rachel's sister.

I hear from Myra they're off to Skye. Rachel and her sister. Escaping the storm. It's probably as well. Though she says you're disappointed she won't be at the lunch.

. . . Kafka? Yes, I've been deep into him; burning the midnight oil.

I'd started to tell you, Oscar. About everything being in the melting-pot once more. Late last night I had a phone-call from Father. He told me Sharon was at his house, with Belinda and Phil. They'd come to stay. You mean for a few days? I said. No, for a while, he said very matter-of-factly; till she sorts out her feelings. She's left Steven.

Then she came on the phone, sounding very cheerful and calm. She'd realised she and Steven weren't suited. I said I agreed with her but was surprised, as only a couple of days before she'd talked quite happily of their plans for Christmas. It was a sudden decision, she said. Something had happened that told her she didn't really know him; and what she'd found out about she didn't much like. She wouldn't explain. I asked why Phil was with her. She said he'd got very upset; refused to stay with Steven or move in with Lilian. So after a lot of rowing with his father and tears, he'd come with them. She didn't mind, he was a nice boy, and good with Belinda. And my father doesn't mind. The school holidays have started, and he wasn't happy there anyway; if necessary he can go to school in Winchester for a while.

I was foolish, Chris, she'd said; but I was right to leave you.

I said, You're not coming back then? My heart sinking lest she say yes, lest she say no. She hesitated for a long time, then said, Not at the moment anyway. I need a period of calm to sort out my feelings. Alan's being very kind.

Dad came back on the phone at the end to say, It's best this way for the moment, Chris, don't you think? Give her time to sort herself out?

I had to agree. It's sensible. We'll be together at Christmas, that's one thing. Dad's still coming to town on Christmas Eve; we won't miss your lunch. Then I can drive with him down to Winchester. I'll make sure I don't drink too much, since he tends to get tanked up as you know. Sharon's parents will be there for Christmas too, alas. It means we'll have to watch a load of trash on TV.

. . . It is! Quite a turn-up . . . Just three weeks.

. . . I can certainly ask her. It depends when her parents are due. Get Myra to give her a call. But could you really stand two children here? Belinda can be very noisy . . . I guess it is, though I never felt Christmas was for me, particularly.

Anyway, it's all over, Oscar. A very brief encounter. She'll almost certainly come back if I really press her. I've been feeling exhausted. Steven rang me this morning; shattered and bewildered at first, but gradually sounding almost relieved. Taken aback, of course, by Phil's departure, but even hedging there, saying if it's what he wants for the time being, he needs a woman to look after him, and Lilian's in no mental state to have him.

Bill Hamilton and I went to her exhibition at Lambeth Town

Hall. The one she organised before she switched jobs. *The Nude as Viewed by the Model*. I thought I should see it before it closes . . . Did she? What did she think of it? . . . It certainly *was* quite powerful. We got into a terrific dust-up – well, Bill did. I'll tell you about that later. As you probably know, there were written comments to each picture telling us whether we should approve of it or not; and I was quite amused to see Lilian's comments on one painting, called *White Shark Devouring Eel*. It's essentially a vast cunt, with teeth, about to swallow a weedy cock. I remember when she first saw the picture, in the basement of some provincial art gallery, back in June, July. She described it to me: a crap painting by some sick guy from Chicago called Steffi Rosenberg. She didn't know anything about him, she was going to find out. She said it was ideal for her exhibition in its misogyny and pornography.

Well, it's now a passionate and powerful assertion of female identity, and Steffi Rosenberg is perhaps the most original of Chicago's Lesbian Feminist collective! What's in a name, eh? I did remember thinking the name Steffi could be female.

There were several lesbian separatists at the exhibition. Kind of SAS androgynes, giving us thunderous looks. Bill and I were the only males there. Bill was drunk, of course, and started talking very loudly. Shouting, practically. I DIDN'T FIGHT FACKING HITLER FOR SOME FACKING NAZIS TO TELL ME WHAT I SHOULD LIKE . . . WE MEN ARE THE NEW FACKING JEWS – WHY DON'T THEY FACKING PUT US IN FACKING CONCENTRATION CAMPS? . . . Well, of course, that got them. Rapists! Wife-beaters! Murderers! Abusers! . . . He even got into a scuffle with one muscular woman. WHY ARE YOU ALL FACKING LEFTIES? he shouted at them. WHAT WAS WRONG WITH MAGGIE? BEST FACKING MAN IN THE COUNTRY! And so on.

I eventually managed to get him out and back to my flat. A bit more sober after black coffee, he said to me did I remember the WAAF officer in the bus? I said yes. He said, All women are officers, Chris, and all men are other ranks. Or that's how it used to be. And there was a very sensitive and subtle balance of power between us. He hadn't minded in the least, he said, when that WAAF officer got him jankers a couple of weeks later for being scruffily dressed.

This morning he gave me a highly intellectual critique of the exhibition. Concentrating on Munch's *Madonna*, which of course Lilian slags off. He called it 'From *Madonna* to Madonna'. I meant to bring it for Myra. I'll bring it next time . . . Oh, he said, there used to be hostility between the sexes but it was all healthily covered up, and it didn't stop men and women behaving graciously to each other. Whereas now you can't stroke a woman's hair without its being a political statement.

He saw the shrivelled foetus in the corner of Munch's *Madonna* as the late twentieth century, haunting the late nine-teenth. He quoted Auden: We must love one another, or die.

. . . Of course it is. We *are* brutes. It's all extremely difficult. I actually agree with much that Lilian says; only not in that context. Art and propaganda don't mix.

So what do I do with Sharon, Oscar? Do I want her? Or only a video of her?

The flat's much too small. Perhaps we could survive together if we lived in a big house. I could work in the basement, and Sharon could leave me a meal once a day at the end of the corridor. I'd shuffle out in my dressing gown to get it – that would be my exercise. Do you remember Kafka saying that in one of his letters to his fiancée? She'll only have to see him, he promises, for an hour a day at most!

Speaking of sinister figures – there's Klaus! That was such an awful, awful shock. I don't know if I can forgive her for that. It was such a beautiful fantasy. Klaus is still very much alive in my imagination. The things they did – no, the things she said they did. Betrayal without pain, only happiness, because it's in the past.

It's more real than anything that *actually* happened to me in Vienna. The past may always be an illusion. Doesn't Myra ever wonder if Auschwitz did not in fact exist – as those neo-Nazi idiots suggest?

I could get to like being able to shut my door and plunge into total solitude. 'A silence deeper than silence, a night darker than night.' Last night I really started to explore the insect image in Kafka and Hitler. The Jew as insect; Kafka

227

as insect. And that disgust with the body they both felt – obsessed with alimentation and excretion. Kafka's Table-Talk would be a very small volume, because nobody could bear to eat with him! Chewing every mouthful into pulp . . . There are such beautiful parallels, Oscar: Vienna and Prague; the tall, Aryan-looking Jew and the squat, Jewish-looking Aryan! I need to know more about Modernism. It seems to me you could consider the death-camps a form of repulsive art. They had a terrible beauty of pragmatic efficiency, with surreal overtones. I mean, the arrival by train, which you normally think of as a homecoming, or else opening up the excitement of a holiday. And the orchestras playing jolly music. The metaphors of purification, the bath-houses and the cleansing furnaces, and – Sorry, I'm upsetting you. Forgive me.

. . . I'm sorry I didn't quite . . . Eichmann was at Theresienstadt, right . . . Listening to the Jewish choir and orchestra . . . It was the Verdi Requiem . . . He applauded, tears in his eyes, yes . . . Then he sent the whole lot off to Auschwitz in the morning! Oh, my God! My God!

. . . I'm sorry . . . Daisy? I don't understand . . . Oh, *Dies Irae* – right!

Pardon? Schiz – schizophrenic existence! You can say that again!

Kafka and Hitler – they're like one person split in two, Oscar, it seems to me. They were both full of the seeds of death. I was reading before I came that horrid passage where he imagines his father executing him; in a machine that slowly rips him in two. Hitler externalised the violence, simply killing twenty or thirty million people, while remaining for most of the time in the best of spirits. – And the way they thrived on cunning; Kafka weaving deceits around his readers and his fiancée, Hitler around Chamberlain.

There's so much, so much – don't you think? Women – their essential contempt for them . . . So much to read, to think about, to write.

But I need space, and peace, in which to do it. Instead, I'm racked with anxiety about money. My first thought, when I heard that phone-message from Lilian, was, My God, how shall I manage without her dough! And I'm *desperately* trying to dissuade Bill from going to live in Singapore, where a rich old girlfriend of his has just been widowed. That's why I spent an afternoon with him. I say to him, You're not ready yet, it's a leap in the dark. But it's I who am not ready, and if he goes *I* shall be in the dark. Living seems *more* expensive than when there were three of us. Because if I go into a supermarket for a pound of cheese I now pick up a bottle of whisky too. The situation's desperate; I'll be forced to sell the flat and move into a bedsit.

My masturbatory fantasies are still full of Klaus and Sharon! Do you think it's possible she was only pretending they didn't have an affair, to punish me?

. . . Yes. Time. Your carp will be ready. Castro's not come; he's getting pretty feeble, isn't he? I saw him hobbling around the kitchen, when I came. The kitchen door was partly open and I saw Myra, stirring the pot. I wondered, does she have an ulcer? . . . Because she was wolfing down chunks of dry bread. It looked strange . . . That's good; but it's bound to be stressful for her; she really doesn't look well.

I ought to have brought a coat; it's quite chilly out. Actually I think I'm feeling slightly fluish.

. . . Well, if you're absolutely sure! I have to admit the smell is overwhelmingly delicious: thank you!

Golders Green
December 18

Dear Lilian,

Thank you so much for your card. Botticelli's *Primavera* is so much more suitable for a Jewish couple than the hosts of bright angels we've been getting, and what more cheerful picture for an old and dying man? You have sent it before, but no matter: a great painting changes with one's moods and seasons, as I'm sure you had in mind.

We are deeply relieved you're okay now. What you did was an understandable reaction to so many painful events in your life. What went wrong between Steven and Sharon? I guess he found he'd made a dreadful mistake. It's very nice that you'll be back in your own home at least over Christmas, and with Steven. A quiet Christmas, as you say. I think we shall all be having a quiet Christmas. Take things steadily, feel your way slowly. You and your husband have started talking, that's the main thing.

I read with interest his piece in the *Observer* last Sunday, predicting that within his lifetime he'd see social democracy, and virtually a common law, prevail from California to the Urals. Well, he could be right. He's a bright chap, your erring but remorseful husband.

Never mind about Phil. He'll be back. At the moment it's possibly just as well he's having a complete change of air. It won't do him any harm. Alan James is a very decent man; he'll take good care of him.

I've spoken to Chris, and I know he's terribly relieved you're all right. I'm a little concerned about him, though. He's becoming obsessional – and dreadfully bitter towards women. Certainly not towards you, though; in fact you must realise he's quite hung-up about you. Of course you're bound to remind him of his mother. That's the essence of his life: the impossible search for his mother.

Please *do* bring Steven and his mother along on Christmas Eve. We remembered you and Steven are vegetarians. I didn't realise who his mother was; I saw her on TV in the Lords debate on abortion, and she was most eloquent and persuasive; and again on *Question Time*; she looks good for her age too. It will

230

be nice to meet her. In addition to yourselves it seems there will be Chris and his father, also Charles and Andrea Dahl and their son Tristram. You met Charles and Andrea at Brighton. Confidentially, Charles is to get a K in the New Year's Honours Lists. I'm not sure that drawing a fat salary for plodding on in the civil service for thirty years is a sufficient reason to give someone a knighthood, but there you are! They're very 'wet' Tories, but nice enough. And Tristram is a brilliant young cellist; we've persuaded him to perform for us.

I now recall Steven knows Andrea quite well: aren't they on some legal working-party? I think she mentioned it to me at Brighton.

I had hoped Rachel Brandt and her sister would be able to come. I know you and her sister Sarah Fitzpatrick are 'enemies' at present; but perhaps it would have been a chance to shake hands. She lost her eight-year-old daughter from leukaemia a few years ago, and has used writing to struggle back to life. This was her first piece in a national newspaper. I truly don't think she knew what she was doing, and was stunned to wake up and find she was a national pariah. As a result she's plunged into quite a deep depression. I'm not blaming your organisation; I certainly wouldn't agree with Levin that liberals have grabbed hold of this case because it's less of a problem for them than Rushdie v. Muslims; the Turban article was very unfortunately worded, but I would blame the editor rather than the inexperienced author.

Anyway, Rachel has taken her off to the Hebrides for a couple of months. Maybe it's just as well.

I'm sure you'll take to Tristram. And his playing really is first-class. Talking of music, we hope you will accept the enclosed CD of the Walter-Ferrier *Song of the Earth* we played at Brighton. It's a very ancient recording, but the sound has been upgraded by one of those modern technological miracles. It's not a Christmas present, Lilian my dear, just a personal gift to you; so play it straight away and think, a little, of me. I watched your response to it at Brighton, and you had tears in your eyes. I was moved by that; I think you were responding not only to Mahler's glorious and tragic music but to the German, even if you didn't understand it. *Ich suche Ruhe für mein einsam Herz . . .*

Rest I am seeking for my lonely heart . . . Could one imagine a more perfect word for rest than *Ruhe*, with all its richness and longing? It's a most heavenly language, even though John Fowles says in one of his books that it's the natural language for executions.

So play this CD; if not all of it then the last part, *Der Abschied*, Farewell; play it and remember, whatever happens, I have loved you. – Still do, in fact. (Myra, who somehow understands my feeble distorted grunts and is typing this, understands my love for you also, and approves.) I love you not only for yourself as you are, but because you bring back the dead to me.

If you should wonder why I, an English Jew of Czech origins, love the German tongue so much, I should tell you that the Jews of Czechoslovakia were torn between the Czech, German and Yiddish tongues; members of my family living there spoke Czech as their first language, but it was the language of Goethe and Heine that they read with the deepest, heartfelt pleasure.

Forgive these ramblings. We look forward to seeing you on Christmas Eve, about twelve. We're hoping it will cheer us up. A very dear old friend of Anton Becker's, and later of us too, Marie Charpentier, has died in Paris. She was an excellent fiddler, and could have played professionally; but instead she became Secretary of the Communist Party in Paris. Well, now she is gone, like communism itself. I've heard there's likely to be a *putsch* in the Soviet Union in a few months' time, but even if it succeeds they'll never bring back the old idealism. The Russians will be able to choose between chocolate chip and raspberry ripple icecream, but they'll slowly lose their love for Pushkin and Tolstoy.

Myra has been very depressed recently. She corrects me that she has *always* been depressed. It's true that holocaust survivors never really escape depression, though Myra has put on a really good show. But underneath – well, for most understandable reasons we've never been able to lead a very active sex life, for instance. However, sex isn't important. Her present depression is only worse because survivor-depression worsens as one ages. And *I* am a burden.

That's why we thought we'd have a few friends in. And we'll try to make it jolly.

SCREAM

Myra corrects me again, rightly. Sex *is* important; and we've had wonderful sex. On occasions she can be Chernobyl . . . And we still have a rich fantasy-life, on that borderland where memories and imagination meet.

One never recalls an actual fuck; what one remembers are images of desire. As on that long-ago evening with you, Lilian, which has given me unforgettable erotic images. Your shoulder almost touching mine on the sofa, and the air filled with your scent; a crossed, elegant leg, black stiletto moving slightly to the jazz-beat; your face expressionless as you wondered if I would dare to put my arm around you. The soft cloud of your shampooed hair, melting through my fingers; the deep blaze of your brown eyes, the brush of your tender, menthol-scented mouth (you occasionally smoked Consulates then); and after that, as I have told you before, the wonderful, unexpected sight of you undressing; that slight thrust-forward of your stomach as you fought your trapped dress; your rounded thighs stressed by blue suspenders which, their clips catching the light, pulled into arcs your seamed nylons; then, when you sat, the tug of your fingers at your earrings; your perfect, somewhat heavy, breasts emerging from your brassière, bobbing slightly as you stood again to slide down your white panties . . . That triangle of lush hair . . . A slight shyness still; every motion, pure natural grace.

All this will be anathema to you, no doubt; but Myra nods, she saw you when you tried on the dress she made for you; she was conscious of your beauty too.

Shalom,
Oscar

4

Dear Chris,
I agonised over what card to send you, but in the end my imagination gave up and it's the same old Nativity. Thanks for the drink the other night, it was most enjoyable seeing you at home. Hope your cold is better. See you at Oscar's on Mon. and then we'll make a fresh start in the New Year.

Love and Happy Christmas,
Lilian

Skye,
Hebrides
Dec. 20

Dear Dr Jacobson,

I was thrilled to get your letter and gift. Thank you. The only thing about London I miss here is my contact with you.

Sarah is feeling a lot better. The cottage is small and damp, on the edge of the sea so the wind batters us constantly. Sometimes it's quite terrifying, in fact. But we keep a nice fire going and when the weather eases we go out for a walk in the few daylight hours. It's very healing, the solitude and wildness. And even, in a strange way, the darkness. There's mercifully no TV, just our radio and cassette recorder. And so you couldn't have chosen a better gift. I'd never heard the *Four Last Songs* before; they are beautiful and heartbreaking. We both listen with tears in our eyes, thinking of Ruth; but it's good for Sarah; she says she feels she is only now mourning properly.

You will know *I* am convinced 'the soul will fly free, in the night's charmed circle, *tief und tausendfach zu leben* . . .' As you say, what a rich language it is; and how sad that it's also capable of a word like *Vernichtungslager*. You told me once it was a word full of poetry and enchantment for them; surely that can't be true?

I wish you and Mrs Jacobson a very happy new year, and send you my love. Hope to see you in a few weeks, and also that you're wrong in believing you've undertaken your last analytical session. I need you! I pray for you.

Rain has started to lash down, but we're going to put on our souwesters and walk to post this. I hope your lunch party goes well; I'm sure it will.

Yours,
Rachel

PS. Must tell you a dream that won't surprise you: I was in a urinal, standing beside my father, and peeing in 'competition' with him.

PICTURES AT AN EXHIBITION

Winchester,
Jan. 13 1991

My Dear Oscar,

We arrived back here last night, collecting Phil from Hertford on the way, and I was deeply moved to find your letter and parcel awaiting me. There seems so much to say – and Dad's old Amstrad is unfamiliar to me. I am still trying to cope with all the shocks, starting with those two WPCs at my door on Christmas Eve when I was expecting a somewhat tipsy father to be standing there.

People on the whole have been kind, other than the media – and the police, of course, for a few grim days. Mavis and Fred were wonderful to us, but of course their little house is terribly cramped and I was glad when we left Northampton behind. Dad's girlfriend, Deirdre, had kept the house aired and put some food in the fridge. Obviously the Braithwaites have been very kind and hospitable to you, but I can understand your relief at hearing you're to be allowed back into Padernice. Even with all its reminders of that ghastly scene, and as you say with the ghost of poor old Castro asking where his bowl is. How kind it was of Rachel, to have offered you a retreat in Skye.

The media of course have been fiendish. We've taken about ten calls today, now they know where we are. Poor old Rhodes, the Tory tabloids have really had a ball with him. Wonder how much the *Sun* paid Caufield's ex-wife for that little exposé? I only met the Dahls a couple of times, but they struck me as a pleasant couple. The imputation that Dahl betrayed secrets to the Soviets sounded absurd, even without the ludicrous suggestion (in the usual sly way to cover against libel charges) that you had something to do with it as his therapist. I suppose it was fair game to bring up his part in the Keeler business. I hope you didn't read the very nasty piece hinting that Andrea Dahl was once involved with you, that Tristram was more than your godson, and so this gave you a hold over her husband. If you did read it, I hope you treated it with contempt. Right up to the usual standard of *Sunday Times* investigative journalism! Journalists are gross – anything to sell papers. Even the *Guardian* waded in; someone, wondering rhetorically how as a JP she could sentence prostitutes, given her wild reputation in the sixties, quoted *Lear*:

> *Thou rascal beadle, hold thy bloody hand!*
> *Why dost thou lash that whore? Strip thine own back;*
> *Thou hotly lust'st to use her in that kind*
> *For which thou whippst her!*

And made equally sour remarks about their wealth, asking how she had the nerve to send poor youngsters, fiddling a few quid on benefits, to prison. Trust the *Guardian* to sound morally superior! I don't know that their journalists are on the breadline!

The important thing is, neither of them deserved their fate. None of them did. It was, as you say, so entirely random and pointless. I'd have been there myself, despite my bad cold, if I hadn't feared to pass it on to you. It makes me, in a curious way, guilty. And how ironic that you only invited the Dahls because you wanted Tristram there; and then he was saved by a late invitation from Edward Heath to play in his Christmas orchestra. 'Bladder of pompous vanity' – I liked that.

It's all, as you say, a mystery. 'Behold I tell you a mystery.' It's exactly the theme of your notes for what would have become *Goethe's Tree*. How can I thank you for sending the notes? I was overwhelmed. Are you sure you won't be able to write the book yourself? I can only say I will try my best to do justice to your ideas. You rightly guess they are close to mine. I agree with you that both Nazism and communism were in their way 'rational' theories, developments of the Enlightenment, based on eugenics and egalitarianism respectively; but proved so monstrous that they brought their own destruction upon them. But our present liberal fascism, as you suggest, is so eminently reasonable that who could choose anything different? Who could object to a humanely controlled market economy? To rational laws governing the relationship of the sexes? To the unity of Europe? I liked this: 'There are no more gods and heroes. Just two billion years of Jacques Delors and John Major, until the sun mercifully swallows our poor planet, dying of *ennui*.' Wonderful!

But I think you are right too in predicting explosions

of individual and street anarchy, all over the world. Drugs, serial killers (of both sexes), and epidemics of psychopathic destructiveness like the one in your house. Criminals will be the new saints and saviours. 'Because ultimately humanity can survive Hitler but not Delors. Delors doesn't exist in the unconscious; Hitler does. The rational is much more terrifying. Whom the gods wish to destroy they first make rational.' Your mind, Oscar, has not been the least affected by your illness. I have been invited to write an article for the *Observer*, on the psychology of such murderous random attacks, and with your permission I would like to quote your above remark.

I had no idea your grandfather was a rabbi. I'm sure he would have been proud of your embryonic book. Like its author, your notes have wit as well as profundity; I loved your grim little story about the lovers who had read over and over *The Joy of Sex*, until they had perfect sexual bliss, giving rise to a terrible mental oppression in which they started to loathe each other! And that joke about the Munch exhibition (I mistyped Munich!); followed immediately by a very serious observation – 'People had passions then; passionate, tortured souls; no consensus sex, coalition sex, with emotions as paralysed as my body.'

Well, it is full of riches. I could go on quoting back to you all day.

It must have been painful for you to give me your account of Christmas Eve; but I am grateful. I can well imagine Lilian and Steven and his mother going on and on about the Poll Tax, education, the health service, inadequate arts grants, etc., until you were sick and tired of it and tried to lighten the atmosphere with Strauss and carols. No, you're right, it wouldn't work! I thank God Myra took your hint and said you needed some fresh air. How dreadful to return and find Castro lying in the hall, covered in blood.

And I simply can't begin to imagine your feelings when you entered the lounge. Yes, I think I remember *The Human Mountain* at the exhibition, and I can imagine the bodies striking Myra in that way, heaped together. There have been snide remarks, too, made about the fact that they were shot with your own revolver; or rather your souvenir Lueger. But it was perfectly natural that someone should ask if you weren't scared of break-ins, and for Myra to produce the revolver and say, Not with this. I can picture her saying it; she's very strong; has to be, to have endured what she did. Which is truly *un*imaginable: I curse my stupidity in not realising why she was gnawing at dry bread. I can begin to understand, from your words, how she's played a role. To be in a gathering and to wonder how much Zyklon-B it would take to kill them; and how much manure, grease, etc., they would produce – God, it's another world! As you say, how laughable the rumours that she's slightly mad!

I recall your moving compliment to her in Brighton. That she was your Death and the Maiden, Dance of Life, Madonna, Lonely One, Sick Girl. Yes, you were lucky to find her; but she was equally lucky to find you, my dear old friend.

That *Lear* quote in the *Guardian* reminded me of something you said to me after Rachel's vampirism. With amazing generosity you said she'd cut through the crap for a moment; that all the party-babble about wicked taxes and who-was-bonking-whom was as if, amidst the cosmic tragedy of *Lear*, we saw Cordelia trotting along to marriage guidance with her hubby, and complaining that he spent no time on foreplay. You said life isn't really *here*, and only survivors like Myra – and Rachel in her moment of dementia – knew where it really was. I didn't altogether understand you, but I do now. God, we thought *she* had been violent!

I'm as puzzled as you by the word-game Father and the others were playing, when they were so brutally interrupted. I can't shed any light on it. You say they'd only jotted a few of their names down? Father wasn't a man to enjoy that kind of thing, and I wouldn't have thought Lilian and Steven were either. You may recall how Lilian reacted at Brighton when someone – I think it was Naomi – suggested a game of Consequences.

I'm glad to hear you say none of the guests showed any sign of imminent destructive mania during lunch, and you're sure the assault came from outside. Certainly Dad was in good spirits before he left the flat (not that he could have been responsible; he could hardly have scalped himself, poor old chap). I'm sure you're right that everyone there had enough violence in him, and self-hatred, to want to produce mayhem ending in suicide;

but hardly in those circumstances – full of good roast beef and Sainsbury's claret, with Christmas lights twinkling and *Silent Night* playing. Also, when one considers all the mutilations and the sexual evidence, it's inconceivable.

The brutes who got in – presumably anti-Semitic youths – might have posed as carol-singers. And it's very possible that, drugged up as they must have been, the sight of the revolver 'triggered' off more than they'd intended.

I don't want to say much about the police questioning of me. I'd like to try and forget it. Their only 'evidence' was the O-negative blood-type of the sperm found in Lilian. I tried to point out it wasn't that rare a group. Well, in the end they let me go. I felt like Kafka, where he describes being bound by a rope round his neck, then pulleyed up through various floors of a house until just a morsel of bloody flesh emerges on to the roof.

The most horrific moment of all was when they played a tape of one of your sessions with Rachel. The one in which she said she heard my father saying Belinda was his child. The police were arguing that I'd found out about it and went berserk as a result.

More painful still was when Sharon admitted it was true. Or *may* be. Can you imagine how I felt at that moment? She confessed she's griefstricken for my father, and as good as admitted I'd always been second-best for her.

And yet – you will understand – there was also a peculiar masochistic *thrill* when I heard her say that . . .

And the one good thing about staying with her parents was that we were forced to share a bed. And she talked, and talked, and talked. About Klaus, about Steven, about my father! I realise she's entirely faithless and deceitful, yet – or therefore? – I love her very deeply.

She tried for a while to 'sugar the pill' for me (and lessen her guilt) regarding Belinda by saying Alan had told her he wasn't my biological father. That he'd said my mother had had an affair and the chap had got her pregnant. Some rugger-playing architect, she said, after I pressed her. I got extremely angry with her; apart from my fantasy about you I'm not interested in finding myself fathered by some stranger. Better the devil you know . . . Anyway, she admitted at last it wasn't true.

It actually cleared the air a little. We decided we couldn't stand to live in London after this, and should move here. We're going to have Phil with us too; the poor lad doesn't want to live with his gran. And he's very taken with Sharon. We'll see how it goes.

In a way I have everything I've ever wanted: country house, Daimler, lovely five-acre garden, fame of a kind, some splendid antiques. And yet I feel I have nothing. I feel hollow.

An 'existential void' – as you say about the West. I loved your comment that communism, by enslaving people, allowed them to be spiritual and free. We're enslaved, in contrast, by trivia, by the mad pursuit of personal happiness, diversions. As if by a black swarm of insects. (You told me once, long ago, how you'd dreamt the name 'Padernice', meaning purification, in an insect-dream.) I think Sharon realises that now too; she feels she's suffered a kind of summer frenzy. According to her it began when I'd been in a frenzy myself – imagining you'd said I was heading for a psychosis. She started to feel she couldn't cope with me – and there was Steven, seeming to offer some escape.

She wrote her letter to him on this Amstrad. Despite the fact that she feels no personal sadness at his death, I have been searching the Limbo files in hope of resurrecting her letter! Crazy! But she's promised to go into minute detail about the sex with Father, Steven and Klaus – who was very real. She'll also let me 'dress up' occasionally. She found that amusing. She doesn't understand that I find it creative rather than erotic.

I've been avoiding one topic. Brearley, the Gauleiter who interrogated me, told me about my mother's relationship with Myra. He had in front of him statements you both made at the time of her disappearance. I think Brearley was trying to get me to say I blamed you and Myra for losing her. I mean, for my losing her. It didn't work, because he could tell it was a complete shock to me. He read out Myra's statement that she *definitely* had plans to go to Canada, since she couldn't cope with the lie she was living with my father.

I only wish you had been more definite with me. And been open about their relationship. But I've come to terms with it. I have the impression you've had to set up a strong defence. No doubt also you wanted to spare me knowing my mother was at least bisexual. Anyway, it's all far in the past. It explains why she left, which is some relief – though not why she chose to leave me behind.

I agree with you absolutely that I'm not cut out for psychotherapy. I shall write – and, bless you, you have given me an enormous start. You've helped me to realise my mother's departure affected me so much that I have always to be *on the point* of losing her again – in the shape of Sharon.

My obsession blinds me to too many things in others. It is unforgivable how I never, in over six months, uncovered Lilian's longstanding liaison with her farmer uncle. I also didn't make enough of her discovery that her early childhood was in Nazi-dominated Europe. As you say, it may help to explain her authoritarian streak.

It was brave of Myra to attend her and Steven's funeral. How touching that you arranged for her body to be covered in lilies. Yes, I think Lilian might have been happier if she'd stayed with art. I'm sure it has consoled Myra. I didn't know she decided to be an artist through you, through drawing for you someone you'd loved and lost. That's a beautiful story.

Sharon wants me to drive into Winchester for a take-away, so I must finish. We've been busy today, unpacking our stuff and so on. I hope your return to Padernice will not be too harrowing. Go right past the lounge into your study, and put on that record. It sounded to me a very healing thing to do. I remember you playing *On Hearing the First Cuckoo in Spring* to Dad and me, after we'd returned from a test match at Lords. I'm sure that would have been the Beecham recording; it was scratchy even then – but so lyrical and poignant.

I realise I haven't thanked you for the second precious gift, the case-study made by an Auschwitz survivor from your cousin's buried notes. I have put it to one side; I don't feel I am strong enough yet to read it. You honour me with it.

I miss seeing you; but we shall stay in touch. My love to Myra. I am confident you will hear the real cuckoo again. You must survive this. We need you.

With warm regards,
Chris

Padernice,
January 22 1991

Dear Phil,

My wife and I have not had the pleasure of meeting you, but
have heard a lot about you from your dear mother. You have
suffered a terrible loss, and we send you our deepest sympathy.
It will take time but we are sure you will find the wounds
healing, especially as you are in such good hands. The one
consolation for us from the tragedy has been that fate spared
you, Chris, Sharon and Belinda from being present.

I was delighted to hear from Chris, who phoned us yesterday, that you have been accepted as a day-pupil by Winchester
College, and that you seem to be settling in very well there. It
is also some consolation that you are financially secure thanks
to the Appeal Fund in addition to your inheritance. The English
are remarkably generous, especially when a disaster occurs
around Christmas. But money, of course, does not begin to
compensate.

Live cats' heads are guiding missiles on to Baghdad. (Chris
will know the reference.) We feel we have lived long enough
in this world. I am only anticipating death by a few weeks
or months. Of course there will be some who will think our
decision proves that Wiesenthal is right. (I'm sure you will have
seen the newspaper reports or rather rumour-peddling.) I've no
idea why people think KGB documents from the Baltic States
are any more reliable than released CIA documents! Do they
think my mother, a shrewd down-to-earth Birmingham lady,
didn't recognise her own son! I can't believe my cousin, Chaim
Galewski, was a collaborator. And in any case, I am not him!

We pray the rising generation – yours – will make a better
job of it than we did.

Would you please pass on to Chris the enclosed book? Tell
him it was a present from Chaim, signed by him; and that I
thought the *Metamorphosis* a fitting bequest in view of his change
– and ours.

We are content that everything else in our house burns with
us. Except for this woodcarved head, which depicts myself
when much younger. I looked at it and thought: I know who
should have this. It will mean nothing to you at the moment,

Phil, but I assure you it is connected to you. I have made arrangements for you to learn the truth about it at a later date; meanwhile you can see it as a puzzle.

I wish you all the best.

Sincerely,
Oscar Jacobson

Death is nothing to be frightened of. Your parents are at peace. 'Yet a little sleep, a little slumber, a little folding of the hands to sleep . . .' You will find, when you have lived to a ripe old age like me, that life seems in retrospect like a vague and incomprehensible dream.

MADONNA

'The voice said, Cry. And he said, What shall I cry? All flesh is grass, and all the goodliness thereof is as the flower of the field: The grass withereth, the flower fadeth: because the spirit of the Lord bloweth upon it: surely the people is grass.'

Dr Lorenz murmured this, his face gleaming with sweat from the heat of the flames; the mountain of bodies never seeming to diminish; nor, nearby, the mountain of shoes, clothing, toys, that the girls of Canada were labouring to reduce.

His lament was for a soldier, Rommel, who had died of wounds inflicted by enemy strafing. This had been the gloomy message Dr Rohde had brought, arriving late at the ramp. Though from our point of view it was good news, I felt a tinge of regret. He'd been one of the Germans I'd admired before the war, along with Bertolt Brecht, Fritz Lang, Thomas Mann, Marlene Dietrich.

The summer, *die letzte Sommer*, wore on. Still the naked living skeletons in the hospital block, their oedema-swollen testicles swinging, their bald skulls bobbing and shaking, chests pathetically thrust out, stick-limbs flailing weirdly, attempted to run past Dr Lorenz at the block-selection. And still he would place their cards on the pile for special treatment.

Still he was unfailingly courteous at the ramp, separating the sheep from the goats, right or left, with a twitch of his crop. Assisting old ladies with a hand under their elbow; patting a child on the head, saying, 'You'll be okay; it's nice where you're going.' And still, climbing out of the Red Cross truck, entering the building where the Hungarian Jews were undressing before their shower, he would say to this or that person, 'I'm sorry it's so crowded; please remember your peg-number so you can find your clothes again.'

Indeed, it was with yet more frenetic energy and sense of purpose that he did these things: cramming more and more bodies into the bath-house, until – when the moment came to pull back the bolts – the corpses were erect, unable to fall; blue, and with excreta and menstrual blood trickling down their legs. Supervised the flinging of more and more corpses into crematoria or into burning pits. And I understood him; understood his sense of mission, his conviction that this was for the greater good of humanity. We were on opposing sides, but I guessed I might do the same, if it would lead to the triumph of communism. You couldn't, as Stolb said to me once, make an omelette without breaking eggs. It was just the wrong omelette, sauerkraut instead of bortsch.

Stolb left, taking his wife and Elli with him; as far as I could tell, he'd deserted. Lorenz sent his wife and family back to Berlin. Only one child remained – Renate Tillich. And one night, I heard, when Tillich was on duty in the bath-house, his wife took Renate to see it, and even held her up to peer in at the corpses: telling her she must remember this and be proud.

There was a strange occurrence, a touch of humanity. It involved Alma Rosé, a German Jew. Alma was a distinguished violinist and a niece by marriage of Gustav Mahler. She led the Auschwitz camp orchestra. One afternoon, while I was helping Dr Lorenz to administer phenol to some prisoners, Rohde dashed in with the news that Alma was critically ill. Lorenz was so distressed that his needle struck the Mussulman's rib instead of penetrating the heart. He had to repeat the action. Then he dashed off to the women's hospital-block to see if he could help save her life.

Several hours later word filtered through that she was dead. The SS doctors were distraught.

No one ever found out why she had come down so suddenly with fever and stomach cramps. Well-fed, well-housed, well-dressed (comparatively speaking), she'd been in perfect health. The day before, she had been told she would be released from the camp to go to perform for the front-line troops. It was unheard of, to release a Jew. Alma, a fervent German patriot, had been beside herself with joy, not only at being released, but at being so honoured as to play for brave German soldiers.

Judith told me, behind a stack of suitcases that night, after she'd made love to me listlessly – it was always so: I ascribed it to fear and undernourishment – Alma had turned up, radiant, wanting to share her wonderful news with the Kapo of Canada, her best friend. The Kapo, Judith said, had pretended gladness and invited Alma to dinner; but you could tell she was eaten up with envy, and the girls of Canada believed she poisoned Alma. It's possible.

Anyway, on the morning after her death, Litai, Lasalles and I were allowed to go to pay our respects. We found her lying in state on a bed in one of the hospital's offices. Girls of the orchestra, in their navy-blue skirts and white blouses and stockings, lined the catafalque, staring at their saviour, weeping. They wept for themselves too, not knowing what would happen to them. Tillich, Rohde and Mengele stood at the foot of the catafalque, caps off, at attention. Tears trickled down Tillich's and Mengele's faces. Alma looked more beautiful than she had in life – she'd really been rather plain. Very dignified, almost smiling. Her large strong hands looked especially beautiful; they were crossed over her breast.

Some SS man had touchingly placed a lily in her hands. And the whole bed of state was piled with a profusion of white flowers; mostly lilies. The SS had sent a truck into the town to buy all this mass of flowers from a florist; bought up the whole market stall! The sweet, fresh, innocent smell of lilies masked, while we stood by Alma, the smell of roasting flesh.

Flowers for a Jewess. She was the Shekhinah, mother of all things, the madonna, the virgin of Auschwitz. No medieval troubadour, no Wolfram von Eschenbach, mourned for his Lady more than these death-camp doctors. For a moment, as we stood there, death meant something.

How they love their music, the Germans.

I found myself wondering what music was playing behind Alma's white, impenetrable brow.

I said as much to Lorenz, in his house that evening. The house seemed melancholy, cold, barren, without the cheerful presence of Frau Lorenz and the children; and he looked lost. He was drinking a lot. 'What music,' I asked, 'was playing in her mind?'

'It could have been this, Chaim,' he replied. (He occasionally called me Chaim in private.) He went to his shelf of records and selected one. He put it on the gramophone. The music was scratchy, even by the standards of 1944, but instantly I recognised and was swept away by the closing bars of Mahler's *Das Lied von der Erde*. I thought of my father's suicide in the face of intimidation and financial ruin; of my mother, sisters and wife (with our baby in her arms) entering the gas-chamber; and choking tears filled my throat. '*Still ist mein Herz und harret seiner Stunde! Die liebe Erde allüberall blüht auf im Lenz und grünt aufs neu! Allüberall und ewig blauen licht die Fernen! Ewig . . . Ewig . . .*'

The anguished, lyrical contralto voice, above the throbbing strings: 'My heart is still, and waiting for its hour! Everywhere dear Earth grows green afresh in Spring! Everywhere, for ever, horizons are bright blue! For ever . . . For ever . . .'

Ewig . . . Ewig, repeated over and over again, dying away into nothing. Lorenz's eyes were wet.

'My son; my dear little boy,' he murmured.

He added brokenly, 'I only had the chance to see him once, when he was three. His mother wrote often, though, and spoke of him. He was . . . he was born slightly handicapped. I didn't . . . I didn't realise I cared for him so much, until that telegram came.'

As he removed the record from the turntable his eyes strayed to a photo of his wife and the two children I knew and was fond of. He was wondering if he would ever see them again.

He loved children, and not only his own. I was to see that love again, in Belsen, one year later, when he handed to Judith a starved and filthy Renate Tillich to clean up and feed. I am sure it wasn't only self-preservation that made him promise to find a home for her, so giving his old colleague a better chance of escaping. Though he wore a different uniform and a neat moustache, and spoke in what sounded like excellent English, I saw the same tenderness in his eyes, putting Renate into Judith's stick-like arms, as on that night of Alma's lying-in-lilies. And I guess, from the choice of an English name that he later offered to his driver (along with documents and cash), he was remembering this day.

We drank rather a lot. I was feeling shaky following an incident in the hospital-block, and was grateful for the chance to drink. During the night I'd been violently woken up to find Lasalles and Litai holding me down, with the sharp edge of a knife at my throat. Distorted rumours of the experiments I'd helped to conduct with Stolb had filtered through to them. I remained calm; told them if they were going to kill me it would be much better to choose a method that could allow my death to be ascribed to natural causes. Then Gilchik had woken up, gently remonstrated with them, and they'd let me go.

After Lorenz and I had drunk most of a bottle of coarse vodka, I stumbled upstairs. Having relieved myself, I glanced into Irmgard's room. It had been stripped bare. I recalled her fair hair outspread on the pillow, and was touched by the memory. I hoped she was all right. This, for her, had been home and security.

I felt a little guilty. I'd observed Frau Lorenz packing, and heard Lorenz ordering a car and escort to drive them to Berlin; I'd reported it, as was my duty, to the underground. Yet it was extremely unlikely that they'd managed to get a message out to the partisans; or, even if they had, that the partisans would have bothered themselves with a harmless woman and her children.

When I came downstairs, Lorenz, slumped in an armchair, was running a hand over the carved head given to him by Frau Tillich. He had brought everything he cared for into his study; said he didn't like sitting in the rooms once filled by the loved voices. 'Frau Mahler admired this piece,' he said. 'She came to play for us one day. It was wonderful. Even the children were very moved by her playing. We offered her tea. She felt tremendously honoured, it was clear. She said what a noble race the Germans are; that even a busy, fairly uneducated housewife like Frau Tillich had real artistic talent.' He pulled himself up in the chair to pour himself another drink; offered me the bottle. 'What was very clear also is that the poor woman felt completely German. It's strange, isn't it?'

A lump came into my throat. How could I begin to explain to him that it wasn't at all strange? Slowly, falteringly, I described my own situation, as a young medical student in Prague. Evening after evening in cafés, with other German-speaking friends, trying to forget the Czech babble around us by sharing our enthusiasms – for Schiller, Heine, Beethoven . . .

'I'm a patriotic Czech,' I said; 'yet, above all, I feel German.'

'That's astonishing! You're a surprising fellow, Chaim!'

You could not, he said, escape the innate superiority of the Aryan. He would give me an example. He'd visited Treblinka, just before its closure. Stangl, a very decent fellow, had told him how the work-Jews had reacted when transports had resumed following a long fallow period. 'They cheered, he said, when one of his men gave them the news that tomorrow they'd start rolling in again! They were beside themselves with joy! Because, of course, they hadn't had much food since the rich Jews from the West had stopped coming; they were quite hungry. They must also have been frightened that they might not be needed much longer. It's understandable, up to a point. But to cheer, knowing thousands of men, women and children were on their way at that moment! Well, it's inconceivable that Aryans would have acted in that obscene way.'

While agreeing, I pointed out that they'd mounted a rebellion and broken out. That had been quite brave. Many had died for their comrades. Lorenz conceded the point. It had been too little, though, and too late. 'Stangl told me their passivity had caused him to stop thinking of them as human. Especially the Eastern Jews; he'd had to take more care with the Western transports. You should have seen what he'd done with the station: flowers! a clock with false hands!'

Some five years later in my Damascus surgery, staring at a tall, dark, hook-nosed Austrian who was complaining about stress-related symptoms – he was working too hard, as usual, for a knitting company – I thought of the tubs of flowers, the surreal clock he'd once created – and of skeletal Jews rejoicing because the transports had started again.

I spoke to Dr Lorenz of Franz Kafka, who had felt very much as I and my friends did about German culture. He wrote the name down in a notebook. He would read him. Well, no, he probably would never have the chance to. Gloom settled on him again, though only for a few minutes. Then he gave a slight but almost tender smile, saying how much he appreciated my company; how, if only things had gone well, such good people as Alma Mahler and I would surely have been leaders of a small Jewish colony; somewhere like Madagascar. I felt tears prickle behind my eyes, at such evidence of his respect.

'Odd,' he said. 'I called her Mahler instead of Rosé!' He narrowed his baggy eyes and smiled. 'You would make something of that, wouldn't you?'

I gave a shrug. Still blinking tears back, I felt no interest whatsoever in the doubtful mechanics of analysis. He continued,

'It's the association with the wonderful music we listened to, I imagine . . . Though actually, it wasn't *Das Lied von der Erde* that was going round in my head, but one of his symphonies; the Symphony of a Thousand. Do you know it?'

I shook my head.

'I heard it once in Vienna. Why was I thinking of it just now? – It hasn't entered my thoughts for years. It requires a vast orchestra and choir, hence the title. It ends with a most beautiful setting of the Chorus Mysticus from *Faust* . . . "*Alles Vergängliche/Ist nur ein Gleichnis . . .*"' He stopped, forgetting how it went on. Annoyed with himself, he made to stand up and go to his books; but instantly I continued for him:

> '*Das Unzulängliche,*
> *Hier wird's Ereignis;*
> *Das Unbeschreibliche*
> *Hier ist's getan;*
> *Das Ewig-Weibliche*
> *Zieht uns hinan.*'

'Ah! Yes!' His shirt swelled between his loosened tunic and a blissful sigh burst from him; he threw his head back and closed his eyes. I knew he was hearing again, like music, those divine phrases – as was I. In my heart, my mother, Marie, and Gita my wife blent into one . . . 'All that is transient/Is but a symbol; All that's inadequate/Becomes fulfilment; The indescribable/Here is revealed; The ever-womanly/Leads us on high.'

His eyes, opening, were moist. He leaned forward to clink glasses, saying, 'To woman. To Alma.' Then, sensitive to my feelings, 'To both Almas – yes?'

'Yes.'

'Goethe wrote those lines at Buchenwald, and knew he'd finished his great masterpiece. So he relaxed, for a few weeks, in the bosom of his family, and then quietly died, at eighty-two. Dropping as peacefully as an acorn. That's how my mother died, they said.'

Evening shrouded into night; we became quite drunk. We remained in the realm of poetry. He declaimed Shakespeare:

253

'To be, or not to be, that is the question . . .' I envied his knowing Shakespeare in the original. He owed his English, he said, to the years in the Austrian gaol; his communist cell-mate had taught English in a school. Lorenz admired the English; or had done; now he cursed them for not realising they were fighting the wrong nation.

In return I quoted what little Czech poetry I knew. Then some Baudelaire that Marie had taught me; but Lorenz didn't know French. After this he produced, triumphantly, some 78s and put one of them on. I was astonished and moved to hear a Czech song that I knew almost by heart, from a song-cycle by Janáček. 'How did you know that's one of my favourite works?' I asked. Smiling, he said he'd enquired of Gilchik, and then asked Rohde to try and get hold of it in Berlin during his leave. He'd wanted to thank me for my friendship and help. I felt the tears I had fought back surge free, as the tenor voice, singing in German, soared.

When the last record ended, the young man disappearing with, as Lorenz remarked, impossibly high notes, we lapsed into silence. Each locked, I guessed, within his own memories of love's delirium.

– Or of sacrifices made; for he broke the silence by saying, 'There's so much I wanted to do with my life, Chaim. I've got talents, only there's been no chance to develop them. I wrote a little too, in my Austrian cell. And now you've made me interested in psychology. I'd never have *dreamed* there's so much that is hidden, like the Nibelungen treasure, in the recesses of one's mind! If I had lived, I'd be tempted to leave the heart and turn to the mind.' For instance, he now knew why he'd thought of the Mahler symphony and hence misnamed Alma: Tillich had been arguing that more people, as many as a thousand more, might be crammed into the bath-house. 'It was bothering me even as we spoke of Alma, since it would cause much unnecessary suffering; yet I know we have a big problem. I was thinking of her girls in the orchestra, who looked so sad and so pretty: they might be among them, some day soon.'

Yes, the mind was extremely complex; even more than the heart, lungs, and circulation.

He gave a grim chuckle. 'I might even have read your Freud! . . . Joy! Ah! I've experienced it, in the distant past.'

I hadn't seen his real self in this accursed place, he said. Normally he was quite a lively fellow. I'd noticed that, I responded, in watching him play with Irmgard and Seefried. As if to demonstrate his liveliness he put on a dance record, followed by *Lili Marlene*. His eyes became misty as he listened. How he longed for his wife, he confessed. They'd had good sex since the headaches had lifted. He was very much in love with her still. She was a beautiful woman, didn't I think so? So soft and plump. I nodded.

'But I've been unfaithful.' He rubbed his swollen eyelids. 'I slept with Irma.'

I held out my glass for him to refill it, waiting for him to say more, but he remained silent, head bowed. 'It's natural,' I said; 'don't blame yourself too much.'

'You're a good fellow, Chaim. I feel closer to you than almost anybody.'

Suddenly he leaned across and gripped my hand; swallowed it rather in his, roughly, almost as if we were to arm-wrestle. Then as suddenly he jerked away.

'I'll do my best for you. When the end is near the crematoria will be blown up and the fit prisoners marched west; but I'll keep you here, don't worry. You'll stand as much chance as I. Better, in fact. You'll be a hero to the Soviets – a red triangle; they'll hang me. Well, what does it matter?'

Had he considered, I asked, putting his services at the disposal of the Red Army? Many were doing it. If the chance occurred I'd intercede for him. That was generous, he said; but he couldn't imagine such an eventuality. Although, as he'd said many times, he admired the toughness of communism, its intellectual conviction. Thanks to his Austrian cell-mate, he couldn't see national socialism and communism in quite such black-and-white terms as most did; both systems, at least, were for the masses against the privileged few. Rather communism than liberal democracy, that was for sure.

The distant sound of a train, growing and then stopping, with a hiss of steam. Gloomily he shook his head. 'Too many are coming. We can't cope.' And indeed Auschwitz was panting, choking, labouring: reminding me of the old nag whipped by the scrap-dealer in my native town.

His face, in the half-light cast by a lamp, wore a perplexed look. 'What we have done,' he murmured, 'was necessary; even enlightened. Truly constructed around Goethe's tree. Yet we shall be misunderstood. People will call us doctors who killed instead of healing. They won't realise we've been healing too, in a larger sense, by killing Europe's plague bacillus.'

I nodded sympathetically; then, after a decent interval, said, 'I'd like to hear about you and Irma. If you care to talk about it.'

He shifted uneasily. 'Oh – well, it was all right. It was even more than that while we dined and drank and flirted. And when she undressed.' He opened his silver cigarette-case and extracted two cigarettes, holding one out for me. 'But then, guilt overcame me. It was just a moment, a gesture. She sat, when she was naked, to take off her earrings; and for some reason that simple unerotic act reminded me of Gudrun.

'Well, I might as well tell you. About our first meeting. It was in a crowded tram. We were both standing, pressed against bodies, facing each other. There were several people between us, but slowly, for both of us, there ceased to be anyone else in the tram. We just gazed and gazed at each other, without smiling. It was a complete trance. And then, with her right hand, she unclipped her earrings, and smiled at me. She told me later they'd been hurting. But for me that act had been like undressing for me, and I felt shivers run all through me.

'It was in Dresden. She was there on holiday. It's a beautiful city.'

Even so, in spite of his guilt, he had fucked Irma Grese.

'I wish Gudrun would write, to let me know they're okay.'

'Well, it's only a week,' I said.

'Yes. Yes. I'm sure they're all right . . . How's your girl? Is she enjoying Canada?'

I nodded. It was the best place in the camp. Except for the fear. They weren't allowed to survive long there.

'That's what I meant to say to you,' Lorenz said, leaning forward to stub the half-smoked cigarette. I made a mental note to grab it for Litai. 'I think I shall need to – extricate her from the Kommando on Thursday.' His eyes pierced me.

'Ah! Thank you.'

His gaze shifted; he looked embarrassed. 'I was wondering – you say she's good at drawing likenesses?'

'Yes – excellent.' My sphincter muscles tightened momentarily on the sketch of Elli. Dear Elli.

'I merely thought – if I gave her photos of my wife – that she might make some drawings from them. You know – erotic drawings. Do you think? They would be a comfort to me. I wouldn't need to go to other women, I'm sure of it.'

I said I thought she'd be glad to do that, and would do it well.

'That would be wonderful! And making her even more – you know' – he rolled his hands before his chest – 'fleshly, like she was before Hadamar.'

'She could do that.'

'Frau Tillich can draw well, but I hardly like to ask her.'

'Judith will give you exactly what you want.'

His eyes glowed. 'That's good! That's very good! It wouldn't be anything – distasteful.'

He sighed. 'I've only loved two women in my life, Chaim. Gudrun is one; the other was Lotte, the girl I met at the farm. She was a Jew. Highly assimilated, but a Jew. I had to let her go. I hated doing so; Jewish females have a very strong sexual instinct; they even smell of sex, don't you think?' He looked into my eyes and I shrugged. 'I think she passed me at the ramp, a year or so ago. It was hard to tell; but she was the right age. She certainly gave no sign of recognising me. She had a baby in arms and a boy of ten or so; I had to – you know . . .'

'I know.'

He looked perplexed, weary; his eyes closed.

Later, in the stillness of our hearts: 'You know, one of my grandparents was Jewish, Chaim. One. Only one. My paternal grandfather.' And he repeated, in slightly incorrect Yiddish, the opening words of the *Shema*.

Yet the next morning – or perhaps two days later – anyway, a beautiful fresh summer morning – he was standing at the ramp, ramrod stiff, directing operations. I happened to be walking in that direction, heading for Canada. Everything seemed normal at first; the flames leapt from the pits and spat up from the crematorium stacks; smoke billowed, fleering across the sun. Yet something was different. As I approached, I saw that there was no selection; all were being directed towards death, towards the pyres. And instead of the choking moans one was used to hearing from the crematoria, the cries were now loud and agonised. Then I saw why this was so. The walking corpses from some Hungarian ghetto were being grabbed by SS soldiers and hurled straight into the flames. Men, women, children, babies, all went in.

Just across the low fence from a crematorium, the girls of Canada, free from work until the luggage was brought from the train, were sitting on the grass, talking and even laughing. Sight of them must have reassured the straggling walkers, heading for that strange glow in the sky, that strange, unearthly screaming noise. The girls, quite neatly dressed, looked as if they were having a picnic. A picnic on grass. *Die liebe Erde blüht auf im Lenz und grünt aufs neu!* It couldn't be too bad. A couple of the girls even waved to them. I saw Judith among the cheerful sprawlers. I waved to her. She didn't see me.

The Canada girls, chatting, laughing, singing, taking a bite to eat, out of supplies brought by the last consignment, knew they might be in the flames themselves tomorrow, and if not tomorrow it would be soon (I had no intention of telling them how soon); but for this moment they were alive and the sun was shining. I walked on towards the ramp. *'Raus! Raus!'* I heard. 'Leave your luggage! Move!' The striped-uniformed skeletons of the service Kommando, weaving among the dazed arrivals, dragging corpses aside, piling up cases.

Lorenz saw me, and nodded curtly. He was sweating; a lock of black hair trailed across his forehead. He looked ruffled, even upset. His stick was pointing right, right, right; and he wasn't offering any reassuring words.

I came up to him. 'What's wrong?' I asked.

'Some damn fool in the Sonderkommando. Apparently his wife and child were on this train. He rushed up to me, screeching, begging me to spare them. Of course I told him I couldn't, it was impossible. Told him to be a man. Well, he threw himself into the flames after them. Madness! It's upset me for some reason.'

'But why are they being thrown in alive? Couldn't you at least shoot them first?'

'The Red Army's crossed the border into Hungary. We've got two hundred thousand coming in the next two weeks. What else would you have us do? There's simply no time! No time!'

Exasperated, he turned his back on me, his baton pointing right, right, right.

I smiled feebly at a little cloth-capped boy, clutching his mother's hand, who looked scared. Then I strolled off towards the picnickers.

I said to the girls as I came up to them, 'Hello, it's nice for some!' And two or three of them, gay in their blue polka-dot dresses, smiled back, decently rearranging their skirts as I sat down. One or two even coquettishly tossed their hair, which had grown to a reasonable length. It was such a pleasure to sit on grass; to feel it cool and sharp against my palm. I tried to join in a Polish folk-song. Judith broke off a small piece of cheese for me and I ate it with relish.

I returned to the Mussulmans, coughing and groaning in their beds. Dr Lorenz called in an hour later and, exhausted though he obviously was, operated with his usual care and dedication on a factory-worker's crushed hand.

When dusk fell, and the sky was filled with the red glow, I came back to Canada. Another train had arrived; I saw Mengele's elegant form, silhouetted against the fire. Judith stole out to me. She pulled off her dress and was naked underneath. Her cold lips clove to mine; and this time, despite the continuous screams of the dying, she made love with a devouring intensity that previously I had only observed. But afterwards she screamed too, without a sound. I cradled her and stroked her skull, the hair downy as a baby's.

The tall flames leapt and spat; burnt flakes rained unnoticed on us, as if from the faint but serene stars.

'Canst thou bind the sweet influences of Pleiades, or loose the bands of Orion?'

Ewig . . . Ewig . . .

PATTERNS OF AN
OBSERVED DISTURBANCE

Patterns of an Observed Disturbance is a remarkable and explosive thriller set partly in the Nazi death-camps, partly in modern Britain. At its centre are an elderly neurologist, David Epstein, and his wife Sara, an interior designer. David is semi-paralysed as a result of multiple sclerosis. Behind the couple lies the giant shadow of the holocaust. While David, a British Jew, was spared its effects personally, fighting instead in the Battle of Britain as a brave and decorated pilot, the European branch of his family perished in the camps. His Polish cousin Moshe was a prisoner-doctor trying his utmost to save lives but inevitably compromising with evil. David has come to identify strongly with Moshe, who did not survive.

Sara Epstein, for her part, is secretly tortured by memories of surviving at the expense of other members of her family. She still keeps a piece of bread about her person at all times, fearful of starvation; still calculates how much gas would be required to kill all the people in a theatre or cinema. Deeply depressed by her memories, and by the burden of caring for David, she transforms a Devonshire summer house-party to a mayhem of rape, mutilation and murder. Her victims, six in number, and randomly chosen apart from David's daughter Yseult, symbolically represent the six million Jewish dead. Instead of the disbelieving silence that followed the holocaust, this comparatively small-scale atrocity attracts enormous world-wide media attention. A drug-crazed anti-Semitic gang is blamed, though never identified or discovered. A few weeks after, David and Sara commit suicide by burning their cottage to the ground.

However, questions remain. There are the persistent rumours that locals in the Devonshire village have seen David walking with Sara late at night. Can it be that his paralysis is psychological and spasmodic, an unconscious attempt by his failing body to comprehend the deathliness of existence in the camps? Or is his illness a cover, assumed in hope of escaping prosecution for some crime committed earlier in his life? Specifically, are David Epstein and his Polish cousin one and the same person? Did he fully collaborate in the atrocity in Devon, or even instigate it? Were the couple bound together by some earlier atrocity at Buchenwald, in which David saved her life at the expense of her soul; and did she now demand retribution? These are questions that their nephew, Charles Vane, sets out to solve, in a quest that leads him across Europe and into nightmarish continents of the imagination; leads him too into the murky shadows of his own mind, an obsession with the mysterious Karl, in Berlin, his wife's lover.

It is Karl, grandson of a former Luftwaffe ace, who leads Vane deep into former East German territory, to a village cemetery, and points out a gravestone marked with the name of Squadron Leader David Epstein . . .

This gripping novel, blending Le Carré and Kafka, is sure to arouse fierce controversy, since its plot echoes fictionally a real-life tragedy that English readers, in particular, will remember: the London murders of December 1990 which have become known as the Christmas Massacre. The author himself suffered in that tragedy, his father being one of the victims; he was himself, briefly, a suspect. But James has taken the reader far beyond even the sensational facts of that unsolved crime. A surviving prisoner-doctor writes in a letter to Vane: 'Snow has settled outside my bedroom window. A raven sits on a branch. There is no colour in the landscape: it's very like Auschwitz in winter. In other words, it's home. If you spent any time in Auschwitz, that becomes the home you can never forget.' But in a sense, James suggests, the camps are a common home to everyone who lives under their evil and enormous shadow. The mentality that shaped them, in the cause of a perverted 'reason', is still with us. In the words of the surviving prisoner-doctor: 'Whom the gods wish to destroy, they first make rational.'

Christopher James was educated at Shrewsbury School and Oriel College, Oxford. Subsequently he trained as a psychoanalyst, first in Vienna and then with Dr Oscar Jacobson in London. He lives in Winchester with his wife, daughter, and adopted son. *Patterns of an Observed Disturbance* is his first novel.

THE KISS

Am I talking too much? I don't know what you expect by way of background. I didn't intend to bore you with politics; I've never been interested in politics; but it's painful to see what's happening, to see Europe in the figure of the monstrous Kohl or his kind. Our people used to have a refreshing innocence; now all that has been destroyed – along with our jobs. I can sympathise with the right-wing extremists who are attacking immigrant hostels, even though I deplore it. They feel dispossessed. We had some nasty petrol-bomb attacks in Leipzig, just before I came away. It was very upsetting seeing the swastika, and hearing the chants of *Sieg Heil* – but they were youths without jobs, without hope. So one has to understand.

We even have Jews in our street coming back and demanding houses that have been lived in by my neighbours for fifty-odd years!

Not that I'm against the Jews. Nor was my father; he would play chess every week with a Jew called Bechstein, a very nice old man. I'm an internationalist. But also a patriot, and now my patriotism has nowhere to go.

Do you mind if I smoke? Really? I know it's bad. I've given up several times.

Please tell me when you'd like me to stretch out. I thought you'd want me to do that from the beginning. I'm glad you didn't; it's nice to be able to look you in the eyes for a while. You have such kind eyes, Dr Becker.

I didn't want to tell you too much about me in my letters. I know you fought bravely for the Wehrmacht in the war, and were anti-fascist – as I am, of course; but I thought with my background you might become prejudiced against me. Incidentally, my father did a lot of good work bringing war criminals to justice. Nobody mentions that about him any more. It was he, for example, who found out Tillich – who we're hearing so much about – was alive and in Bolivia. This was back in the sixties. Only he was instructed to bury it; apparently his extradition would have endangered a Soviet agent in the West. Tillich's had a charmed life until now; he was actually interrogated by a British intelligence officer, but bribed him into letting him escape.

267

PICTURES AT AN EXHIBITION

I can't thank you enough for replying in so generous a way, to a complete stranger. Those press allegations against you, when your photograph was published in Europe, must have been very painful for you. Imagine for one moment believing you were Mengele! It was all media hype – is that the Western term? – simply because of a report that I.G. Farben, the Auschwitz factory, had provided Saddam Hussein with his chemicals. There was great hysteria; people were afraid Germans would be expected to send troops to Saudi. Mobs were breaking windows in Berlin in protest – it was almost a *Kristallnacht* atmosphere there, quite sinister. The whole Nazi past came up yet again, and the stupid rumour about you fitted in. Mengele advising Syrians.

It's easy enough to say almost *any* elderly man is Mengele. Who of course is dead. There's no agreement about what he looked like. Some who knew him at Auschwitz said he was short, swarthy and dark-haired; others that he was tall, blond and blue-eyed! So their reports of his alleged crimes are likely to be equally suspect. I'm not saying that they're all untrue. Not at all.

Others said you were Dr Lorenz. Well, that name rang a bell with me; I had a photo of him in an old album of my father's, taken early in the war. I compared them both and there was of course no resemblance whatever! I think I have it with me, actually, in my bag . . . Yes, here it is. By the way, I can't agree that he's kicking a Jew in that photo: it seems to me he was having fun with him, perhaps had just kicked a ball. What do you think? . . . Good, yes, it's obvious really. Anyway, I forgot about it again, and you were completely exonerated. It turns out Lorenz was hanged by the Russians. And then that ex-colleague of my father hinted that you were in touch with a Jewish scholar in Paraguay, an Auschwitz survivor, who'd written with some understanding about the doctors who worked there, and I thought I'd write to you and ask for his address. I'm so glad I did.

You really think I'll find a talk with him helpful? It's wonderful that he and his wife are here too. I liked them a lot. Especially his wife; she's a most intelligent woman. She and I had a long talk after dinner, when you were out walking. On their way here they saw the big Berlin exhibition of Munch's paintings.

I've seen reviews of it, I really must go. She made Munch live. Apparently she had something to do with the film that's on with it. I only know *The Scream*. I gather the exhibition is to mark the centenary of one of his first major European exhibitions, in Berlin in 1892. It was closed down after a week because his art was said to be corrupt. Mrs Orenberg and I had a friendly argument about censorship. I feel very vulnerable on that issue, having worked in that field. But surely one can't allow *everything* to be freely available? We have our young people to protect. Mrs Orenberg disagreed strongly, but in a pleasant way. Only I hope I didn't offend her.

I liked Rachel Brandt too. She was obviously so thrilled to meet Dr Orenberg at last. She tells me she'd never have persuaded the Ukrainian government to make that house a holocaust museum if he hadn't pestered them with letters. I just hope she doesn't come back in five years and find it's a pig-sty again, or whatever it was.

Though I do wonder if it does any good to keep dragging up the holocaust. It was war, there were atrocities on both sides. Look at what happened to Lorenz's wife and children. They were leaving Auschwitz by car, for Berlin, in 'forty-four, only the communist underground got word of it to a partisan group and they were ambushed. Frau Lorenz and the little girl were raped before being shot. Whatever Lorenz may or may not have done, that was obscene. My father found that out. It's in my mind today because Dr Orenberg asked me if I had any information about them. He's intensely interested in Lorenz and has been trying to trace him. Because of the rumours that he'd survived and was living with a Jewess; and because some survivors say he was a decent person.

When I told Dr Orenberg what had happened to Lorenz's family he had tears in his eyes and couldn't continue the conversation. A Jew! A camp survivor! It gives hope for humanity, don't you think? But doesn't it also show it's wrong to keep the holocaust alive? What do you think?

Mrs Orenberg told me her husband lost his wife and three young children. She said you never stay quite sane after such a loss. You survive like a ghost, she said; or like a neat little museum smelling of polish and bleach.

There's Herr Braun and his colleague, taking the air. I don't like him; have you smelt his breath? . . . Those clouds look threatening.

I was pleased to hear Mrs Brandt say one of the former Wehrmacht chaplains was going to be officiating at the dedication, along with a rabbi and an orthodox priest. As I understand it, they tried their hardest to save the children. I'm sure it will be very moving; are you positive you don't want to go with them?

Would you mind if I opened a window? I don't want my smoke to trouble you and it's rather stuffy in here. I hope you'll like Yalta; I've been coming here for the past thirty years, to this very hotel. It used to be a holiday dacha for GDR officials and their families. Most of the staff are the same, and they very kindly let me come this year again at a reduced rate. I was so pleased they could find you a room, it will make it so much more convenient. I didn't know if you'd be – forgive my rudeness, I was thinking of your age, but you're marvellously fit. Seventy-five? No, I can't believe it! And your German's so good, even after speaking mostly Arabic and French for so many years. And attractive. That's what struck me when you called from Damascus. Attractive voices are very important, don't you think? . . .

Thank you, it's kind of you to say so. I *used* to have a good head of hair, but I'm afraid now there are – what's that English song? – 'silver threads among the gold'. I *feel* more attractive – or at least less depressingly middle-aged when I'm here. The Black Sea is such a paradise after Leipzig, you can't imagine! Only there are more and more Germans coming here, especially with the situation in Yugoslavia – and I used to enjoy getting away from them! I think you were very wise to leave! This place is becoming a new playground for them. And this year it's all shoes, shoes, shoes; a convention of shoe-makers! Fashion-shoes! Herr Braun offered me some free samples at breakfast this morning – heels three inches high. I told him I was perfectly happy with my comfortable flat shoes, thank you very much. So he said – leering at me – we have shoes of all kinds, Frau Koch, let me show you them . . . A poor East German, a Cinderella . . . And what else would he have shown me! What would he expect in return for his precious shoes! And I might well end up with more than shoes . . .

I probably shan't come back here again.

– I was thinking, I occasionally go to a lovely little fishing village in Yugoslavia. It's so tragic, what's happening there. Serbians dying in cattle-trains and concentration camps. One of my friends has a ghastly photo, cut from a newspaper, stuck on her fridge door. It was in most of the Western papers – a man who's all ribs and skull and eye-sockets, a prisoner of the Serbs, with cancer, but they won't treat him because he's a Muslim. My friend says she's deliberately put it in the kitchen so her children will realise how fortunate they are.

God in Heaven, it's like the last eighty years haven't happened! It's like a recurrent nightmare . . .

But, you see, here in the midst of Europe – death-trains and death-camps. It shows what war does.

Where was I? – My memory's terrible these days. I remember: why I need to have a long talk with Dr Orenberg. You see, I'd always been told my father had been anti-Nazi and worked for the resistance. But after his death I discovered he'd served at Auschwitz. It's been very hard to come to terms with, even though logic tells me the horror must have been exaggerated somewhat, and that many perfectly decent Germans must have had to do things they didn't want to do. And I guess my father couldn't bring himself to tell me. I've never discussed it with my mother, she's not been in good health for years and I haven't wanted to upset her.

But this is what I didn't want you to know about. Forgive me. If you want to walk right out of the room I shall understand.

And to know you are willing to work with me! . . . Oh, that doesn't matter, experience isn't everything; maybe Dr Orenberg would have been more professional, but he praised your abilities highly. He told me you'd helped cure him of morbid obsessions, even though you'd never analysed anyone before, and in the most appalling conditions – disease and hunger and so on. And you cured him finally by playing an aria from the *Messiah* on the gramophone, he said! Oh yes, he couldn't praise you enough.

I'm sure such a gift doesn't disappear just because you felt there was more need for ordinary doctors in Syria. I understand your urge to do penance for Germany by working in an underdeveloped country: it was a noble sacrifice. I already feel a sympathy with you; and it's so wonderful you're willing to give up your entire holiday, and without payment! I'll try to make it up to you in some other way . . . No, I shall insist. All I shall want from Dr Orenberg, when he comes back from that village, is an afternoon's heart-to-heart talk. In any case I shouldn't think he'd be fit enough to take an analysis. He's quite frail, isn't he? Except – again – his voice; that's youthful, like yours. But apart from that . . . he and his wife were out playing table-tennis this morning before breakfast; but he really didn't look up to it.

. . . I'll be fine; just give me a moment . . .

You're being so kind to me . . . I'm sorry. I'm remembering when I played tennis and table-tennis with my father here. We did have such wonderful family holidays. Why do all the good things have to end?

Yes; thank you. It's stupid of me to get upset. My friends usually say I'm very unemotional. My parents always taught me to control one's emotions. I think that's why my marriage failed and I didn't get on with my son.

Do you have children? . . . I probably shouldn't have had any. My son and I haven't spoken for about ten years. It's awful, awful. Who is to blame? Me, I suppose. And his father. You try to do your best for your children, but you seem to take a wrong turning somewhere.

I certainly can't blame my own upbringing. My parents loved each other and loved me. I felt secure. Oh, there wasn't much to eat, and living conditions were pretty awful; but I wasn't unhappy. My first years, the first years I remember, were actually spent in the Soviet Union. Not anywhere scenic like this – a small nondescript town near Minsk. There were lots of former German officers and their families, sharing an old house. We had one room, and about ten families shared the kitchen and bathroom. It was freezing in winter and stifling in summer. But of course there was a lot of comradeship, and I had many 'aunts and uncles', as well as other children to play with. The men weren't there very much, they spent most of their time at a nearby training centre; training for the Stasi, I realised later.

We children were taught mostly by our mothers, each according to her talents; though there was a local teacher, who came to us three mornings a week and taught us Russian and the basics of Marx-Leninism. She was a war widow, yet treated us pretty well, considering.

We moved to the GDR when I was seven. I grew up certain my father had been anti-Nazi. That gives the wrong impression; it's like saying I was certain the sun was hot; I simply took it for granted. Until . . . Well, that was – I learned about it in a very dreadful way. After his death I was going through his effects. There were suitcases and filing cabinets I had to break open. I found stuff he probably should have destroyed; probably *would* have done if he'd felt any warning of a heart-attack, but he'd been in excellent health. There was one thing in particular, a reel of film. I borrowed a projector and played it.

I'm sorry. No, I'm fine now. You needn't be afraid I'm going to be shedding tears all the time. But it was just so totally unexpected. It was a pornographic film. Very amateurish, black-and-white. There was a naked girl lying on a bed. And sitting on one side of it was a man in an SS uniform, and on the other a very thin man in a striped uniform; very short crewcut hair, almost bald in fact; he looked like a concentration camp inmate. Well, another very skinny man, also naked, was brought in by a soldier, and though there was no soundtrack it was clear the SS officer was threatening this man with his revolver, making him lie down and make love to the girl. She was a willing accomplice. They made love, though the man looked absolutely terrified. After about five minutes or so he looked as if he was coming, and then – I couldn't believe it, it was sheer horror – the SS officer put the gun to the back of his neck and shot him.

I forced myself to sit and see it through. Another man was brought in, in fact there were seven or eight all told. And exactly the same thing happened; only sometimes the SS officer fired the shot and sometimes he gave his revolver to the prisoner and *he* shot him.

I thought – I hoped – it had nothing to do with my father. That perhaps it was evidence he'd found against some Nazi war criminal and just stowed away. But I knew I was kidding myself.

You couldn't see the SS officer clearly, his back was usually turned to the camera; but I could see his face enough to know that it almost certainly was my father. Yes, I'm certain. It was my father.

I had a nervous breakdown. A very deep depression. I didn't work for a year. That was seven years ago but I suppose I'm still not completely over it.

Dr Orenberg said I must understand the pressure people were under. Quite decent people. Your mind could split in two, he said. Do you think that's true? Can you say anything that would make me feel better about my father, Dr Becker? Can you, as a decent German, forgive my father? I suppose that's really what I want: forgiveness for my father.

. . . Yes, all right . . . Quite comfortable. Well, perhaps that cushion, thank you. I can see why analysts prefer their patients to be lying down; one is more relaxed. And just to hear the voice; not to be watching your face for signs of disapproval or even disgust. Yes.

And now, what happens? Do you ask me questions? Do I just say whatever comes into my head? What do we call each other? Dr Becker sounds terribly formal, and I hate you calling me Frau Koch, it reminds me too much of my ex-husband. That's another story; you'll hear quite enough about him in the next four weeks. Do you think you can help me in four weeks? Well, I hope so, and we can carry on by letter as you say. But anyway, please call me Alma, if you don't mind . . . That sounds better. It's soothing somehow. Suddenly I could almost drift asleep. You remind me of my father when you say it. I loved him very much; I've never been able to love anyone so much as him, that's my problem. Part of my problem. I have many problems. I'm very screwed-up. You'll soon find that out. Music is a great solace; I wondered if you'd mind my putting on a tape, very low? Thank you. The Goldberg Variations . . . Heavenly.

You'll start me off crying again. That was wonderful! I wasn't imagining it, was I? You did lean over and kiss me on the forehead, didn't you? That's one of the most wonderful things anyone's ever done to me! You're such a kind man. I'm sure you're going to help me.

So how do we start? With a dream?

CONSOLATION

'The cries of the children,' said the aged German bishop, in the crowded museum, 'will be heard no more. For those of us here who were involved, innocently, and who fought with all our strength to save them, there is but one consoling thought . . .'

A NOTE ON THE AUTHOR

D. M. Thomas lives in Truro, Cornwall, the county where he was born and grew up. *Pictures at an Exhibition* is his tenth novel. He has also published several volumes of poetry and translations of Russian poets. His third novel *The White Hotel* was shortlisted for the Booker Prize and has been translated into twenty languages.